Tom Clancy's
POWER PLAYS

CUTTING EDGE

CREATED BY
TOM CLANCY
AND
MARTIN GREENBERG

WRITTEN BY
JEROME PREISLER

PENGUIN BOOKS

PENGUIN BOOKS

Published by the Penguin Group
Penguin Books Ltd, 80 Strand, London WC2R 0RL, England
Penguin Putnam Inc., 375 Hudson Street, New York, New York 10014, USA
Penguin Books Australia Ltd, 250 Camberwell Road,
Camberwell, Victoria 3124, Australia
Penguin Books Canada Ltd, 10 Alcorn Avenue, Toronto, Ontario, Canada M4V 3B2
Penguin Books India (P) Ltd, 11 Community Centre,
Panchsheel Park, New Delhi – 110 017, India
Penguin Books (NZ) Ltd, Cnr Rosedale and Airborne Roads,
Albany, Auckland, New Zealand
Penguin Books (South Africa) (Pty) Ltd, 24 Sturdee Avenue,
Rosebank 2196, South Africa

Penguin Books Ltd, Registered Offices: 80 Strand, London WC2R 0RL, England

www.penguin.com

First published in the United States of America by Berkley Books 2002
First published in Great Britain by Penguin Books 2002
1

Printed in England by Clays Ltd, St Ives plc

Acknowledgments

I would like to acknowledge the assistance of Marc Cerasini, Larry Segriff, Denise Little, John Helfers, Brittiany Koren, Robert Youdelman, Esq., Danielle Forte, Esq., Dianne Jude; the wonderful people at Penguin Putnam Inc., including David Shanks and Tom Colgan; Joel Gotler and Alan Nevins. But most important, it is for you, my readers, to determine how successful our collective endeavor has been.

—Tom Clancy

ONE

IT WAS THE GOBLIN THAT LED THEM TOWARD DISAS-ter.

Cédric Dupain was at first merely curious as their strange caller glided into his probe lights—though fascination was quick to snare him. One of his job's strongest lures was its promise of the unexpected, and Cédric took pleasure in discovery even when it was accompanied by considerable risk. He had been at his profession for over a decade, longer counting his three consecutive tours with the French Navy. All those years, so many dives, and nothing he'd encountered in the depths had yet given him real cause for fear.

Cédric cut his thrusters, turned his head, glanced through his faceplate at Marius, and saw he'd also come to a dead stop in the water. Then he reminded himself that *faceplate* was the wrong word. The correct term for the clear hemispheric panel was dome port. Just as the hardsuit's exterior was called a pressure hull, and the glovelike hand sockets were called manipulator pods. A man who put great value on precision, Cédric knew it was also somewhat inexact to say that he and Marius Bouchard were functioning as divers—or that their suits were, in fact, suits at all. Both men would be more aptly considered pilots operating anthropomorphic underwater vehicles, submersibles that could descend to six hundred meters—two thousand feet, as Cédric's American instructors would measure it—beneath the ocean's surface.

The nomenclature had been a headache to learn, but for Cédric it was an important reminder. The world below was a world apart, and his hardsuit had more in common with a spacesuit than an ordinary diving rig. Indeed, his ability to walk the seabed was as remarkable as an astronaut's to stride across the pitted surface of the moon. He did not want to let caution slip and forget for a moment what damage the crushing pressures of the deep would wreak on vulnerable human bodies.

Cédric stood motionless. He'd already located and videoed the source of the problem that had prompted an emergency repair call to the *Africana*, a medium-tonnage cable ship Planétaire Systems Corporation had contracted to maintain its undersea fiberoptic lines. But sights like the one now before his eyes gripped him with a kind of joyous awe, and were what truly pulled him to the cold depths. That he earned an excellent wage was only a convenient, if fair, rationale for doing a job he would have paid every last euro of his own to carry out.

Perhaps twice his size, the goblin came closer, cutting a slow circle through the dusky water. Cédric watched as its orbit tightened to within seven meters of him and suddenly broke, the goblin turning away, its abrupt change of direction propelled by a chopping flick of its tail.

The hardsuit's mini-POD seemed to be working perfectly.

Cédric remained watchful. Shoulder mounted in front of his thruster pack, his xenon lamps played over the veering goblin's long body. He noticed a pink lacing of blood vessels under its smooth, whitish gray skin. Noticed racks of sharp white teeth on its protrusible jaws, thrust out of its open mouth on reflex like jagged spring-loaded clamps. Noticed tiny lidless eyes on either side of the thick, flat growth of meat and bone bulging from its snout . . . eyes that passed over him with an interest he couldn't have described and an attitude it was impossible to gauge. There was expression in them, yes, and intelligence, but of a trackless alien variety.

Cédric could see why the Japanese fishermen who'd discovered the species had chosen its name: *Tenguzame*, goblin shark. He decided right then that it might be the most spectacularly hideous creature he'd ever seen—with the possible exception of his songful operations manager topside.

"Just *look* at that thing, will you?" he said over his communicator. Though the words to Marius hardly required secrecy, he had used their closed subchannel. It was something of an amusement. Gunville couldn't resist eavesdropping from the ship's control room, and Cédric couldn't resist thwarting him. "I expected we might run into bulls or tiger sharks . . . didn't think these monstrosities climbed above six hundred leagues."

"It must have been drawn to the cable." Marius's digitally transmitted voice was free of distortion. "Wouldn't be the first time, judging by the number of teeth we saw in the segment that went bad."

"That's no explanation."

"Why not?"

Cédric hesitated a moment. Though a good and dependable fellow, Marius had been on the job less than a year, and his occasional obtuseness could be a frustration. It was true sharks sought out hidden prey with specialized sense organs, nerve-filled pores called ampullae of Loranzini that detected the electrical fields radiated by creatures of the deep . . . and every other living thing, for that matter. And while the fiberoptic strands at the core of the submarine lightwave cable gave off virtually no stray emissions, the current flowing through the copper tube *around* the fiber—in these older repeatered systems, any-way—did indeed generate a low-frequency field that would sometimes confuse a shark into mistaking a seg-ment of cable for a potential meal.

This, of course, presumed the SL was functional, un-like the ruptured cable that had caused a partial telecom-munications failure for many thousands of the region's broadband-reliant users. And there Marius's supposition strayed from logic.

"The wire's dead. Shorted-out," Cédric said, trying to check his impatience. However slow on the uptake Mar-ius might be, some allowance had to be made for his relative inexperience on the job. "There isn't any voltage to stir up the beast's appetite."

Marius didn't look surprised behind his bubbled acrylic dome port, and Cédric wondered for a moment if he might simply take amusement from hearing him state and restate the obvious. An odd thought, and improbable, but not out of the question. Could it be that he was being made a goat?

Cédric chased the question from his mind, having more serious matters to occupy it. Such as why the goblin at least *appeared* to be going at the cable. Ignoring him, it had swum off toward the sandbank on his left, assumed an almost vertical attitude in the water, and then angled its horny snout down toward the crippled fiber.

Cédric watched the shark resume stitching into the bot-tom sediment. He remembered that in the early days of submarine cable installation—around the late 1980s—it had been common to find dozens of shark teeth imbedded in sections of damaged line. That problem had been solved by encasing the cables in multilayered armor—a tough yet flexible sheath of plastic laminate steel wrapped in a thick nylon roving. The sharks would still bite, but their teeth rarely penetrated to the electrified copper.

Rarely wasn't quite the same thing as *never*, though. As Cédric and Marius had discovered earlier.

Still, Cédric was convinced the shark attacks were only half the story, and that the initial cable fault could be blamed on drag trawlers or dredgers—long-line fishing vessels that dropped heavy nets down to the seabed for tuna, mackerel, cubera, and, in the case of the dredge boats, shellfish. In addition to Gabon's domestic fleet, the boats came from countries as far to the north as Morocco, Nigeria, and Libya, and as far in the opposite direction as South Africa. They came, as well, from outside Africa's continental boundaries—Europe and Asia in particular. Fisheries based in Cédric's native France sent their vessels here. As did companies in Japan, Korea, China, Germany, and the Netherlands. Most were licensed for deepwater operations in the Gulf of Guinea, but there were enough illegal ships that would trawl the spawning grounds nearer the coast, where tight zoning rules had been placed on commercial fishing . . . the Chinese being the worst offenders.

Cédric knew environmental impact was part of the reason for the restrictions. Fishing accounted for two thirds of Gabon's economic production, and low yield had been a problem in recent years. But another serious concern was protecting the submarine fiberoptic network that represented a cooperative investment of nearly a billion dollars for local businessmen and their foreign partners in the broadcasting and telecommunications industry.

Unfortunately, policing the seaways was an impossible challenge for Gabon. A runt of a nation, its navy consisted of five hundred men, a couple of patrol boats, and the same number of amphibious hovercraft. This paltry force could not by any stretch keep up with poachers who were skilled at evasion and equipped with state-of-the-art countersurveillance apparatus.

The damaged cable Cédric and Marius been sent down to examine had been terribly mangled—evidence that it had gotten raked up from its shallow burial trench by bottom dragging gear, most likely the saw-toothed iron plow bar of a clam and oyster dredge. At that stage, the cable's surrounding nylon yarn would have been easily shredded and gashed. Cédric could see how the breach could go as deep as the third layer of armor. He could further imagine a shark attack, or series of shark attacks, finishing the destructive work once the outer armor was compromised.

Which still left him with a significant unanswered question. The goblin . . . what would have brought it here *now*, attracted it to a lifeless cable?

A moment later his puzzlement deepened. The shark had continued hovering in the water several yards away like a clock hand pointed to the numeral six, its nose down, its tail fins aimed toward the surface. Cédric saw it lunge straight for the seabed now, its thick, horny snout appendage drilling deep. Sediment billowed up in a turbid cloud. The goblin darted back up and sliced a rapid circle around the spot where it had struck, row upon row of fangs spiking from its open mouth. Then it speared into the sand sheet again, prodding the thick silt and muck, churning more of it from the bottom with repetitive jackhammer thrusts.

"Je ne comprend pas," Marius said over the pilot-to-pilot. "Our ugly friend's in quite a froth."

Cédric was thoughtful. "We need to have a look at what's agitated it."

"Are you sure? I don't know I'd want to approach the creature if it was in a *sedate* mood."

"We saw a repeater in the cable about forty meters

back. They're spaced fifty meters apart. Unless my estimate's off by a long throw, we'll find another over by
the shark."

"You think that could be what's making it act up?"

Cédric's shrug went unseen inside the bulky aluminum
alloy shell of his hardsuit.

"The laser pump's an expensive contraption, Marius.
I'd just as soon spare it from becoming an hors
d'oeuvre," he said. "Besides, it may be holding a residual
charge. That could prove your idea about the cable at-
tracting it to be half right. Or less wrong, anyway. And
I figure you'd enjoy the chance to call me an ass."

"In this case, I'll settle for thinking you one."

Cédric chuckled a little. "Is your POD toggled on?"

"Yes, but—"

"Then we won't have to get too close. You saw how
it turned from us before."

Marius fell silent, conversely indicating his doubts
weren't *at all* quieted. But Cédric was reassured by how
well the protective oceanic device had performed on the
goblin's approach. Designed to irritate the same sensory
organs that allowed sharks to home in on their kills, the
POD emitted a 360-degree electrical field that had ap-
parently caused their unwelcome welcomer sufficient distress to make it avoid them.

"Come on," Cédric said. "I'll lead the way so you
won't be the first of us to get chewed to pieces."

Before Marius could finish voicing his sarcastic thank-
you, Cédric depressed the pedals inside the hardsuit's
oversize Frankenstein boots—he'd never been told what
to properly call the encasements for his feet—and activated his thruster unit.

Its motors engaged with a gentle kick. There were two
blade-driven thrusters oriented for horizontal movement,
another pair for vertical propulsion, any of which could

be used singly or in combination to allow full omnidirectional control. Now all four whirred to life at once.

As the motor vibrations steadied to a faint pulse, Cédric lifted off the seabed in underwater flight, his body remaining in an upright position. Marius swept along behind and to port, careful to stay wide of his backwash.

They closed distance with the shark in a rush and immediately caught its awareness. It withdrew from the sandbank and swung around to regard them, its small round eyes cold and alert, gleaming in its ghastly head like chips of black mirrored glass.

The men assumed stationary hovers, their horizontal propellor blades slowing.

"Why hasn't your friend left?" Marius said.

"*Our* friend," Cédric amended. "Give it a chance to react to our electronic security blanket."

The shark kept watching them, turned in their direction, stilled by their intrusive presence.

After several long moments it lunged.

Cédric released a gasping exhalation. He heard Marius blurt a stream of invective in his earbud. Its stiletto-toothed mouth agape, the shark came on fast, straight— and then veered away with a lashing herky-jerky motion barely three meters from where the two men hung suspended over the sandbank.

Cédric watched it disappear from sight, felt the knot in his stomach loosen, and took a deep breath of the hardsuit's recycled oxygen.

"Tell me something," Marius said. The scratchy tremor in his voice was not due to any transmission breakup. "What's the effective range of our PODs?"

"Seven meters."

"The shark should have been informed of that specification, don't you think?"

Cédric grunted in response and thrust forward through

the water. Marius followed. Seconds later they reached the churned up patch of seabed that had been the target of the goblin's battering frenzy, eased off their footpads, and made a floating descent.

Cédric had scarcely alighted when he saw evidence that his suspicions had been on the mark. Plucked from the unsettled deposits was a cable segment with a lumpish bulge in it, often described as resembling a snake that had swallowed a rodent—a repeater case. It must be what had aroused the goblin's attention, he thought. No great surprise there, though Cédric made a mental note to corner one of the ship's cable technicians and find out for sure whether the component could hold a charge despite a widespread systemic power failure.

He was still examining the length of cable when something unusual *did* catch his eye. Very unusual, in fact.

Cédric looked down at it a moment, baffled. Not far from the repeater, a section of the cable remained partially buried under a thin layer of sand and clingy vegetation. He reached down to clear the material away with his robotic prehensor claws, his fingers working actuators inside the manipulator pod. Then he scrutinized his discovery from a graceless bent-at-the-knees position—the hardsuit's limited number of hydraulic rotary joints did not permit bending at the waist.

"Marius, come have a peek," he said.

Beside him, Marius assumed a comparably awkward stance to look at the watertight rectangular box.

"A splice enclosure," he said. "I didn't know the wire had old repairs."

"It doesn't. Or it shouldn't. None."

"You're positive?"

"None," Cédric repeated. "You can take a look at the grid charts once we're back on the ship. But trust me, I'd remember. I've been maintaining the cable almost

since it was laid." He carefully extracted the splice housing from the mud with his prehensors. "Something else. The enclosure doesn't look like any type Planétaire's used in the past. It's very similar, yes. Not identical."

Marius produced a confused frown. "Do you think it has some connection to the service failure?"

"No. You saw where a dredge frame tore up the cable. That was unmistakable."

"Then what are you trying to say?"

"I'm not certain." Cédric paused. "But this is a damned mystery."

Marius's frown deepened. "Do we tell Gunville about this now or later?"

Cédric silently withdrew a hand from the sleeve of his hardsuit and flipped a switch on the radio console illuminating its inner hull's chest piece. The diver-to-surface channel opened up with a faint hollowness that he always associated with holding a paper-cup-and-string telephone to his ear in childhood.

"Now," he said at last. "We'd better let him know right away."

In the *Africana*'s monitoring operations room, Captain Pierre Gunville already knew.

His eyes circles of bright green fire in a smooth, mocha brown face—at fifty-two years old, Gunville was sufficiently vain to pride himself in a complexion free of lines, wrinkles, or sagging skin—he stood watching an alarm light flash on a signal column in front of him, sliding his right forefinger over a rudimentary mustache, and silently mouthing the words to a folk ballad he'd learned long, long ago. Its expression of a heart captured by desire, of grace through love's devotion . . . not in the five hundred years since the song's composition had anything surpassed it.

"Belle qui tiens ma vie, captive dans tes yeux, wui m'as l'ame ravie, d'u souris gracieux . . ."

"Sir, Dupain's hailing on the transceiver." Seated with his back to Gunville, one of the half dozen handpicked crewmen at the consoles glanced over from the marine radio's surface station, his earphones pulled down off his head. "How do you want me to respond?"

The red alarm light continued its steady blinking. Gunville stood in his customary place at the operation room's rear, moved his finger back and forth over the faint dash of hair above his upper lip, and whispered remembered verses of song. He'd been growing the mustache for less than a week, and it was at the irksome stage where it was neither here nor there—an adolescent's whiskers. But Jacqueline had told him she found mustaches appealing on men of his type, though she hadn't elaborated on just what type that was, and by her lack of specificity might as well have said she found it appealing on a *mulâtre*. Gunville could read between the lines and accept social enlightenment for the theatrical prop it was. Still, he had to admit to being beguiled by the siren. And everything balanced out in the end. Gunville would show her the fullness of his passion, then leave her stung by his spite.

"Sir—"

"I know. Dupain calls." Gunville was disappointed by Andre's skittishness. The find below had been anticipated. Only its timing had been at question. "You can tell him I'm busy with a mechanical problem at the aft crane. Or in the engine room. Or that I'm holding a conference, or napping in my cabin. I don't care what you say. Just stall until this problem's been solved."

"Yes."

Gunville looked at him.

"Another thing," he said. "Contact the tether winch

detail. I want to be sure there are no unassigned hands on deck except the tenders. No witnesses, *comprendez-vous*?"

After a moment's hesitation, the radio man nodded, put the cans over his ears, and returned his attention to the console.

Gunville studied the back of his head. Andre was a likeable sort. Married, young children. Of Bantu descent, as had been Gunville's mother. And he'd worked aboard the *Africana* for years. But the nature of the ship's business had rapidly evolved, and it seemed Andre had failed to adapt. Gunville himself felt a great deal of stress, but also realized that he simply had to bear it, putting confidence in his new business alliance and their joint ability to execute contingency plans.

It was sad, he thought. So sad.

Andre would have to go, but at the same time he could not be allowed to move on elsewhere. Leaving him to become a casualty of change. A failure of evolution like poor Cédric and Marius.

Gunville took a mournful breath, reached down into his memory, and again began to move his lips in a low whisper: *"Libre de passion, mais l'amour s'est fait maitre, des mes affections, et a mis sous sa loi . . ."*

Immersed in the song's romantic sentiment, finding comfort in its lyrics and melody, he soon felt very much better.

The yacht rolled over the calm, dimpled sea between the quays of Port-Gentil and the long band of oil platforms extending southward off the Gabonese coastline. These resources, trading port and near-shore petroleum fields, framed an economic success that gave the little nation's citizens average head-for-head incomes surpassed only by South Africans among their territorially advantaged regional neighbors.

Though of high style, the yacht, or *super*yacht—as the vessel's 130-foot length, structural enhancements, and sophisticated onboard technologies truly classed it—was not at all a conspicuous sight as it ran a gentle northerly course toward the Gulf of Guinea, waters abounding with giant blue marlin, tarpon, and other potential brittle-scaled, rubber-finned sportfishing trophies. Individual opulence sparkles amid general prosperity, and the few may taste rare luxury where there is common satisfaction—the queen bee in her honeyed chamber knows.

Inside the *Chimera*'s four spacious decks, every detail was of plush yet tasteful elegance. There were lacewood and sycamore finishes, walls covered with embroidered Canton silk damask, marble veneers imported from the stone quarries of Pordenone, Italy. On its exterior starboard quarter, a single touch of ostentation flared at the eye: a decorative painting of the ship's mythological namesake, a creature with the head of a lion, body of a goat, and a sinuous serpent's tail. In this particular depiction, the monster was shown breathing flames.

The owner of the yacht had an appreciation for fables, relishing the age-old stories for their grand scope, color, and subtext. He had much the same fondness for wordplay. Constrained in manner, offering a dispassionate face to the world, he was a man who privately enjoyed the artful lark, the inside jest, the nuanced turn of phrase.

Etymologically, *Chimera* is the word root of *chimerical*, an adjective that can be used to describe something—or someone—of a nature that is deceptive and slippery to the mind.

In ichthyology, *Chimera* is a genus of fish, distantly related to the shark, that has existed in the world's oceans for four hundred million years—a phenomenal triumph of survival attributed to its swimming at great, lightless depths beyond the safe reach of those who would hunt and trap it.

In genetic science, a *chimera* is defined as an organism spawned of two or more genetically distinct species. Chimeral plants are propagated by horticulturists and fancied by collectors. Laboratories have created mixed-species test rodents in vitro. Fueled by calls for artificially grown transplant organs and tissues, recombinant-DNA technologies have produced the means to spawn human-animal chimeras through manipulation of embryonic stem cells. Some have been given European patent approvals.

A man of disparate business interests, the yacht's owner was the prime, and silent, financial backer for a Luxemburg-based biotech firm that held two species-joining patent claims. It was a minor gamble for him, a diversionary fling, but one that might yield profit over the stretch. And in this adventure, too, he saw subtle shades of meaning. Sometimes in his secret reflections, he would imagine himself the spawn of a paternal pig and mother rhea, a flightless bird of garish plumage. On these instances, he saw the comedy of life to be blacker than clouded midnight and as fiery-sharp as the point of a cauterizing needle.

Now he was a tolerable distance from such thoughts. On the large flying bridge of the *Chimera* he sat on an elevated mango-colored sofa to one side of the pilot-house, his right leg hung over his left, his thin fingers laced together on his lap, watching the slow slide of sea and shore through a panoramic curve of windows. He was dressed lightly for the torrid heat in a pale blue, short-sleeved, collared shirt; cream trousers; and tan deck shoes. Around his neck was a mariner link necklace with a small pendant charm, both of them hand-tooled out of silver from Bolivia's cooperative Cerro Rico mines. Another of his quirkish notions, the ornament was a representation of the miner's god, whose shrine occupied a niche behind the entrance to every dangerous sulfur-stinking shaft—a horned, squatted, vaguely wolfish being with a phallic thrust between its thighs, said to hold the power of life and death over the impoverished, ragtag *campesino* workers who labored to extract his mineral bounty, placating him with gifts of coca, tobacco, and pure-grain alcohol and honoring him with orgiastic celebrations of vice and excess.

Like many gods and monsters of folklore, this lord of the underworld was known by more than one name. Mountain villagers descended from the Inca called him Supai. Most Bolivian peasants knew him as El Tío. The sly uncle who cast a neutral eye on virtue and sin, caring only for tributes offered. A demon that desperate men had sainted in exchange for his inconstant favors.

The owner of the pleasure yacht knew, and he well understood.

He looked out the bridge's sweeping windows, past the stations where his helmsman and engineers sat in their epauleted white uniform blouses. Looked out at the sun-stippled water and the crowded international harbor and the fixed oil platforms standing with their tall booms, derricks, and wellheads.

Here was wealth, he thought. Tremendous wealth, all visible right on the surface. But none of it interested him. The treasure that had made his migration to Africa something more than a flight from the wide nets of his pursuers, the continent's greatest bounty, was the light pulsing through fine veins of glass that ran deep where the sun did not reach.

There was no chance in the world that he would let anyone stop him from tapping it.

"Casimir," he said, his tone soft. "Are you ready?"

His pilot had a brief exchange in the Bandgabi tribal dialect with a man at the console beside him. Then he nodded.

"Yes," he said, switching to English. "We've completed a modem upload-download test . . . real-time streaming telemetry and multimode sensors are online . . . everything checks."

"Why haven't you deployed, then?"

"Gunville. We were waiting for his confirmation."

"And he's given it?"

"Just now," the helmsman said. "His men are in position aboard the *Africana*."

The yacht's owner unlaced his hands and fluttered one in front of him. He was eager to be rid of those glorified utility workers below.

"Take us on to the next stage," he said. "Please."

An instant later he felt the mildest of bumps run through the yacht, and focused his eyes on the monitor boards.

The killfish had launched from its chamber.

The deployment chamber in the *Chimera*'s lower starboard hold was little different from a torpedo tube, but the minisub housed within bore no resemblance to a conventional weapon or remote underwater vehicle. Nor was there was anything conventional about it.

What it looked like before ejection was a metal shoebox with a considerable distension around the middle, as if it had been overfilled until its sides were pushed outward. As it left the chamber and its lateral, rear, and top stabilizer/orientation fins unfolded, its appearance grew closer to that of a fish with an egg-swollen belly.

Each of these comparisons was appropriate.

The killfish was full and, after a fashion, pregnant.

•   •   •

"What's holding up Gunville?" Marius said.

"I don't know," Cédric replied. They were back on their closed voice link. "Andre told me that he's gone to the engine room. Some kind of problem."

"Bullshit. They've got phones in there, and he could reach for one if he chooses," Marius said. "I'll bet that son of a bitch is on the pot with his trousers around his ankles, serenading his true love."

Cédric grinned. And fondling it, no doubt—*l'e petite amour*. He wasn't about to argue Gunville's case, though.

"We've been down at extreme depth for almost four hours," Marius said. "Why push things to the limit? We should video the splice and call it quits."

"Let's not work ourselves into a premature snit. *Five* hours might be pushing." Besides, Cédric thought, the repair technicians might prefer to receive live imagery from them, observe his curious find from angles of their own choice before lowering their grapple to raise the cable. "We're bound to hear from the songbird any minute. Meanwhile, we can still do what you suggest, take some pictures—"

Cédric became distracted by a sudden movement at the far right periphery of his vision. He cocked his head inside the dome port for a better look, but it reduced his field of view just enough so he realized he'd have to turn his whole body.

He applied the slightest bit of pressure to his left foot-pad for a thruster assist and was nudged the opposite way.

A quick spin of his blades, and Marius shifted to face in the same direction. "Don't tell me the shark's returned in spite of our PODs being activated."

"Probably not. Whatever I glimpsed didn't seem that large."

Cédric was quiet for a moment. There weren't many

forms of aquatic life down here that presented even the slightest hazard, but he was always on the lookout for an unusual specimen, making him an underwater equivalent of a bird-watcher, he supposed. Though it seemed a stretch to believe he'd have two exceptional sightings in a single dive, maybe he'd gotten fortunate. The Ogooué Basin was stocked full of unique tenants, including deep-water octopuses and nautiluses.

He scanned the underwater dimness, kicking his shoulder lamps to their brightest settings with the touch of a switch inside his hardsuit. Then his gaze fixed on a speedily approaching object about six meters distant at three o'clock.

He raised an arm to point. "Marius—"

"I see it," his partner said. "What the hell is that thing?"

Cédric's silence did not stem from any lack of desire to respond. He simply hadn't the vaguest clue.

For an instant he entertained the thought that he really *had* lucked into another sighting. That whatever was coming toward them was a strange, wide-bodied fish to be imaged and subsequently identified for his personal archive of marine animals. As it got closer, however, he realized it was neither fish, nor cephalopod, nor any other type of living creature.

"I think—Marius, it looks like some kind of unmanned probe."

"But that doesn't make sense . . . we'd have been informed if one was operating in this area."

Cédric was silent again. Marius was right, it didn't make sense. Just as a splice that shouldn't have been in the cable made no sense. Yet there it was lying uncovered on the seabed only a few steps from where he stood. And there in the bright fan of his lights was an autonomous

underwater vehicle unlike any he'd seen in his entire diving career.

Then it struck him that it did resemble *something* he'd
seen before—and that flash of sudden recall instantly
branched off into another like electronic data through a
signal splitter. Cédric's first clear memory was of a fish
he'd often spotted skimming through the sea grass while
on a year-long Planétaire telecom project in the Carib-
bean. His second was of an article he'd read mentioning
the same creature—a fish, family Ostraciidae—in one of
the scientific monthlies he read with compulsive dili-
gence. *National Geographic*'s French edition, perhaps,
but that didn't really matter. The important things for him
were that the boxfish was distinguished by the hard outer
carapace that deterred predators but also made its body
rigidly inflexible . . . and that the boxfish's means of lo-
comotion, which gave it exceptional stability and maneu-
verability despite the unbending armor, had been studied
by American military researchers interested in using it as
a model for the steering and propulsion systems of future
generation AUVs.

All this passed through Cédric's brain in milliseconds,
flashing along parallel but independent paths of recollection toward a sharp, startling convergence as he focused
on the robotic craft bearing toward him. If he'd had time
to consider them, the implications of what he saw might
have caused a slow trickle of fear to filter through his
surprise—but he didn't.

When fear *did* overtake him it would be in a cold,
blustering rush.

The AUV had closed to within five meters of the hardsuit pilot and leveled in a stationary position. Cédric noticed a small lenticular window on its underside, a nubby
black projection at its front end, and did not like the looks
of either.

Then an opening appeared on the starboard side of the vehicle's flat hull. Cédric would never know whether the hatch, lid, panel, or whatever it was had recessed into the hull or sprung inward like a trap door—it happened too quickly for him to tell. The opening appeared. And before he could react, a compartment *behind* the opening released its implausible contents into the water.

The twenty or so dispersing spheres looked to him like metal ball bearings, although they were somewhat larger than racquetballs in size. Each of them had four tiny screw propellers—one on the upper axis, one on the lower, another two on opposite points across its diameter.

His eyes wide with amazement, Cédric thought crazily of a toy called a Pokéball he'd once gotten his youngest nephew for his birthday, something that opened up like an egg to release a little cartoon imp.

He was still thinking of it when the spheres assembled into tight cluster formation and came swarming toward the spot where he stood with his dive partner.

"Cédric . . . what's going on?" Tension brimmed in Marius's voice. "What are those things?"

Cédric couldn't waste an instant with guesswork. He switched to the diver-to-surface freq.

"*Africana*, we have a situation," he said.

He got an earful of silence in response.

"This is a mayday, *Africana*. Repeat, mayday, can you read?" he said.

More dead silence from topside.

"God damn it, come in, what's wrong with you up there?"

Still nothing. And the rapidly moving spheres were almost on them.

Cédric abandoned the radio, looked at Marius. He had no shred of a plan in his head, and the knowledge that their thrusters weren't designed for speed hardly inspired confidence one would come to him. But Cédric had been a navy man for a very long time, and he did not like it at all that the lens-shaped aperture and black projection on the minisub were reminiscent of the guidance and homing packets of seeker torpedoes.

The robotic swarm meant danger.

"We have to get away," he said. The declaration sounded blandly, hatefully obvious. "Try to—"

They were the last words he managed to get out of his mouth before the spheres came swooping down on them.

He felt three quick, clapping thumps on the back of his thruster unit, a fourth against the POD encasing his right hand, followed by a fifth and sixth on his left. There were some hard claps to his chest and the side of his neck, and the next instant a staggering *thump thump-thump* against his foot that almost threw Cédric off balance into the muddy sediment.

"My God!" Marius shouted over the comlink. "They're sticking to us. *Sticking!*"

More of the obvious. The globes were clinging wherever they struck. Cédric could see them becoming affixed to the same areas of Marius's hardsuit as his own, fastening themselves to its thruster pack and dome collar joint, bunching onto the prehensors of both extremities like crops of giant metal berries. He simultaneously realized they *weren't* attaching to Marius's upper arms and legs, points that had also escaped contact on his suit.

Again Cédric had no chance to wonder what this implied. He was far too cognizant that if either of their hulls suffered a breach, its internal environment would be displaced by sixty atmospheres of pressure—a compression so vastly beyond human tolerance that it would pulp its occupant's internal organs and burst the very walls of his blood cells.

He felt another of the spheres hit his back. How many were on him now? Ten, twelve?

Beside him, Marius was close to panic. His arms rose and fell against heavy water resistance, rose and fell, flapping in what looked like slow motion as he tried to shake the spheres from his gripper claws.

Cédric knew he was scarcely further away from losing his composure.

"Marius, hold still, I'll try to pull them off you," he said. "We need to stay calm, try and get them off *each other*."

Marius met his gaze through their rounded dome ports, gathered his wits enough to stop the furious paddling of his arms.

Cédric reached out to Marius with his lefthand prehensor, testing its mobility with his individuated finger control rings. He was somewhat amazed to find that he could still open and close it despite the weight of the spheres attached to two of its four stainless-steel claws.

He clamped the gripper around a sphere lodged at the base of Marius's neck, gave it a strong tug. It didn't budge even a little. He tugged harder, microelectromechanical sensors inside the control rings transferring his exertion to the claw as increased output. The sphere would not yield, and now Marius was screaming again, unnecessarily reminding him that it was sticking, it was *sticking*, the damned thing wasn't coming off. Cédric could feel himself start to nervously perspire inside his suit and added a prying motion on his third try, straining the gripper's servos to their limits.

The sphere finally detached from the collar joint—but by just the slightest bit. A few centimeters at most before clamping right back *on*, pulling along Cédric's MEMS-aided gripper claw with a powerful attraction that jerked his arm up and out toward Marius.

All in a moment's span his relief had budded, bloomed, and turned to ash gray wilt as fear blew through his heart in a killing frost. He could neither separate the sphere from Marius, nor himself from the sphere, which now joined them as if . . .

Cédric blinked with the last meaningful realization of his life. Another that seemed so glaringly evident, he could only wonder how it had not dawned on him much sooner.

"They're magnetized," he heard himself tell Marius in an almost matter-of-fact tone.

Marius's eyes were full of terror and confusion behind his view port. In fact, it almost seemed to Cédric that his features had drawn together into a bold, hanging question mark.

Cédric was wondering just what sort of answers were expected of him when the spheres fastened to the hardsuits exploded, and the rushing sea took his thoughts.

"Well, Casimir? My curiosity pesters."

"We have total success. The neodymium hunter swarm has acquired and neutralized its targets."

The yacht owner's eyes were brilliant ice. "Would damage imagery be too tall a request?"

Casimir's attention held on the monitor and control boards.

"It could be done," he said. "The killfish has been recalled beyond the outer edge of the blast zone, and its backscatter sensors show a high density of suspended particulate matter within the zone. But we could task it—"

"No need, bring it back in," the yacht owner said. "Laziness of imagination is a common failing in this day and age, Casimir. We mustn't allow ourselves to submit."

"As you wish."

The yacht owner reclined on his pale orange sofa, his bone-thin form barely impressing weight into its cushions.

"And his spirit moved upon the face of the waters," he said in a near undertone. *"Fiat lux."*

Casimir's head turned briefly to regard him over a white uniform epaulet.

"What was that, sir?"

The yacht owner passed his fingertips through the air.

"Old words from an old and very fascinating story," he said.

TWO

From the *Wall Street Journal* Online Weekend Edition:

UPLINK INTERNATIONAL TO COMPLETE
STALLED MARINE FIBEROPTIC NETWORK
*Experts Agree Venture May Plunge Telecom Giant
into Choppy Seas*

SAN JOSE—In a move analysts believe marks a critical and risky juncture for the world's leading telecommunications super carrier, UpLink International announced earlier this week that it has concluded a long-rumored deal with Planétaire Systems Corp to pick up some very large pieces left by the France-based company's financial tumble.

Once UpLink's primary European rival, Planétaire has been the most recent telecom industry player forced to make sharp operational cutbacks during a period of global economic uncertainty that has seen many established technology firms struggle and fail. While many in the financial sector expect industrywide earnings to improve at least marginally over the next quarter, Planétaire's losses have been deeper than some due to a combination of heavy capital borrowing—said to have exceeded $1.5 billion U.S.—for its construction of a submerged fiberoptic cable ring in the waters around Africa and steep declines in revenue from its cellular telephony service elements.

Although the specific terms of the pact have not been disclosed, insiders report that UpLink has acquired all of Planétaire's existing "wet highway" and terrestrial fiber network equipment and facilities in equatorial African nations, considered some of the most underserved markets on earth, in part due to the region's continuing political and economic instability. Speaking on CNN's *Moneyline* program, however, UpLink vice president and frequent spokeswoman Megan Breen gave high marks to the groundwork laid by Planétaire and expressed confidence in her firm's ability meet any challenges it may face.

"Planétaire has enjoyed tremendous past success, and I'd be pleased if our agreement allows it to consolidate and direct its assets toward a bright future," she said. "Our companies have been very competitive, but at the same time worldwide connectivity is a goal we've always shared, and UpLink is wholly committed to building upon Planétaire's established infrastructure on the African continent."

Ms. Breen emphasizes that commitment is long term, extending into the next decade and beyond. "It's really a logical outreach for us," she said. "Our driving corporate philosophy, and the core belief of our founder Roger Gordian, is that the introduction of modern, reliable Internet and telecom services to developing countries parallels the emergence of America's rail and telegraph system over a hundred years ago and can bring about comparable industrial, political, and social progress."

But some have suggested that Gordian and company

will have to navigate rough waters in a period of rapid financial sea changes—and beware of sinking beneath those shifting currents. The expansion mentioned by Ms. Breen would put considerable strains on the resources of any firm, even one as globally dominant as UpLink. Much of Planétaire's African network is already connected to Europe via seabed fiber cable and there is speculation that UpLink plans to thread a transoceanic line to the Pacific Rim. This ambitious effort would require retrofitting decades-old portions of the system with high-capacity, next-generation equipment and undersea cable—a high-priced undertaking.

Marine maintenance also can be expensive. Less than a year ago Planétaire incurred multimillion dollar repair costs when a segment of cable was damaged off coastal Gabon, the small equatorial nation where its African network hub is located. Two specialist deepwater divers were accidentally killed while investigating the service disruption. Although the tragic incident is presumed to have no bearing on Planétaire's regional pullout, it does point toward the complexity of initiating cable projects in inhospitable and sometimes dangerous environments . . .

"What's wrong?" Pete Nimec said.

"Hmm?" Annie Caulfield said.

"I'm wondering what's the matter."

"Nothing's the matter."

Nimec was otherwise convinced.

"Come on," he said, shaking his head. "Something is definitely the matter."

Annie looked over at him. Nimec looked back at her. She was holding the ladle. He had the spatula.

"What makes you think that?" Annie said, a trifle distantly.

"This right here makes me think it." Nimec raised the spatula and wobbled it in the air between them. It was a proffer of evidence, his smoking gun, courtroom exhibits A through Z rolled into one.

Still looking somewhat preoccupied, Annie regarded him without comment as a bright, warm, daisy yellow torrent of east Texas sunshine washed through the window of her kitchen, where they were at the electric range fixing breakfast, Annie with her blond hair spilling mussily over the collar of her bathrobe, Nimec already dressed in Levi's and a T-shirt, Annie's kids in their pajamas at the opposite end of the house, just stirring under their bedcovers, this being Sunday morning after all.

"You'd better flip that thing," Annie said finally. She nodded toward the sizzling dollop of pancake batter she'd ladled onto the hot skillet in front of him.

"You sure?"

"Unless, of course, you have some reason for wanting to serve Chris and Linda burned pancakes—"

"Ah-hah. Got you. There it is," he said.

"There *what* is?"

"More proof that you're upset with me." Nimec gave the implement in his hand another little shake. "I'm using a metal spatula right here. And the skillet's your expensive nonstick. Means I'm supposed to use a Teflon-coated spatula or screw up the finish, right?"

Annie looked at the blade of the spatula with surprised recognition.

"Yes," she said. "It does."

"Ah-hah," Nimec repeated, and gave her a look that meant his case was closed, open and shut.

He reached past Annie, slipped the spatula into a wall-holder jammed with cooking utensils, pulled a coated spatula from it, and immediately turned the pancake onto its unbrowned side.

"I don't understand," she said. "If you know you aren't supposed to use my metal one—"

"It was a test," he said before she could finish her question.

"A *test*?"

"Right," he said. "I grabbed it to see if you'd notice, and then remind me which spatula I *am* supposed to use."

"Oh," she said.

"But you didn't," he said. "Notice or remind me, that is."

"No, I didn't . . ."

"And you always do," Nimec said. "From the very first time I stayed over. Except once when we had a fight, and you got quiet like you've been all morning."

Annie watched him transfer the finished pancake to a serving tray and then motion for another ladleful of batter. She dipped into the mixing bowl and poured some onto the pan.

"Okay, that's plenty, or the middle won't get done," he said. "Now how about you tell me why you're mad."

"I'm not—"

"You are—"

Annie's sharp look abruptly silenced him.

"That was you and not a Pete Nimec look alike in my bed when I awoke, oh, forty minutes, an hour ago, wasn't it?" she said.

"What's that got to do—?"

"Did the actions I initiated at the time *seem* angry?"

Nimec felt an embarrassed flush in his cheeks. "Well, no . . ."

"Because if they did, we were having a very serious miscommunication."

"No, no. Your, uh, our, communication was fine. Great, actually—"

"So when, and why, do you believe I would have gotten offended?"

"Angry," he clarified.

"What*ever*," she said.

Nimec looked at her a moment, then sighed.

"When you got so quiet afterward," he said, "I wondered if it could have anything to do with my asking you to take Chris and Jonathan to see the Mariners next weekend. Which I wouldn't have done, except that I promised to take them myself, and got Gord to swing those lower box tickets for me."

A moment passed. Annie chin-nodded at the pancake cooking on the skillet. Nimec tossed it.

"Pete," she said. "Why in the world would I mind going to a ball game with my own son?"

"Well, Jon's *my* son . . ."

"Our respective sons, then," she said, and suddenly hesitated. "Jon doesn't have a problem with me, does he?"

"Annie, you know Jon's wild about you."

"I *thought* I knew . . ."

"He is. Crazy wild, in fact. Don't ever worry about that."

"So what exactly do you feel would be the problem?"

Nimec shrugged.

"I don't know," he said. "Though I figured you might not appreciate having to fly all the way to the West Coast with me gone. Or maybe just having to sit through nine innings of baseball, not really being that familiar with the game . . ."

"The boys are always happy to explain its ins and outs to me," she said. "Last time I got the lecture on the cutoff man, backup cutoff man, and the superduper Zimmer-Jeter rover play for when they both miss a throw. And I'll be sure to use lingo like 'lights-out' and 'good stuff' and yell like a maniac whenever Ichiro's at bat."

That produced a faint grin on Nimec's face.

"Guess you *are* pretty good," he said.

"Guess I am." She smiled a little, too, and gestured at the range. "We'd better get the next pancake on."

They did. Nimec watched Annie go through the simple routine of dipping the ladle into her mixing bowl, and pouring the batter into the center of the pan, and rotating the ladle to spread the batter evenly. He watched her and noticed the golden highlights in her hair from the flood of morning sun through the window, and recalled all at once how those accents had seemed a deeper burnished color when he'd held her against him in the flicker of a bedside oil lamp the night before.

"Annie . . ." he said softly.

"Yes?"

"Please help me understand what's bothering you."

She looked up at Nimec's face, and he looked down at hers, their eyes meeting, the two of them standing there by the stove in a kitchen filled with what had become a familiar yet preciously special aroma of weekends spent together after weekdays working in different cities, different states, thousands of miles apart, Annie at the Johnson Space Center in Texas, Nimec at UpLink's main headquarters in California, thousands of miles, so many thousands of miles between them.

"Africa," she said after a long silence. "It's being worried about you going to Africa. To Gabon. A stone's throw from the Congo, where tribal armies that have spent the last quarter century massacring each other in civil wars are usually also in-fighting just as brutally."

"Annie . . ."

"And it's being selfishly, *clingingly* worried about how much I'll miss you."

Silence.

Nimec looked at her, breathed.

"Annie, I'll only be away a few weeks. There's nothing to be afraid of—"

"Like when you were in Antarctica last year? For only a few weeks. An entire continent where people aren't even supposed to have guns, and Cold Corners station was attacked by a small army. Hired *commandos*. You and Meg could have been killed. UpLink has enemies, Pete. That's just how it is. UpLink has serious enemies around the world and I accept it. But don't expect me not to worry."

Nimec said nothing for a while. Then he suddenly moved closer to Annie, dropping the spatula on the counter beside the range, taking the drippy ladle from her hand to let it sink into the mixing bowl, wrapping his arms around her waist and pulling her to him.

"If not for us crossing paths in Antarctica, we wouldn't be together," he said. "That's the other side of it."

"I know, Pete, but—"

He gently held a finger to her lips, silenced her.

"I try to be careful," he said. "Always. But these days I try even harder. Before, I wouldn't care if I was in the field a week, a month, six months. In San Jose, it wasn't much different. The job was everything, my whole life, and the rest was filling time. All I'd come home to on a Friday night was that pool room you're always threatening to disinfect. Now, Friday afternoons at the office, I can't wait to get to the airport. Can't wait to get things done and come back to you. And that's how it'll be in Africa. I'll get things done, and I'll come back."

Annie looked at him, still silent. Bright blue eyes holding on his brown ones. Blond hair shining in the sun. Then Nimec saw her smile and felt her press more tightly against him.

"I love you, Pete," she said, her lips brushing his chin.

"I love you, Annie," he said, his throat thickening inside.

"I smell my panny cakes!" Chris shouted from down the hallway.

Annie smiled.

"Little guy's up," she said in a furry voice.

Nimec winked at her.

"I hope you mean the kid," he said, and reluctantly pulled himself back to the stove.

" 'Plunge telecom giant into choppy seas,' " Megan Breen read aloud, her head bent over the *Journal* piece, an errant tress of hair slipping across her cheek. " 'Navigate rough waters . . .' "

" 'Beware of sinking beneath those shifting currents' happens to be my favorite," Roger Gordian said.

"Ouch." Megan tucked the loose strands behind her ear. They were the rich reddish brown color of midautumn leaves. "Talk about stretching a metaphor, I can almost hear this one groaning."

"And begging in vain for a merciful end," Gordian said.

"Until it lapses into tortured incoherence," Megan said.

Gordian turned from where he stood by the coffee maker in a corner of his office.

"We'd better quit while we're ahead," he said. "You'd almost think the article was written by our old friend Reynold Armitage, wouldn't you?"

Megan sat nodding in front of Gordian's desk. She put her hardcopy down on it.

"Now that you mention it," she said. "What was it he called us in print? 'A growing monstrosity'?"

" 'A growing, *failing* monstrosity,' " Gordian said. "You know, I actually found myself looking for Armitage's byline after scanning the article. But he seems to have pretty well faded from sight since we beat the Monolith takeover attempt."

"Amen," Megan said. "May destiny's sails sweep him along a course far from ours—"

"Megan—"

"Sorry," she said. "It scares me to think I'm becoming so impressionable . . . could be it's all that time on the ice."

Gordian opened a tin of green tea beside the coffee maker, spooned some into his cup's ceramic filter, held the cup under the machine's hot water tap, and ran steaming water over the loose tea leaves. Then he covered the teacup with its lid and looked halfway around at Megan.

"Like some coffee?" he asked, and nodded toward a pot on the warming tray.

"What's the roast?"

"Excuse me?"

"The roast," she said. "I was wondering if you can offer me any of that great Italian coffee you always used to make or if it's more of that weak stuff your dear, sweet, gustatorily desensitized personal assistant's been brewing."

"No idea, I stick to my ocha these days . . . strict orders from Ash," he said, sounding oblivious. "I can ask Norma—"

Megan hastily flapped her hand.

"That's okay," she said. "I'll pop out to Starbuck's later on this morning."

Gordian shrugged, returned to his side of the desk, sat. There was a box of assorted doughnuts to his right. He peered inside, selected one with chocolate frosting and rainbow sprinkles, and took a bite as the tea steeped on his blotter.

"Are the doughnuts permitted by Ashley's dietary edicts?" Megan asked.

Gordian chewed, swallowed, gave her another mild-mannered shrug.

"I haven't mentioned them to her," he said, his expression all innocence. "Her big concern lately seems to be that I get my tea polyphenols. Something about their antioxidant and antiviral properties."

"I see," Megan said. She was thinking that the boss *did* seem incredibly hale and hardy. Perhaps not quite back to the robust fitness he'd exuded before the disease—really an attempted assassination with an insidious bioweapon—that nearly ended his life almost two years ago, but immeasurably better than when she'd left for her nine-month stint in Antarctica. His hair was all gray now, true, and you could see more scalp underneath, but there was little else in his appearance to remind Megan of the anemic fragility he'd shown throughout his early recuperative period. He looked, in a word, restored. And while Megan wasn't inclined to dispute the beneficial properties of tea tannin, or flaxseed oil capsules, or whatever else Gord's wife incorporated into his therapeutic regimen with each of her frequent trips to the health food store, she believed that Ashley herself—her unfailing devotion and perseverence—had been at the true center of his comeback. Ashley, yes, without question, and the combative spirit that beamed from his steely fighter-pilot's eyes and had sustained him through five years of nightmarish captivity in the Hanoi Hilton.

"So," Gordian said now, lifting the filter from his teacup and placing it on a small tray near his elbow. "What are your thoughts?"

Megan looked at him, pulled her mind off its momentary detour.

"About the article, you mean," she said.

Gordian nodded. "*Articles*, plural. And I'm referring to their journalistic merit rather than prose stylings. A

lot's been written about our African plans since we laid
them out to the financial press, and none of the pieces
I've seen is applauding our judgment."

Megan shrugged.

"You'll notice the total absence of shock on my face,"
she said. "Those pieces might give a rosier view of things
if the splendid and talented wordsmiths behind them
bothered with their *easy* homework. . . . And what gets
me ticked is that it wouldn't mean shelling out so much
as fifty or sixty expense-account dollars for one of those
overpriced country investment guides. Any legitimate reporter has budgeted—id est, free—access to online information services. What would it take to find an
economic profile on Gabon? Or West Africa in general?
A five-minute search, and they'd have loads of data about
the oil and gas field development that's been going on
offshore . . . especially Sedco Chemical's licensed acreage blocks."

Gordian abruptly broke into a grin.

"Fiery," he said.

"What?"

"You *don't* look shocked," he said. "I'm just hoping
the flames you're spitting won't set off the sprinkler system."

Megan felt a smile steal across her own lips.

"Maybe I don't have much tolerance for people who
run on negative charges. Less than ever after Cold Corners, and seeing how everyone there came together to
tough out the worst of situations," she said. "But it's like
Alex Nordstrum says. After the military contracts Up-
Link landed a decade ago, you could have gone into
instant retirement. Spent the rest of your life chasing hot-
air-balloon-around-the-world records, climbing mountains in the Himalayas, crossing the Atlantic in replica
Viking ships . . . what Alex calls jolly follies. The nay-

sayers don't carp about anybody who makes that sort of choice. I'm not sure I particularly wish they would. You've stayed in the real world, though. Put everything on the line to make a difference, corny as *that* sounds. And they're always expecting you to fall on your face."

Gordian raised his teacup, inhaled the flowery-scented steam wafting up from it, and sipped. He put down the cup, took a large bite of his doughnut, chewed quietly, swallowed. Then he dabbed a bright pink sugar sprinkle from the corner of his mouth and had another sip of tea.

"Megan, I'm flattered, but these are my questions," he said after a while. "First, do you think we're getting in over our heads with this fiber project? And second, can I assume the more conscientious homework you implied the newsies should have done relates to Dan Parker holding a chair on Sedco's board of directors?"

Megan looked at him for about thirty seconds, thinking.

"I'll try to roll my answers together," she said. "I studied the figures we received from the number crunchers, and gave Vince Scull's risk-assessment report some careful attention. Then I factored in Murphy's Law and concluded our spending in Africa's going to *surpass* what the negative-charge people expect by two to three billion dollars over the next couple of years. To be honest, four billion wouldn't surprise me if we start integrating our broadband fiber and satellite facilities. That would deplete us to an extent we might not be able to sustain, even with the credit guarantees we've secured from Citigroup." Megan paused and leaned forward. "That said, we also have a great shot at success. But I really believe it hangs on doubling up our projects in the Ogooué Fan. And *that* means we need to clinch the deal to wire Sedco's deepwater platforms to each other and then build the cable out to their land-based offices. The advance capital from Sedco can carry us for a minimum of two years, and by then we should be seeing a slow but steady return on our African telecom expenditures as a whole."

Gordian had moved his cup of green tea—still about two-thirds full, Megan noticed—aside and out of his way on the desktop. Now he reached for a second doughnut and got started on it.

"Qualified optimism," he said after swallowing a mouthful of fried dough, grape jelly, and chocolate frosting. "Is that how you'd describe your Monday morning outlook?"

Megan shrugged.

"I'd say it's considered optimism," she answered. "There's a difference."

Gordian sat, nodded, and ate his doughnut.

Megan looked past him out the office's polarized glass wall at Mount Hamilton in the southern distance, its great flank rearing over the Diablo Range like a hump of bunched and knotted muscle. It was a clear, sunny day and she could see the Lick astronomical observatory domes gleaming white on its four-thousand-foot summit. The view reminded her of something.

"I stopped by Pete's office on the way to mine, but he wasn't there," she said. "Do you know if he got hung up in Houston?"

Gordian shook his head. "Pete took a long weekend," he said. "He'll be leaving for Gabon with the advance team on Friday, and wanted to spend some extra time with Annie Caulfield."

Megan smiled a little, her expression hinting at an unstated thought.

"They've become quite an item," she said.

"Seems the case." Gordian looked at her. "It's interesting to me how they got together romantically. The circumstances, that is."

Megan tapped the corner of her mouth with a fingertip. "What do you mean?" she asked.

Gordian finished his second doughnut, reached for a napkin, wiped his lips, and then tossed the crumpled napkin into his wastebasket.

"They first met in Florida. When Pete went down there to help investigate the space shuttle tragedy at Cape Canaveral," he said. "It was clear they worked well as a team, but kept their relationship all professional at the time. Or didn't go too far beyond that, anyway."

Megan looked at him.

"You never can tell. Pete's such a tightly corked bottle, it's almost impossible getting him to spill anything about his private life."

"I think I had a bit of an inside line," Gordian said. "Annie and I stayed in contact afterward. UpLink having so many ties to NASA, and she being an executive at the JSC, of course . . ."

"Right, of course . . ."

"Annie would often ask how Pete was doing, ask if I'd say hello to him for her, that sort of thing. And I'd always pass along her best wishes."

"Right . . ."

"Although Pete never commented or showed much reaction," Gordian said. "Then after a while Annie *stopped* sending her regards but would still occasionally mention Pete during our conversations. For the most part wanting to know if he was okay. So I can pretty safely conclude they lost touch."

"Well," Megan said. "That seems a logical guess."

"It does," Gordian said. "And it's the reason I find it so interesting that their love bloomed amid the frozen wastes an entire year later, excuse my stale poetic instincts."

Megan caught a quick glance from him.

"Why the look?" she asked.

"I was just wondering if you had any insights," Gordian said. "Given that you were with the two of them at Cold Corners."

Megan quickly shook her head.

"No," she said. "No insights."

"You're sure? I can't shake this hunch that something or some*one* helped coax them along . . ."

"You're asking the wrong person," she said.

"Oh," Gordian said. "Because I know you're about as close to Pete as anyone. Besides Annie, naturally. And that you've become very friendly with *her* since Antarctica . . ."

"I was too busy with my responsibilities as chief administrator to put on a second hat."

"Second hat?"

"As in social director."

"Oh," Gordian said.

"Or matchmaker, if that's what you're suggesting . . ."

"Then it was long-time-no-see, I love you for the two of them?"

Megan shrugged.

"I suppose," she said.

Gordian shot her another glance. "That sounds very un-Nimecian, so to speak."

"Like I said, you never can tell." She shrugged again. "I'd better get back to my office, there's a ton of paperwork that's been waiting since Friday."

Gordian nodded, watching Megan rise from the chair opposite him.

"However their match got made, whoever may or may not have given it a kick start," he said, "it's wonderful to see Pete and Annie happy."

Megan paused in front of Gordian's desk, a dark mahogany affair roughly the size of a fifteenth-century Spanish war galleon.

"Yes," she said, struggling against an insistent grin. "It really is, isn't it?"

Port-Gentil sits on the low-lying Ile de Mandji finger peninsula of Gabon amid estuarine swamps and deltas that swell to flood levels in the rainy season, the drainage channels describing its neighborhoods joined by small bridges that are more pleasantly—and safely—crossed on foot than in one of the city's speeding, careening taxis.

No such bridges span the social divisions between district borders. In the fringe neighborhoods of Salsa and Sans there is unemployment and periodic lawlessness. Street crime may be scurrying or savage as opportunity bids, the hustle alternating with the gun.

Downtown in elegant colonial homes, ears sensitive to mannered conversation are deaf to far-off sounds of crime and looting in the night. Was that a crash of breaking storefront glass beyond the canal? A woman's pitched scream? *Ce n'est rien*, leave it to the gendarmerie! Instead, enjoy the gentle clink of the champagne flute, the cognac snifter. This is where the magnates and government officials thrive—an upper stratum of wealthy, educated *functionairres* molded and hardened over a century ago, when Gabon was the capitol of French Equatorial Africa. This, too, is home to the expatriates: bankers, investors, industrialists, and technical engineers drawn by the country's oil and precious mineral reserves.

Their nights are calm and long in comforts, their days busy and filled with enterprise.

The man in the panama hat and white tropical-weight suit had found Port-Gentil a good place to settle. Here he had eluded his enemies and was able to move with freedom, delving into currents where he could satisfy his innate drive to achieve and attain. When not aboard the *Chimera* attending to his dark occupations, he liked to stroll the city's conspicuously miscellaneous districts and take in their skewed contrasts: mosque and casino, skull cap and pomade, luxury hotel and hovel, sidewalk café and fetish market. Often he stopped outside the large church where worshipers raised their voices in a fusion of Christian hymns and animistic chants, hedging their bets by musically praising Christ as they recalled ancient initiations to the Cult of Fire.

The market was among his favorite spots, a crowd of outdoor stalls lined up in aisles in a section of town called Le Grand Village.

Today there had been a bad moment during his walk. The blazing dry-season heat took his mind back to Bolivia, and the time he had turned his face to the sun and burned away his rage, feeling the layers of skin redden and blister in its searing exposure. Such flashes of that memory were exceptional for him. He had suffered the annealing pain, scoured the leftover contaminants of defeat from within himself, and gone forward with things. But the disappointing news from America had caused the past to seep into his mind lately, and for those few seconds it had found a particularly deep route of entry. At the Beacon District sidewalk stand where he had stopped for *pain beurre* and coffee, he paid the vender his coins and left the breakfast sitting on his cart. The African street had faded around him and he was again on the veranda of his Chapare ranch house, his dull-eyed, placidly stupid heifers grazing in the distance. And his face was on fire in the sun.

Then his brief opening to the recollection shut tight, and it was Bolivia that evaporated from thought. He had continued to the market for the item he wished to pick up before calling on his governmental contact at city hall.

Once there he had gone directly to a merchant of charms and ritual medicines known among the circumspect for his choice stock, transported from around the continent in defiance of endangered species and antiquities laws that intimidated others—all of it stored in barrels, baskets, cartons, crates, burlap sacks, even rusted cans arranged beneath his stall's straw canopy. He trafficked in back-room merchandise while lacking a back room, pawned smuggled hides and relics with his left hand, and common medicinal powders and charms with his right . . . sometimes shuffling items from one hand to the other.

That this merchant was an ace of the swindle just gave bargaining with him a crisp edge. His combination of guile and brazenness merited appreciation and kept the man in the white suit's own cunning instincts honed.

The dealer sat in his simple kaftan behind a wide display board mounted on loose foundation stones, and cluttered with animal skulls, horns, and hooves. Carved wooden masks hung from one of the thick canopy poles, bunches of desiccated lizard and mammal cadavers from another.

He acknowledged his customer with a quick smile of recognition.

"Je suis heureux de vous voir."

"Merci, vous êtes très aimiable."

Their polite exchange of greetings out of the way, the man in the white suit had been specific about what he wanted to acquire, and the merchant was quick to declare he could provide it. Indeed, the desired commodity was not, strictly speaking, black market; legalities only discouraged the practice by which it was obtained and put it in short supply. He had turned from his display board, knelt on his haunches, and then begun moving and shifting the containers, taking occasional furtive glances over his shoulders at passersby. The man in the white suit kept an observant eye on him. Soon the merchant located the carton he'd been seeking, unfolded its flaps, pulled a coffee can from inside, took off the can's plastic lid, and extracted a sealed plastic bag that had been folded double and packed in sawdust.

He blew bits of shaved wood off the bag as he got back to his feet and returned to his customer.

"It is in here," he said. "Forty years old, maybe older. There aren't many to be found these days. It is valued by collectors—"

The man in the white suit had stared him into silence.

"I am not a collector," he said and held out his hand. "You will vouch for its place of origin?"

"The highlands in western Kenya, near Lake Victoria."

"I see. It is Gusii, then."

"Yes. From a warlord, I am told."

"By who?"

"The *omobari omotwe* himself," the merchant said. "He still lives to curse those Red Cross and missionary doctors who stole his patients."

The man in the white suit had taken the bag, opened it, removed the article inside with his thumb and forefinger, and given it a careful inspection. The shape, feel, and coloration were right; after a few minutes he'd been convinced it was authentic.

"Tell me your price," he said, and slipped it back into the bag.

He had paid what the merchant asked without dickering and left the market for his appointment downtown.

Etienne Begela's title was Minister of Economic Development, and his office was on the fifth floor of town hall, a building of tall colonnades and marble walls that reflected the august sensibilities of the French governors for whom it was originally built. The man in the white suit had announced himself at the main security desk and waited less than a minute before the guard who phoned upstairs motioned him toward the elevator.

Now he took the short ride up, walked through a hall in profound need of air-conditioning, and turned a bend. A young woman approached, rushing toward the car from which he had just emerged—Begela's aide. Her gaze averted, she nodded her head in acknowledgment as she swept past him.

He returned the minor courtesy, sensing her nervousness.

Another turn of a corner and he saw Begela at his door, leaning out into the corridor.

"Mr. Fáton," the minister said. "*Bonjour*, do come in—"

The man in the white suit disdained physical contact, but allowed for local custom and shook Begela's extended hand. The Gabonese were demonstrative in their airs, offering the firm grip and steady eye as they connived.

As he entered Begela's office, Fáton noticed a cup of steaming coffee and an open records file on the aide's unoccupied desk. Not to his surprise, she had been hastily dismissed.

Begela showed Fáton through to his inner office, pulling its door closed behind them. Fáton had seen the room before, a typical high-ranking bureaucrat's sanctuary, its walls fortified with certificates of education and accolade, photographs of Begela posed alongside his ministerial cohorts, a flagpole in the corner—in this instance brandishing the green, yellow, and blue national stripes.

Begela gestured toward his desk with a sweeping wave of his arm.

"Please, please have a seat," he said, his too-loud voice

another example of that nettlesome overexpressiveness. "I know why you've come, but let me reassure you that I did my best in Libreville."

"Your best?" Fáton lowered himself into a chair, removed his hat, and watched the minister round the desk to sit opposite him. "It seems, Etienne, that the unwanted newcomers face no greater problem than to choose their lodgings before arrival. Are you going to tell me that is all I was to expect from you? After listening to your pledges? After what I have spent?"

The minister looked at him. His skin was chestnut brown, his face a long oval. With its flat cheeks and narrow eyes under high, arched brows, it seemed an animated version of a Congolese mask Fáton had once purchased for himself at the fetish market.

"I've kept my promise," Begela said. "Nothing in life is certain, and in the capitol this is particularly true. Some members of the National Assembly have been swayed by UpLink's—"

Fáton's hissing expulsion of breath instantly silenced him.

"Watch your words," he said. "That name is vile to my ears, and its mention further erodes my confidence in you. Only a fool would think this cubbyhole secure as we sit here."

Begela opened his mouth, closed it.

"Monsieur Fáton, I share your disappointment with the results of my trip," he said at last. "My ties to factions within the assembly have tilted the balance of important decisions affecting Port-Gentil in the past, and I was frankly convinced they would do so again in this instance. It was indicated to me that your, shall we say, financial incentives, would be the glue for a political coalition that could block the Americans from finalizing arrangements with my government. But in the end the

assemblymen who signaled they would act in your—
our—favor backed down. As did a fellow minister in the
Office des Postes et Telecommunications . . . someone
with whom I have a clan affiliation and whose promises
are normally trustworthy. No offer was enough. The president and prime minister are adamant about welcoming
those we wish to keep out. They control the ruling party,
and the party holds more than half the assembly's hundred and twenty seats. And, needless to say, the assembly
controls the OPT."

"Ah," Fáton said. "And what am I to take from this
lesson in Gabonese civics? Other than further evidence
that your prating assertions of influence meant nothing.
That you failed me."

Begela shook his head in denial.

"It may be true we cannot keep the Americans out of
this city at present," he said. "Their future is anything
but inevitable, however. Port-Gentil is many kilometers
from Libreville. And I have recourse to ways of making
their time here most unpleasant."

Fáton traced a finger around the brim of the panama
hat on his lap.

"If by that you mean your pathetic assortment of
greased gendarmes, technicals, and militiamen, then you
are once again exaggerating your reach," he said.

Begela continued shaking his head, his hands on the
arms of his chair. "With utmost respect, I think I know
something about my own people—"

"Perhaps so, Etienne. But you know nothing of the
enemy's strength," Fáton said. "I cannot afford another
fumble . . . which brings me to the reason for this call."
He paused, his eyes on Begela's. "I've picked up a gift.
A piece of history that I hope will benefit you. Help you
avoid similar misjudgments from this point onward."

Fáton reached into an inner jacket pocket for the plastic bag he'd brought from the fetish market, removed what was inside, and leaned forward to set it down on the desk.

The minister's high, curved eyebrows became more pronouncedly elevated. A bleached white color, the object was a smooth, not quite flat disk perhaps four inches in circumference.

"What is this?" he said, drawing back with an involuntary start.

Fáton kept his gaze on the minister.

"Come now," he said. "I shouldn't have to tell a man of your erudition and deep cultural roots."

Begela shuddered a little. He was taking in quick snatches of air, as though short of breath.

"C'est un rondelle," he said.

"There you go," Fáton said. "My source assures me it was taken from the skull of a Gusii chieftain. I cannot offer independent verification, but that's of trivial consequence with something of this rarity. As you can see, it is close to a perfect circle. I also think it worth appreciating the even, regular scrape marks around its edges, where the cranial hole was made. All in all, a beautiful specimen. One that would have required an expert bit of filing and scraping with the *omobari*'s knife."

Begela stared at the object, his hands still gripping the arms of his chair.

"Why?" he said. "Why do you come here with such a thing—?"

"I shall not repeat myself," Fáton said. "Surely you know that a patient would be trephined to rid him of demons believed to have lodged within his skull. Similar practices were used in medieval France when surgeons looked to remove *pierres de tête*—stones of madness—from the brains of idiots and the delusionally insane." A thin smile touched his mouth. "I don't know if any were ever found, Etienne. But your people are enamored of French tradition, yes?"

The minister sat in silence. Beads of sweat had gathered in the depression above his upper lip.

"Take it," Fáton said. "Carry it as a talisman around your neck, or in a pocket over your heart. How you wear it is not my concern . . . just so long as it stays on your person." He continued to smile faintly. "May it guard your head against poisonous thoughts, and serve as a reminder of what can happen to a man who succumbs to them."

Begela looked at him. Then he slowly lifted a hand off his chair, reached toward the desk, and closed his fingers around the rondelle.

"What should I do next?" he said in a dry rasp. "About the Americans . . ."

"You needn't do anything for the moment—but I appreciate the fact that you've asked. It already signifies a new mental clarity." Fáton rose and put on his hat. "Between us, I've planned an intense study of the enemy that should determine our tactics against him in coming days. Find what he treasures most, and you've identified his greatest vulnerability. Take it from him, and you hold the key to his defeat and destruction. It is a simple doctrine that can prove complicated in execution . . . but a game without challenge is hardly worth playing, don't you agree?"

The minister had lowered his eyes onto the back of his own clenched, trembling hand.

"Quite so," he said.

Fáton stood before the minister's desk, his smile growing until it showed a row of small, even teeth.

"I'm glad we agree," he said in an indulgent tone. "It seems to me we've made progress here today. And progress, Etienne, is always a delightful lift."

● ● ●

The adoption center was at the end of a long dirt and gravel drive that led off the coiling two-lane blacktop between Pescadero Creek County Park and Portola State Park, a short fork in the road to the southwest. Julia Gordian considered herself fairly adept at following directions, but because the sign marking the drive was obscured by a thick outgrowth of oak and fir, she had missed it at first and had driven twenty minutes past her destination to the Pescadero Creek Park entrance. There a helpful ranger at the admissions gate had steered her back around, advising her to stay on the lookout for a PG&E roadside utility station about an eighth of a mile before the unpaved turnoff.

The utility station was nothing more than a green metal shed with a concrete apron that almost blended into the woods to the right, and Julia spotted it only at the last instant. But soon afterward she'd seen the sign with the wood-burned depiction of a greyhound on a rustic post amid the trees. She had swung her brand new Honda Passport onto the mostly uphill drive, muttering a stream of obscenities at the pebbles spitting up from under the vehicle's tires to pop and rattle against its windows, and sparing some choice words for the jutting branches on either side as they raked across its shiny silver finish.

Julia drove slowly along. She had just strung together a phrase pairing synonyms for the excretory functions of various farm animals and a particularly objectionable sex act between human family members, when two buildings came into sight ahead of her—a small frame house with a neat lawn to her left and a flat-roofed prefabricated aluminum structure some yards beyond it. There were five greyhounds cavorting in a large pen behind the house. Two of them were fawn colored, two were roans, and the odd dog out was a tawny brindle. It hardly surprised Julia that none of the greyhounds were gray.

She rolled the Passport into a dusty, weed-smattered parking area by the prefab, cut the engine, grabbed her handbag off the passenger seat, strapped it over her shoulder, and got out. The plain metal sign above the building's open door read:

PENINSULA GREYHOUND RESCUE AND ADOPTION CENTER

As she started toward the building, a man in blue jeans, a plaid work shirt, and a baseball cap with a well broken-in bill appeared in its entrance, and then came down the two wide front doorsteps to greet her.

"Julia Gordian?" he said.

She nodded. "And you must be—"

"Rob Howell, pleasure to meet you," he said, smiling an instantly likeable smile. A lank six footer with a dark scruff of beard, he held a cell phone in his right hand, offered her the other. A pair of heavy rubber gloves was stuffed into his back pocket. "Today's my day to clean the exercise area out back. Cynthia . . . that's my wife . . . saw you drive up and called to let me know. I'll introduce you later, when she's through feeding our six-month-old."

Julia nodded again and stood quietly in the warm sunlight.

"So," Howell said after a moment. "How was your trip here?"

"Oh, great," Julia said. "Very relaxing, in fact."

"Any trouble spotting that sign down the hill? Guess it's kind of hard to notice sometimes. With all the branches I'm always forgetting to trim—"

"No, no, I saw it just fine." She nodded over toward the house. "Those are beautiful dogs back there . . . are they up for placement?"

"Actually, they're our personal brood. Rachel, Monica, Phoebe, Ross, and Joey. Don't ask how we got stuck with them—"

"What about Chandler?" Julia said. "I assume they're named after characters from that TV show *Friends*. . . ."

"Right, that's it."

"And Chandler being the sixth, well, friend . . ."

"Cynthia and I try to leave an open slot. Just in case another dog turns out to be irresistible," Howell said with another smile. "You have, what, two ex-racers of your own?"

"Jack and Jill," Julia said. "Which means a third pooch would have to be named Hill or Pail of Water. If I use your general naming formula."

"There's a lesson in that for prospective adopters, I suppose," he said. "Stick to nursery rhymes with lots of characters—"

"And sitcoms with large ensemble casts."

Both were grinning now.

"Follow me," Howell said and nodded toward the center. "We should talk about the job."

The area just inside the building's doorway turned out to be a combination waiting area and supply-and-gift shop. There were folding chairs to one side of the room that Julia guessed were for visitors, a counter and cash register, and walls lined with all manner of greyhound-related merchandise: books on the breed's history and care; porcelain statues and life-size posters of greys; ashtrays, coffee mugs, pens, beach towels, cooking aprons, sweatshirts, T-shirts, jackets, and even socks featuring their likenesses. There were also leashes, collars, and coats as well as plenty of general dog health and grooming items.

Howell had noticed Julia looking around the place.

"Every cent we make here at our In the Money

store . . . that's a little play on words, since racing grey-hounds get retired, really discarded, by their kennel own-ers and trainers after they've finished *out* of the money once too often . . . goes toward the upkeep of our facility and maintenance and veterinary expenses for the dogs," he said. "We do lots of mail order and are just getting into online sales."

Julia faced him, impressed. "That's quite an opera-tion," she said.

Howell stood at one end of the counter, an elbow rest-ing on its edge.

"Right now, it's tough," he said. "Cyn's got the baby on her hands, and I'm a night auditor over at a hotel out near San Gregario Beach. But we try our best to juggle everything."

"There are no other volunteers?"

Howell shook his head.

"We used to have a couple of regulars, super folks," he said. "A college student who came in two, three af-ternoons a week. And a woman who'd help us out Sat-urdays. But the kid transferred to an out-of-state school, and the woman's a single mom who's had to take on a paying weekend job to make ends meet." Howell shrugged. "When she couldn't cut the schedule anymore, I decided to put up fliers in pet stores."

"Like the one I saw," Julia said. "How's the response been?"

He wobbled a hand in the air.

"I'd categorize it as lukewarm. There've been a few candidates, besides you. They were all well intentioned, bless 'em. But being a dog lover or even somebody who's put in hours at an ordinary animal shelter, isn't necessarily enough of a qualification. People who haven't had experience with greys don't expect the kind of work that's involved after we rescue them from the track. The dogs are sick, malnourished, and covered with open sores from being cooped up in wooden boxes whenever they're not racing. They've spent their lives in what amounts to a state of sensory deprivation, and it's easy to lose patience with a seventy- or eighty-pound, five-year-old adult that's basically a puppy in terms of behavioral development. They aren't housebroken. They need to be taught how to walk up and down stairs. They've never seen windows before and think they can jump right through glass. They're traumatized, afraid of everything. And with good reason. Maybe sixty percent of them have caught regular beatings from their handlers. I've got to figure, though it's not as if anybody's going to fess up to it. The dogs come in with gashes, bruises, torn ears, even broken teeth and ribs."

Julia nodded.

"Jill couldn't do stairs for six months," she said. "And Jack must've been very badly abused. He'd wake up from a dead sleep and spring onto all fours, screaming, his eyes bulging. The sound of those screams, God, it was so horrible. So *human*. The first time, I was sure he was in excruciating pain, having some kind of physical seizure. I think it was the middle of the night. My husband . . . well, my ex . . . phoned the veterinary clinic's emergency number, but before we could reach anybody, Jack settled down. From then on, I'd try to soothe him whenever it happened, talk to him the way you'd talk to a person who's had an awful nightmare. That worked okay after a while. But he still has occasional episodes."

Howell gave her an assaying look from where he stood against the counter.

"Guess I don't need to worry about your experience," he said.

She smiled. "Guess not."

Howell was silent a moment.

"You want to know the hardest thing about running this show?" he said at length. "For me and Cyn, anyway?"

She nodded again.

"It's letting go of the dogs once we've gotten them healthy," he said. "We find that handling more than fifteen or twenty stretches us thin, though we've boarded as many as thirty at a time. Every grey we save arrives with a whole set of problems and needs lots of attention. Some are here months, even years, before we find a suitable home, and they can grow on you. One-on-one. But you have to be able to keep a certain distance, almost a doctor-patient relationship, and that takes a strong kind of person. You invest too much of yourself in a particular animal, you're going to have your heart broken more than a little when it's placed."

Julia looked at him.

"Or wind up living with the whole cast of *Friends*," she said, thinking she'd managed to survive her disastrous seven-year investment in a *marriage* that had been liquidated when Craig decided to take a sudden hike on her—talk about having to let go and learn to cope with heartbreak.

The room was quiet. Howell leaned against the counter, a thoughtful expression on his face. Julia heard the distinctive throaty woofing of a grey somewhere out back of the building, followed by that of a second dog. Then the overlapping, explosive barks of what sounded like at least three or four more of them.

"Rolling thunder," Howell said. "They've been stuck in their kennels all day, and are letting me know they want to be let out to do their business." He pushed himself off the counter. "You have time to help with that right now?"

Julia smiled.

"Sure," she said. "Whatever dirty job you ask of me."

Howell motioned toward the door.

"C'mon," he said. "We'll work out your schedule while we walk."

THREE

SAN JOSE, CALIFORNIA
MADRID, SPAIN
GABON, AFRICA

WEARING PROTECTIVE GOGGLES AND EARMUFFS, THE two men stood ready, their knees bent, hands wrapped around the butts of their weapons.

Then they heard the double beeps in their electronic muffs, a cue that their timed session had started.

They sighted down the shooting range's raceway lanes. Now, or maybe an instant from now, their targets would begin moving at changing speeds and angles in computer-generated, randomized tactical scenarios.

In Nimec's lane, inconspicuous lights dimmed to simulate crepuscular conditions. It was dawn or twilight, and the big bad wolves were out on the prowl.

Nimec saw a metal practice figure shaped like a male head and torso swing up at a firing point in front of him, snapped the muzzle of his Beretta 92 toward it, and squeezed the trigger. The exposed target turned edgewise on its pneumatic actuator stand, avoiding the first 9-mm round. Then it began to duck down. But Nimec's second shot tagged its flank before it could reach concealment.

He had no chance to congratulate himself. Another target had emerged from the left side of his raceway lane and charged. Nimec shifted his aim as Metal Man reversed and started to retreat, covering ten feet in about a second. One shot, two, and then the third stopped Metal Man dead in his tracks.

Fast SOB, Nimec thought. He drew a breath, sliced his gaze this way and that. Another target leaned out from against the wall—a shoulder, a head. His gun crashed, good-bye Charlie.

In the next lane of the newly overhauled indoor course, Tom Ricci stared into different lighting conditions. Diffuse, full. It could have been the artificial illumination of an office building, a warehouse. Or—

No, not there, he didn't want to go there.

Ricci held his FN Five-Seven by its stippled grip, waited, his nose stinging from the nitrate smell of propellent powder. He'd aced a pair of badguys that had sprung into sight back at the end of the lane and expected more of them, knew there'd be more, *wanted* more.

Ricci kept waiting, concentrating, eyes hard for the kill. He tasted acid at the root of his tongue and liked it.

Then, about forty feet down, here was pop-up badguy number three. Dead center in the lane, cutout gun in hand, got himself some balls, this one. *Okay. Okay.* Ricci aimed, eager to take him.

And suddenly his mind turned the hated, unwilling loop. Could be it was the preprogrammed lighting. Or maybe that was groping for a reason. Ricci wouldn't think about it until later. *Office building, warehouse . . . germ factory.* Right now he was back. He was there.

Northern Ontario. The Earthglow facility. Déjà vu all over and over and over again—

Together they move down the hall. Ricci in the lead, followed by Nichols, Rosander, and Simmons, three members of the Sword rapid deployment team assembled at Ricci's unrelenting insistence. This is their first mission as a unit, and it is one hell of a nasty biscuit: They have penetrated the heavily guarded facility seeking a cure—

or information that might lead to a cure—for the lab-engineered virus with which Roger Gordian has been deliberately infected. Around them are austere gray walls, doors with plain institutional signs. Ricci slows before each sign to read it, then trots forward, seeking the one they need.

The corridor bends to the right, runs straight for twenty feet, hangs another right, then goes straight again for a short hitch and angles left. The men sprint around this last elbow and see a bottleneck elevator. An arrow below its single call button points downward—a sublevel. On the wall next to the button is a glass plate, what Ricci believes to be an electronic eye, hand, or facial geometry scanner. There is a biohazard trefoil above the elevator's shiny convex door. The sign beneath it reads:

RESTRICTED
BSL-4 LABORATORIES
AUTHORIZED PERSONNEL ONLY

Ricci feels a cold tack push into his heart. While no medical expert, he's done his homework in preparation for the raid, and knows that BSL-4 is the highest level of safeguard for personnel working with dangerous pathogens. It occurs to him that this may well be the birthplace of the mutant virus that is turning Gordian's internal organs to bloody sludge in a San Jose hospital bed. He also realizes that the killer, who Rollie Thibodeau—Ricci's co-supervisor of field security operations—calls the Wildcat, is likely one of the authorized. Ricci detests the name Thibodeau has attached to him, thinks it sounds too much like a badge of honor. But then, he and Thibodeau are on very different pages about almost everything.

Ricci lets these thoughts have their unpleasant mo-

ment, then he looks at Rosander and Simmons.

"We have to separate," he says. "Somebody could come up this elevator, surprise us from the rear. It's got to be watched while I scope out the rest of the hall."

The two men accept his orders in silence. Then a thumbs-up from Rosander, his eyes fastened on Ricci's.

"Good luck," he says. "Chief."

There is pride and respect in Rosander's voice as he addresses Ricci with that informal designation of rank. Chief. Even if there were time, Ricci knows he could never express how much it means to him. He is not the share-and-bare-it-all type. Not by a hobbled man's mile.

He nods, claps Rosander's shoulder, shifts his gaze to Nichols, who is young, green, and has made mistakes in training that might have gotten someone else dismissed from the team. In fact, the kid had been prepared to lay his head on the chopping block afterward. But Ricci had seen some of his own fire in Nichols's eyes—only a cleaner, brighter, untainted flame—and convinced him to stay on.

"Ready?"

"Yes, sir."

Ricci nods again.

"Come on, it's you and me," he says, and they hurry on along the corridor, leaving the other two men behind to guard their rear.

Though Ricci cannot know it, the next time he sees them they will be dead on the floor near the elevator, Simmons bleeding out from multiple bullet wounds to the side of his rib cage, Rosander with a crushed windpipe, and his brains oozing from a point-blank gunshot to the head meant to finish him off like an animal in a slaughterhouse pen.

And that will not be the worst of it. Unbelievably, unbearably, not the worst . . .

Ricci heard the flat, electronically baffled report of his gun through his earmuffs—a sound that tugged him from the sinkhole of memory with his finger still tight on the trigger. He took in the present like a drowning man starved for air as the third firing-range badguy went down, caught by a single clean shot. The Five-Seven raised level with his chest, Ricci stood waiting, ready, wanting to stay fluid as the tac sequence progressed. To keep his mind on the controllable here and now, and resist the desirous undertow of the past.

A second ticked by. Ricci breathed, exhaled. Ready. Steady. A crouched figure appeared from the right side of the course, the computerized lights dimming around it for a little added mischief and chaos. *Go!* Ricci swiveled his extended arms, sighted over the nub of his gun barrel, and bang. Crouching badguy was no more.

Ricci held a motionless shooter's stance. Took another breath. Kept trying not to think but to *be*. Here, now. In the moment, as the movie stars liked to say. Then a fifth badguy sprang out at him, standing at full height, facing Ricci from the middle of the corridor—

No, no. The firing lane.

Ricci swore to himself. Just what moment had he been in?

He got that biting, bitter taste in his mouth again, his gun swinging into position, his finger starting its deadly squeeze . . . and stopping.

Another figure had sprung up out of nowhere directly in front of the badguy. A woman, her painted-on eyes wide, her painted-on mouth gaping in a silent scream, the expression a cartoon facsimile of terror. Ricci held his fire. This was goddamned unexpected. Sure, why not? *Unexpected* was the whole point of this exercise.

Clever fucking software.

Practice badguy, practice hostage.

Ricci hesitated. *Tick-tick-tick.* Decision time. Now thought had to reenter the process. And with thought came a backslide into the choking memories of Ontario, and his dash through that final passage with Nichols, deep in the hornet's nest, desperate to find what he needed to save Gordian's life, uncertain whether he'd even know how to recognize it, or the place where it would be stored. Ricci's helmet gear had provided wireless audiovisual contact with Eric Oh, an epidemiologist who was coaching him from three time zones away in California, and who Ricci had been told *might* know if they were very lucky—

On his right, behind a thick plate-glass inset, Ricci sees a large room filled with equipment that seems to indicate he's getting hot. Tanks, ducting, air feed, and intake pumps.

"Doc? You with me?" he says into his helmet mike.

"Yes. You're looking at the microencapsulation lab. This can't be far from where they'd keep the cure."

"Right. Assuming there is one."

Silence to that remark.

Ricci looks at the solid concrete wall ahead of him with a stitch of apprehension, hustles along at a trot. The problem is he's running out of hallway. Three, four more office doors on either side, and that's it. Dead end. If he doesn't find what he needs here, it's doubtful he can shift the hunt to another part of the facility without turning all his men into casualties. He can almost feel the weight of their lives on his shoulders.

"Ricci, wait, slow down!" Eric's voice is loud, excited in his comlink's earpiece. "Over on your left, that door!"

He stops, turns, scans the sign above it:

POLYMERASE ACTIVATORS/ANTIVIRALS

"Tom, listen—"

"You don't have to translate," Ricci says. "We're going in."

He quickly moves to the left of the door, waves Nichols to the opposite side, tries the knob. Locked. Stepping back, Ricci aims his weapon—it is a compact variable velocity rifle system subgun with adjustable lethal or nonlethal settings—at the spot below the knob, squeezes off a staccato burst, then kicks out at the door. It flings inward without resistance, the lock mechanism in fragments from his shots.

They scramble into the room, Ricci fanning his outthrust gun to the left, Nichols buttonhooking to the right of the doorway, looking sharp, his technique perfect.

The office is unoccupied, its lights off. Ricci finds the wall switch and they come on.

He is seconds from a decision that he will always wish he could unmake.

The mid-size room is windowless, partitioned into four central soundproof cubicles that enclose counters and computer workstations. The double-depth multimedia filing/storage units built into the walls are six feet high, with slide-out drawers and rotating shelves in steel housings. Quick access systems, no doors, no locks. It doesn't surprise Ricci. The staffers allowed into this office, this entire wing of the building, would have wide clearance anyway.

He moves deeper into the room, turns to Nichols.

"You better stand outside in the hall, watch my back," he says, forking two fingers at his own eyes. "Keep alert."

It seems a fundamentally obvious and sensible call for Ricci. He does not know how long he will be in the room. He doesn't even know exactly what he's looking for. But *he does know he'll be vulnerable and distracted while he forages around in here. Watch my back, keep alert. Obvious.*

Nichols looks at him with an expression that Ricci notes without quite being able to characterize it. In months to come, on the countless nights of poisoned sleep when that moment replays itself in his thoughts, he will understand it is plain and simple gratitude—for the second chance Nichols has been given, and the confidence being placed in him.

·The moment passes. Then the kid gives Ricci a crisp little nod that has about it the quality of a salute, turns, and goes back through the door toward his encounter with the Killer, and the hail of bullets that will rip the life out of his body . . .

Ricci was jolted back to the reality of the firing range, this time by his heart's heavy beating. He'd gotten caught somewhere between past and present again, as if they had converged around him in a kind of dizzying overlap— the dashed, rudimentary lines of the target figure's face becoming the sharply defined features of the Killer as Ricci first saw them years ago. He had never gotten his chance at that savage monster inside Earthglow, but there had been a time long before that, when they had grappled hand to hand in yet another faraway place, fighting to an impasse at the Russian Cosmodrome. There, as in Ontario, the Killer had escaped him, vanishing into the benighted Kazakhstan mountains amid the fierce, final combat of what would be logged in Sword's mission files as Operation: Shadow Watch.

Now Ricci stood with his hands wrapped around the butt of his gun. The Killer had started to retreat, backing slowly away down the lane, using the hostage figure as a shield, keeping her in front of his body. He was about a foot taller than Screaming Woman, easily a foot, and

Ricci was convinced he could take him down nice and clean, do it without so much as ruffling her hair. One shot to the head, over and out. But there would be an undeniable risk to Screaming Woman. Say the Killer was holding her at gunpoint, the weapon's snout pressing into her back. Say he had a knife against her throat. Ricci knew her situation was chancy even if his marksmanship was true. A slight jerk of the Killer's hand, an automatic dying spasm, could result in Screaming Woman becoming what Ricci had called a civilian casualty when he wore a detective's badge. On the force, protection of the innocents overrode your pursuit of the guilty. When losses occurred it was despite every intent and effort to avert them. But would a loss in this case be unintentional or incidental?

Ricci stood there with his hands around the gun, its trigger a tease to his finger. The finger moving slightly back, increasing its pressure—

"Tough choice. Good thing you don't have to make it."

Ricci turned his head toward the sound of Nimec's voice. He had stepped over from his firing lane, the earmuffs off, goggles down around his neck, his Beretta already holstered at his side.

Ricci looked at him but didn't say anything. His features were blank.

"Didn't you hear the beeps?" Nimec said. He was tapping his unprotected ear. "We're done."

Ricci stared at him in silence a while longer, his Five-Seven still held out, the pupils contracted to black pinpoints in his ice blue eyes.

Then he looked back down the firing lane.

The lane had gone completely dark, its target and hostage figures fixed in position. A lighted red sign high on the back wall was blinking the words:

Auto Timeout

Ricci slowly lowered the gun and slid it into his leather.

"Yeah," he said. "Done."

Quiet hung over the room, as rife in the air as the smell of discharged ammunition.

"Tom, we need to talk," Nimec said. "Let's get out of here."

"Here's fine."

"It might be better to do our old usual tonight. Sit down in my pool room over a couple of Cokes."

"Here's fine," Ricci repeated, his tone no more expressive than his features.

Nimec almost felt as if he'd phoned one of those automated customer service lines and gotten stuck on the starting option. He studied the rough, jutting angles of Ricci's face and shrugged.

"There's some general stuff I'd like to cover," he said. "With me going to Africa, it'll be you in charge—"

"And Thibodeau," Ricci said. "He'll make sure I remember to pull the store gate at night."

Nimec inhaled, exhaled.

"Thought I rated better than that sort of comment," he said. "You were gone a long time. I know what it took for you to leave. How much it took out of you to come back without finding our man. But we have to put it away for now. Move on."

Ricci nodded, seeming to look straight past Nimec at some point several feet behind him.

"Sure," he said in his null, automatic tone. "Got anything to mention besides?"

Nimec considered whether to push ahead. Though Ricci had returned from his alligator hunt three months ago, it mostly felt as if he were still elsewhere. And that sense of his continued absence just intensified when you tried stepping close to him.

Finally Nimec shook his head.

"Maybe later," he said, and glanced at his wristwatch. It was almost eight P.M. "I'm driving on over to HQ. There're lots of odds and ends that need wrapping up before my trip, and I might as well get some things done while the building's quiet. You want to stay, work in some more practice, that's fine with me. I won't worry about you pulling the gate afterward."

Ricci stood without moving and watched as Nimec turned to leave the room.

"Pete," he said.

Nimec paused near the door, looked at him.

Ricci nodded toward his darkened shooting lane.

"I've got a question," he said. "Strictly about procedure."

"Go ahead."

"That hostage situation before the timeout," Ricci said. "If you're in my place when it comes up, how would you handle it?"

Nimec thought about it a second, then shrugged again.

"Hope to God I never have to find out," he said.

The personal ads appeared on the first Thursday of every month in newspapers throughout Europe. Although each entry was different from the preceding month's, its content would be identical to those printed on the same date in various countries and languages. In Italy the personals ran in *l'Unita*. In Germany, *Die Zeit*. The *London Times* carried them in Great Britain, *Liberation* in France, *El Mundo* in Spain, and *De Standaard* in Belgium. Because Cyrillic script had to be avoided out of practicality, the ads were placed in English versions of Hungarian, Czech, and Russian papers—the *Budapest Sun*, *Prague Post*, and

Moscow Times, respectively. Also for practical reasons, the Greek daily chosen to print them was the German-language *Athener Zeitung*. As in eastern European nations, the character sets unique to Greece's alphabet would interfere with a consistent application of the simple code embedded within the messages. And a code without fixed rules amounted to no code at all.

For some time now the recipient of these secret contacts had rented a luxury suite in a restored nineteenth-century home on the Gran Vía in central Madrid. Built as a manor for relatives of the second Bourbon Restoration king, Alfonso XII, it was now occupied by an apartment hotel of four-star excellence and high discretion, appropriately named La Casa Real—The Royal House. This was the busiest part of the city, and he had once explored the idea of settling into the quieter but equally lavish Barrio de Salamanca east of downtown. Both had residences to his liking, and cost was not a factor. His sole concern about Gran Vía had been the dangerous number of eyes that might slip onto him. In the end, however, his instincts snarled at the soft faces of the *pijos*, or children of affluence, who dallied in the bars and cafés of the latter neighborhood, and he had decided it would be better to hide in full view at the city's center than to hear their bleating voices and smell the mother's-milk stink coming off their pores.

La Casa Real held a further advantage of convenience for him. It was a short walk west to the green line Metro station or east to the Iglesia de San Jose on Calle de Alcalá. Past the church on that same street was the circular Plaza de Cibelles, where its statue of the Roman fertility goddess Cybele—known as Rhea to the Greeks—sat in her stone chariot hitched to stone lions on a stone island from which her naked stone cherubs, their forever-young, never-innocent faces bloated like the faces of dying cats, poured their bowls of water into the surrounding fountain pool. There at the lower rim of the fountain he could bear right into Paseo del Prado and then cross the green toward the great old art museum, where he would admire Brueghel's *The Triumph of Death* in its ground-floor Flemish gallery, only paces beyond the Puerta de Goya entrance.

These past days as September rain clouds arrived to douse the summer heat, he had been drawn to another destination at the corner of Calle del Arenal and Calle de los Boradores, in the ancient district north and west of Gran Vía—Iglesia de San Ginés, whose bell tower struck its Sunday calls to worship mere hours after the Joy Eslava discotheque in its shadow had its last call for drinks, and the Saturday-night crowds that flung heatedly across its dance floor emptied, staggering and shuffling, onto the streets. With the lens of his digital camera, he had photographed the church from every angle to capture its solid ledges and brickwork, the architectural repetitions that hinted at that deep-rooted Moorish tendency to hold fast, the forceful and domineering thrust of the tower's spire. Back in his suite, he had used the images for detailed reference as he sketched out plans for a wooden scale model of the church.

Without any previous experience, Kuhl had scrupulously crafted three such models during his extended hibernation. The gothic Saint Jean Cathedral of Lyon was his first; if his goal was to task himself, he would move with audacity to capture a resplendent citadel of heaven, an archbishop's throne. The next church he had built was the Basilica of Santa Croce, where the bones of Galileo, the seeker of answers accused of heresy, and Machiavelli, the seeker of power banished for conspiracy, lay entombed. His most recently completed model was the Church of Saint Thomas, in Austria. The small, severe building was a relatively undemanding bit of work for him, but he had known that in advance, having mastered his woodcraft long before the project was undertaken. And the church's cloistered austerity had seemed a perfect expression of his circumstances as one year of withdrawal and cover made a slow passage into another.

A man who hungered for action, Siegfried Kuhl had needed to remain dormant. It was an adaptation that ran against his innermost grain, and he had often thought of surfacing to face the Sword operative whose seething cathexis of revenge had made his pursuit of Kuhl a constant threat. But Kuhl had been advanced a handsome sum to vanish from the face of the earth, with additional payments of one million dollars a year deposited to a numbered Swiss account in monthly installments. A soldier of fortune by self-definition, he was bound to honor this contract—and his sponsor's exceptional reach of imagination, his resourcefulness, was no less an inducement than the monetary retainer. There was in him nothing of the mediocre or the common. His mannered delicacy enframed a hot rebellion against the boot of order that Kuhl recognized and found impressive. While the payments toward their unwritten agreement continued, he would stay out of sight, and attempt to stanch the dreams of combat bleeding into his mind.

Kuhl's work on the model churches was the wrap, the tourniquet he applied, a means of control that had come to him in an unexpected, almost startling moment of revelation back in Lyon. He did not know what precipitated it. Saint Jean Cathedral was on the Saône not far from his hotel, and Kuhl had passed it along the river walk many times before the day he paused to gaze up at its buttresses and pinnacles, its transept spire piercing the sky. All at once, Kuhl believed he had come upon an understanding of the aggressive vision it must have taken to conceive and raise so magnificent a structure . . . a thought followed immediately by his own visions of the torch, the bonfire, and the raised sword. What furies of the human soul must have needed such an elaborate, soaring cage? How great a will to contain them must have driven its construction? And what if its *de*construction were achieved with comparable purpose and discipline? What measure of will would that be? What consecration of the fervent thing within?

Kuhl had decided to put himself to a private test. Soon afterward, he started his model of Saint Peter in his hotel room, working at a sunlit window that overlooked the site where one of Caesar's lieutenants had founded the city, declaring it a home to his veteran warriors. And his work in each of its phases had been ongoing ever since.

Here today, however, Kuhl had no room in his affairs for the final camera shots of San Ginés tower he felt were necessary for the accurate weathering and detailing of its twin on his scale miniature. Nor was the Breughel a present lure to him. Leaving his hotel at six A.M. under a Madrid sun that had arisen hot and contemptuous of autumn, he had instead gone toward Calle de Alcalá and the San Jose church, a structure of lesser distinction than San Ginés that interested him only because of the daily hours its diocese kept and how they in turn determined the hours of a sidewalk newspaper and magazine stand down the street from its steps.

In Madrid even churches neglected by travel brochures held valuable art and artifacts, and admittance was generally restricted to scheduled prayer services to ensure the presence of a watch against thieves who might drift in among the worshipers and sightseers. It was unusual for a church to open its doors before nine or ten o'clock in the morning, but Iglesia de San Jose was an exception, opening at seven to accommodate legions of international travelers, VIP businessmen, and morning traders at the nearby stock exchange in this most visited district of the city.

The news vender outside Iglesia de San Jose capitalized on its early hours by getting a similar jump on his sales. He received the morning papers well before any competing dealers in town and would arrive at his stand at the break of dawn to set up his display racks and have them filled for his sidewalk trade as the congregation moved on from its prayers at the church.

Kuhl presumed the vender had convinced his deliverymen to make him the first stop along their routes with ample greasing of their palms, but that was of no importance to him. The relevant point was that it enabled him to pick up his first-Thursday-of-the-month copy of *El Mundo* almost as it shipped from the press. The window of opportunity for which the personal ad would be useful was an hour, not one second more or less. Precisely when that hour commenced was part of the information relayed by the code, and any chance that Kuhl could miss it was eliminated by his getting hold of the paper on release.

The electronic editions of *El Mundo* and other papers that Kuhl read for the communiqué in his scattered lodgings across the Continent would not do. Their posting times could be irregular, and the Web sites sometimes went down. Moreover, the online sites were not uniformly comprehensive. Some of them omitted personal columns, and some offered partial or alternate listings. For Kuhl to be confident, his sources had to be dependable. Thus he relied exclusively on the print versions of the newspapers.

This morning Kuhl's brisk pace had carried him to the stand as its owner was still slicing open the wide plastic straps of his newspaper bundles. With a few minutes to spare before the papers were separated, he had turned into the church and paused at a side altar to light a votive candle for a lover he remembered with particular fondness, and whose life he had reluctantly taken to preserve secrets of which she had known far too much, leaving her body in the beautiful rolling hills of Castilla y León in the Spanish countryside. The votive was a memorial Kuhl believed she would have appreciated.

Now he came down the porch onto the street, noticed *El Mundo* had been put out for sale, took a copy, dropped his pesetas into the vender's hand, and pushed his way back through the thickening foot traffic on Calle de Alcalá to Casa Real. Waiting for a stoplight to change at the street's busy intersection with Calle de Hortaleza, Kuhl folded it open to the classified pages and traced his eyes down columns of personal entries. Most were straightforward casts for sex or companionship that shared a certain banal, desperate vocabulary. There were the people seeking long-term partners, thrill dates, discreet adulteries. The common descriptions of age and appearance, and predictable mentions of candlelight, music, and travel.

Kuhl found the entry meant for his eyes in the third column. Adhering to the established format, it was a brief *lettre d'amour*, identifiable by distinctive matched, reusable pairs of sender and recipient names chosen from a list of twenty-four he had committed to memory—twelve of them male, twelve female. In fact, mnemonic triggers were the basis of the code. Information stored away in his mind provided the context for its key elements, making it absolutely foolproof. Kuhl knew the first letter of the recipient's name always corresponded to a time at which he would, if necessary, have the ability to reach his sponsor over a secure Internet live conferencing connection. The letter "A" matched with one o'clock, "B" two o'clock, "C" three o'clock, and so forth. Whether the start time for the viable SILC was before or after noon depended on the sender's first initial: a vowel pointed to the morning while a consonant marked it for the afternoon.

Here, Kuhl instantly noticed that the ad began with "My Darling Anya" and ended with "Your Unforgetting Lover, Michael-Sebastian."

These routine elements of the message elicited no reaction from him besides a rapid noting of the timetable. The short window of contact would open at one o'clock Greenwich Mean Time that afternoon—the GMT standard was used, again for consistency's sake—and shut at two o'clock after the predetermined hour passed.

It was something in the body of the message that quickened his pulse.

The text between salutation and closing said:

Our ardor lifted me to a place beyond the stars, and I cannot bear the fall now that you are gone. Could we have gone too high, too fast, too far? Did our hearts burn too brightly for their flame to last? As I must endure the lonely darkness of love's ashes, I think it would have been better if we had taken flight without them.

Kuhl stared at the newspaper, his eyes locked on a brief possessive phrase in the message's fourth and last sentence.

Love's ashes.

Moments passed. Kuhl kept staring at the paper, at that pair of simple words, the sounds of automobiles and pedestrians in the intersection tamped and dulled by the bloodrush in his ears.

Love's ashes.

Together they formed a second mnemonic. Codewords

he had hoped for, but never truly allowed himself to expect.

Kuhl thought of the flame he had lit in the church, that tiny surrendered spark of memory and passion. Then he closed his newspaper and resumed walking quickly toward his apartment hotel as the traffic light across the street changed from red to green.

For the next several hours he would do nothing but wait in his suite to make contact.

"This place is exquisitely nifty," Megan said. "All we need now is for the Blob to come glooping over us."

"The what?" Nimec said.

"The Blob," Megan said. "As in that old fifties make-out movie. Starring Steve McQueen and a thousand tons of gelatin."

"Oh, right," Nimec said. He was staring out the windshield of his reconditioned '57 Corvette roadster at an orange neon sign shimmering the words BIG EDDIE'S SNACK SHACK into the night.

Megan looked at him from the passenger seat.

"The gelatinous lump was known to be gracious and humble in real life, but tended to play very slimy characters. I suppose it was the usual Hollywood typecasting."

"Hmm."

"Winning an Oscar for its role must have been some consolation, though," Megan said. "The story goes that nobody in the Academy knew whether to nominate it for best actor or actress, so they created some kind of special category. Best Performance by an Amorphous Gender-Neutral Green Thing."

Nimec kept gazing silently at the entrance to the drive-in restaurant as a pretty, ponytailed carhop who seemed about the right age for a college sophomore came roller-skating out to the car.

He pushed in a chrome dashboard knob to douse the lights and glanced over at Megan.

"What are you having to eat?"

"I'm torn between the fried popcorn shrimp and fried clam strip baskets."

"That time we stopped in Maine a couple years ago, you told me you didn't like clams."

"*Whole* clams," Megan said. "Much too chewy."

Nimec looked at her.

"Let's get one basket of each and split them," he said.

"Yum, yum," Megan said. "And don't forget our side of potato skins. And my Diet Coke. While you're treating, dear man."

He grunted and rolled his window halfway down. Rockabilly music burst into the 'Vette from speakers above the diner's wraparound awning—somebody who sounded like Buddy Holly but wasn't.

"Hi." The carhop outside leaned toward him with a pad, a pencil, and a very cute smile. "Will the two of you be needing menus?"

Nimec told her they wouldn't and placed their orders and watched the carhop roll off across the parking lot with the diminishing clatter that skate wheels make when spinning away over paved surfaces.

Then he became quiet again.

"About the Blob winning an Oscar," Megan said. "A nonhuman superstar of undetermined sexual identity must have caused quite a ruckus at the time. This was 1957 or '58 and couldn't have been more than three or four years after the McCarthy hearings, blacklisting . . . did you know even Lucille Ball came under investigation, by the way? *Lucy*, of all people in the world. But what's odd about how it came about was that Desi—"

"Meg, give me a break." Nimec glanced over at her. "There're some things we need to discuss."

She gave him a look of mock surprise.

"No kidding," she said. "Here I thought you only dragged me out of my apartment at ten o'clock at night to go hot-rodding around the Bay Area and chowing down fast food."

Nimec sat there unconsciously tapping the steering wheel.

"Ricci was over at my place before," he said. "I asked him to come for shooting practice at the range. Figured it might loosen him up, get him talking. The way it did sometimes before he left here."

"And it didn't work."

Nimec shook his head no.

"A big piece of him's still gone," he said. "Maybe most of him. He won't tell me what he's thinking, or what he's feeling. I can guess some of it. But just enough to know he isn't right."

"Does it worry you?"

"Some, yeah," Nimec said. He moved his shoulders. "Could be I'd feel different if I wasn't heading off for Gabon the day after tomorrow. Once Ricci got back, I had myself convinced the normal routine would help him. You start on an everyday grind, it can smooth the edges from the outside in."

"And you haven't seen any change?"

"Not for the better." Nimec said.

Megan mulled that over.

"I haven't missed getting nicked by those edges you mentioned," she said. "But I also haven't been back in SanJo very long, and it's an understatement to say I'm not close to him. I don't believe he likes me too much. Sometimes I doubt he even respects me." She paused. "I suppose that's my way of making excuses for leaving you stuck with a problem that really needed attention from both of us."

Nimec looked out over the sportster's hood scoop and through the restaurant window and watched its short order cooks working over their deep fryers and grills. Big Eddie's was a family business that had first opened its doors when Eisenhower was president and stayed under the same family's continuous management for going on half a century. It still held annual sock hops and for all Nimec knew Big Eddie, if he'd ever existed, continued to run the show. Though more likely it would be Big Eddie Jr. or Big Eddie III.

"Don't sweat it," he told Megan. "You've had to make your own adjustments. I can see the boss handing over more responsibilities to you. See him easing himself out of things little by little. He's still Gord. He's looking healthier. But he isn't what he was before the bio strike. And he won't be again, will he?"

Megan looked at him.

"No," she said. "He won't."

Nimec sat facing the windshield for several moments, then turned partially toward her.

"So you see where I am tonight," he said. "Thinking about changes. The ones that are happening, and the ones that aren't. And none of it's in my control."

Megan nodded. The carhop rolled up with a tray of food in disposable containers and hooked it over the half open window. She reached into her apron pocket to fill her hand with tubs of cocktail sauce, tartar sauce, and ketchup, set them on the tray with the meals, and then asked Nimec if he cared for anything else besides the check. He told her he didn't, noticed her sweet, easy smile again, and added a generous tip to his payment.

Megan held a hand out over the stick shift.

"Okay, pass me the greasy delights," she said.

They leaned back in their bucket seats and ate quietly.

"I'll tell you something," Megan said after a while. "When you wanted to bring Tom Ricci into a command position with Sword, I was convinced he'd never work out, and went along with the move assuming you'd eventually see how wrong it was. Yet now I feel I'm having to defend the rightness of your choice to you. Tom came through tremendously in Kazakhstan, and then again in Ontario. He lays everything on the line, and it's probably true that sometimes not all of him comes back from it. But if that costs us, imagine what it has to cost him. How hard it must be to live up to what he demands of himself."

Nimec considered that a second. He dipped a shrimp into some tartar sauce with his fingers and put it in his mouth.

"You'll need to keep an eye on Ricci while I'm gone," he said.

"Yes."

"There's a lot of anger and frustration between him and Rollie Thibodeau, and I can see a blowup in the making. It's pretty clear from all the little things. Like how they say each other's names. And the way they act whenever they're together in the same room. You're going to have to watch out for that, too."

"Yes."

They ate some more of their food. Outside, the Buddy Holly simulacrum had done a gradual fadeout and Elvis Presley, the genuine article, was singing about how he couldn't help falling in love with someone.

Nimec looked at Megan.

"I've also got a personal favor to ask, if you don't mind," he said.

She nodded.

"It involves Annie."

Megan waited.

"Before she came along, I'd almost forgotten what it was like to worry about anything or anyone besides UpLink," Nimec said. "I've had to rethink that, though. Take a new look at my responsibilities. What they are, and what they should be. I figure Africa's probably going to be business as usual. But you know how it is."

Megan nodded again.

"Yes," she said, "I do. You can't afford to let things slide."

Nimec paused, transferred his food container from his lap to the top of the dash, and moved forward a little in his seat.

"Jon's got his mother to take care of him, and I know he'll always be okay," he said after a bit. "With Annie it's different. She's tough. Good at handling things, been relying on herself a long time. But I don't want her to *have* to do that anymore. Don't want to be thinking there's a chance she's ever going to be alone."

Megan gave him a third nod.

"Annie's my friend, Pete," she said. "More, she's one of *ours* now. Package deal. You know what comes with that."

He looked at her, then grunted.

"She'll be in town a couple of weeks from now, staying at my condo with the kids. Hers and mine. We were supposed to see a ball game . . . and if you have time—"

"At your service," Megan said. "I'll invite them over for dinner and ask if they want to stay overnight. Annie's been scoffing at my claim to virtuosity in the kitchen, so it'll give me a chance to show her up and feed the brood all at once."

"Uh-oh," Nimec said. "Double jeopardy."

"Is this what you consider being grateful?"

"No," he said. "Realistic."

Megan stretched her lips into an exaggerated frown, reached for his food container, and set it back onto his lap.

"Eat a clam, buster," she said.

Madrid. One o'clock in the afternoon. His model church on a table near the apartment window, Kuhl's curtains were drawn, a pale light filtering through their sheer white fabric to throw a shadow of the church, still towerless, onto a wall and corner of the ceiling. Under a fluorescent swing-arm magnifier clamped to the table, the tower subassembly awaited his last touches of detail.

Across the room, Kuhl sat at a notebook computer joined to a cable Internet connection, his eyes fastened to its screen as he clicked onto a private conferencing site and typed in his security key. Headset on, he waited a moment and was forwarded to the next level of channel-specific authentication.

The prompt for his first spoken pass phrase appeared.

"On Maple White Island," he said into his headset's microphone.

Another moment passed. Kuhl sat in the cropped shadow of his church. His computer's client software converted his analog voice signals into a binary stream that was encrypted and transmitted to the server.

He was prompted for his second pass phrase.

"Deep in the Brazilian jungle," he said.

Kuhl waited. The prompt for his third and last pass phrase flashed onto the computer screen.

"Professor Summerlee found the Lost World," he said.

Kuhl waited again. The three-step process ensured exceptionally accurate client verification, allowing the server's voice biometric program engines to conduct a comparative analysis in much the same way that a fin-

gerprint would be scanned for its unique characteristics—
his words broken into phonemes and triphones, basic
units of human speech that were analyzed for their dominant tonal formants and matched against a digitally
stored speech sample in the database.

Kuhl's identity confirmed, his computer showed the
ENTRY ALLOWED notification. A brief animated icon
flashed onto it: the Chimera of Greco-Roman legend
standing in profile, its lion's head twisting toward him,
its jaws splitting open to breathe a great billow of fire
that went curling and churning across the display until it
became a coruscant sheet of orange. The orange quickly
dispersed in brilliant slips and shreds and left only the
monstrous head of the lion—now static except for a pair
of sparkling ember-red eyes—facing Kuhl onscreen.

Then an electronically altered voice in his earpiece, its
frequencies bent and phased to a low pitch:

"Siegfried, at long last," Harlan DeVane said. "How
splendid it is to hear from you."

In the study adjoining his yacht's master stateroom,
DeVane sat very still as the wall-mounted plasma display
went dark. Then he slid off his headset, lifted his wireless
computer keyboard from his lap, and put it on the richly
inlaid walnut table beside him.

A chill smile trickled across his face. The user icon
Kuhl had chosen for himself was a nice bit of drollery
that suited his temperament as well as DeVane's animation did his own personality . . . or at least a part of it.
The chimera was an amusing outlet, but Kuhl had no
similar touch of flash, no taste for the razzmatazz. A bar-
barian warrior who stood out of his time, he could have
been a Viking, a Saxon, a Mongol Khan.

DeVane reclined in his chair, his elbows propped on
its armrests, fingers woven into a cradle under his chin.

If Kuhl was surprised by his activation notice moments earlier, it had not showed. But the actual mission assignment—that had given him quite a shot of juice. Not even the digital processing that stripped all mood and emotion from the human voice had concealed Kuhl's eager satisfaction over his instructions. The words DeVane used were deliberate echoes of comments he had made to the good economic minister Etienne Begela in his governmental office—why bother to fiddle with something that worked?

"Find what Roger Gordian most loves, and we will know his greatest weakness," DeVane had said. "Strike at it, and we will have struck at his heart."

"I will be moving on from here right away, then."

"Yes."

"To America."

"That's correct, Siegfried. America. Where Gordian's heart *is*. And where opportunity is a wild running horse to be roped and ridden."

Kuhl had asked only a few practical questions after that.

Though far away, DeVane had felt his arousal.

Slowly now, he let his eyes glide over the row of four African masks aligned on the wall above the plasma screen. There was a reptilian gold fetish mask that Ebrie chieftains had carried to laud the killing of their tribal enemies, a blockish, primitive Dogon hunter's helmet worn for protection against the spirits of slaughtered prey, an Ashante ghost mask with curling horns and sharply filed teeth, and the Fang Ngi secret society mask of which Begela's face had somehow reminded DeVane—or more accurately, Mr. Fáton—at their recent appointment in Port-Gentil.

Gerard Fáton. Jack Nemaine. Henry Skoll. The Facilitator. *El Tío*. All of them were masks of DeVane's creation, available to him when necessary. Even his Harlan DeVane identity was a guise of sorts. Form-fitted, true. Designed and developed around basic elements of his personality. Yet no less a careful invention than the others, a role he had learned to play fully and well . . .

A vivid memory bobbed up into DeVane's thoughts and he closed his eyes as if to stave it off, his fingers unmeshing, pressing lightly against his temples. He sat a while in quiet struggle with himself. It was useless, though. Impossible. The recollection pulsed with a kind of independent, insuppressible life.

DeVane knew he could only let it unfold and hope it did so quickly. He lowered his hands from the sides of his head, rose from his chair, strode across the carpeted floor, and drew the curtain back from a brass opening porthole.

Sunlight washed over him. He lifted the porthole and stared outside without seeing anything. Fresh sea air breezed through into the study, but DeVane's nostrils registered heavy urban smog as the images and sensations came on.

First, the building.

It always started with the building.

As he'd approached from the street, it had seemed to rise infinitely above him.

Nervous, he had walked through the entrance to a security desk and told his name to a uniformed guard who consulted a visitor list, cleared him for entry, and then pointed him toward the elevators.

His stomach had lurched as the car sped him up to a corporate suite filled with employees. They were darting busily between doorways, though he'd sensed their quick, concealed glances. It was as if they were the inhabitants of a lush, sheltering forest, unsure what to make of the stray and anxious creature that had wandered in from some outer barrens.

He had stood before the receptionist, again given his name, and she had risen from her chair and shown him to the office of the man he had learned was his father.

The glass boardroom table was long, dominating the room. There was a smaller table in a corner, a vase with fresh flowers, a coffee urn, some comfortable looking chairs. Shelves of books, many of them leather bound, on a wall near the chairs. He had guessed this to be some sort of informal greeting area, used for pleasant talk.

It was unoccupied as he entered, and there was no smell of brewed coffee in the room.

After several minutes the father had entered and stood regarding him from the head of the long glass table. He, the son, waited beside a window looking down on the great city skyline's tallest office towers. None of them were close to reaching its height.

Instructed to sit at the foot of the long glass table, the son watched the father he had never met before that moment, the stranger with a face so much like his own, settle into a chair at its opposite end. He was a tall man, his posture very rigid. They had seemed separated by many miles. The father wearing a perfectly tailored suit of some fine, light fabric. The son hoping the sleeve of his sport jacket would not ride up to show the frayed threads on his right shirt cuff. He had saved to buy the jacket for their meeting. The old shirt was his best. There had been no money for another after he bought the jacket.

The father observed the son across his long glass table and asked why he had come to him. His voice was calm and without inflection. His exquisite suit was like soft but impermeable armor. He truly seemed miles and miles away.

Seated by the window, the son answered him and wondered if his voice would fail, fall as short of reaching the father's chair as the tops of the skyscrapers below. Still, his request seemed a fair, even modest one. The son knew of a deep and broad accumulation of family wealth, but did not then appreciate its meaning, and would have mistaken its neglected leavings for the brightest and rarest of jewels. The son knew of respected legitimate children, but he did not then consider himself their equal, let alone their better by vast degrees.

The thrust of what he wanted was recognition.

The father looked at him without any whatsoever.

"Listen to me this once, because once is all you get," he had said. "You have no place here, no help, nothing to gain. Your mother is a piece of loose candy in a common bowl. Any man can reach into it for her, and I may have had a taste. If the bowl was passed to me or put in easy reach, why not? I can't be sure. Hard candy, it's a cheap temptation. Sweet but uninteresting. Meant to be indulged and forgotten."

The father had stood, then. His gaze flat and noncommittal, no room in it even for contempt.

The son had hated his eyes for their resemblance to his own.

"I'll give you some advice, off the record," the father said. "Go about your life, make what you can of it. But know your boundaries. Don't look past the rim of the bowl. Don't expect to share my name. And don't ever dare to return here. I said this was your one and only chance, and I meant it. If you try to see me again, contact me in any way, you'll be pissing in a very goddamned strong wind."

The father had allowed a few seconds to pass, as if to make certain his warning had been absorbed. Then he waved his hand toward the door in a gesture of dismissal, held it out until the son had risen from his chair and turned his back.

Now, as the memory finished running its cold, cold course through his mind, DeVane lingered by the *Chimera*'s open porthole for several moments, as he had lingered before departing the table of his father those many years gone by.

He realized his pallid hand was spread open in front of him, looked down at it with constricted anger, and lowered it to his side. Then he shut and latched the porthole, and pulled the curtains across them with a sharp jerk of his wrist, expelling both breeze and sunlight from the room.

Traces of his memory stayed in the air with him somewhat longer.

DeVane had listened carefully to his father's words, let them sink in and work their changes. He had remembered them, as advised, and in that sense proved himself an obedient son.

But he had bided his time—and returned.

And when he did, the wind, that *goddamned strong wind*, had been blowing relentlessly in his favor, feeding his sails all the way.

FOUR

AS HE LUGGED HIS FEET TOWARD THE RIO DE GABAO
Hotel's atrium and wearily braced for the dinner reception organized by his cultivated Gabonese hosts, Pete
Nimec pressed a multifunction button on his wristwatch
twice to check its Annie-Meter, which was not what the integrated feature was actually supposed to be called. What
the feature was supposed to be called, going by the user's
manual he'd barely skimmed, was either "To-Do List" or
"Reminder Calendar" or "Countdown Alarm" . . . or
maybe something else kind of similar he'd given up trying
to remember.

There were, Nimec thought, too many brand names
and trademarks and jargonese catch words for all the
countless gadgets floating around these days. Or possibly
it just seemed there were too many when you cruised
into your forties, and were old enough to remember a
time when the pocket transistor radio was considered a
modern marvel, and the black-and-white portable television became an affordable household fixture that would
eventually render the behemoth family console obsolete.

Still, the name game seemed complicated to Nimec.
Even his digital watch wasn't a watch, or exclusively a
watch if you wanted to be nitpicky. It was, rather, a
WristLink wearable minicomputer with a high-res color

liquid crystal display panel and infrared data-transfer port, designed and marketed by no lesser outfit than his own employer, and sporting everything from an integrated 5× zoom digital camera with sufficient built-in memory to store a hundred fifty snapshot images, to a personal global positioning system locator, to satellite e-messaging software, an electronic memo pad, address book, onboard video games, and—proving it could still could be used as a timepiece by Cro-Magnon throwbacks such as himself—programmable displays for every time zone in the world and a receiver module that synched it to the National Institute of Standards and Technology's atomic clock out in Boulder or Denver—Nimec forgot which Colorado city—rendering it accurate to the split second by an official federal government agency. Besides touting these many bells and whistles, the watch, or wearable, was certified waterproof to a hundred-foot depth and furthermore had come to Nimec free of charge, being one of his occasional deluxe perks as Roger Gordian's security chief.

Yet for him the best of the gadget's features was its Annie-Meter.

As he called it.

Nimec had set it shortly after leaving Houston for San Jose earlier that week. To be more precise, Nimec had set it fifteen minutes after Annie dropped him off at the airport, where she'd sent him on his way with a deep, sweet, shamelessly immodest kiss through her car's open passenger door as he'd leaned in across the front seat from the curb . . . a kiss whose taste had lingered all the while it took Nimec to reluctantly pull himself and his carry-on bag from her car, turn through the terminal entrance, obtain his boarding pass from the clerk at the departure gate, and finally sit himself down in the passenger waiting area to fool with the watch's push-button menu controls.

The Annie-Meter, so-called, looked to unknowing eyes like an electronic calendar. What you did with it exclusively, if your name happened to be Pete Nimec, was first scroll to the box around the date you left Annie, whenever you left Annie, and record the exact, official NIST time you made your generally romantic farewells. Then you went to the screen that allowed you to specify the expected duration of your time *apart* from her and entered that information, inserting a little check mark beside the ALARM option—which, thanks to shareware Annie's son had downloaded from the Internet overriding the WristLink's preprogrammed selection of beeps and musical tones, would sound a bleeping rendition of the Temptations' "My Girl" on the day you were scheduled to see Annie again. Next up, assuming once more that you were Pete Nimec, was to open another dialogue box and checkmark the COUNTDOWN option enabling you to monitor, with a quick and convenient glance, the exact, official NIST number of days, hours, minutes, and seconds that were left until you got to hear that blessed melody. Finally you made absolutely sure both your farewell and return-to-Annie dates were highlighted in valentine red on the calendar, push-buttoned your way back to the device's normal watch face, and that was that.

Nimec had last consulted the Annie-Meter riding the elevator down from his guest suite in UpLink's reserved upper-story block, and noted he was twenty-three days, one hour, and an odd bundle of minutes from reuniting with his honey bun. Meaning that by the conclusion of the obligatory dinner reception, possibly sooner if it didn't drag on too long, the number of days would be reduced to twenty-two and change. That was, he acknowledged, parsing things a tad. But as Tom Ricci had advised back when Nimec was entirely confident Ricci had his head on straight, you had to count your gains in small steps.

He entered the atrium now, joining the twenty-five or so attendees who'd gotten there ahead of him. All but one were men in suits, and half of those were UpLink corporate officials and high-level technical consultants focal to the fiber ring deal. The sole woman present was Tara Cullen, the project's network operations manager . . . and a sleek, standout blond, as the thick cluster of smiling African delegates around her had clearly noticed. Nimec saw three or four members of his twelve-man security team interspersed throughout the crowd, lapel pins on their jackets—the triangular pins' engraved and laminated design showing a broadsword surrounded by stylized satcom bandwidth lines.

Everyone from UpLink looked about as zonked as Nimec felt. He had wanted representatives from his Sword contingent at the gathering as a gesture of courtesy, but because they weren't part of the business delegation had seen no reason to trot out the entire bunch. He'd thus asked for only a handful of volunteers, having allowed those who preferred to skip the festivities do so after their long, taxing haul from California. Starting tomorrow his group would have its work cut out conducting surveys of UpLink's new onshore and offshore facilities and laying the groundwork for site policies, procedures, and equipment. Let them relax while they could.

Aside from a fleet of black-tuxed, white-gloved servers weaving about the room with trays of hors d'oeuvres and cocktails, the rest of the people Nimec scoped from the entryway belonged to the Gabonese welcoming committee: politicians and administrative appointees led by Etienne Begela, who Nimec's well-studied contact brief tagged as bureaucratic head of the telecom regulatory agency in Port-Gentil.

Now Begela looked over at Nimec, excused himself from a group of UpLink executives he'd engaged, and approached with his arm outstretched.

Nimec went forward to meet him. The atrium was awash with sunlight even though it was almost seven in the evening. It gleamed off the silver trays and table settings and spilled through the glass-paneled ceiling onto exotic blossoming floor plants, which Nimec didn't recognize in the least and which seemed almost too outlandishly tall and lush to be genuine.

"Monsieur Nimec, hello, it is a pleasure." Begela pumped his hand, offered a huge white-toothed smile, and introduced himself in French-accented English. Nimec wondered briefly how the minister had identified him right off, then guessed one of the execs had pointed him out. Either that or Begela had been pretty good about reviewing his own background files. "I hope you are finding your accommodations satisfactory after such a lengthy trip, and would like you to know I've personally selected those hotel staffers who will be attending to your party throughout its stay."

"I appreciate that," Nimec said. "Everything's great."

And the hotel *was* very nice—elegant, in fact, Nimec mused. Though even a jungle hut and straw cot would have been agreeable to him after his latest marathon global traverse. This one ranked way ahead of SanJo–Malaysia on the all-time fatigue scale, and seemed a close runner up to SanJo–Antarctica. How many hours had it spanned? A glance at his superwatch would of course tell him to the exact, official NIST atomic minute, but Nimec had the sense that knowing the answer to that question would make him feel even more wiped out than he currently did. There had been the United Airlines charter out of San Jose airport—well, playing the name game again, Norman Y. Mineta San Jose International Airport, as the city council had rechristened it a couple of years back in honor of the former mayor—at six thirty in the morning the previous day. That had taken his group to their connection at O'Hare in Chicago, where they had boarded a UA international flight to Paris de Gaulle after a five-hour layover. Arriving in the glorious City of Light around seven the next morning after a full day of travel, they'd barely had a chance to toss back some Mc-Donald's coffee and hit the terminal restrooms—which had been the high point of that little interlude, and no more glorious than visits to *salles de bains* the world over—before hustling aboard an Air France A340 for another seven hours in the wild blue yonder, and finally touching down at Leon M'ba Airport in Libreville at around five in the evening. From the nation's capital they'd flopped onto a waiting Air Gabon Fokker 28 that had shuttled them to Port-Gentil, where they'd hustled into their rooms, and, each in his or her own dog-tired way, prepared for the banquet.

"When you've rested up, we shall have to familiarize you with our city," Etienne Begela was saying now. "You'll find it delightfully captivating, I'm sure. I'll show you our government offices tomorrow, and can recommend places to shop, dine, even enjoy some sightseeing if the desire strikes. And I have people ready to assist your group in whatever other ways may be needed."

Nimec gave the minister a nod.

"I look forward to all that once I've recharged," he said. "We'll try not to be too much of a nuisance."

A pair of waiters glided over and surrounded Nimec with their carefully balanced trays of appetizers. One held a selection of pâtés, thin-sliced sausages, truffles, and chilled poached salmon. The other had something hot,

what looked like escargot stuffed into sauteed mush-
rooms. Nimec found himself disappointed. The offerings
looked tasty enough. And he'd done his homework about
the long French tradition here. Gabon had been visited
by trading ships from Marseilles and Nice since before
Columbus, was settled by colonial forces right around the
middle of the nineteenth century. Still, you could sample
French food anywhere. It was the universal posh cuisine,
and this affair definitely had a high poshness quotient.
Nimec wasn't big on it, however, and guessed he'd
hoped for more regional fare. If you were going to fly a
couple of zillion miles to Africa, you wanted to chow
down on African.

Nimec sampled the pâté and thought it was blandly
decent. But he resolved that he'd have to take Begela up
on his offer of guiding him toward some interesting spots
to eat.

He noticed Tara Cullen passing by with one of the other
Gabonese delegates and waved to catch her attention, figuring it was an ideal chance to provide an intro . . . as well
as an opportune moment to ease himself out of the conversation and into a chair for a while. And maybe see if any of
the penguins were serving coffee. He really did feel head-
achey and bedraggled.

"Tara," he said, "I'd like you to meet—"

"Ms. Cullen and I have already made one another's
acquaintance." Begela flashed his big, overpowering
smile at Nimec, then beamed it onto Tara and snagged
her elbow. "Indeed, though, I feel professionally obliged,
and personally delighted, to take this opportunity to ex-
pand upon it." He nodded at the tall, dark-skinned man
who'd been walking along with her. "Macie Nze, this is
Mr. Pete Nimec, Mr. Nimec, Macie Nze . . . my friend
and fellow in the Ministry of Telecommunications. He
can tell you of our recent trip to the capital in support of

UpLink's agenda." The smile became even more commanding. "And we ourselves must talk later, Macie, no?" he said without elaboration.

Nze gave him a nod and agreed that they should. Nimec thought he looked sort of flustered—or surprised, anyway—wondered about it a second, and then ventured that he probably just didn't appreciate having his blond companion rustled off by a colleague.

As Begela steered Tara toward the bar, Nimec also decided to forget about his quiet cup of coffee.

"So," he said, and extended his hand toward Nze for a fresh round of vigorous shaking. "Tell me about that trip of yours . . ."

Nze did, to neither man's particular enjoyment.

The old Detecto stand-up scale had originally belonged to a Lousiana country doctor, who had it delivered to Roland Thibodeau's appearance-conscious godmother as a lagniappe, a little something extra offered for good measure, when she had bought some nice, new-looking furniture at his moving sale . . . or so Thibodeau recalled her telling him. He had vague memories of his dear Nanaine Adcle Rigaud getting many small, pretty gifts from the doctor before he and his wife left the bayou, pulling stakes for New Orleans all of a sudden. These gifts, too, may have been lagniappes. But Thibodeau had been very young back then, and unclear about the ways of adults.

What he did remember clearly was that Nanaine had always kept the scale against her bedroom wall in the modest settler's house where he was raised from the age of ten, after losing both his natural parents between June and October of 1955—his father to a bewildering freak accident, then his mother in a way that was even more inexplicable to him. *Jus' must've got a special prov'd'nce again' 'em*, was a phrase he'd often heard

muttered among his schoolmates and their families . . .
the first time from a distant relative at Cecilia Thibodeau's wake. Then and later, it had been hard for him to
disagree. If going from fatherless to orphaned in a single
horrible season wasn't smoking-gun evidence of that special prov'd'nce—of Rollie getting FUBARed from a rear
position, as his boys in the 101st Air Cav might have put
it—what else in the wide world would qualify?

The scale's heavy iron upright and platform base were
lilac colored, Nanaine Adele having concealed its basic
physician's white under a paint job of her own lively and
eccentric preference—a coat of paint that was now
chipped, faded, and flecked with rust from top to bottom.
Thibodeau had thought about stripping it a time or two,
restoring the scale to its original condition. A lilac scale
in his office surely did nothing to convey an impression
of red-blooded Cajun manliness, and he sometimes felt
foolish when he pictured himself on it. Lilac was a dainty
color. As Nanaine Adele had been a dainty little bit of a
woman. But it had been her favorite shade of purple,
favorite flower, beloved fragrance of spring. She had
even worn bonnets of homespun, hand-dyed lilac cotton
to church on Sunday mornings.

Thibodeau had let the scale remain as it was. And if
that cast doubts on his masculinity, well, he owed no
explanations to anyone and was sure he'd never left any
questions in the minds of vulnerable or designing ladies.
On the contrary, another expression to circulate around
Thibodeau in the Caillou Bay town where he had grown
up (this when he was a teenager) had been *le cœur
comme un artichaud*. Meaning his heart was like an ar-
tichoke . . . a leaf to spare for every pretty girl around.

Thibodeau hadn't argued that one either. Enough dark-
haired, sultry-eyed darlings had been enthusiastic takers
at the *fais do-dos*, village dances, that went on from sun-

down to sunup, with the main entertainment occurring in the dark, fenced yard behind the barn where the band played loud.

Rollie Thibodeau's sentimental attachments were few but strong, and he'd held onto only a handful of keepsakes from back home. Some black-and-white family photos dulled by time's wasting touch. Paper flowers his mother had worn on her wedding dress, their colors also diminished. A carton of gear his father had used for fishing shellfish while he threaded among the swamps and marshes in his twelve-foot dugout canoe: tall, wooden oyster tongs, rope nets, a tangle of crab line, the bucket in which he brought home his daily catch, one of the traps he would set on the muddy shore along his route to snare muskrats—"swamp rats" he'd called the nasty furballs, though their hides must have fetched a fair rate at market. There was an assortment of other boxed remembrances. And, of course, the Detecto doctor's scale. During his tour as a Long Range Reconnaissance Patrol commander in Nam, Thibodeau had rented storage space for the items in Baton Rouge, where they were kept until his return to the States.

After he was done with the war, and the war done with him, Thibodeau moved around a lot, inside and outside the country. For almost two decades he had capitalized on his elite military background by teaching classes on self-defense and firearms use, occasionally handling personal security, hiring out his services to clients ranging from business executives and Hollywood stars to European and Arab royals. Meanwhile, his boxed up this's and that's had gathered dust in one warehouse or another. Since 1995 or so, right about when Megan Breen roped him into UpLink International's developing security force with a pointed inquiry—If you've got the ability to do something constructive with your life, why spend the rest of it watching to see that nobody pulls the diapers off spoiled princes and princesses?—everything had been stashed away in a cheap concrete storage unit about the size of a walk-in closet at the head of a dreary, unfrequented parking lot a dozen miles outside Los Angeles.

Everything except Nanaine Adele's rusty, peeling lilac-colored scale.

Even before UpLink, that scale had gone wherever he did. Thibodeau wasn't sure why. In his opinion, rearview mirrors were supposed to help guide people forward on the highway of life, not inspect their balky hairs and crooked neckties at its rest stops. He hadn't been back to Louisiana since breast cancer got Nanaine Adele in 1989, and wasn't about to waste a minute longing for Acadia. The relics of the past that Thibodeau held close to him were the useful ones, which was probably the main reason he'd made the scale his constant traveling companion. It was a symbol more than anything else, he guessed. A reminder that the only memories worth carrying around were those that made riding out the present, and maybe the future, a little smoother.

Besides, the damn thing was just plain reliable.

Though never preoccupied with his weight, Thibodeau had kept an occasional eye on it, and always managed to stay in good shape despite the limitless pleasure he took from beer drinking and hearty eating. At six feet, four inches tall, he was the bearer of a wide-boned, chockablock physique, and had sustained a steady-as-she-goes 235 pounds for most of his adult life, packing virtually every last ounce of it in slabs of muscle hardened by regular and diligent workouts.

All that had changed about two years ago, when he'd been sucker punched by a submachine gun round while defending an UpLink facility in Brazil against a terrorist hit . . . a bullet that had gone deep into his stomach, hung a left through his large intestine, and then plowed into his spleen, turning it to mincemeat before finally butting up against the back of his rib cage. There was also plenty of hemorrhaging, and a partial lung collapse to stop the ER personnel who received him from getting too blasé about their task.

For several months after he was shot, Thibodeau's weakened condition had precluded strenuous exercise. Resistance training wasn't worth a thought—in fact, he'd had days when simply raising himself out of bed, or from a chair to a standing position, was a torment. And by the time Thibodeau was at last able to get back into the gym, he'd recognized that his body might never regain all of its lost trunkish strength. There was getting shot, and there was getting gut shot. And more often than not gut shot had a way of leaving you permanently damaged goods . . . special prov'd'nce strikes again.

While on the mend, Thibodeau had been coaxed into accepting what was intended to be seen as a major promotion at UpLink, and gotten a big pay hike consistent with its added responsibilities. He supposed he should have been grateful. That he was wrong to feel privately indignant about a legitimate career advancement. Still, Rollie Thibodeau was nobody's fool, and understood that his physical deficits had factored into the offer. To what degree, he didn't know. And maybe didn't care to guess. Why bother? He had been convinced it was made partly because Megan and Pete Nimec had wanted to remove him from active field duties he could no longer handle with 100 percent effectiveness . . . and nothing would unconvince him.

Specifically, he would become the administrative overseer of a newly created two-man post dubbed Global Field Supervisor, Security Operations.

They could take the man out of the field, but they

couldn't take the field out of his job description, he had told himself.

That smidgeon of gallows humor had given him zero consolation.

Now Thibodeau stood on the platform of his Detecto and frowned—a deep, disgusted frown that pulled the corners of his mouth far down his bearded face. The beard was a couple of years old and neatly trimmed. Over the past six months he had let it fill out to hide his jowly cheeks and the heavy dewlaps under his chin. For a while after his shooting he'd held at his usual 235 pounds in spite of the changes he saw in the mirror—but that was a deceptive measure. Thibodeau's muscles had lost weight as they shrank and deteriorated through disuse, even as the extra calories from his unmodified consumption of food and drink turned to fat. This had equalized things on the scale, and he had grown thicker, looser, and chunkier everywhere on his body without putting on so much as an ounce.

The problem was that it got harder to burn off fat as you lost muscle tone, and it would continue piling on unless you dieted, exercised, or got into a disciplined health routine that combined the two. Thibodeau hadn't. And he'd gained from his 235. The weight had crept up on him slowly, seemed to wrap itself around him like a huge silent slug. The warning signs had been present, of course. His vanishing jaw line, his thickening waist. But as long as he'd hovered within range of that 235 mark, they also had been dismissible. Thibodeau had felt his slacks—and undershorts, to give frankness its due—start to pinch and grab in all the critically, uncomfortably wrong spots. Felt his shirt tighten at the belly, its sleeves constricting around his shoulders and arms. If gradual upward nudges of the scale's lower indicator slide from 236 to 237, 240, and even 245 pounds balanced it, that seemed to fall well within his personal tolerance zone. Especially when he could lower his measured weight by 2, 3, sometimes a notch below 3½ of those apparent pounds by removing his shoes, his shirt, his shoes *and* shirt, and maybe some other articles of clothing if necessary—say after a few days of hearty banqueting, for instance.

Another trick Thibodeau had discovered was to step off the scale and recheck that the arrow on the beam and its frame met exactly. If they didn't, it could throw off his weight reading by a quarter pound or more, and he'd have to fiddle with its balance knob to make an adjustment. And although it distressed him when he'd needed to bump the upper indicator to its 250-pound poise on the bar while standing almost naked on the platform, he'd extended his rather malleable tolerance zone by reassuring himself that he would soon do something to trim down—cut out the andouille sausages and cornbread, switch to a lighter brew, keep his hands from reaching for the refrigerator door late at night.

Soon being one of those dangerous words with a value that was impossible to calculate, and therefore notoriously wide open to interpretation.

According to the scale's measurement beam, Thibodeau was now up to 299¼ pounds. Less than 1 pound shy of the boldly engraved and enameled number *300* on the beam. A tremendous increase of 54 pounds in eighteen months.

That was 299¼ pounds, with every last stitch of clothing except for his socks and boxers stripped off, flung in a large pile on the chair behind him.

"Gone an' turned myself into *un ouaouaron*," Thibodeau said in a low growl, using a Cajun word for bullfrog that reflected the cultural penchant for onomatopoeia, mimicking the sounds made by the creatures at dawn and dusk. "A fuckin' *ouaouaron*," he repeated, inserting a colorful modifier of his own fancy.

He did not know why he'd chosen this particular morning to take his weight. Having acknowledged the need to drop excess ballast, Thibodeau had gotten onto the scale infrequently over the past couple of months to avoid the comedown of reading premature and discouraging numbers. The truth was, he hadn't yet gotten full-swing into his diet. Hadn't really decided which foods would be the best to cut back on or investigated which kinds of beer would be light-bodied, palatable replacements for his favorite malt. He'd been too busy with work, and these decisions took careful forethought. Nobody who rushed into them was ever going to buy a winning ticket.

So why the scale? Thibodeau wondered. Why today? Why climb aboard now, when Tom Ricci, joint holder of the global field supervisor slot, its buck rapid deployment man—and one of Thibodeau's least favorite people in the world—was due for his briefing on the security upgrades implemented here at SanJo HQ while he'd been away on his solo safari for *le Chat Sauvage*? Why the hell do it knowing he was in for certain disappointment . . . and for that matter embarrassment, unless he got off its platform and back into his uniform *tout de suite*?

Thibodeau stood there on the scale another few minutes, looking down at his sadly fallen build. He had fussed all he could with its knob and indicator slides. He was wearing little more than air. And the measurement beam had gone on hanging in perfect, balanced suspension at 299¼ pounds.

Not that he needed a numeric reading to appreciate the indignities he'd inflicted upon himself. It was evident from the bare, bulging pillow of flesh into which his once-taut stomach had grown, the soft rolls of flab above the hips too kindly known as "love handles," and, most depressingly for Thibodeau, the pads of adipose tissue over his breastbone that showed early evidence of transforming into what were sometimes—in a much too crass and *un*kind fashion—referred to as "man titties."

But he'd killed enough time inspecting himself. More than enough. Ricci would be on his way over from his office down the hall, and Thibodeau damned well wanted to be back inside his pants before he showed up.

His lips still pulled into a scowl, he got off the scale to put on his clothes, disconcerted by the loud, banging rattle of its beam and platform bearings as they were relieved of his prodigious weight.

Thibodeau was trying to stuff the middle button of his shirt through its hole when he heard three sharp, brisk knocks at his door.

Tom Ricci, man of action. Predictably right on schedule.

"Un instant," Thibodeau called out, working in the recalcitrant button. "Wait just a minute—"

Ricci gave the door another quick knock, then took hold of the outer doorknob and let himself in.

Again, predictably.

His shirttails out over the open waistband of his pants, Thibodeau looked at him with an annoyance he made no attempt to conceal . . . and a sudden flush of embarrassment that he was hoping *could be* hidden.

"Thought I asked you to hang on," he said.

Ricci stood inside the entry, turned the dial of his wristwatch toward Thibodeau.

"Don't have a spasm on me," he said. "We've got an appointment."

Thibodeau regarded him another moment, disconcerted. Then he inhaled, holding in the breath—and his stomach—as he tucked, zipped, and hooked himself into his uniform slacks.

"Okay," he said on his exhale. He nodded toward his desk. "Grab a seat an' we'll talk."

Julia Gordian felt convinced Vivian was a shoo-in for adoption. There was still the cat test ahead, true, but she wasn't too worried. That was pretty much a guaranteed cinch.

She stood looking out the window of the In the Money Shop at the introduction and walking area next to the center's dusty parking lot, where Viv, a one-and-a-half-year-old grey whose career as a racer had ended after she'd broken the wrong way out of the gate in two of her first three starts, was being strolled around on a leash by her prospective rescuers, a seemingly nice enough family named the Wurmans—mother, father, and eight- or nine-year-old son—from up around Fremont. The dogs were always brought out to the people who came to look at them, as opposed to the people entering the kennels, which was how it usually worked at animal shelters. This was because, in addition to being weak and malnourished, some of the new arrivals had not yet gotten their vaccinations, were susceptible to canine diseases for which human beings might be unwitting carriers, and were therefore segregated until Rob Howell had gotten them checked out by his regular vet and approved as ready for placement. A small handful of visitors would complain about the policy, wanting to have their pick of all the greyhounds on hand, but Rob tended to send that type on their way as politely as he could—his position being that anybody who couldn't find a dog to love among the half dozen or so he was willing to show as available candidates wasn't qualified for greyhound ownership.

Julia supposed Rob's criteria were about the same as those a child-care worker would apply to couples interested in adopting a baby . . . although she'd actually had to wonder a couple of times if *his* rules weren't even more stringently set and enforced.

"You have to start the screening process the minute people leave their car," he'd told her on her first day at work. "Look for a good fit, and don't let your eagerness to place the dogs affect your judgment. Watch how folks act, listen to what they say, get a feel for the vibes they send out to the dogs, and the vibes the dogs send out to them. Much as I want permanent homes for our greys, they're better off as tenants with us than in a *bad* home where they aren't getting proper care."

Watching from behind the shop's sales counter, elbows propped on it beside the cash register, Julia had seen encouraging signs that the Wurman-Vivian vibe exchange was tuned to a harmonious cosmic bonding frequency. Vivian's leash was now in the hands of Papa Wurman, who was smiling over at Mama Wurman, who was beaming right back at him as an excited Junior Wurman crouched beside the dog and gently stroked her sides. Viv, meanwhile, was relishing the attention. A good fit? They appeared to be striking up the very music of the spheres.

Julia realized she'd been humming a melody to herself, recognized it as the chorus to the old Broadway song "Matchmaker," and was starting to wonder how *that* archaic musical strain had managed to surface from the junk bin of her post-Boomer memory storehouse when her cell phone suddenly began to tweedle.

She pulled it from the belt case clipped to her jeans, glanced at the Caller ID number on its display, and smiled as she fingered the TALK button.

"Yente's Canine Dating Service, open sunrise to sunset," she said. "To Life!"

A hesitant, "Excuse me?" at the other end.

Julia chuckled. Roger Gordian. A biz whiz without parallel, but more than a little humor impaired.

"Hi, Dad," she said. "Don't hang up, you've got the right number."

"Oh," Gordian replied. "For a second there I thought you said . . ."

"Just amusing myself. My boss is out back feeding the dogs, and I'm waiting to give my maiden cat test. He wants me to get the experience. We really should have given it to Viv . . . she's one of our sweetest greys . . . *before* a family showed up and fell in love with her, but somebody got their signals crossed. Either they never told Rob they had a cat during their phone interview, or he forgot to make note of it, it's been so crazy around here we can't be sure. Either way I've got to deal with it."

"Oh," Gordian said again. A pause. "If you don't mind my asking, what's—?"

"A cat test's for dogs that may be going to homes where there's already a kitty-in-residence," she said. "You know how easygoing greys are, but problems can happen when some of them mistake cats for bunnies."

"As in *rabbits*?"

"They're used as lures on the course," Julia said. "I think the law in most states is that track owners have to use mechanical ones, and they do during races to keep the police off their backs. But when they're training the dogs out of sight . . . well, never mind, I won't gross you out with some of the nauseating stories I've heard. Bottom line, we need to be sure our dogs are compatible with other pets."

"I hope that doesn't mean there's a supply of disposable cats at the center."

"Nope. Only an ornery old calico named Leona that the people who run this place got from the ASPCA," Julia said. "They keep her safe and overfed for her unfaltering dedication to the cause, don't you fret."

"As long as you tell me not to," Gordian said. "Anyway, if you're busy with things, I can call back—"

"No, believe me, I really was just waiting around for man and beast to get acquainted," Julia said. "What's up?"

"Well, your mother and I were hoping we could see you this weekend," Gordian said. "You could come for dinner tomorrow, naturally bring Jack and Jill, and the three of you sleep over at the house. If you want, of course. Then stick around with us Sunday for brunch and pampering—"

"Sounds tempting, Dad. Especially that last part about getting the princess treatment. But the timing's rotten," she said. "Rob . . . Rob Howell, that is . . ."

"He's your boss, right?"

"Right, sorry," Julia said. "Anyway, Rob works the graveyard shift at a hotel called the Fairwinds, I think it's somewhere on Highway 1. He mainly does audits there, but every so often handles the switchboard and reception desk, too, and I guess he's offered to sub for one of the day clerks for the next couple of weekends—they're buddies and the guy has a family emergency. Besides, Rob has a newborn and could use the extra money."

"Which leaves you running the show at the center."

"All by my lonesome. I wish there was somebody else. Rob's looking for more help. With his wife busy taking care of the baby, though, I can't exactly lay too much on her lap." She paused. "Any chance of us getting together during the week? I'm off Monday and Wednesday, and could meet you at your office for one of those father–

daughter lunches where you lecture me about how I need to find an honest *paying* job."

"Now there's what I call a real temptation," Gordian said. "Unfortunately, I'm out of town from Monday morning until Thursday or Friday. Washington, D.C. You remember Dan Parker?"

Julia smiled. Was it only *her* parents, or were all of them always asking their adult children whether they could remember people they'd known their entire lives? With her father, the person in question was very often Dan, whom Julia had practically grown up around and even invited to her wedding. Her mom was likewise constantly astounded that she had any recollection of her Uncle Will, who had been one of Julia's most dearly loved relatives, and was a frequent visitor to the Gordian home until his death from a sudden heart attack when she was eighteen or nineteen years old. What were they thinking? That their kids went through childhood and adolescence with their memory banks set on auto-delete? That they were oblivious to everything around them until they were, oh, say, forty-five, fifty, or so? Or were these supposed to be trick questions?

"Hmm, Dan Parker," she said, deliberately keeping any trace of sarcasm out of her voice. "He's that buddy of yours from Vietnam, no? The one who used to be a congressman in San Jose?"

"That's right, he was at your wedding reception," Gordian replied, sounding pleased by her name-recognition ability. "These days Dan's an executive with Sedco, the energy firm, and we'll be meeting with the rest of its board to negotiate the final points of a fiberoptic deal."

Julia looked out the window, saw the Wurmans were leading Viv back from the parking lot. "Guess we'd better hold off on making plans till next week," she said.

"I guess."

The shop's front door opened.

"Have to run," Julia said. "Good luck with your trip, Dad. I love you."

"Love you, too, honey," Gordian said. "Oh . . . and *l'chiam*, by the way," he added.

And then hung up.

Julia looked at the phone and blinked in surprise, a grin of colossal amusement breaking across her face.

Parents, she thought.

The wonders truly, truly never did cease.

The same yet different was how Rollie Thibodeau had been trying to characterize the overall facility security picture at UpLink International, and particularly UpLink HQ SanJo, since Ricci's departure.

The same, more or less, insofar as its requirements and policies.

Different, slightly, insofar as their implementation, with heightened emphasis on incident readiness and management.

There had also been some modifications to the electronic security systems—what amounted to minor tinkering in the area of general surveillance and countersurveillance operations, with more significant enhancements regarding the detection and control of chemical and biological threats.

"Some of it's these times we're living in. Everything going on around the world, you got to take extra precautions," Thibodeau said now, looking across his desk at Ricci. "Plus we been bitten once, you know."

Ricci sat motionless. When he answered, it was in an odd, clipped tone.

"Tell me about the techware," he said.

"There's operational gear big and small, but we'll start with the onsite basics," Thibodeau said. "We got new concealed weapon detectors in most of our buildings. And not just at entries. We been thinking about indoor environments. Walk around any floor here and you'll pass through a hidden magnetic scanner."

"I've noticed them at the hallway corners," Ricci said. "I can see where some door frames have been replaced."

"Figured you would," Thibodeau said. "Later on, I'm gonna walk you down to the monitoring station, show you right where they all are—"

"Don't bother," Ricci said. "They're okay. Most people won't spot them. The ones who do would be good enough to make any kind of scanners we install. I just want to know how they perform."

Thibodeau shifted in his chair. He was suddenly conscious of his uniform's too-snug fit, of the too-tight waistband of his trousers around his middle, of the chair's armrests pressing into his fleshy sides. If he pulled up his shirt, he would find little irritated patches of red on his flanks, wouldn't he?

He wondered what it was about Tom Ricci that had set off the heightened sense of his own ungainliness. Or maybe he was just projecting. Ricci hadn't said or done anything that could be taken as a reaction to his size. But Ricci was also just as whipcord lean as he'd been a year ago. While he himself had put on half a hundred pounds.

Thibodeau remembered the rattle and bang of the scale when he'd stepped off it. He adjusted his position behind the desk again.

"The scanners," he said. "They're . . . how can I say it? . . . more *discriminating*. Walkthroughs we had before weren't no better than what they using at commercial airports. You know the problems with them. Can't tell the difference between an Uzi and a set of keys or some pocket change. Can't find where something is on a person's body. And they be screwed up easy by electrical fields. Too many computers or cell phones working around them, we get false alarms. Waste time and resources. These CWD systems we installed can tell the object's size and shape, and pinpoint where it's located. Whether it be under somebody's left arm, strapped around his ankles, or stuffed where the sun don't shine."

Ricci's head went up and down.

"All right," he said. "What else is there?"

"Hate to think about it, but we put a whole response system in place for biochemical incidents," Thibodeau said. "This whole building been outfitted with sensors. Every room. Every office. Rooftop to basement."

Ricci looked at him.

"Hell," he said.

"I know," Thibodeau said. "Cost us a fortune."

Ricci kept looking steadily at him.

"I wasn't talking about what it cost," he said. "I meant this world of ours is fucking hell."

Thibodeau was silent. He'd never much liked Ricci, but had developed a certain trust in him. In his abilities, his self-command in tough spots. Now he didn't know what to think. Ricci hadn't changed on the outside, it was true. Inside, though, something was very different. It was as if those hard, unsharing eyes of his were mirrored glass surfaces. Thibodeau didn't know what was going on behind them.

"The sensors," Ricci said. "They mass spec?"

Thibodeau nodded yes.

"The spectrometry units I've seen look like U-Haul trailers," Ricci said. "They're too big to cart around offices—the military tows them around with Humvees."

Thibodeau shrugged.

"Be true for most of them," he said. "Think it's because of all the air they got to suck in for accurate samples. There's hoses, plus a vacuum collector and a separate laser chromatography unit in the housing. Adds up to a lot of space. The laser machine shoots beams of light through the air sample, and that light bends off whatever particles get caught with it. Then a computer tell us what those particles are, depending on the *angle* it bends at, sort of how our eyes see color." He paused, pulling at his beard some more. "Far's the system goes, you'd have to ask our R and D noggins for every detail of how it works. The handle I got is that it's like an invisible electronic nose, sniffs for germs and chemicals just the way our noses . . . or to put it better, the nose of a trained bloodhound . . . can pick up the smell of things in the air. Special cells in the nose, what the noggins call receptors, they be connected to nerves that can tell the brain what those things are. Then the brain translates the info as smells. Our invisible nose, now, it uses them sensors I told you about—*micro*sensors, they called, made of different polymers—exactly like the receptors. But instead of having nerve connections, they attach to optical fibers. Coat 'em, actually. One coated fiber maybe pick up anthrax or smallpox. Another can recognize the sleeper bug that almost killed the boss. A third can catch a whiff of cyanide, sarin gas, or some other nerve agent that been released—"

Ricci made a slicing gesture to check him.

"Let's skip ahead," he said. "Say we're attacked. The invisible nose twitches, we evacuate, get emergency medical treatment for people we know were exposed, make sure everybody else that might've been affected is examined. That's our immediate response. Now how do we conduct decontamination and site inspection? Who takes charge of the investigation? The feebs and CDC? FEMA? Or homeland security people? We supposed to let them walk right on in, go clomping all over each other's tracks like they did at Gordian and his daughter's homes a couple years ago? Or when they mucked up that anthrax mail probe in '01?"

Thibodeau blew a breath out his pursed lips. "Be quite a bunch of questions," he said. "I guess what happens far as outside agencies depends on the particulars. If there's a threat of public infection, we need to let them know . . . and where chembio's the problem, you have to expect that's going to be the case. But ain't nobody can beat us comes to dealing with problems of multiple jurisdiction. So we try to coordinate, hope they have the sense to work with us and not around us. That way we don't have hassle figuring out how to work around *them*."

"What about the first part of what I asked you?" Ricci said. "Same example. The sensors find a trace of something bad. A strain of virus. Bacteria. Is there some way we can clean the place up before it spreads?"

Thibodeau expelled another breath. He really did hate to think about this subject.

"We installed decon fog dispensers with the capacity to wipe out certain bugs," he said. "Anthrax, that's one of them. Got a long list of others I can show you . . . be *dozens* of others. Once we know the premises're empty, the fog's released, goes all the places the bioweapon would. Air vents, the spaces between computer keys, wherever. They tell me the fog particles are ultra-fine, smaller than the spores. Kills them by breaking 'em down right to their DNA."

"And the bugs it can't kill?"

"Brings us back around to the issue of readiness, an' how we apply policies that're already in place. Somebody walks into the building and we don't like the looks of him, I want him checked out. That's whether he's wearin' a mail deliverer's uniform, got his name on a visitor list, or be the head of a senate delegation. He can walk on air right before our eyes, heal the blind and crippled, say he's Jesus Christ himself in a hurry to announce his Second Coming. We think he looks suspicious, he ain't getting past the guard station unless he's ready to wait for us to feel convinced. And if that means we want to search-wand his robes and examine his sandals for plastic explosives, maybe ask him to give us phone numbers so we can call The Blessed Mother an' Holy Father in Heaven to verify his identity, *suite*. So be it."

"There are going to be complaints," Ricci said.

Thibodeau shrugged.

"Israeli security been handling things that way for years at their airports and main office buildings, and they don't catch no grief," he said. "Ain't nobody's freedoms bein' violated. A person does want to object, it's his or her right to leave. The fancy tech's great. I'm glad we got it. But me, I'm lettin' our people be guided by their own eyes, ears, and noses more'n any electronic ones. Puttin' my stock in the human element."

"You didn't hear me argue." Ricci stared into his face. "I just want to know which element you mean."

The remark surprised Thibodeau, and his expression showed it.

"Afraid I don't understand," he said.

"I think maybe you do," Ricci said. "We can pick and choose our options, or lay them out across the board. I'm curious how it'll be for you when the heat's on."

Thibodeau was silent. He wasn't sure how to answer, truly wasn't sure he'd even gotten Ricci's inference. But his fixed stare and strange tone of voice were unsettling.

Ricci sat watching him a while longer. Thibodeau was almost glad when he finally rose in front of the desk.

"I guess we're done," Ricci said.

Thibodeau looked at him. *Done sounds fine,* he thought. Except they weren't.

"We never did talk about the personal field equipment," he said.

"No," Ricci said. "Maybe we'll make some time later."

Thibodeau wasn't sure why he found himself opening his desk drawer and reaching into it. He supposed that uncertainty was, in its way, a fitting note on which to end their little let's-get-reacquainted talk, which had left him wondering about a lot of things . . . foremost among them the point Ricci had been trying to make, and now his own.

"Might want to keep these handy," he said, and tossed a couple of aluminum squeeze tubes from the drawer onto his desktop. They were about two inches long—the size of toothpaste samplers.

Ricci picked them up.

"What's inside?" he said.

"Guy from special development got them to me a couple days ago," Thibodeau said. "It's wound closure gel. We're getting ready to deliver a ton of it to the military—they already issue something like it to their forward combat troops, but this's supposed to seal the skin better'n any other kind of dressing, keep it clean and breathing until an injured soldier get to a MASH unit. The idea's for all our field personnel to carry the stuff, too. Case somebody gets his hide perforated way I did a few years back."

"How come you're giving them to me now?"

"I got to read over the test reports this week, decide whether to approve 'em for issue," Thibodeau said. It was a truth that felt like a lie. "Thought you might want to have your say."

Ricci examined the tubes in his palm a moment, then dropped them indifferently into the pocket of his sport jacket.

"Decide whatever you want," he said. "I'll stick them

inside my shaving kit in case I nick myself."

Thibodeau shrugged without response, watched Ricci leave the office, then sat looking at its closed door in silence for long minutes afterward, trying to figure out for sure what had passed between them.

In the end, however, he was only positive that it scared the living daylights out of him.

"Looks like we're ready to go," Julia Gordian was saying. "If anyone has questions for me, I'll be glad to answer them after explaining how this works."

This being the cat test, which was about to commence in a restrictively small back room at the Peninsula Adoption Center. Besides a couple of plastic chairs and wicker kitty bed in which Leona the Grouch was now curled, it was occupied by Vivian the Grey, the Wurmans, and Julia herself—a close-quarters environment that was no fluke whatsoever, since forcing Viv and Leona to invade each other's private space would give Julia a very good idea how the dog would behave in a similar, but uncontrolled, household situation.

"There are two parts to the test," Julia continued, holding Viv close beside her on a short leash. She looked alternately from Mr. Wurman to Mrs. Wurman. "In the first, I'm going to bring Vivian right up to the kitty bed and see whether she displays any aggressive tendencies toward cats, which is pretty rare. Most greys are either curious, indifferent, or, believe it or not, even afraid of them, like my own two babies at home. Occasionally they even get frisky—"

"How come you put that bad thing on Vivian's mouth so she can't open it or breathe?" said Junior Wurman . . . whose name, Julia had learned, was actually Thomas.

Julia glanced over at his accusing face.

"A muzzle isn't really a bad thing, and Viv can breathe

through it just fine," she said. "Greyhounds are used to wearing them when they race, and I've only put it on now to make sure Leona doesn't get hurt in case she's snapped at."

Thomas looked mistrustful. "But you told us that wasn't gonna happen."

"I said it *probably* won't," Julia said, and offered a reassuring smile. "We need to be careful, 'kay?"

A halfhearted nod from Thomas. He wedged himself back against his seated parents, still regarding Julia with critical mistrust.

She returned her attention to the adults, feeling a bit like Cruella DeVille. With vampire fangs.

"If all goes well, our next step is to see whether Vivian shows overly possessive traits when one of you holds the cat," she said. "Some jealousy's normal between them, and no different, really, from human sibling rivalry. Viv might show it by starting to whimper or getting down in a play position to catch your eye. If that happens, you need to be aware of it, spread around the affection, and everybody's going to be happy. But it's important to realize we're talking about a big, muscular seventy-five-pound dog that can sprint almost as fast as a Thoroughbred horse, compared to an animal that weighs maybe a tenth as much, and is also a whole lot smaller. A cat that gets caught in a dog's jaws is in serious trouble, and we want to help spare you that kind of unhappy incident—"

"Can *I* hold Leona when we do it?" Thomas said. Which made it twice now that he'd interrupted.

Julia looked at him. Hadn't she mentioned she'd take questions *after* her explanation was finished?

"I think it's best we leave it to your mom or dad," she said. "To be on the safe side—"

"But you said that *thing's* supposed to be on Vivian's mouth to stop her from biting anybody!"

"That's true." Julia was wishing the kid's mother or father would chime in and help her out here. "She can jump at Leona, though, and you might get a little startled—"

"What's *startled* mean?"

"Ah, a little upset, in other words—"

"Won't you have her on a leash?"

"Well, yes—"

"Why'd I be *upset* if Vivian's on a leash and *can't bite* anybody—?"

"It's okay with us if Thomas wants to hold the cat," said Papa Wurman, whose first name was Stanley. He put a hand on his son's shoulder and gave it a doting squeeze. "Desmond, that's our house cat, belongs to him. And Vivian's going to be his new best friend. So how about we let him make the choice."

Julia looked at Stanley. This was not quite the brand of parental mediation she'd had in mind. In fact, the euphonious cosmic vibe Julia had thought she detected in the air earlier was starting to seem more and more like a wild-flying spray of sour notes. She was thinking her emotions might have led her into the very sort of pitfall Rob had warned against—namely getting too enthusiastic about the prospect of finding a home for one of their rescues.

She was quiet a moment. It was Rob who made the final call in a dog's placement. Standard operating procedure was for Julia to consult with him at the windup of every orientation she supervised and give her positive or negative impressions of how it went. Any doubts she might have about people would measure significantly into his own evaluation, and if need be he'd play the stern heavy, explain why a greyhound wasn't a suitable pet for

them, and send them on their merry ways. But Julia
hadn't completely ixnayed the Wurmans, not yet, and
saw no harm in going ahead with the cat test. Nor was
there any hard-and-fast rule to prevent the *kid* from being
the cat bearer. Assuming the test got that far, the way he
conducted himself might even figure into her recommendation.

"All right," she said. "Let's get started."

Vivian passed step one of the test with flying colors.
Her eyes anxious circles, her long tail tucked between
haunches still bald and rash-inflamed from crate burn at
the track, Vivian stiffened with resistence as Julia led her
over to the slumbering Leona's bed and acquiesced only
after some soothing words, a pat on the head, and a
couple of firm but gentle tugs of the leash. When Julia
unwound the leash from around her hand to give it
extra slack, Vivian opted to retreat from the bed rather
than approach any farther. When Julia pulled her closer
to it, and Leona stirred to give the grey a dozy, half-
lidded, let's-get-this-drill-over-with-so-I-can-get-back-to-
my-catnap look, Viv shied off again, turning her head
slightly to avert her gaze.

Julia moved away from the bed and the nervous grey
eagerly joined her, shivering a little, leaning against her
legs for reassurance.

"As everyone could see from her body language, Viv's
reaction to Leona fell somewhere between timid and
downright afraid," Julia said. She stroked the dog's neck
and flank to calm her. "Obviously, that beats aggressive.
Now Thomas—"

"Do I get to hold the cat?"

Julia looked at him, bit the inside of her lower lip.

"Yes," she said, whooshing out a breath. "You get to
hold her. What I'd like you to do is carefully pick Leona
up, then trade places with one of your parents so you can

sit and cuddle her on your lap. When I bring Viv over to you, pretend not to notice us. Just keep petting and talking to Leona. Sound good?"

Thomas responded with one of his impatient, borderline rude half-nods, bent to lift the cat out of her basket, and then sat with it as Mama Wurman—introduced as Ellen—vacated her chair.

Julia shot Thomas's father a glance. She wasn't sure why she'd expected Stanley to be the parent to stand up, but he remained glued to his seat, arms crossed over his chest. And though it had nothing at all to do with their eligibility for greyhound ownership, Julia couldn't help but note that chivalry wasn't a point of emphasis for the Wurman brood.

She stepped forward again, letting out the leash, guiding Viv toward Thomas.

The kid was a natural for the role of animal provocateur, she had to give that to him.

"I love you, kitty-cat," Thomas cooed. He nestled Leona in his arms, scratched behind her ear, buried his face in the thick fur of her nape, and gave her a series of smoochy lip-smacking kisses. "I love you best of all, love you so, *soooo* much—"

All in an instant Vivian launched forward, straining at the leash. She was growling, her teeth gnashing inside the muzzle as she thrust her long snout at the cat. Before Julia could yank her away from him, Thomas screamed and flinched back in his chair, slamming it hard against the wall. Hissing, spitting, her fur on end, Leona took a defensive swat at Viv. Then she sprang out of Thomas's arms to the floor, went scrambling wildly across the room, and bolted out the doorless entry to the storefront with a loud mewling screech.

"The lady tricked me!" Thomas hollered. His face red,

tears bursting from his eyes. *"She knew the dog was gonna be bad and she tricked me!"*

"Thomas, I'm sorry you got frightened, but that's not true." Julia had pulled in the leash, straddled Vivian between her legs, and could already feel her subsiding. "I told you there was a chance—"

Thomas leaped to his feet, and the chair fell over with a crash. Ellen swept him into her consoling arms.

"No you didn't!" he bawled. He'd clenched his hands into tight, white-knuckled fists and was shaking them at his sides. *"You're a liar! A mean, mean liar!"*

Stanley rose from his chair and looked across the room at Julia.

"Under the circumstances, given how my son's been traumatized—"

"A mean liar lady with a bad, stupid dog . . ."

"—I feel it's best we reconsider this adoption," Stanley said.

Julia somehow managed to arrest her smile.

"Mr. Wurman," she said, "I have to admit those were exactly my thoughts."

Macie Nze had done his best to mark the 4×4's route, and by that guess its general destination. The sounds and smells coming through the open front windows made it apparent that he'd been taken into the bush. Deep into the bush to judge from the long, punishing drive, which already seemed to have gone on for half the night. Though his eyes were covered by a canvas hood or sack, he was convinced his captors had headed south for dozens of kilometers, and then east for dozens more, putting him somewhere near the Wonga-Wongé Preserve, if not within its actual boundaries.

Nze had fought to hang on to his wits, stay alert to surrounding noises, keep track of turns the vehicle had made . . . lefts, rights, curves wide or sharp. Orienting himself hadn't been easy. Wherever he'd been brought and held for many hours after his abduction was clearly within the city limits, but he'd been forced to wear the hood the entire time and gotten only a vague sense of his starting point. Yet neither his negated eyesight, his fear, nor his constant discomfort—and occasionally dreadful pain—had stopped Nze from being able to tell when the 4×4 was crossing bridges or stopping at intersections. Or when its tires had left Port-Gentil's paved streets and thoroughfares for the outlying bush country.

The feel of the unimproved roads he'd traveled ever since had held their own clues to his direction. Even a newcomer to the land could have differentiated between highway macadam and rutted wilderness path, and except for his four years abroad at university, Nze, who was a month shy of his fiftieth birthday, had lived in Gabon his entire life. He could identify the *type* of surfaces over which he'd been driven, whether coastal sand or laterite, a soft, iron-rich earth that was typical of inland marshes and lagoons, and would hold moisture through all but the harshest dry seasons. For a while now the laterite had been sucking at the vehicle's wheels, causing it to pitch and yaw, repeatedly bogging it down in claylike red muck.

That continuous rocking was bad enough for Nze, but the jolts he took in the 4×4's cargo section whenever it was pushed out of a bog were far worse, and had wrung stifled groans of agony through the thick band of duct tape over his mouth. After the abductors walked him from his temporary holding place—hooded, gagged, and at gunpoint—they had forced him to squat on his knees in the 4×4's cargo section, and then bound his wrists and ankles together from behind with electrical cord. The first rattling bump had knocked Nze off balance onto his left side, flinging his body against a heavy tire stowed in back with him . . . presumably a spare. He'd remained there since, unable to pull himself up, the grooved pattern of its treads stamping into him through his clothes. Movement just worsened the abominable strain on his neck, back, and legs. And those sudden forward lurches of the vehicle, *mon Dieu*, they were almost unendurable.

And so the drive stretched on. Nze believed daybreak was fast approaching—for whatever it was worth, the coarse, heavy fabric over his face had not completely blocked his perception of light and darkness. Much earlier, before the 4×4 slipped out of the city, he'd distinguished the glow of traffic signals, streetlights, even the occasional glancing headlamp beams of other motor vehicles. Now he had discerned a faint lifting of the black outside the windows, coupled with the sounds of an awakened jungle. He could hear the discord of overlapping birdsong, and had thought he'd recognized a mangabey's shrieky primate cry behind him on the forest road.

Part of Nze's mind yearned for an end to the torturous ride. Another part of him, however, understood how insane a desire that was, what its fulfillment would likely mean for him. He had tried to ignore these emphatic inner warnings, banish them from contemplation, but they had persisted anyway.

Assistant Minister Macie Nze was a man of some fair reason, a trait that would not allow reality to be denied.

If only his capacity for logic and common sense had guided his recent actions, Nze supposed he would never have gotten into this wretched spot. But greed was an imbecilic spoiler that could overcome a person's best instincts. In his case, it had happened once too often.

As the car rolled on over the dirt roads, Nze's thoughts suddenly backtracked to when he'd been taken outside his home all those hours ago . . . and then reversed themselves a little further, to the very moment he was lured into the trap.

The call came shortly after eleven o'clock on what was now the previous night. Seventeen minutes past eleven, to be exact. There was a Berthoud clock on his living-room bureau, and Nze recalled having looked at the antique timepiece as he had reached for the phone, setting down his late-evening glass of wine.

"*Bonsoir*, Macie." The voice in his handset had belonged to Etienne Begela. "*Ça va?*"

"*Bien, merci.*"

Nze had waited. Begela's cordial tone had thrown him off guard, as it had at the hotel earlier that night. His superior in the Office des Postes et Telecommunications, and a Beti Fang of maternal family linkage, Begela had not spoken a word to Nze for weeks before the reception . . . not, in fact, since their tense conversation aboard the Avirex flight out of Libreville after the National Assembly voted its approval of the UpLink licenses. Begela alternately accused Nze of being a bungler and double-crosser for having withdrawn his opposition. Nze countered that political exigency had left him with no choice except to launch a strategic retreat. The Americans' support among the PDG's most formidable and senior members was overwhelming, he'd insisted. Continued challenges would merely label both of them obstructionists to their future sorrow.

"Don't speak to me of sorrow," Begela said once their plane left the Gamba airport runway. "It isn't you who must face our backer."

"He paid us to lobby—"

"He expected us to deliver."

With that curt interruption, Begela had risen from beside Nze to take an unoccupied seat up the aisle, and afterward had presented him with nothing but silence and his back.

Until the 11:17 telephone call.

Last night.

Nze remembered standing quietly with the receiver to his ear for several moments after their exchange of pleasantries. Studying his ornate centuries-old clock. Noting the swing of its pendulum's polished brass rod as droplets of light splashed over it from a chandelier overhead.

"We've gotten a break," Begela had said. "I've met with the individual we spoke about on the plane. Things went far better than expected."

"He doesn't blame us for the vote?"

"Let's say I've managed to raise his consciousness about the Libreville hearing, and our political system in general."

"How so?"

"Our lack of success was a disappointment to him. As is the arrival of the UpLink advance group. But he understands the complexities we dealt with in the capital, has revised his objectives accordingly, and remains hopeful we can barter influence with our opposition, sway them to rescind their decision."

Nze had shaken his head. "With the Americans in our country, I don't see any chance of making inroads—"

"Hear me, *mebonto*," Begela broke in, using the familiar Fang term of address reserved for members of a nuclear kin group. "Our associate still asks for our favors, and we should oblige him. He knows it does not come without ample compensation."

Nze had paused to think. He'd reached for his glass of Clos du Marquis, sipped. Begela's implication was plain. The foreigner had been a brimming well of profit neither of them was eager to abandon.

"Was he specific about what he wants from us?"

Begela gave an affirmative grunt.

"It's best we discuss that in person," he said. "I'll send over my car to bring you to the office."

Nze was surprised. "At this hour? I've just gotten settled in . . ."

"Consider it worthwhile overtime," Begela said. "We mustn't delay. There are steps we can take in the morning that will reassure our backer, yet are consistent with a phased approach that will satisfy your cautious inclinations."

Nze had taken another drink from his wineglass, let the warm and mildly bitter flavor of the Saint Julian grape settle over the back of his tongue.

Ample compensation.

"Give me fifteen minutes to get ready," he'd said at last.

The black Mercedes 500E coupe pulled in front of his colonial townhouse a quarter hour later on the dot, and Nze had noticed nothing unusual approaching it across the empty sidewalk. Begela's personal driver, Andre, had whisked around to the curb, nodding dutifully as he opened the rear passenger's side door.

Nze was leaning into the Benz when he saw the man in its backseat—a man the coupe's double-glazed windows had at first concealed from view. In his dark coverall fatigues, he very definitely was not one of the minister's regular employees.

For a confused, off-kilter moment, Nze had wondered if he might be an official escort of some kind. But then a scent that was at once recognizable and incongruous wafted over him from the car's interior . . . the pungent, leafy smell of khat.

Although the stimulant drug was legal in Gabon—as it was throughout the rest of Africa—Nze knew no ministerial guard would have the effrontery to chew it while on duty.

He'd stopped halfway inside the car, hesitant, suspicion abruptly taking root inside him.

A profanity was husked in his ear: *"Encule-tête!"*

Powerful hands closed around Nze's neck from behind, wrenched it backward before he could react. The hood fell over his head and was pulled down below his eyes, his face. Then Nze was shoved into the rear of the car, where his mouth was quickly wrapped with duct tape outside the sack.

Someone pressed into the car after him and the door of the Mercedes slammed shut.

An instant later, Nze heard the driver get inside.

Nze made smothered sounds through the tape, struggled to move, but could scarcely wriggle his body. He'd been crushed between the man in dark fatigues and whoever boosted him into the car.

An object jabbed into his right side. Hard. The blunt barrel of a gun.

"Ça suffit!" The order to stop squirming had been spat by the same gruff, husking voice he'd heard out on the sidewalk. Again, close against his ear.

Nze became still, heard a different voice from his opposite side.

"Dépêche toi, vas-y continue!" the khat chewer shouted at the driver. Urging him to hurry up, get on with it.

The car had jumped forward into the street.

Nze was certain the hideaway to which they brought him was near the ocean harbor—perhaps a storage warehouse, or indoor berthing space. It had taken only minutes to get there. As they pulled him from the car, guiding him roughly along, he had felt the transition from asphalt to old wooden boards under his feet, smelled saltwater and diesel fuel, heard what sounded like the rhythmical knocking of a ship's hull against its moorings. Then a roll-down security gate being raised on rusty metal tracks in front of him.

He was led indoors. Thrust into a chair. Told he'd be shot if he put up any resistance.

The gate clanged shut.

Nze sat without budging for hours before he was shuffled out into the 4×4. At the time, he had no idea why they had kept him at that interim place . . . but much later, after his captors passed out of the city, he would conclude they had been waiting for the night to run itself thin. It only made sense. The roads leading into the bush were slow to traverse by daylight, and filled with unseen hazards in darkness, becoming more arduous as Port-Gentil's outlying townships and settlements were left behind in the distance. They would have wanted to limit the amount of ground that had to be covered before the first rays of dawn came bleaching through the sky.

Now the sun was up, its heat building in the cargo section around Nze as the 4×4 gyrated along over pebbled, foliage-tangled jungle roads and trenches. In September, the days were quick to grow sweltering, and air-conditioners were useless and unused in motor vehicles. He could feel sweat pouring down his face under the canvas hood, feel the tire rubber wedged against his side getting warm. His entire body ached, besides, and his arms and legs were tingling from lack of circulation.

There was no way to be certain how many men were riding with him, but Nze had mentally indexed at least four voices from snatches of overheard conversation. One of them was very soft, belonging to someone who spoke French with a perceptible foreign accent . . . an American accent, he believed. The khat chewer from the backseat of the Mercedes was also among his hostile, unchosen companions, and Nze did not have to hear the man speak to know it. The combination of his drug of choice's sickly sweet odor and the stultifying heat inside the cargo section had pushed Nze to the verge of nausea. And his constant tossing about hadn't helped. With his mouth taped, he'd been afraid he would choke on his own vomit if the trip stretched on much longer, heaving up what little was left of yesterday's dinner—and fine wine, he recalled miserably, thinking of the glass he had set down to answer the phone.

Nze actually found himself grateful when the vehicle bounced to a halt, its engine cutting off with a shudder . . . and then was struck by how odious his circumstances must be to evoke such a feeling, the constant realist in him serving up another reminder that having reached his destination could not prove a good thing at all.

Doors on both sides of the vehicle opened, shut, and Nze heard footsteps scrambling over earth and scrub toward its rear. The cargo hatch was lifted. Arid—but fresh—air wafted through, easing the stuporous, khat-smelling heat around him.

This time Nze could feel no gratitude. He had already wasted his meager quota.

Hands seized the back of his perspiration-soaked shirt, pulling him from the open hatch like a trussed animal. Nze landed on his shoulder with a thud that knocked the wind out of him. He felt somebody take hold of the cords around his wrists, heard machetes hacking at foliage as he was dragged blindly over what seemed to be a rough footpath. Pebbles and thorns skinned his hands. A spiny clinging vine caught his left pants leg, raked it upward, and tore the flesh above his ankle. At some point he had lost one of his shoes, the foot that wore it twisting sharply. It had elicited a muffled whimper from him.

Nze did not know how far his abductors pulled him as

they tramped on through the brush. Fifteen meters, twenty, perhaps farther. He did not know.

Suddenly, they stopped.

Nze was grabbed by the shirt collar again, pulled up onto his knees with a vicious jerk, and steadied from behind so he wouldn't keel over, as he had in the four-wheel drive.

The tape around his hood was torn off. Then the hood itself.

Up and off.

Nze's eyes filled with an explosion of glare. He grimaced as they adjusted to the daylight, blinked away stinging tears.

Swooning from fatigue, his vision a watery blur, Nze still found he could discern a great deal about his surroundings. He was in a small circular clearing, its edges shagged by high thickets of Marantaceae with dark green leaves the size of elephant ears. The clearing's plainly defined boundaries and trammeled-down carpet of sedge suggested it was man made, slashed out of the forest with machetes like those his captors had used on the trail. Around and underneath Nze, the sawgrass growth was especially scorched, almost black, giving it the appearance of a large stain spread across the ground.

Then he spotted the tire lying in front of him. Doubtless the *same* tire that had been jammed against him in the cargo section for many hours. A portable metal gasoline can was beside it. A row of men nearby to the right, their knees level with his eyes.

He raised his head for a look at their faces. There were four of them—Andre in his conspicuous chauffeur's suit, and two Bantu with semiautomatic rifles slung over their shoulders, dressed in coverall fatigues identical to those worn by the khat chewer. Nze could not see the latter, but thought he might be responsible for the shadow falling over him from behind . . . and realized now that he was not the group's only user. As the minister knelt there before them, one of the Bantu removed a wad of the drug from a banana-frond wrapping in his hand, passed it to the other tribesman, then got a second wad and put it in his mouth with two fingers.

They chewed and watched him with hyped, bright eyes.

Nze looked away from them to the group's single white, a lance-thin man in a safari jacket and bush hat. His eyes were pale blue, his skin the color of chalk.

Nze at once saw the camera hanging over his chest from a neck strap. It was a 35-mm with a large objective lens.

The white met Nze's gaze with his own, studying him. Both hands in the gusset pockets of his jacket.

"Bienvenue," he said in the lightly accented French that Nze remembered from their trip. *"Por le maia distance, se bien regarder á la lumière du jour."*

Nze was silent.

"I assume you've guessed who I am," the white said.

Nze gave a slow nod.

The tire, he thought.

The gas can.

The burn-stained ground around him.

He felt himself trembling with fear.

"Let's hear you say my name," the white said. "It's been a grueling ride for everyone. But worn out as we are, we must strive to be polite."

Nze started to answer and his voice cracked. He wet his parched lips, tried again.

"Gerard Fáton," he rasped.

The white continued regarding him steadily.

"There you go," he said. A trace of a smile on his lips. "Monsieur Nze, you should be honored that I've come down to say good-bye to you, and capture the moment so that it will be remembered and appreciated."

Nze's trembling worsened. He couldn't make it stop.

"I've done nothing . . ."

"And your doing nothing has cost me."

Nze shook his head.

"What happened in Libreville . . . I did my best," he said. "My arguments were defeated . . . but your desires weren't made clear to me until very late. Too late. I had to rush to understand them . . . to prepare. If I'd had more time—"

Fáton vented a sibilant breath through his teeth.

"Lie to me once more, and I'll have your hands separated from your wrists to make the burning worse."

Nze was shaking uncontrollably. There was no denying what was planned for him. He felt his bladder release and hardly cared that his abductors could see the moist stain spreading across the crotch of his pants. He could live with the shame, if he could somehow find a way to live at all.

"You changed your vote to curry favor with some no-rate government connivers," Fáton said. "Vulgar *rustres*. Rubes and yokels who play act at being Mandarins."

"I'll try again," Nze said. "I can do better. Much better. I never meant to give up, you must believe that—"

"Stop. Now. You offend me." Fáton shut his eyes, inhaled through his mouth, stood quietly holding his breath. After a long while he expelled the air from his nostrils, raised his eyelids with a kind of reptilian slowness, and went back to staring at Nze.

" 'I don't see any chance of making inroads'," he said. "Does that statement ring familiar to you?"

Nze's face showed the anxious terror of a captured animal. Familiar? Of course it was. Of course. Here was another piece of the trap's framework. Fáton was simply repeating words that the assistant minister himself had spoken to Etienne Begela over the telephone what seemed a hundred years ago.

Fáton stared at Nze for a brief moment longer before turning to the small group of men beside him.

"Let us necklace this faithless swine and be done here," he said.

Even as he spoke, one of Fáton's armed guards went to the tire, crouched over it, and began filling it from the can, working the spout through a hole that had been gouged into the tire's sidewall. He poured until the can was almost empty, took a handkerchief from his pocket, soaked it with whatever was left of its contents, and wadded it into the hole, leaving a small wick of cloth hanging out. Finally he tossed the can into the brush and was joined by another of the guards, who helped him lift the tire off the ground and carry it toward the patch of blackened sedge where Nze knelt helplessly and watched.

Nze tried to move, knowing it was futile. The khat chewer from inside the Benz—or whichever of his captors was standing behind him—had taken fast hold of the electrical cord that bound his arms and legs. He could only squirm with impotent terror in that solid, unbreakable grip.

The tire was lowered over Nze's head to rest around his shoulders. Fuel sloshed inside it, the stench overwhelming him.

He sobbed.

"Very good," Fáton told the pair of fatigue-clad men. Then, to Nze, in a tone of calm gratification: "You were warned about lying twice, little piglet."

Nze sobbed openly.

Fáton was looking past his shoulder.

"Omar," he said, *"Coupez ses mains, si'l vous plaît."*

Omar, cut off his hands, please.

Nze felt a sudden swish of air, glimpsed the bright sun-sparkle of the rising machete blade. He was already screaming when it came down on him with a quick sweeping motion, his cries loud enough to startle a drove of birds from their perches in the hemming brush. Cold pain sledged up from his wrists as the machete carved into them, penetrating deep, momentarily snagging on something, a resistant knot of muscle or bone. It was wobbled from side to side, and then pushed through with a sickening wet crunch. An instant later the coldness turned to pulsing heat.

Nze howled at the top of his lungs, his blood soaking into the thirsty blackened ground. The shadow of the khat chewer, the machete wielder, *the butcher who had maimed him*, folded and unfolded as he crouched behind Nze, and rose again, and then dropped both severed hands in front of him, let them fall together inches from his knees, crimson streaming from them, tatters of meat flapping wetly around the stubs of his wrist bones, the second and third fingers of one hand twitching like the legs of a dying crab.

Through a haze of suffering and weakness, Nze watched Fáton slide a fist from his right gusset pocket and hold it out before him like a sideshow magician engaged in an amusing bit of hocus pocus. Then he spread open his fingers to display the wooden matchbox in his palm.

"Allumettes," he said. Again with that even, satisfied calm. "Here is some humane advice, *mon ami*. As the diesel oil inside the tire bursts into flame, it might be desirable for you to take good, deep breaths of smoke. This goes against involuntary reflex, I know. The fumes will be quite hot, and are apt to sear your throat and lungs. But if you do manage to control yourself—deep breaths, I remind you—they will render you unconscious

before the melted tire rubber and burning fuel start to run over your body. They cling to the flesh, you see. And I imagine it must be quite agonizing when flesh cooks."

Fáton's left hand appeared from inside his jacket, produced a match from the box, and flicked it against the striker.

Its head budded orange and he moved to within arm's reach of Nze.

Nze looked at him, tears streaming down his cheeks, his nose and throat clogged with mucus.

"Please, I beg you—" he began.

Fáton frowned with disapproval, touched his flickering match head to the wad of cloth.

"Here, at least, my labor has not been in vain," he said, and stepped backward as the makeshift fuse ignited with an audible whoosh.

The fuel inside the tire caught almost at once, fire gushing out the large hole in its sidewall, then gnawing through in other places, rapidly tracing its way around the circumference.

Moments later the whole tire went up with a combustive roar. Nze gasped for air and felt broiling heat fill his mouth. Choking on his own scream, he struggled grotesquely to tear free of his bonds with fingers he no longer had, the blaze ringing him in, raking him with its vicious talons. Blots of diesel fuel and gummy, liquified rubber dribbled over his skin, bonded with his skin, ate their way down and down and down into his skin. He could hear his blood sizzle in that blasting, torching heat as the fiery mix splashed the raw bloody stumps of his wrists.

The lids burning away from his eyes, wilting off in curled, blackened strips, Nze endured several remaining instants of sight before the eyeballs themselves were cooked in their sockets—a brief staring agony of horror

in which he could see Fáton through breaks in the sheet
of flame, standing with his camera raised, his pale lips
drawn into a leer beneath the wide, black circle of its
lens.

Then Nze's throat finally unlocked to release the
scream that had been trying to force its way out. His body
its own raging pyre, he continued screaming for some
time, bellows that went climbing high into the air with
the flames and smoke. Fáton was cognizant of them long
after he and his men had returned to the 4×4 and swung
back around onto the snaking jungle trail.

Nze had not taken his advice about the deep breaths,
it seemed . . . and, in Africa as perhaps nowhere else on
earth, one's mistakes bore the harshest of all possible
consequences.

FIVE

VARIOUS LOCALES

ON HIS LAST EVENING IN MADRID, SIEGFRIED KUHL
sat facing his high terraced window above the Gran Vía
and watched the sunset bathe his completed scale miniature of the Iglesia de San Ginés in deep burgundy light.
Against the wall near the apartment door were his few
articles of luggage. Beside his chair was a large paper
shopping bag that contained a purchase he had made at
an art-supply shop some blocks from La Casa Real.

He had moved with haste to close out his affairs here,
and it had now come down to his final act before leaving.

As his eyes took in the miniature, Kuhl thought of the
long effort it represented, the concentrated application of
his learned skills. Its piece-by-piece construction had
been painstakingly slow, but impatience rather than patience had held him to it, an irresistible drive to see the
model take on finished shape from its raw makings. He
thought of the hours he had spent sketching plans from
the digital reference images stored in his laptop computer, of the careful fabrication of its segments with his
saws, rasps, files, gouges, chisels, and wood knives. He
summoned back to his very fingertips the tactile impressions of working his materials, methodically hand carving unformed balsa to replicate the church's brick and
tile facades; its crests, moldings, and traceries; its every

architectural feature and texture—even cutting small pieces of glass to fit its windows.

Inside his church, Kuhl had re-created San Ginés's three arched naves and the figure of the Virgin Mother in her apparition as the Lady of Valvanera, patroness of remedies, whose grace was sought for healing and protection in war. There, it was said, a group of assassins had once stolen into the vestibule and murdered a young man as he knelt before the Lady in adoration, leaving his headless corpse to be discovered at her feet, and his spirit to haunt the aisles with ghostly elegies to a transgression unpunished . . . and, Kuhl imagined, a restless anger at reverence scorned and unrewarded.

After detailing the model to his satisfaction, Kuhl had sanded and primed its subassemblies for the paints he had mixed to create the earth tones of its outer walls, the darker colors of rail and roof, dome and steeple, as well as the age-tarnished iron bell in the proud tower of San Ginés, and the crucifix raised high above all. He had applied his coats of paint with precise brushstrokes, done his staining and streaking with a sponge applicator to approximate the effects of age, sun, and soot. Then he had used clever dashes of color to hint at the rare artwork decorating the interior walls—canvases by El Greco, Salvatierra, Nicolás Fumo, and a reproduction of a work by the Venetian master Sebastiano Ricci that had been destroyed in an eighteenth-century fire. Ricci, whose devout paintings commissioned by the authorities in Rome contrasted strongly with his reputation for impiety and willful defiance of religious law.

Kuhl stared at his miniature from his chair across the room, his eyes fixed on the bell tower he had epoxied to its rooftop just minutes before.

Like flames, the westering sunlight boiled through its semicircular arches.

With the dying of the day, Kuhl's period of latency had also reached its end. Minutes from now he would depart for Barajas airport and exit the country using a fraudulent identity and supporting documents—one of many aliases he'd seeded around the world and kept in reserve for when he received his signal from DeVane. Thousands of miles away, Kuhl's cell of sleeper agents in America had been activated and made rapid arrangements for his coming. On his specific instructions, they had secured a base that fit his cover and conformed nicely with his tactical imperatives. It would provide crucial seclusion, exploitable terrain, and at the same time place him within close reach of his potential target or targets.

Find what Roger Gordian most loves, and we will know his greatest weakness. Strike at it, and we will have struck at his heart.

Kuhl was confident of achieving those objectives. He had compiled a thorough mental dossier on Gordian, and knew Harlan DeVane's intelligence was still more comprehensive. His American operatives had also supplied useful information. Much had been readily acquired, for despite his estimable regard for UpLink International's corporate security, Roger Gordian had put limited emphasis on his individual *secrecy*. Kuhl had found this unsurprising. Gordian was a prominent businessman, someone who led a highly public life. Whose success depended in part on his accessibility, and a reputation that inspired widespread confidence. His background was common knowledge. His personal and professional linkages were to a considerable extent open, apparent, exposed. Some of them had already come under Kuhl's pitiless lens, and he believed their order of importance in Gordian's life to be a relatively simple determination. Once he was convinced beyond doubt of the link best broken, it would be no less simple to assess its vulnerabilities, and learn whatever remaining facts he needed to move with potent, decisive speed.

He moved his glance to the clock on the table next to him, then returned it to the miniature of San Ginés.

The hour and minute had come.

There was only one thing left for him, one thing before he closed out.

Kuhl slid his hand down to the shopping bag he'd leaned against the foot of his chair and took hold of its handle. Then he rose and went over to the worktable where the church of his diligent fashioning glowed bloodred in the ashes of nightfall.

He stood there looking down at it, appraising its every feature, recalling the intensity of his labor with a sense of powerful and intimate connection. Feeling an investment of self that in some indescribable way connected him, in turn, to the old church on Calle del Arenal, after which his exacting replica had been crafted.

Calle del Arenal, the Street of Sand, ancient cemetery of Jews, their dust and bones razed at the order of an inquisitor tribunal.

Kuhl thought of the lustful dancers at Joy Eslava, gathering in the shadow of the cross like freed birds outside a cage that had held them from flight, as if that near reminder of confinement somehow added fervor to their kinetic mingling.

After a moment, he reached into the shopping bag for the sculptor's mallet he had purchased at the nearby art-supply shop. The iron head did not weigh much—one and a half pounds, to be precise—but it was quite sufficient to do the job intended for it.

He leaned down, placed the shopping bag on the floor next to the table, and opened its mouth wide. Then he straightened, raised his sculptor's mallet over the church, and with clenched teeth brought it down hard on the newly completed and attached bell tower.

It took only a single blow of the mallet to drive it down through the model's splintering roof to its inner core. Three additional blows reduced the entire miniature to crushed and unrecognizable scraps of colored wood.

Kuhl did not pause to regard its shattered remnants, merely cleared them from sight with a broad swipe of his right arm that sent them spilling over the edge of the work table into his shopping bag.

Brushing the last pieces of the obliterated church off the table, he lifted the bag again, carried it to the door of the apartment, gathered up his luggage, and vacated without a backward glance.

Kuhl left the shopping bag in a waste receptacle in an alley behind the building, and could feel the tightness in his jaw starting to relent by the time he hailed a taxi to the airport. His existence in Madrid was indeed closed out; he had been released for a mission that he almost believed himself born to fulfill.

Across the ocean, Big Sur awaited.

"I'm telling you, Gord, no qualifications, this is the juiciest steak I've ever eaten," Dan Parker said, and swallowed a mouthful of his food. He had ordered the prime New York strip with a side of mashed potatoes. "I feel like we haven't been here together in years."

"That's because we haven't," Roger Gordian said. He had gotten the filet mignon with baked. "Three years, if you're counting."

Parker looked up from his plate with mild wonder. "No kidding? *That* long?"

Gordian nodded, pressing some sour cream into the potato's flesh with his fork.

"That long," he repeated. It *was* a bit hard to believe.

Lunch at the Washington Palm on Nineteenth Street was once a regular monthly appointment for them, but that was before Gordian's illness. It was also before Dan had lost his congressional seat in Santa Clara County, having succumbed to the political fallout for helping Gordian lobby against indiscriminate dissemination of U.S. encryption tech abroad. This had proven a resoundingly unpopular stance among his constituents in Silicon Valley's software industry, who, with the exception of UpLink International, had not seemed to care a whit whether the al Qaedas, Hamases, and Cali Cartels of the world had access to products that could thwart the best surveillance efforts of global law enforcement, their rationale having been that the terrorists and drug lords could get their hands on similar encoding programs from foreign countries, or bootlegged copies of U.S. programs regardless of legal obstacles. If you can't beat 'em, join 'em for a buck, Gordian thought, even if they're planning to flood your borders with heroin or level the foundations of Western civilization.

"A lot's happened to keep us busy," he said.

"Truer words have never been voiced." Parker tipped his head toward the good-humored caricature of Tiger Woods on the wall above their formerly usual corner table. "At least Tiger's still here with us."

"That he is. And for my money the kid's a permanent fixture."

Parker grinned. The sports and political cartoons mounted everywhere in sight were a tradition at the restaurant harkening back almost a century to the original Palm on Manhattan's East Side. Before Woods rose to fame on the green, his current spot on the wall had for over a decade been occupied by the caricature of a retired star football player who'd been well-loved by fans young and old until he was accused of a grisly double homicide, one of the victims being his ex-wife and the mother of his children. Then the football player's picture had come down and been replaced by a drawing of a television sportscaster who was soon to be booted from his job after allegations that he'd taken large bites out of his mistress while dressed in women's clothing, or something of that nature. Woods had replaced the sportscaster on the wall around 1998, and remained there since, even though the sports commentator had eventually found sufficient sympathy among fans and network executives to be restored to his approximate slot on the airwaves.

Now Parker reached for his martini to wash down another chunk of steak, drank, produced an *ahhh* of sublime relish, and set his glass down on the white tablecloth.

"Okay, Gord," he said. "We've talked plenty about my chronic political hankerings. How are *you* these days?"

"Very well," Gordian said thoughtfully. "Older," he added with a slight shrug. "And . . ."

His reflective expression deepened but he just shrugged again and cut into his steak.

Parker waited for about thirty seconds, then gave him a vague gesture that meant "What else?"

Gordian studied his friend's curious face.

"Sorry, I didn't mean to keep you in suspense," he said. "Couldn't come up with the exact word. You know how it is with me."

Parker smiled a little. A brown-haired man of middle age and medium build, wearing a black hopsack blazer, pale blue shirt, and gray flannel trousers, his appearance was unremarkable in almost every respect until you inevitably noticed his eyes. In them was a look Dan had not lost since his days as wing man to Gordian in their hundreds of sorties over Nam, flying F-4 Phantoms through waves of antiaircraft fire as they searched the forested ground for VC entrenchments. It was a look so similar to the look in Gordian's eyes that people would sometimes mistake the two for brothers.

"Granted, self-expression isn't your most notable personality trait," he said. "You want to try taking a stab at it anyway?"

Gordian hesitated, his knife and fork suspended over his plate.

"It's a kind of feeling. Or my wanting to hold on to a feeling, if that helps at all," he said. "I don't think I can explain it any better. But sometimes when I'm getting out of bed on a workday, and my blanket's tossed off, and I have one foot halfway to the floor, I look over at Ashley, and I'm perfectly content with how things are at that split second. It gives me incredible peace of mind knowing I don't really have to leave her for UpLink to be okay. More than okay. That everything I've built is strong enough to stand, to grow, if I decide to stay right there in that house." He paused, sipped his drink—mineral water with a lemon twist. "On the other hand, I don't want to stay put, become complacent. Don't want to *stop*. And that's as essential to the mix as any sense of accomplishment or fulfillment. Wanting to stop and not stop . . . to keep attaining things and at the same time let go. I honestly *don't* know the word for the feeling, Dan. It might sound like there's some contradiction in it, but I'm not sure. And I want to figure it out, find whatever will let me keep riding it."

Parker chewed his food quietly a minute, glanced at his martini, and frowned. There was nothing left of it but the rocks. He caught a waiter's attention, motioned to his glass, and continued eating in silence until his refill arrived.

"The part about not leaving home might have to wait," he muttered half under his breath, taking a deep sip of the cocktail and swallowing the words with it.

Gordian looked at him. "What was that you said?"

Parker flapped a hand in dismissal.

"Time for that later on," he said quickly. "Right now, I'll make you a proposition. After we're done with business here in the capital, I'll head back home to Saratoga, think about the word that keeps hiding from you, *le mot juste*, see if I can draw it out into the open. Meanwhile, you turn that resourceful steel-trap brain of yours to pondering how I can get back to where I belong."

"Congress."

Parker shrugged.

"Public service," he said. "I'm open to broad and innovative suggestions."

Gordian paused again. Then he reached for his lemon water and held it out across the table.

"Okay, settled," he said. "Can do."

They clinked glasses, then sat a moment.

"We should get on to the capital business you mentioned," Gordian said.

Parker nodded.

"In my opinion, your coming here to make a closing pitch without a whole army of experts was a stroke of inspiration," he said. "It's going to make all the difference in the world."

Gordian smiled. "Dan, we've already toasted to our deal—"

"I'm serious," Parker interrupted. "Sedco's about oil. It's no insult to my fellow board members to say that's what interests them. What they know. They've read the UpLink prospectus, the analyses and recommendations prepared by our advisory panel. They don't need technical lectures on the ins and outs of fiberoptic communications. They don't even have to appreciate all their properties, advantages, and capabilities. It's enough for them to understand offshore drilling operations are becoming more computerized practically every day, and that high data transmission from the rigs to our onshore facilities is a necessity. Wiring up our platforms to your African telecom ring isn't just to our benefit, it's inevitable."

"You're convinced a majority of the board sees it that way?" Gordian said.

"Totally," Parker said. "The few fence straddlers or outright dissenters might need some help trusting the rest, and maybe themselves. That's what *you're* about, Gord. Inspiring trust and credibility." He paused. "It's a very big reason I think your coming here alone was so important."

Gordian rubbed his chin. "What's your slant on them? The possible opposing voters?"

"There aren't many, for one thing. I'm betting Bill Fredericks will need the most persuasion. With him, resistance to progress is a sort of reflexive crusade. He was a Sedco executive when the fossil fuel we sell was still living plants and protozoa—"

"I think it's made from plants and bacteria . . ."

"Protozoa, bacteria, flying aardvarks, what-the-hellever," Parker said. "Point is, Bill seems to be the only member with a problem getting a basic grasp on lightwave systems . . . which is no shocker to me, having been to his home. Don't even try bringing up video conferencing to him. His phones have hammer and bell ringers, and I swear to God I saw some with rotary dials. He refuses to use e-mail or even check out the Internet. Mention increased bandwidth, and he thinks it's got something to do with his wife's rings and bracelets. Doesn't see anything wrong with sticking to the marine radio links we've been using for decades and probably wonders what the hell's wrong with using Morse code to contact the mainland."

Gordian laughed.

"I'll try to be extra attentive while nursing him along," he said, and finished his lunch. "Who else?"

"Paul Reidman. He's savvy. Keen on the corporate security aspect, likes the idea that tapping a data stream carried as pulses of light is a damn hard task, going to be almost impossible when we get to practical photon encoding in the next few years." Parker sipped his drink. "Reidman can be fiscally myopic, worries about short-term unit costs versus a reasonable investment in the future. But his stinginess cuts both ways. He's seen the reports showing that postinstallation maintenance of undersea fiber systems is relatively cheap. Average is something like two, three major faults every quarter century, right?"

"Three, according to our preliminary risk assessment," Gordian said. "We should have an update from Vince Scull soon . . . he flew out to Gabon separately from the rest of the advance team, but should have joined them by now. Also, we're in the process of contracting a repair fleet for guaranteed rapid deployment."

"Stress that to Paul. Remind him that Planétaire already had one of those statistical faults back in May, trimmed your odds some," Parker said. He saw the wry amusement in Gordian's face. "What's to laugh at?"

Gordian shrugged a little.

"I was thinking you truly *are* made for the campaign trail," he said.

Parker was unabashed. "I'm not trying to exploit anybody's misfortune. Not gleefully anyway. But it's the kind of market research that can sway Paul."

Gordian shrugged again.

"I wasn't being critical," he said. "Just making an observation."

"Good, you know how sensitive I am," Parker said.

He eyed the last morsel of his steak. "While we're on guarantees, give me UpLink's capacity timetable."

"We can promise an initial secure multimedia transfer rate of between one and two terrabytes per second. Phone, video, Internet, or any combination thereof. After a year of upgrades we should be up to four terrabytes. By 2005, we can virtually assure you almost ten. Looking at the startup number, Megan Breen's favorite example is that it's equivalent to millions of simultaneous telephone calls, a ten-mile high stack of printed material, and twenty feature films."

"Every second?"

"Right."

Parker mouthed a silent *wow*.

"Make sure to refresh Paul about that, too." He lifted his fork, then noticed Gordian glancing across the table at his plate. "What is it?"

"If Ash were here, she'd tell you to leave the gristle," he said.

That elicited a snort from Parker. "To which I'd respond that it's lean gristle."

Gordian smiled, watching him eat. "All right. I've checked off Fredericks and Reidman for extra handholding. Any others?"

"You persuade those guys, you're in crack-dandy shape."

"Good," Gordian said. "Then I've only got two more things on my mind."

"Shoot."

"I've wondered about your being taken to the carpet for a perceived conflict of interest."

"You mean my urging along the fiber installation?" Parker said, and pushed his cleaned-off plate to the side. "That'd be ridiculous. If anything this is a clear instance of *coinciding* interests."

"I know. It's why I said *perceived*."

"Don't waste another minute thinking about it, Gord. Our friendship's no secret. And I don't believe anybody at Sedco would question my integrity."

Gordian nodded. "All right, next," he said, "I want you to explain your half intentional slip up. That comment about how my staying home will have to wait."

Parker cleared his throat.

"I thought I said later on that one—"

"You did." Gordian looked at him. "I'm saying give it to me now—"

"Gord—"

"Now, Dan. Your conscience is crying out to you, begging to be heard."

"You sure?"

"Absolutely. You wouldn't have made that blatant fumble unless you wanted me to ask about it."

Parker sighed.

"Okay, you win," he said. "The fact is that the company president and veep, who, as you know, are huge UpLink supporters, met a few days ago and came up with this idea for an event that would celebrate our new relationship. Working on the supposition the deal gets signed and sealed, needless to say, they put in a conference call about their idea to Hugh Bennett—"

"The chairman of Sedco's board?"

"Right, King Hughie, the board chairman, who is also prepared to advise we move ahead with the fiberoptic system install. And *he* was seriously taken with their idea."

"They want press coverage, photo ops," Gordian said. "Understandable."

Parker gave a nod.

"Sedco's got terrific competition for offshore oil prospecting licenses in West Africa," he said. "Some of the industry biggies involved in the bidding are Exxon, Chevron, Texaco, Elf Aquitain. There are state-owned companies—Petroleos Brasileiros out of Brazil, as a for-instance—and their subsidiaries. They've been leasing huge, contiguous blocks of deepwater acreage all down the equatorial coast from Nigeria to Angola. Some of these sites are what geologists call elephants . . . expected to yield upwards of a billion barrels of petroleum. Two blocks found by Texaco in the Agbami Basin—that's off Angola—are geared to produce a hundred fifty thousand barrels a day before this year's over, and might very well double that output when their operations are in full swing. To stay in the game, Sedco needs to raise its stock market profile. A headline-making affiliation with Up-Link would accomplish that in a snap. Help us work with the U.S. Department of Energy to secure underwriting loans from OPIC."

Gordian thought a moment. The Overseas Private Investment Corporation's political risk insurance to American companies making investments in emerging nations couldn't be undervalued.

"And if it motivates African governments that want in on our fiber ring to give Sedco's bids and development proposals added consideration—"

"Then all the more reason for King Hughie to feel enthusiastic . . . and to do everything he can to make sure his enthusiasm becomes contagious with his boardroom colleagues," Parker said.

Gordian drank the rest of his water with a twist.

"I gather Bennett would appreciate my attendance at this festive pageant of chief executives," he said.

"I'd go so far as to say he's going to hint at how *much* during tomorrow's meeting with you," Parker said.

Gordian lowered his glass. "Any inkling where the festivities would take place?"

Parker looked at him.

"In Gabon," he said. "On one of our wellhead platforms."

Gordian stared at him across the table.

"Who's turn is it to pay for our lunch today?" he said.

"Yours," Parker said.

"Right answer," Gordian said. "Now let's hear who's actually picking up the tab."

"Guess I am."

"And who's going to pay the next *dozen times*," Gordian said.

Parker expelled a breath.

"Ah, me again, I guess."

Gordian nodded once.

"Shall we call it an afternoon?" he said.

Parker looked around for the waiter, made a scribbling gesture in the air to indicate he wanted the check.

"You know, Gord," he said. "I would genuinely like my conscience to go *screw* itself."

Pescadero, California. Nine o'clock in the morning. Felicitous sunshine greeted Julia Gordian as she left the house for her morning jog, setting off honey gold highlights in the blond streak she'd Clairoled into her dark brown hair. The streak was new, as was her retro sixties' shag, and she thought the combination made for a pretty spiffy look. It had occurred to her that the streak would bug her father when he saw it for the first time next week, which was unquestionably part of the kick. Immature, yeah, sure. But Julia had been bugging him on a constant basis since she hit puberty lo those many years gone by, and at thirty-two years old, an independent woman, figured she could do so however she wanted without hearing about it. Besides, Dad was at his most adorable when he overcompensated, tripped all over himself trying not to *show* he was irritated.

Julia could hardly wait until she unveiled her shoulder tattoo, a discreet little Japanese kanji symbol that meant "freedom."

Accompanying her today, as every day, were her two rescued greyhounds—Jack, a brindle guy, and Jill, a teal blue gal. Julia did her stretching routine in her thickly hedge-rimmed lawn while the greys did their business out back. Then she hooked them onto a retractable leash with a two-dog attachment and started out onto the sidewalk, turning left toward the corner of her residential block.

A Subaru Outback drove by, heading in the same direction, slowing imperceptibly as it passed her.

Click-click-click.

This brilliant A.M. Julia had on black body-hugging athletic shorts, a black sports bra, a waistpack water bottle, Nikes, and a lightweight white pullover top to foil the early chill and neighborhood oglers . . . particularly Doug, the house dad across the street, who always seemed to be coming out to fetch his newspaper from the doorstep when she trotted past.

And here he was now, right on the mark. Just once, Julia thought, you'd think he'd be changing a diaper or giving the kid a warm bottle.

She ignored him as usual and concentrated on working into a rhythm. The less fretful of the two dogs, and the smoother runner, Jill trotted right along at her side, eager to bask in the gushy praise she would receive for keeping a cooperative pace. Meanwhile Jack was cantering a little ahead of them to show his alpha-ness—and inevitably run himself into a tangle around a tree after getting spooked by the fluttering shadows of its leaves . . . or, worse yet, buzzed by a winged insect, the most fearsome of all God's creatures from his neurotic perspective.

Julia got to the end of her block and hung left on Trevor Avenue, which by no coincidence happened to be where her favorite pastry shop was located, its hot cinnamon-raisin muffins beckoning from their giant display basket in the storefront about a third of a mile farther along her route.

Paused at a stoplight on the corner of Trevor, the Outback's driver waited for the signal to turn green, then made the same left as Julia. His digicam ready, a man in the front passenger seat raised it to his window and snapped off a second rapid series of shots as the vehicle reached her.

Click-click-click.

The vehicle passed Julia again and drove off down the avenue.

Another would pick up her movements later on.

Jean Jacques Assele-Ndaki was one of 35 highly ranked Gabonese officials to find a copy of the photograph in his mail. Of those men, 16, including Assele-Ndaki himself, sat in the parliament's 120-member lower chamber, or National Assembly. Another 6 held seats in the Senate, its 90-member upper chamber; 4 were secretaries in the presidential cabinet; 4 headed important government agencies. The remaining 5 recipients were *ministres delegues*, or economic ministers appointed to manage and regulate the partial privatization of national industries that had been under full state control before Gabon's economic restructuring program commenced in the mid-1990s.

In each case, the photo was enclosed in a plain manila envelope and neatly taped between two rectangular pieces of cardboard to protect it from damage in shipping. Adhesive labels on the envelope's lower left- and right-hand corners read *"Personnelle et Confidentiele"*—

Personal and Confidential—so it would be opened only by its intended recipient. Their typeface, and the type on the separate address label, was a common boldface Times Roman font produced by an equally common make and model of computer printer. Even the ink-jet cartridge used was of an ordinary, commonplace variety. None of the envelopes bore a return address. And none included a worded message.

The ghastly picture of Macie Nze was a clear enough communication without one.

Although an inspection of their coded postmarks would reveal they were deposited at Libreville's main postal center on Boulevard de la Mer sometime after the last batch of mail was sorted and processed on the evening of September 26, and before the first batch was loaded onto delivery trucks early on September 27, not even the most sophisticated forensic tests would have shown evidence of handling on either the photographs or their packaging. There were no latent fingerprints, biological samples, trace fibers, or minute particulate materials from which useful information could be extracted. It was as if the mailings had been prepared under aseptic laboratory conditions.

Of course, few, if any, of the public officials to receive the envelope would have considered informing the authorities about it for a moment. They had far too much to lose from any sort of police investigation into their surreptitious contacts and affairs.

Because Assele-Ndaki's office headquarters was located near the start of the mail route in the Quartier Louis, his deliveries would generally reach it before he arrived for the day. This pleased the assemblyman, whose bent was to read through his morning correspondence over a cup of strong mocha-flavored coffee and a crème tart bought on his way in, at a patisserie on a side street off Boulevard Omar Bongo.

The contents of the manila envelope, however, had left Assele-Ndaki wishing he had never opened it. Not today, nor ever.

While Assele-Ndaki's terror on discovering the photograph was characteristic of all those who laid eyes on it, the horror that descended on him went many shades deeper, and his grievous sorrow was something entirely of its own. He and Nze had known a close fraternal relationship that went back to childhood. Born into political families, they had grown up neighbors in Port Gentil, where their elders had often socialized. As boys they had attended the same primary and secondary schools, played soccer on the same youth league. They had shared a dormitory room at the Sorbonne in Paris, graduated that esteemed historic university with advanced economic degrees, and after returning to Gabon held executive positions with the nation's largest energy and ore mining firms. Some years afterward they had found their lives again intertwined, as both gained National Assembly seats in the same constitutional election.

And together they had attended a string of secret meetings with Etienne Begela and other principal government figures, gatherings at which they were persuaded to accept handsome financial inducements from the *blanc*, Gerard Fáton . . . grafted to thwart UpLink International's overhaul of their country's telecommunications system. Begela had drawn Assele-Ndaki and his longtime friend into the conspiracy, just as he had doubtless courted the rest of its participants. But Assele-Ndaki would blame no one except himself for his decisions. They had not resulted from any form of pressure or coercion. Rather, he had been enticed by the easy money . . . and, to be truthful, succumbed to the excitement of slipping across lines of ethics and legality, a visceral delight in probing his untapped capacity for craftiness.

Now that thrill had been replaced by the sickening realization of how mad his actions had been. *Their* actions—his and Macie's, perhaps the actions of the rest as well. It had almost seemed a game until their chamber of parliament convened in Libreville for its vote. The amendment they had drawn up to stall legislation that would ensure the extension of UpLink's temporary operating licenses for at least the next quarter century contained what they had fancied to be marvelously clever revisionist language. But when the president had gotten wind of their intentions through his cadre of appointed loyalists—Gabon's constitution, drafted under his sharp authoritarian eye, allowed him to handpick nine assemblymen to chair key law-making committees—the authors and supporters of the proposed amendment had been cautioned to desist in far blunter terms than their artful bill flaunted. The choice presented them was stark. They could move forward with their obstructionist plans and invite the scrutiny of the ministry of justice. Find their government and business dealings, financial records, even their sexual activities open to rigorous investigation. Their every affair delved into without deference to social position or regard for privacy.

Or they could instead go with the existing bill. And also go about their lives unburdened by inconvenient, embarrassing disruptions.

The amendment had been scrapped, and UpLink's regulatory approvals given easy passage through the Assembly.

What Assele-Ndaki and his friend had failed to grasp—what none of the amendment's sponsors had understood at the time—was that they were in greater jeopardy of being rolled over by the inexorable force that had driven them on until that point. The *blanc* would tolerate nothing but their moving forward once they had committed to his agenda, would simply plow them down in their tracks if they dared halt or turn back.

Now Assele-Ndaki felt his skin prickle. Beads of sweat slicked his forehead, gleamed on the broad slopes of his cheekbones. Macie. Poor Macie . . .

He had been murdered. Made a gruesome example. Inquiry and scandal were the tools of politicians. And the *blanc* was not that.

Assele-Ndaki shuddered, staring at the photo of Macie on his knees with the blazing necklace around his shoulders. Macie burning like a human candle, his face contorted in dying agony behind licks of gasoline-charged flame. Macie burning with his hands cut off at the wrists, dropped on the ground where he could see them as the fire rose around him and the life broiled from his flesh.

An example, Assele-Ndaki thought again.

Though numb with shock, he retained full command of his instincts for self-preservation. Examples were by very definition meant to serve as warnings, and he would not have been sent the photograph if it was too late for him to avoid sharing Macie's fate. There was still a chance the telecommunications legislation could be defeated, or become so deeply mired in the parliamentary process that the net result was the same. While it had cleared the National Assembly, its ratification would require Senát passage, normally a rubber stamp vote to satisfy the president's will. But Assele-Ndaki had many confederates, some of them quietly aware of the *blanc*'s maneuvers. If the venerable *senateurs* ruled to overturn the bill after their chamber deliberations—*if* enough of them could be persuaded to vote against it—it would be kicked back down to the lower parliamentary house and resubmitted to committee for changes. Then the amendments could be reintroduced, the process for all practical intents and purposes started from the beginning.

Assele-Ndaki's heart was racing. It was a plan of abject fear and desperation, he knew. All those who undercut the president would pay the consequences. They would be probed, censured—their personal reputations impugned, their careers in government run into the dirt. Some stood to lose everything. Were Assele-Ndaki's wife to learn of his own extramarital proclivities—

Everything, yes, the amendment's proponents would lose everything.

Except their lives.

Assele-Ndaki gazed at the photo of Macie in his smoking ruff of flame and felt a fresh bout of horror and grief.

Better to walk in disgrace than suffer death. Especially *that* kind of death.

He set the photo into a drawer, reached a trembling hand out toward the telephone—but his secretary buzzed his intercom before he could lift the receiver from its cradle.

Senateur Moubouyi was on the line with a matter of pressing urgency, she informed him.

Were his mood less oppressively bleak, Assele-Ndaki might have smiled.

He had, it seemed, been beaten on the draw.

Nimec had arranged for them to meet the cable ship's captain and project manager at ten P.M. in a dinner club called Scintillements. His name was Pierre Gunville, and for some reason Vince Scull was having a hard time with that. Scull also had a problem with the name of the club and the fact that their meeting was not taking place in an office building during normal work hours. Nimec could not say these complaints surprised him. Aggravation was Scull's emotional springboard. If the day ever came when he wasn't simmering with annoyance, you had to figure it might be worth consulting Nostradamus to see whether it was an omen of something or other being seriously amiss with the world.

Scull had begun his grumbling the second he met Nimec in the corridor outside their guest suites at the Rio de Gabao Hotel. Stepping into the elevator now, he jabbed a thick finger at the LOBBY button and continued to bitch and moan without respite as the doors slid closed.

"So why the hell doesn't any of this crap bother you?" he said.

"Which crap do you mean?" Nimec said. "Just so I'm straight about it."

"This guy with the fucked-up name, this fucked-up place where he made our appointment to meet him, this fucked-up *time* for it when I'm just off the plane from Paris," Scull said, recapitulating his whole bilious list of complaints. He rubbed a hand over his scalp to smooth down a strand of his nearly extinct hair. "That's what crap, Pete."

The car started on its way down. Nimec tried without luck to think of a convenient blanket response, decided to tackle things in reverse order.

"You could have flown Air France with the rest of us, gotten here a couple days ago," Nimec said. "Nobody twisted your arm into waiting around for a private jet charter."

"Is that goddamn right?"

"Right."

"Well, I'm not going to get into how much I paid for my membership on that service," Scull said. "An expense the boss might've offered to shoulder, incidentally. At least *halfway* shoulder."

Nimec gave him a look. "That's asinine. If you have a fear of flying . . ."

"How many million times we been through this? I'm *not* afraid—".

"Okay, we'll say you've got issues with commercial airlines," Nimec said, loath to step into that sucking bog of dispute. "It's your problem, you pay."

Scull sneered.

"My problem, you want to call it that, is with how they run their security," he said. "You're the expert. Tell me you feel safe flying the terrorist-friendly skies."

Nimec leaned against the handrail on the back wall of the car, glancing up at its floor indicator panel. The number twenty-four flicked by. Eleven down, twenty-three to go.

"I don't waste energy worrying about what I can't control," he said. "DeMarco's got the right take on it, you want to know what I think. If terrorist incidents in the air were the norm, they wouldn't make headlines. The only reason they're on the six o'clock news is because they don't happen every day."

"Like floods, earthquakes, and volcanic eruptions, huh? A guy walking aboard with a Semtex bomb in the heel of his shoe's just another act of God."

"Do us both a favor and let it go, Vince."

"Let *what* go? It was me who was at those negotiations in Paris all last week, while you were still cooling your heels at the home office," he said. "If somebody hadn't sewn things up with the Nautel's cable-maintenance fleet, we wouldn't be going to see Captain Gunslinger tonight."

"The boss had other negotiators there taking care of things," Nimec said. "You enlisted."

"That's where you're dead wrong, Petey," Scull said. "I'm the company point runner. The forward scout who's supposed to go conning for buried mines. The risk assessment man. Which means—"

"It's your job to assess risks," Nimec said, completing the familiar mantra. He checked his Annie-Meter. Too long to go. Then he glanced at the floor-indicator panel again. Ten, nine. Almost at the lobby. He would have to settle. "Fact is, Vince, you're earning the salary that pays for your executive jet plan tonight. We'd need to talk with Gunville even if his outfit wasn't contracted. Right now our teams just mean to use Nautel for support ops. But two divers from the *Africana* got killed while making repairs on the same fiber line we're planning to send our men down to survey. I know the company line about what happened to them. I read the press accounts. And I still want to sound him out. Hear the story straight from his mouth. Because it's *my* job to keep our people as safe as can be when they might have to put themselves at risk."

"Did you hear me say I had a problem with that?" Scull thumbed his chest with indignation. "How about we get back to what I asked in the first place, you don't fucking *mind*."

Nimec shrugged mildly.

"The Gabonese are late eaters," he said. "Nine, ten o'clock at night's their usual dinner time. It's also the custom to invite foreign business guests out for a meal. Entertain them. And the place we're meeting Gunville is supposed to be pretty decent." He paused. "You ought to enjoy yourself while you can. Be glad it's not two days from now, when we have to head into the bush to check out the new ground-station facilities."

"I'll be gladder if we could stick to the point." Scull rolled his eyes. "Scintillements, you know what it means? Sparkles. Probably has those laser lights flying around over the walls and ceiling, make you feel like some nut-case with a big crayon covering them with colored squiggles—"

"I'm not sure that's how it'll be. I picked up a tourist brochure in my room, and there was an ad—"

"Come *on*. Since when are you so gullible? Must be the settled life affecting you."

Nimec looked confused. "Settled life?"

"I just asked you not to stray off the topic. You want my advice on this love thing you got going in Texas, we can do it later," Scull said. "The club, Petey. Focus on the club. Think about its name a minute, then tell me you expect good eats. They can be pretentious as they want dressing it up in French, I still say it belongs on the marquee of some poky Brooklyn disco like the one that used to be run by the Russian mob punk you took down . . . what the hell was it called, by the way?"

"The Platinum Club."

"Yeah, that's it . . ."

"Vince," he said. "French is the official language here."

"So?"

"So maybe it's you who should use your head." He shrugged again. "Nobody's dressing anything up. Nothing fancy or pretentious about it to their ears."

"Still worse," Scull said. "If the owners of the joint *know* the customers know what the name means, how good can it be? And speaking of bullshit handles, what's with this Captain Guns-at-the-hips? If you think you're gonna find *that* one on his birth certificate, guess again." Scull made a rumbling sound. "Reminds me of a guy I met at a party once, introduced himself as John Wildlife. No shit. Right away, I peg him as some dilettante rich kid whose moneybags parents stuffed a fortune into his mountaineering knapsack, or maybe into his kayak when he was about to paddle off down the Snake River. Had to be a fortune. Startup capital to help him found one of those tree-hugger nonprofits in D.C. . . . Georgetown, no less. Guy's got a whole floor of offices on Sixteenth Street for this foundation—you know what rents are like over there. And the reason? Just so he can take a vacation from his *recreational* activities every now and then, pull himself out of the white-water rapids long enough to dry off his ass. John Wildlife, will somebody please fucking spare me—"

Their elevator stopped at the lobby with a soft *ding*. As its doors swished open, Nimec saw the concierge flash a hospitable smile from his desk and expelled a sigh of relief. Scull had ceased his tirade.

"Come on, Vince." He exited the car. "Let's find ourselves a taxi."

Scull followed a step behind him, frowned.

"I'll be happy if we get a driver who doesn't take us for a couple of greenhorn suckers," he said.

The concierge took pains to be helpful as the two Americans came across the lobby from the elevator. Did they need their currency exchanged? he enquired in studied English. Would they like particular directions somewhere? Were there any special room-service orders they might wish to place with the staff in advance of their return?

The first man to pass his desk—Monsieur Nimec, executive suite 9—declined with a polite thank-you. The new arrival—Monsieur Scull, who had insisted on an immediate room change from suite 8 to suite 12 on check-in, stating the former was incommodious and noisy—merely shook his head in the negative and followed the other toward the entrance.

The concierge did not let the second guest's scowl leach any of the obliging geniality from his expression. He was skilled at his job and knew how to keep his poise.

The concierge's eyes tracked them as they strode to the hotel entrance and a doorman in a braided, epauletted uniform held open its large glass doors. Then he reached for his telephone, tapped in a number, left a brief message with the person who answered, and hung up.

With their backs to him, the smile he offered the men had fled his face.

Out front, the doorman hastened from beneath the hotel's regal red-and-gold awning, hailed one of several waiting curbside taxis, and opened its rear door for the UpLink representatives. Then he asked their destination—again in their own tongue—was given it by the tall, narrow-jawed man who had led the way through the entrance, and helpfully communicated where they were going to the driver in his native French.

The taller of the men tipped him and climbed into the taxi. His stocky companion packed himself into the backseat next, slamming the door shut before the doorman could close it for him, albeit in what would have been a much gentler manner.

With his gratuity tucked into the pocket of his colorful uniform jacket, the doorman watched the taxi pull away down the boulevard. A moment afterward, the second in the queue of parked taxis slid up to the hotel entrance.

This time the doorman opened its front passenger door and leaned all the way inside.

"Scintillements," he instructed the driver.

"*Ce voir Gunville?*"

"*Ce n'est non l'affair.*"

They made brief eye contact. Then a silent nod of acknowledgment from the driver, and he faced forward, his hands on the wheel. Who the Americans were meeting was truly none of their affair; it would be best for them to know only what was necessary.

The doorman straightened, pushing the door shut.

A second later, the taxi swung from the curb and slotted into the light traffic a short distance behind the vehicle carrying Nimec and Scull.

• • •

The ocean waters of Gabon are blessed with mild currents, and so the *Chimera* floated gently tonight above the Ogooué Fan, a wide belt of alluvial sediment sloping toward the oil-gorged offshore basins beyond land's end. Here, four months ago, Cédric Dupain and Marius Bouchard had come to sudden death at three hundred fathoms, but the explosions and pressure that left their bodies in shredded ruin caused no visible disturbance to the surface tranquillity.

Life's worst acts of violence may be hidden, silent, and deep. Known as the spawning ground of abominations, it is a place where perpetrator and victim meet and witnesses attest to nothing, where crimes committed beget atrocious intimacies, where guilt makes its slippery escape through wormholes bedded in shame.

In his yacht's stateroom bed, Harlan DeVane lay facing its raised porthole and wished hard for sleep to take him. Though shut tight, his eyes were grazed by the navigational lights of the buoys and platforms outside to the west, and the running lights of the great sluggish fuel tankers at near-rest between them. Some nights their flickering glow would lull DeVane into temporary oblivion, but now, on this night, they only prodded him back from its edge.

The porthole's thin translucent curtains swirled in drifts of warm sea air. Naked atop his sheets, DeVane felt the satin breeze slide over his legs and chest, felt the soft, rhythmic rocking of his yacht trying to ease him into darkness. But his body remained stiff, unrelaxed. He had tried to keep his thoughts on business, settle himself by planning for imminent discussions with his clients. There had been little to consider, however. His offering of the current information crop would be a take it or leave it proposition. He had lost much of his fortune and face after the Sleeper virus debacle and been put in a ticklish position with the disappointed buyers of its genetic activators. And yet he had misled none of them. The failure had not resulted from a default in supplying the product, nor a deficiency in its performance, nor any misrepresentation of its ravaging potential. In his line of work, there could be no guarantees against countermeasures taken by the enemy. UpLink International had been the stumbling block, and he fully meant to remove that impediment. He would not repair the damaged trust of his clients by becoming a markdown distributor, a light-palmed haggler like the market venders in Port-Gentil.

With these matters determined to his own satisfaction, the memories had been aroused to work their penetrating, uninhibited will on DeVane. Even those that sated were small molestations, arsenic pleasures.

Now they flashed an image of the brownstone in New York City onto the screen of his mind, a vivid memory of how it had looked to him on first sight. This was thousands of miles and two years to the day after he had sat at the long glass table in his father's tower, hiding his threadbare shirt cuff beneath the sleeves of his cheap jacket. DeVane had known from the moment of his expulsion that important lessons could be taken from it. In the time that passed he had concentrated on extracting every one them, seen that his processing of the information had grown full and complete. None of that time was wasted with idleness.

His appearance had changed . . . no, he had *transformed* himself. That was the primary lesson DeVane had learned: Transformation was necessary for those born outside the fortresses of power to succeed. The faceless unknown must fit themselves to suits that would let them belong.

The suit DeVane had worn as he strode toward the

brownstone on Manhattan's Upper East Side was tailored and padded black wool crepe, his shirt woven gray cotton, his silk hand-knit necktie smartly knotted and dimpled. He had walked in his oxfords just once before to give their leather the suppleness of light wear, then polished them to a soft, rich gleam. Strapped casually over his shoulder was a Coach Hudson briefcase.

DeVane had obtained the expensive clothes and briefcase with money from items stolen and fenced in another city. His hands had become skilled at using the lock pick and shim, at gaining furtive entrance to unoccupied homes. The tower had pointed DeVane's way toward an understanding that his sense of entitlement was a dead skin to be shed . . . and had eventually led him to appreciate that merit did not open doors, but only gave one a chance at staying in the room. He had realized, too, that there was always more than a single door, a single room. For the faceless unknown, cunning and deception were the true keys to the kingdom.

Hocus pocus.

Pausing in front of the nineteenth-century town house, DeVane had noted its every feature with an obsessive attention to detail. A low wrought-iron fence stood between the small flagstone court and sidewalk. A spindling bamboo plant, striped green and yellow, grew from a concrete bed by the front steps. The leaded casement windows had black-barred gates and interior shutters. The door was dark paneled wood with a heavy horseshoe knocker, brass knob, and a pear-shaped light fixture above it. On the jamb, an intercom. There were ornate floral designs on the projecting cornices.

DeVane had looked up at the light fixture amid the busy brush and bump of sidewalk foot traffic and recalled seeing its photograph in a guide to ornamental antiques written by the homeowner. Her name was Melissa Phillips, and she had authored numerous magazine articles and three books on related subjects. Her most recent book had appeared a decade earlier, shortly before the passing of her husband, an executive editor at a famed and venerable publishing house who had been much older than she.

Before his trip to New York, DeVane had learned everything he could about the widow. She had led a reserved, if not quite withdrawn, existence since the end of her marriage. She was reputed to be a mild eccentric who fancied herself as something of a bohemian. There was a small circle of friends with whom she had regular get-togethers, most of them women, socialites she had known for years. Although she possessed abundant financial means, Melissa Phillips would sometimes rent out luxury suites in the spacious town house she had inherited, placing advertisements in the *New York Observer*, a weekly Manhattan newspaper with a large upscale readership. The monthly rates were expensive as listed, but Phillips's leasing of the apartments sprang from a desire for companionship rather than income, and she showed a softness, even a patronlike generosity, toward a certain type of prospective occupant . . . or house guest, as she preferred to call each of her renters. Young people who aspired to careers in the arts often struck an empathic chord in her. Budding writers, musicians, dancers, and stage performers made for colorful house guests and lively evening conversation, and she would on occasion adjust her rents downward to ease their financial burdens, or in some cases defer its due date when their pursuit of the muse ran them lean.

The widow had shown a special affection for gifted, interesting men in their twenties and early thirties, and it was to them that her kindness was most often and fully extended.

DeVane had learned of this preference after reading an archived article taken from the *New York Post*'s Page Six, well known for its gossip columns about celebrities and members of Gotham society.

It had seemed a shining gift to him.

On the brownstone's front stoop, he announced himself to a servant over the intercom and was told someone would be down to admit him in a few moments.

When the door opened, DeVane was not surprised to see Melissa Phillips herself standing in the entry. She was an attractive woman. Small framed, thin, her blond hair just slightly laced with gray.

The widow had appraised him with intent, pale blue eyes.

"Hello, Mr. Nemaine," she said, and smiled. "I'd thought your appointment at that literary agency might delay you . . . it can be horrible getting up here from downtown."

DeVane shrugged, returned her smile with one he had studied on other faces and taught himself to reproduce.

"A playwright's timing has to be perfect, and I try not to miss my beats," he said, taking her extended hand. Her fingers were long, slender. "It's an honor, Mrs. Phillips. You have a distinguished reputation as a benefactress of the arts."

A glint in the widow's eyes. They met his own.

"I'm charmed and flattered to know my efforts are appreciated," she said. "And please call me Melissa . . . I'm not *that* much older than you."

DeVane stood with her hand in his. Behind her, a glimpse of a high-walled entry parlor of palatial dimensions. He was struck by the burnished gold chandelier that hung from its vaulted ceiling, clean white candles in its curved, graceful arms.

She noticed him looking in through the halfway open

door, and glanced over her shoulder to see what had caught his attention.

DeVane was quick; he had worked hard at perfecting the cheat.

"I apologize for becoming distracted, but the chandelier is magnificent," he said. "Gilded wood, isn't it? I'd imagine it must date back to the English Restoration."

Melissa Phillips faced him again, impressed.

"Very close," she said, and opened her door wide to admit him. "It's British. From the early eighteenth century, though. You'll find it even more beautiful at night with the candles lighted."

He had nodded and entered.

As DeVane followed her into the parlor, he had felt almost like a treasure hunter who had unearthed a trove of wealth he had sought for a lifetime—struggling, digging, boring past endless layers of dirt and stone to expose it—and now that he had broken through, now that it was within reach, had discovered it contained an even greater hoard than he had allowed himself to envision.

He wanted to see every prize, take it all in at once . . .

But here Harlan DeVane's string of memories broke off like a film reel that had run out inside a vacated projection booth.

In his cabin on board the *Chimera*, his body had finally released its tension and let him plunge into dreamless sleep.

"I gotta admit, Petey, you were a hundred percent right about the Gabonese having a knack for entertaining their visitors," Scull said cheerfully, his voice raised above the piano-accompanied singing from the club's round central stage. "If I'd realized *how*, you wouldn't have heard me complain."

"Great," Nimec said.

"Also, you should've told me the cooking was Senegalese. Didn't I hear you mention that you been wanting to try African food for the longest time?"

"Could be you did."

"Well, that goes double for me, believe it or not. Which is why—"

"I would have told you," Nimec said. "If I'd known."

"But what about that ad you read?"

Nimec snapped a look at him.

"I suppose I missed the part about the cuisine," he said. "I had other priorities on my mind."

"Hey, don't get defensive on me, I'm just saying it's too bad you *didn't* know." Scull slurped from his spoon. "Anyway, this fish soup's delicious. The spices, boy, they've got a sneaky kick. The heat kind of creeps over your tongue, front to back. Then wham!"

"Glad you're enjoying it."

"I'll have to remember its name. Better yet, I should ask the waiter to scribble it on a piece of paper for me, *tiébou dienn*, right?"

"I think so."

"Because it's one I don't want to forget. When you get down to the rice and stuff at the bottom, take my word, it's freakin' *bliss*—"

"I'm glad."

Scull looked at him. "You already said that."

"Said what?"

"Forget it. How's your chicken *yassa*?"

"Good."

"So why the long face?" Scull said. "Gunville couldn't have steered us toward better eats. Doesn't have a bad set of pipes, either. Though, you want me to be truthful, I'd still prefer he wasn't singing in French so I could understand the words."

Nimec didn't answer.

Scull shrugged, dunked his spoon into his bowl, slurped. Nimec looked at him across the table, trying to decide whether his effusive praise of the food and song offered at Scintillements was authentic, a vaudeville routine intended to needle him, or perhaps a typically obnoxious Scullian mixture of the two. Regardless, Scull had succeeded in wearing his patience down to the thinnest of tatters. Or contributed to it, at least.

He turned toward the middle of the room, which neither sparkled, glittered, nor squirmed with crayon-colored lasers but instead fit the travel brochure description to its very letter. *A sedate, softly lit, classic dinner club atmosphere.* Around the stage were about thirty tables filled with well-dressed men and women, an appreciable percentage of whom were expatriates from the United States and elsewhere. On stage, Pierre Gunville, crew master of the *Africana*, sat on a stool beside the baby grand, vocalizing a sentimental ballad he'd introduced as being about love gained, betrayed, and forsaken—speaking French *and* English for the benefit of his multinational audience. Gunville was clad in a black tux, wing-collared white shirt, and black cravat that had been gradually undone over the course of his performance to reveal a thick, braided gold chain around his neck. It was the most ostentatious thing about the place.

Nimec ate his food, listened, and waited. When he and Scull had arrived at their reserved table earlier, Gunville had come over from the stage—where he was doing a sound check or something—proclaimed his great delight at making their acquaintance, and guided them through the menu, recommending his favorite house specialties. He had then explained that singing at the club was both his joy and sideline, a bit of diversionary moonlighting to compensate for the ennui and accumulated pressures of his hard, extended stints at sea. It was his wish, he'd said, that they enjoy the first of his two half-hour sets during dinner. He would promptly rejoin them for a drink at intermission and be pleased, indeed eager, to discuss whatever matters were on their minds relating to his primary vocation.

By that, Nimec assumed he had meant his captaining of the *Africana*.

Now Gunville's sad screnade seemed to be concluding. Or crescendoing. Or whatever the hell love's-loss songs did when they finally wrapped up. The pianist, whom Gunville had introduced only as "Maestro," struck a resonating minor chord on the keyboard, added a blue trickle of melody. Then Gunville dramatically rose off his stool, lifted the microphone close to his mouth with his right hand, clenched his left hand into a trembling impassioned fist at his side, and ended his number with a sustained, sonorous note and a dashing full bow. Nimec noticed his lingering eye contact with a woman seated alone at a little table for two near the stage, her hands raised higher than the rest as patters of laid-back but appreciative applause spread throughout the room. She was blond, shapely and had on a sleeveless dress with a plunging back line.

Slipping the mike onto its stand now, Gunville thanked the crowd for their kind and wonderful reception, *"Merci, merci beaucoup mes amis!"* Then he gave the blond another glance, momentarily touched a hand to his heart, and exchanged intimate smiles with her before stepping off the stage.

An ardent fan, Nimec thought.

He watched the balladeering skipper approach his table and take a chair.

"Gentlemen," Gunville said, still slightly breathless from capping off his set. "I do hope your reviews will be lenient."

Scull looked up from his soup.

"You can lay it on me anytime, mister," he said.

Nimec wondered if murdering a colleague in public would disqualify him from his position at UpLink.

"It was nice listening," he said, and paused. "As long as we've got you out of the spotlight, though, I wonder if we could get right to some things that apply to our immediate business."

"Of course," Gunville said. "And these would involve the cable inspection you plan to launch from the *Africana* when it returns from dry dock next week?"

"Some," Nimec said. "If you don't mind, I also want to ask you about the accident back in May. I'm sure it isn't a subject you much like talking about—"

Gunville raised a hand.

"A difficult affair anyone would choose to leave in the past, but I can certainly understand your concerns," he said. "Permit me a moment to order a drink, and I'll try to answer as many questions as possible."

Nimec gave a nod. Gunville motioned over a waiter, asked his two visitors whether they might care for anything. Nimec declined. Scull ordered a Courvasier. Gunville got himself a scotch on the rocks.

"What occurred was no less unexpected than tragic," Gunville said after the drinks were served. "Cédric Dupain was the lead diver and one of our best. I believe he had more than two decades of experience between his military and civilian careers, and I'd worked with him in the waters of three continents. He was the first aboard my ship to be trained at piloting single-operator deep-water submersibles—"

"They're what's known as hardsuits in the trade, right?"

Gunville nodded.

"Remote vehicles are more often used these days. Ma-

chines do not share our susceptibility to the hazards of
the deep, and there can be no comparison between losing
a piece of hardware and losing a human life should some
misfortune occur. But our perception, judgment, and
manual dexterity remain irreplaccable qualities that robotic craft cannot share. And the hardsuit's safety record
is impressive in calm conditions. I've heard of only a
single critical incident before the tragedy that took Cédric
and his partner, Marius Bouchard."

"Was Bouchard as good a diver?"

"He lacked the seasoning, but was a trustworthy professional. We send no one down to work at seven hundred meters without comprehensive training and stringent
certification."

"The day those men were lost," Nimec said. "What
went wrong?"

Gunville drank some scotch, lowered his glass to the
table.

"A freak calamity," he said. "They were troubleshoot-
ing for the source of a partial system failure and discovered a fault in the cable, a segment that runs along the
bottom of an underwater ridge primarily composed of
mud and sediment. We believe the damage had been
done by sharks. Soon after they tracked it down, there
was the apparent submarine equivalent of an earth slide."

"Anything like that ever happen before? I mean, without your divers getting hurt?"

Gunville shook his head.

"It is what made the incident so shocking. Had it been
a massive collapse, I might have perhaps reconciled myself to their deaths . . . gotten my mind around it as you
Americans say . . . more easily. When you know someone is in a building that has collapsed, you immediately
prepare for the worst. But imagine learning a person has
been killed after being struck by a few crumbled bricks

or something that has fallen from a construction scaffold. In this case two people. The slide was confined almost to the precise area where Cédric and Marius were working."

"I wonder what touched it off," Scull said. He raised his eyes from his soup bowl. "Reports I've seen all say the fan's tectonics are real stable."

Gunville looked at him.

"That is correct," he said. "Our best guess is that it was progressive erosion. There are natural interactions that can change the features of the undersea landscape even in salutary conditions. Tidal flows, gravitational effects, storms, scavenging or colonizing creatures. This creates nonconformities. Areas of deterioration that may go undetected, particularly if they are small. Over a long period of time an overhanging portion of the shelf was undermined, fractured, and simply gave."

Scull grunted. He ran his spoon around the inside of his bowl to clean off the last of the *tiébou dienn* and put it in his mouth.

"Did you have any seismographs taken afterward?" Nimec said. "Would've helped rule out any chance there was a minor quake."

Gunville shook his head.

"Planétaire Systems saw no reason for it," he said. "Frankly neither did I. The event was localized. Its causes were apparent from subsequent inspection by divers and ROVs. And we were confident of the seismological data already compiled." He reached for his drink. "You must also understand my own immediate priority was recovering the bodies of my crewmen."

"Sure," Nimec said. "We're not trying to second guess anybody."

"Still makes sense to do a comparative geological work up," Scull said. "With all the offshore rigs popping up in the Ogooué, you want to be sure the drilling hasn't moved things around, loosened them like people sticking their toes into sand castles."

Gunville looked at him.

"I agree with your suggestion. If Planétaire hadn't pulled out of the region, it is likely a new survey would have been conducted by my employers at Nautel. Unfortunately, without their finances . . ."

"UpLink will get one ordered," Nimec said.

"Excellent." Gunville sat quietly a moment, then glanced over at the stage. "I hope you will forgive me, but I must prepare for my next set." He offered the men a courteous smile. "I'm certain we'll be talking again over the next several days."

Nimec nodded.

"You bet," he said. "We're very grateful for your time."

Handshakes around the table, and then Gunville was off across the room.

Nimec saw him move toward the blond at the foot of the stage, dawdle there to speak to her.

"Hot stuff," Scull said, following his gaze. "If I could sing like him, I'd be picking up broads left and right, too."

"Don't remember you having trouble on that score when you were married."

"Which time?"

"I could probably take my pick."

Scull shrugged.

"That was all before I lost my boyish good looks," he said.

They were silent a bit.

"Okay," Nimec said, and pointed his chin in the direction Gunville had gone. "Give me your impressions."

Scull pointed to Gunville's half-full scotch glass. "Didn't finish his drink."

"I noticed."

"Sort of left me feeling he gave us the bum's rush."

"Yeah."

"Meanwhile, he's over there talking to the blond, plenty of time for *her*."

"Yeah."

Their eyes met.

"Can't figure what it might be, but I think our fucking crooner Romeo's got something to hide," Scull said.

Nimec nodded.

"You and me both," he said.

Port-Gentil. Headquarters Police Gabonaise. Forty-seven minutes past midnight. His shift long concluded, leaving him drained from overwork and nerves, the normally starch crispness of his officer's uniform gone as limp as he felt, Commander Bertrand Kilana slouched before a computer screen behind his locked office door.

The air in the room was stale with sweat, ground out cigarette butts, and paper cups of cold, half-drunk coffee. One of the cups on his desk had begun leaking from its bottom, but Kilana had not noticed the spreading brown ring of wetness around it. Nor would he until tomorrow morning, when he returned to the office after too few hours' sleep. By then the coffee would have partly soaked through a stack of his important case documents and the pages of a favorite investigative reference book, then dribbled down to the floor to leave a dark, permanent stain on his rug. Kilana would find the paper cup empty and curse himself for having neglected to dump it.

On Kilana's monitor now, a live-streaming Internet surveillance video from the Rio de Gabao Hotel showed two of the Americans under observation exit an elevator that had risen to its luxury suite level and return to their separate rooms.

The commander identified them, tentatively, from his matched listing of UpLink personnel and their suite numbers. This information was stored in his computer's encrypted database, but for the sake of convenience he'd kept a hardcopy on hand beside his keyboard. According to this printout, the men were Peter Nimec—suite 9— and Vincent Scull—suite 12.

He did not know, or wish to know, where they had been tonight—only that they had left shortly before ten, and stayed out for some three odd hours. He did not know their positions with UpLink, though that information could be easily obtained from departmental sources. He did not even know with absolute certainty why he had been instructed to maintain a constant watch over them.

Kilana kept his eyes on his role in the plot and let its other players worry about theirs. It was what he'd been told to do. It was also what was very much safest for him.

Kilana palmed his mouse, moved the cursor to the toolbar of his Internet Service Provider's browser and clicked FILE → ARCHIVE → SAVE. When the dialogue box opened to request a file name, Kilana typed in the word *hibou*, followed by the number twelve.

Hibou is the French word for "owl."

Now Kilana clicked again, and the hidden camera's real-time images of the men were stored as a high-resolution, compressed audio/video DivX file on his database. He then took a rewritable DVD from the rack on his desk, slipped it into the computer's burner drive, and returned to the toolbar.

Several mouse clicks later, he had merged the night's dozen *hibou* surveillance files from the hallway outside the Rio de Gabao's luxury suites into a single large file on the disk. Also on the disk were separate files from inside the suites themselves, designated *faucon*—"falcon" in French. These included an exceedingly interesting video of Tara Cullen—suite 5—as she showered and prepared for bed, which Kilana had given a number of successive replays, watching it for his personal enjoyment while a freshly lighted cigarette burned down to a charred, unsmoked stub in his ashtray.

With the files copied, Kilana removed the disk from the drive tray, put it into a jewel case, and turned off his computer. Then he rose, made a perfunctory attempt at smoothing down his rumpled, sagging uniform, abandoned all hope of it, and left the office, snapping out the lights as he went through the door.

In the parking lot, a courier waited in the shadows near Kilana's automobile. The police commander knew this man's face but not his identity. More willing ignorance; it was well within Kilana's power to learn everything about him, from his grandmother's maiden name to his favorite pissing hole.

Passing the jewel case to the courier without a word, Commander Kilana watched him leave the parking area on foot and then disappear into the night.

After a few moments, he got into his car and drove home, ousting from his mind an intrusive guess about the DVD's eventual destination.

Yes, the less he knew the better.

Except, perhaps, when it came to the beautiful occupant of luxury suite 5 at the Rio de Gabao Hotel.

SIX

CALIFORNIA
GABON, AFRICA

IT WAS EIGHTEENTH-CENTURY FRANCISCAN PADRES
at the San Carlos Barromeo Mission, outside what would
become the city of Carmel, that gave the vast, cragged
stretch of the central California coastline its original
name: *El País Grande del Sur*, or the Big Country to the
South. As U.S. western expansion brought the wagon
wheels of American settlers rolling into this territory, its
Hispanic friars, their numbers and influence already on
the wane, must have been chagrined to hear the place
name anglicized, abbreviated, and vulgarized to Big Sur.
But then, it may be surmised that waves of gold-rushing
Forty-Niners, and the subsequent annexation of California by the Colossus of the North, would have soon made
any consternation over such a thing seem trifling to the
manifestly destined extreme.

The rental cabin Kuhl's sleeper agents had acquired
for him in Big Sur perched on the edge of a precipitous
gorge three thousand feet above sea level, its western
windows offering a wide view of the Pacific Ocean beyond the canyon, its isolation guarded by a thirty-foot-
tall iron entry gate a full mile down the ridge's eastward
slope. Built in 1940 as a secret getaway by one of the
state's early millionaire lumber barons—and currently assigned by family heirs to the management of a real-estate

company specializing in wilderness properties—the furnished cabin was a large two-story structure of stone and Douglas fir logs with open interior spaces, a central spiral staircase, French doors, and upper and lower balconies that extended past the sheer western cliff to overhang the long, empty plunge of the canyon. Access from the limestone gateposts was confined to an unmarked strip of winding dirt road circumscribed by thirty private acres of oak and redwood forest, vertical shale outcrops, rolling fields, and scattered swift-moving streams that ceaselessly chattered, splashed, and tumbled down deep, steep cuts in the wooded mountain slopes.

Behind a high west window on the second floor, Kuhl sat in a supple leather chair watching the commercial van's arrival through his binoculars. It pushed uphill between the trees at an engine-grinding crawl, its wheels occasionally sinking into loose, crumbly ditches in the access road. The road's narrowness would not have allowed even two small vehicles to pass in opposite directions, and it had recently become rutted and washed out after a spate of heavy late summer rainfall. The Realtor's offer to fill and regrade its surface had been declined by Kuhl's representatives. Their employer sought a period of complete escape from distraction, they emphasized. The noisy repair work would have impinged on the first week of his stay at the very minimum, and he was adamant about requiring uninterrupted solitude.

A ten-thousand-dollar deposit left on his lease had ensured that complete deference was given to his wishes.

Now the van came jolting and bumping over the final few yards of the path. Kuhl wondered whether its rough trip up had agitated the occupants he assumed were riding in its cargo section. This was no bit of idle musing. He must have absolute confidence in their reliability. If they showed any sign of unrest he would notice it, apologize for the driver's trouble, and send him back on his way.

After several moments, Kuhl lowered his binoculars to the windowsill. The van had reached the cabin and pulled to a stop on the unmanicured grass beside his own Ford Explorer. The words ANAGKAZO BREEDING AND TRAINING painted on its flank were easily legible to his naked eye.

As the driver got out, Kuhl rose and turned to the man who had been standing behind him near the window.

"Stay out of sight, Ciras," he said. "I'm going down."

Ciras nodded. He was slender, almost delicate looking, with shiny black mongoose eyes, dark curling hair, and olive skin. There was about him a keyed, alert stillness that was all contained energy. He rarely seemed to move unless necessary. When he did, it was in darting bursts. On a crowded Munich street once, Kuhl saw him turn on a Verfasungsschutz intelligence agent who had been trailing them, and slice open his belly with a sweep of the knife so quick its blade was never glimpsed in his hand.

At the foot of the spiral stairs now, Kuhl heard the bell chime and crossed the main room to open the door.

"Mr. Estes, hello," his visitor said. Tall, bearded, and stocky, he wore a short-sleeved chambray shirt, denim trousers, and western boots. Under his arm was a black portfolio briefcase. "Sorry if I ran a little late, almost got stuck a couple times . . ."

"The drive can be tedious. I saw your difficulty coming up." Kuhl let him enter. "You must be Mr. Anagkazo."

The man stood inside the entrance and held out a hand.

"John's fine," he said. "A lot of people maul the second name, and I've had more than a few of them tell me I should change it to something easier to remember. For business's sake. But the line I always come back with is that we've had it in the family a while."

Kuhl slipped a smile onto his face.

"It is Greek, yes?"

"You got it. My great-grandparents came over from Corinth."

"A magnificent city."

"So I hear," Anagkazo replied. "I'm kind of embarrassed to say I've never made the trip. All kinds of relatives there I'd love to meet, but it's always one thing or another keeps me tied down." He glanced into the living room. "You're a professional photographer, right? Bet you get around some."

Kuhl looked at him. He had deliberately placed his camera on a mission bench against the wall—not the digital, but a 35-mm Nikon. Beside it in a deliberate clutter were accessory cases, a light meter, a folded tripod, and scattered rolls of Kodak film.

"Some," he said after a moment.

The visitor angled his head back toward his parked van. A second man had exited and was striding around its right side.

"That's Greg Clayton, my best trial helper," Anagkazo said. "It'll take him about five, ten minutes to get suited and ready for the demo." He hefted his portfolio case. "Meanwhile, we probably should sit down, go over a few things. I'll show you the pedigrees and trial certifications, answer whatever questions you have about my program."

A pause. Then Kuhl said, "I've owned Schutzhund trained dogs before. My assistant made that clear in your conversations, did he not?"

"He did. Well, generally—"

Tired of the man, wishing him gone, Kuhl remembered these banalities of interaction were woven into the fabric of his camouflage veil. "A Rottweiler and a German shepherd—at different times," he said. "Please, though, have a seat."

Anagkazo stepped through the room, lowered himself into a rustic oak couch, and regarded the camera gear again. He seemed intrigued.

"Here to shoot anything special?" he said, unzipping his case. "If you don't mind my being curious."

Kuhl looked at his visitor from an armchair opposite him.

"No, not in the least." He smiled. "I'm working on a book to be published in Europe. A pictorial record of my modern-day journey over the Royal Road."

"*El Camino Reál*, sure. Connects the old mission chain from San Diego to Frisco," Anagkazo said. "I guess you'd find most of those settlements along Route one oh one. Or near it. There are maybe twenty altogether, that right?"

"Twenty-one."

Anagkazo nodded, his brow creasing with interest.

"You know, I've heard San Antonio de Padua's something else," he said. "It's way out past my breeding farm in the middle of nowhere. A hassle to reach because you've got to take a twisty local road, G-sixteen, leads you through the mountains. But seeing it must give you an idea how tough life must've been for those original Spanish priests."

"Yes," Kuhl said. "I'd planned on making the drive."

"Just don't forget to pack lunch and a coffee Thermos," Anagkazo said. "Also better make sure you have loads of identification. There's an army base, Fort Hunter Liggett, in the Ventana backcountry. Government land covers maybe a hundred seventy thousand acres, believe it or not. Most of it's plain wild. The base itself was deactivated almost ten years ago, but they still use it for military reserve and National Guard drills. There are tanks, choppers, fire ranges, ammo dumps. I hear they conduct some special-op training, too, though they keep that part sort of hush-hush." He produced a pocket folder embossed with his company's name from the briefcase on his lap. "The reason I say to bring your ID is that the mission happens to be smack in the middle of a valley on the base's land. You actually need to drive through a checkpoint to visit it, and security's gotten tighter nowadays. Like I told you, it can be a challenge."

Kuhl had reason to be amused.

"But worthwhile, I think," he said. He took the pocket folder from Anagkazo, opened it, and hastily riffled through the thin stacks of clipped-together documents in its sleeve. "All the paperwork is in here?"

"Pedigree records, award certificates, and point breakdowns for every phase of training. Everything signed and sealed by Schutzhund master officials," Anagkazo said. "I included our owner's information packet and guarantees of course—"

"The dogs have Level-Three titles?"

"And other special ones besides," Anagkazo said. "You're getting really terrific animals. Lido, Sorge, and Arek. They're littermates, pure-black shepherd males from west German working lines. The dogs have to be a minimum of twenty months old to qualify for Level-Three certification, and I spent an extra four months training them for advanced titles in protection and tracking. You won't find too many around that have earned the trial scores they did." He shrugged. "But I should show and not tell. Greg must be set by now, and you're probably anxious to meet your new best friends for yourself."

Kuhl looked at him.

"Yes," he said. "Very much so."

They rose and went toward the door.

On the grass about thirty feet from the cabin, Anagkazo's helper had gotten the three coal-black German shepherds out through the van's side panel. A broad, hulking man who stood well over six feet tall, he waited beside it holding them on a leather multiple-dog leash clipped to their steel choke collars. Motionless, they sat side by side at his heel.

Kuhl studied Clayton's oversize flannel shirt and baggy coveralls, noted the odd bunching over his arms, legs and chest, and realized his huge appearance was due in some measure to concealed body padding.

Anagkazo turned to Kuhl outside the cabin door. "Your assistant told me you'd be interested in protection," he said. "Alone up here on the mountain, that's a sensible requirement. Having owned Schutzhunds before, you're probably familiar with what I'm about to say, but some people don't appreciate that effective guard work goes with obedience and control"—he interlocked two fingers—"like this. You can't separate them. Over-aggressiveness is considered a flaw either in a dog's inbred disposition or trained behavior. It shouldn't display *any* aggression unless ordered. They're protection dogs, not guard dogs in the ordinary sense . . . they only do what their owner tells them, won't attack anyone without his direct command."

Kuhl gave him a silent nod.

"We're going to demonstrate how those important qualities I mentioned combine in a simulated protective engagement," Anagkazo said. "The reason Greg's wearing a hidden bite suit, and not the ordinary kind that would fit outside his regular clothes, is because an *intruder*'s going to be dressed in regular clothes. We want to be sure our dogs will perform under realistic conditions. It's part of the extra training I mentioned before, and not even necessary for Level-Three certification." He paused. "Don't be disturbed when Greg brings out his pistol. It's a Bruni practice gun . . . looks and sounds like the real thing, but chambered for firing blanks."

Kuhl smiled at him. "Thank you for the warning," he said.

Anagkazo waved to his helper as a signal to get started. Let off the leash, the dogs remained heeled in position at Clayton's side until Anagkazo called out to them. Then they sprang onto all fours and came rushing over to him at once like a midnight wind.

"Sit," he said in a firm voice.

The shepherds obeyed without hesitation. Kuhl studied them. They were truly impressive: wide-boned, thick-furred, and muscular, with triangular ears erect above the domes of their large shaggy heads.

Anagkazo signaled again.

"Okay, Greg!" he shouted. "Roll it!"

Clayton reached into a pocket of his coveralls for the training handgun. Kuhl noted it was indeed an accurate replica of a Colt 9-mm semiautomatic.

Both hands around its grip, tilting its barrel slightly upward, the helper raised his gun, pulled the trigger. A shot cracked into the air, loud, its echoes bounding off and away into the nearby trees.

Kuhl's eyes went to the dogs. They were still. Perfectly still beside their trainer, facing Clayton across the grass.

In this way, and perhaps others, Kuhl thought, their attitude was reminiscent of Ciras.

Clayton gave the high-country silence scarcely a moment's chance to settle back down around the cabin, and then shattered it with a second round of gunfire, a third, a fourth.

More echoes reverberated through the treetops, scaring up birds everywhere on the ridge.

Kuhl watched the dogs.

None of them had shown any sign of startlement or so much as flinched. They just sat there staring at the man with the gun, their bright brown eyes fixed on him.

Kuhl looked at Anagkazo. "They are in complete control of their natural impulses," he said.

The breeder nodded.

"And without fear," he said. "You'll see what I mean."

Anagkazo waved a hand above his head yet another time. Clayton stepped toward the cabin, his pistol thrust out before him, the uptilt of its snout now barely perceptible even to Kuhl.

Two shots crashed from it.

"Attack!" Anagkazo commanded.

The dogs hurtled forward, racing straight at Clayton, making no sound, midnight wind. The pistol was fired again, a series of rapid bursts, but they did not stop, kept on charging in his direction.

He lowered his gun as the dogs reached him, aimed it at them.

They lunged. One of them drove high, rose onto its hind legs, and Kuhl saw the flash of bared white fangs as its massive black jaws clamped over Clayton's gun arm below the elbow. Another shepherd went for his right thigh. The third, his left ankle. Clayton twisted his body, shouting loud threats at the dogs, pulling them around with him, *dragging* them around with him, but they hung on, silent, silent, throwing their combined weight against him, finally making him lose his balance, forcing him off his feet. As he dropped hard onto his side, the pistol flew out of Clayton's grasp, landed several feet away in a patch of grass.

From Anagkazo now: *"Hold!"*

The three German shepherds released his helper, backed off, and got onto their haunches without turning away from him, staying within a yard of the spot where Clayton had fallen, forming up in a close ring around him. They were still silent, their thick wooly tails whipping back and forth over the ground.

Anagkazo turned to Kuhl.

"Fearless, as promised," he said. "They won't budge until I call them down."

"And if the intruder were to run into the woods?" Kuhl was watching the dogs. "Try to escape rather than press ahead toward a confrontation?"

"As long as you give the command, they'd track and find him no matter where he hides," Anagkazo said. "Bear in mind you don't have to be in danger or any extraordinary circumstances to get the same level of obedience from them. It extends to their routine behavior. Whether it's walking beside you on the street, retrieving a Frisbee at a picnic, whatever. With these dogs there's no negotiation."

Appreciating that last phrase, savoring it, Kuhl waited a long moment before he offered the breeder his reply.

"Excellent, Mr. Anagkazo," he said, then. "Truly excellent. That is just what I'd wanted to hear."

Steve DeMarco was one of nine members of Sword's advance team to have met the plane out at the landing field.

A Boeing 737 freighter, it had flown in with about twenty thousand tons of cargo for the satcom ground station and fiber network head-end center going up near the Sette Cama Forest thirty miles south of Port-Gentil. The bulk of its load consisted of parts ordered by the horde of engineers, plumbers, and other specialized utility systems experts at work in the compound's buildings. There were pallets of everyday office fixtures, including desks, chairs, computers, LAN modems, phones, fax machines, copiers, paper, toner cartridges, and so on. And there was an initial shipment of expensive upgrade and replacement components for the Planétaire optical communications infrastructure, such as long-haul light amplifiers, wavelength division multiplexers, demultiplexers, and routing devices. The telecom equipment alone was worth upward of a couple million dollars, which would have been reason enough for fully three-quarters of Nimec's security contingent to be on hand for the Boeing's reception.

And they had another.

A comparatively smaller portion of the valuable cargo transshipped to Gabon via UpLink Europe had been requisitioned by the Sword boys. This ranged from electrified perimeter fencing, ballistic glass panels, and concrete Jersey barricades for vehicle entry points to fancier hardware like fixed intruder-alert systems, countersurveillance sweep units, mobile robotic guards (dubbed "hedgehogs" by Rollie Thibodeau), and many of the same weapons and chembio threat detectors Thibodeau had described to Tom Ricci during their brief, strained catch-up session at UpLink San Jose. Also arriving with the Sword req were the first three of what would eventually grow into an entire fleet of armored-and-modified-to-order Land Rovers, and a delivery of weapons and gear Nimec's team had been licensed to use for personal and facility defense under special agreement with Gabonese authorities. Among these were several crates of conventional firearms, third-generation "Big Daddy" variable-velocity rifle-system submachine guns, and other lethal and less-than-lethal munitions.

Once the goods had been unloaded they were expedited to temporary warehouses, checked in, sorted, and prepped for final transport—and that was where Steve DeMarco and his teammates entered the picture. Everything was eventually headed out to the Sette Cama for on-site storage and distribution, begging careful supervision as the first loads were transferred onto off-

road trucks and heavy lift choppers by airport personnel.
Four of the Sword ops had ridden with the wheeled convoy along remote jungle roads, which might present
tempting ambush points to thieves and hijackers. Each of
the two birds making the initial air run had swept off
with a guard of its own. As agent in charge, DeMarco
had also assigned three men to the warehouse beat until
the rest of the freight was cleared out of them, a process
expected to take seventy-two hours at the very least.

With things well under control at the airport, DeMarco
had gotten into his company vehicle and driven back to
the Rio de Gabao. His plan was to freshen up in his room,
then grab a bite to eat at the hotel restaurant before giving
Pete Nimec the lowdown on the successful transit operation.

He would wind up with a whole lot more to tell him.

As he got out of the elevator, DeMarco's curiosity had
nudged him to give one of the new pieces of equipment
that had arrived with the 737 a quick test. Though far
from the most expensive or important item in the shipment, it was nonetheless a nifty little gadget . . . assuming
it worked as touted. At a glance it appeared to be a long,
thin silver cigarette lighter. Another version of the same
device, designed to look like a key chain fob, had been
chosen by some of the ops. To each his own.

Whichever outer configuration was preferred, the miniature guts of the thing remained the same. Its true function was neither to fire up a smoke nor to help a person
locate keys buried in a trouser pocket—although the latter was something the fob did quite handily because of
its shape, perhaps accounting for its favored status in
contrast to the fuel-less, wickless, single-purpose mock-
cigarette lighter version. The device's *true* function, at
any rate, was to snoop out hidden surveillance cameras.
Inside the case was a very low frequency directional re-

ceiver sensitive to electromagnetic emissions in the fifteen- to twenty-kilohertz range, corresponding to VLF levels radiated by the horizontal oscillators that typically allowed remote-operated cameras their side-to-side movement. The detector had two switchable modes of alert. At the touch of a button, it could signal the presence of a hidden camera with a discreet pulse similar to that given off by a cell phone set to silently vibrate, or sound a series of beeps through an attached headset. The closer it got to the source of the low-band radio emission, the faster a tiny red LED on the case would blink, allowing pinpoint location of the camera . . . in theory, insofar as DeMarco was concerned for the present. His trust in any gadget or weapon had to meet the same standard he applied to women: He would reserve judgment until he saw how well it treated him.

Thus, DeMarco's test. On his first day at the hotel, he had noticed a couple of minidome cameras in the hallway outside his room. The first to snag his careful eye was mounted flush with the ceiling near the elevator bank and might easily have been taken for one of the domed light fixtures with which it was aligned in a long row. The second minidome was more visibly mounted about two feet to the right of his door—and four or five feet above his head—in a corner formed by the juncture of the wall and ceiling. Neither bothered him by its presence. Quite the opposite, in fact. The Rio was a five-star hotel catering to upper-echelon international travelers. And any decent lodging nowadays was obliged to provide security for its guests. At its most basic, this would consist of an in-house security staff and twenty-four-hours-a-day, seven-days-a-week video monitoring of common areas.

DeMarco's idea was to give the camera near his door a covert pass with his detector simply to find out whether it would buzz and flash its little indicator light as touted.

If the gadget worked, he would accept the good things he'd heard about it. Make it his steady, so to speak. If it didn't, he would have to reevaluate their relationship and likewise warn his men against putting too much faith in it.

As the Dylan song went, just like a woman.

Now DeMarco turned down the hall toward his room, the locator nestled in his right palm. At the door he took his swipe-card key from his shirt pocket with his free hand and inserted it into the reader, simultaneously thumbing on the locator to pass it under the camera, keeping it turned away from the bug-eyed enclosure . . . just a weary guest about to give himself a little neck rub after a long morning of hustle and bustle.

The gadget began to vibrate in mid-pass.

Good, he thought.

DeMarco brought it down between his shoulder blades with a smooth movement, raised it, slid his eyes onto the LED. It was blinking rapidly. He made an adequate show of massaging himself through his shirt, then lowered his right hand to his side, away from the overhead camera, and took another peak at the red light. The blinking slowed, stopped.

Even better.

Satisfied he'd gained a trustworthy companion, De-Marco pushed open his door and stepped into the room. He headed straight over to his dresser and tossed the card key on top of it, already unbuttoning his shirt below its open collar, eager to get under the refreshing shower spray and rinse the sweat and airport dust off his body. Although it was still well before noon, the outside temperature had to be somewhere in the upper eighties, and the soupy humidity made it feel even hotter.

As he went to put his camera locator down beside the card, his finger on the power button to click it to the OFF setting, DeMarco felt a sudden vibrational shiver from it, and realized the LED was blinking through his fingers again.

Rapidly.

Very rapidly.

His brows arched. Red light flickering between his knuckles, he continued to feel the silent pulsations of the locator's alert signal. Then he thumbed it off, his eyes cutting left and right, taking in the room—its walls, ceiling, furnishings, picture frames, mirrors, central air-conditioning unit. Everything.

DeMarco swore inwardly. Not moving his lips. Betraying no hint of surprise through a muttered word or gesture.

After a moment he finished undressing, went into the shower, and turned on the tap, feeling tense and exposed, trying his best to act as if nothing were amiss.

His equipment tryout had proven to be more informative than he'd bargained for. A lot more.

He would have to talk to Pete Nimec right away.

After a night of bad dreams, Julia Gordian had hoped to shake off her mild funk at work Sunday, but the chill, gray weather was doing nothing to give her a lift.

The shelter had been quiet since she'd arrived, Rob off to do his double-duty accounting out at the San Gregario Beach resort, Cynthia dealing with a colicky infant in their house down the lane, leaving Julia to mind things alone. She was okay with that part, but would have been happier if it weren't such a slow day for adoption prospects. There were no appointments scheduled for that morning, and only two penciled in for the afternoon. Quiet, and the low mist pressing against the shop window added to her downbeat mood.

Julia knelt over a bulk order of dog kibble delivered

the day before, slid a box opener between the carton's taped flaps, spread them open, and did a quick count of the three-pound bags inside against the total listed on the packing slip. Behind the counter with her, Vivian loafed on her cushion, raising her head off her crossed paws to nuzzle the carton with mild interest.

"Thanks for the hardy assist, Viv. But everything's here," Julia said, scratching the grey behind her ears, which were folded like a bow on a bonnet—the left ear flipped limply to the right, the right flopped to the left, the two overlapping over the fine, tawny fur betwixt. "No shortages to report."

Viv produced a kind of whistling yawn, stretched, and rolled onto her back. Since being rebuffed by the Wurmans she had become Julia's honorary sidekick, winning the position through charm and sympathy.

Julia smiled at her with affection.

"The tummy rub has to wait, kid," she said. "I've got to earn my nonsalary."

Julia reached into the carton. And while she unpacked and filled the shelves, found herself thinking about the dreams.

They had plagued her every so often since her divorce from Craig. Less often recently, but it seemed their run had not quite concluded and would recur for disturbing encore presentations anywhere between once and twice a month. Julia never knew what events would stir up the pockets of unconscious turbulence or why she'd go plunging into them on any given night. And she was stumped by their power to throw her out of whack almost two years after she'd last had any direct contact with her former husband. They were, like most dreams, insipid. Formulaic variations on a stock theme; confused, weak, even silly recalled in the light of day. But the sleeping mind was both captive audience and uncritical judge of its own regurgitated material, and they had once again kept her tossing and turning in bed.

Leading off last night's bill had been the creepshow she thought of as *Julia Can't Find Her Home*. The title said it all. She'd been driving home from somewhere—home being the residence Julia had shared with Craig for their entire six-year marriage—then swung off the usual highway exit and suddenly found herself in the wrong neighborhood. Or, to be more accurate, in a weirdly transformed version of what she somehow knew to be the *right* neighborhood. The street layout was vaguely familiar. There were landmarks that seemed to belong where she saw them, houses she seemed to recognize, but they had been altered in some uncertain way, and shuffled around like pieces on a Monopoly board. As Julia turned corner after corner, her initial bafflement escalated to panic. There was no sign of her driveway, her front yard. She was lost. The house wasn't anywhere. *She* wasn't anywhere. She couldn't even retrace her route to the highway. She was without any sense of direction, her bearings gone, driving up and down increasingly alien and unknown streets, circling them in a futile, endless search for a home that had vanished.

That realization had awakened her with a scream, prompting a trip into the kitchen for a glass of cold water. It hadn't ended the nightmares, though.

Julia in a House Full of Strangers . . . Almost! had followed shortly after she'd fallen back asleep. In this dream, the beleaguered heroine arrived at her residence without any trouble, but opened the front door to find it filled with complete strangers. As she rushed through its interior she saw people everywhere. Cozying up on the sofa, at the refrigerator, seated in the dining room, chatting and laughing in the halls. None of them knew her. None was interested in knowing her. In fact they didn't seem to notice her at all, just went about their affairs as if she were invisible. She'd wandered the house like a ghost, found herself outside her bedroom. The door was wide open. Inside a couple was vigorously making love, tangled naked in the sheets. The lights were on. They ignored her when she appeared in the doorway. Julia could see the woman's back, see a man underneath her, his face blocked by her riding body, his ecstatic groans muffled against her breasts. It had sounded like Craig. It had sounded exactly like Craig. And that had brought Julia back to reality with a start, left her crying into the pillow of her own darkened bedroom for perhaps half an hour.

At least she had been spared a reprisal of *Nobody Knows Julia*, a subtler but equally disturbing script in which she would come home to find her former in-laws watching television in the living room. In these dreams, they would acknowledge her presence with cool detachment and instruct her to leave at once. Their devoted son and his wife were returning any minute and would not appreciate uninvited visitors, particularly a strange woman drifting in off the sidewalk to cause trouble for them. When Julia insisted she *was* his wife they would quietly repeat that she had better vacate the premises for her own good and then would turn their attention back to the tube. Again, as if she were no longer there. The volume on the set was turned up loud. And whatever they were watching had a laugh track.

Julia sighed. Her urge that dreary morning had been to pull her blankets over her head and stay put. It had been a powerful temptation she'd felt many times before. But she had resisted it today, as she'd always done, except for a couple of instances in the weeks immediately after she learned of Craig's affair. Dreary or not, it was a *new* morning, and she had her responsibilities. Her work at the shelter was for a good cause, one very personal to her. It was also insurance against the deadly appeal of her drawn window shades, blanket, and pillow.

Finished replenishing the shelves with dog food now, Julia sidled around the counter, inspected its adjoining showcase, decided it looked sort of bare, and went into the little side stockroom for some dental and nail trimming kits to fill it out. Despite the store's limited front space, Rob was nitpicky about keeping at least one piece of every item he carried on display, but worrying about two jobs and a baby seemed to have spun his attention kind of thin. Yesterday he had driven out thirty miles along his way to the Fairwinds before realizing he'd forgotten an important ledger. He'd needed to return home for it and arrived at the motel over an hour late, aggravated and embarrassed.

Julia was reentering the storefront with a handful of supplies when she heard the sound of an approaching vehicle. *Don't tell me Rob's come back ledgerless again*, she thought . . . and then told herself she didn't want to jinx him by even half seriously considering it. No sirree, not this morning. What more fitting, lousy capper could there be to it than the poor, overworked guy having to double back after another bout of absentmindedness?

She glanced out the window and was pleased to see it wasn't his Montero, but one of those Subaru 4×4 utility wagons . . . an Outback. It had pulled up to Rob's house, a thirtyish clean-shaven man in a tan leather car coat and jeans stepping out to ring the door bell. After a moment Cynthia appeared on the front porch, babe in arms, and pointed him toward the shelter.

Back in his wagon, the driver rolled into the parking area near the shop, then got out again and came hustling over through the fog, which was now starting to turn into a fine drizzle.

He pulled open the door and leaned inside. Cut in short, purposely mussed snippets, his hair was already sprinkled with droplets of moisture.

"Hi," he said, and glanced at his wristwatch. "I didn't know your Sunday hours, but figured it was after eleven, and took a chance. The woman in that house told me you're open."

Julia waved him in out of the wetness.

"Sure, come on in," she said. "We're just slow this morning."

He entered, paused, quietly looking around the shop.

Julia set her stockroom merchandise onto the counter, stood with her back to it. "If there's anything special I can help you find, let me know," she said.

He gave her a smile, gesturing with his chin.

"Actually," he said. "I'm interested in somebody like your friend over there."

Julia looked around, momentarily puzzled. Then she laughed. Vivian had gotten off her cushion and stuck her head out from behind the counter.

"Oh, sorry, I didn't realize . . ."

"Pooch is a little shy, huh?"

"Don't let Viv fool you, she knows how to get her way."

Now the guy chuckled, too. "Especially with you, I'll bet."

"I guess."

He put out his hand.

"Barry Hughes," he said.

"Julia Gordian," she said.

They shook.

"So," he said. "Tell me what I need to do to rescue a greyhound today?"

Julia hesitated, did a quick memory check, and glanced down at the open schedule book beside the cash register.

As she had thought, there were only the couple of afternoon appointments, and neither of them was for anybody named Hughes.

"Sorry," she said. "I don't see you listed . . ."

"Oh," Hughes said. "Do I need to be?"

"I'm afraid so," Julia said. "Other than for buying supplies or gifts, that is." She paused, her brow creasing. "You mean you didn't know?"

Hughes shook his head.

"I'm always noticing the sign for your shelter on the road," he said. "Figured I'd drop by whenever I could."

Julia produced a sigh. "I really *am* sorry," she said. "We have a lot of dogs that need placement, but there's a telephone screening process. It's given to every candidate owner before they come look at the greys."

Hughes shrugged.

"I'd be glad to answer any questions right here. If you'd like to ask them, that is—"

"I'd like nothing more," Julia said. "It isn't my choice, though. You'd need to speak with Rob Howell. He's the shelter's organizer and conducts all the phone interviews himself."

"Oh," Hughes said again. "Mr. Howell available, by any chance?"

Julia shook her head. "Best thing would be to give him a ring. Monday through Friday."

"That's kind of difficult for me . . . I'm a power company technician, always climbing utility poles, crawling around people's basements, running everywhere on emergency calls," Hughes said, and frowned. "You sure you can't grab hold of him for a few minutes?"

"I would if the timing weren't so bad," Julia said. "Unfortunately he'll be out the next two weekends."

Hughes made eye contact with her.

"And I couldn't ask for an exception—"

"As I said, there's nothing I'd prefer. But I'm new at the job. And rules are rules."

A pause.

"Well," Hughes said, and expelled a long breath. "I guess I'll try back another time."

Julia pulled a business card from the holder by the register.

"In any event, why don't you take this," she said, handing it to him. "It's got our regular business hours. Phone and fax numbers, too, of course."

Hughes reached for his billfold and slipped in the card.

"Thanks." He motioned toward the counter again. "Maybe I'll get lucky, and nobody else will take your adorable friend before I have my chance at her."

Julia glanced over at Vivian and was mildly surprised to see she hadn't come out from behind the counter, but was poking her head out around its side, sniffing away, her ears flat back against her head, the bonnet bow undone. Viv didn't often lay on the bashful routine *that* thick.

"Maybe," she said, feeling an odd twinge that she immediately chalked up to her own growing attachment to the dog—another violation of Rob's thou-shalt-nots. The two of them really had become chums, but she had to recognize somebody *would* take her one of these days. And that it would be very much for the best. "Anyway, I hope you give us a call. Our rescues desperately need good homes."

Hughes nodded, gave her another smile, and left.

A moment later Julia turned from the door and got back to work.

In the Outback, the man who'd introduced himself as Barry Hughes passed the Howell residence, reached the bottom of the lane, turned left, and then drove west over the blacktop toward the coast.

His own particular morning's work was over, and it could not have gone any better.

"So what do you think?" DeMarco said.

"From what you tell me," Nimec said, swatting away a mosquito, "we've got some worries."

"Yeah."

"Serious worries."

"Yeah."

"Which you obviously know, or we wouldn't be here," Nimec said.

DeMarco nodded but said nothing.

They were standing together on an aged steel footbridge over a drainage channel in the city's Romb'Intchozo precinct, their elbows propped on its pedestrian guard rail. In the rainy season, the channel would be gurgling with overflow from the flooded Ogooué River delta. But this was a different season, and the water below them was low and still and muddy. Insects swarmed around thick clottings of food wrappers and other paper litter that floated on or just below the surface.

Nimec wished he hadn't worn short sleeves. Or that he'd splashed on some pest repellent.

"Hell of it is, I can't think of anything but the obvious," he said after a long silence. "We need to find out who's put a watch on us. How wide it is. And we need to find out the reasons why. What they'd have to gain."

DeMarco nodded again. He felt a tiny stinging bite on his bare left forearm, slapped his right hand down on it, examined his palm, and saw the mosquito's wings, legs, and carapace mashed together in a smear of blood. He scraped it onto the guard rail with a sense of vengeful reward.

"Damned bugs," he said.

"No pun intended, I hope."

DeMarco puzzled a moment over the vinegary humor in Nimec's tone, then got it.

"No," he said with a thin smile. "None."

They stood looking out past at the stagnant, refuse clogged, insect-teeming murk under the bridge.

After a while Nimec decided on the first step in what he supposed might be labeled a plan.

Or something close to one.

The Ogooué Fan. Eighty leagues below sea level. Fifteen feet long, its leech-white outer hull devoid of markings, the deep submersible had passed beneath the sand ridge's crumbled terrace to assume a stable automatic hover close to the ocean bottom.

In the steel-walled forward pressure cabin, two men in overalls that matched the color of the craft's fiberglass exterior occupied its command station behind a hemi-spheric acrylic viewport—the large half bubble allowed for wide field, low refractory visibility, giving a near il-lusion that there was nothing to separate them from their aqueous surroundings. One of them sat in the pilot's chair, ready to take manual joy-stick control of the craft and push its ducted, silent-running, eight-horsepower electric thrusters to a speed of better than ten knots in the event that sudden detection or imminent threat drove them to launch an escape. Behind the backup controls to his right, the copilot monitored his frontal and overhead status boards and handled their periodic radio commu-nications with the surface team.

The four crewmen in the aft pressure chamber also wore pale overalls. Two had manipulated the clawed ro-botic arm that had plucked the segment of fiber cable from its bed of sand and sediments. Their companions behind a separate instrument console had followed the marine cable's exposure with the deployment of a tubular protrusion from the submersible's underbelly midway between bow and stern, running it to the rubbled sea floor, mating it to what almost appeared to be an ordinary splice enclosure in the line. But the bidirectional data port in the enclosure's upper surface would be certain to draw attention from a knowledgeable eye such as Cédric Dupain had possessed . . . and indeed *did* when he'd spotted its watertight cover some months earlier, making the discovery that would seal his and Marius Bouchard's fate.

Had Dupain lived long enough to further scrutinize it, his inquisitiveness would have surely led him to find the data port and the special multifiber coupler fitted within the splice enclosure: a microchip-activated beam-splitting pod that, when switched on, would tap into the lightwave signals passing through the cable and divert a fraction of them into the optical fibers of the extended feeder tube. Because the pod had been built into the system near a splice housing known to Planétaire's, and now UpLink International's, system managers, the temporary signal degradation would be considered unremarkable. The heat-fusing of fiber ends at splice points will always result in some attenuation of signal strength, intrinsic losses that are ignored within certain established levels, and there would be many of these points along the route of a typical long-distance network's architecture.

At each parasitic siphoning off of the cable, its flood of raw high-speed data was transmitted from the submersible's array of receiving/buffering computer terminals to Cray superprocessors aboard the *Chimera* using a direct, narrow-targeted underwater-to-surface Intranet link maintained via an extremely high frequency (or EHF) acoustic telemetry modem and on-hull antenna about the size and shape of a carrot. Were they to hear a mission-abort command from the pilot's chair, the men at the aft consoles would be responsible for disengaging the feeder tube and, if time and opportunity allowed, retrenching the cable to hide any visible sign of their tap.

Although these emergency measures were practiced in drills, the reality was that their implementation never had been required. A cautious and prudent man in any circumstance, Harlan DeVane was at his best functioning in the depths.

As DeVane himself often mused.

Port-Gentil. Late Sunday afternoon. Pete Nimec and Vince Scull strode through the main lobby of the Rio de Gabao to the street, past the accommodating concierge, the smiling doorman, the ready taxi drivers parked near the entrance.

On the pavement they turned right and started walking unhurriedly toward the big outdoor market at the north side of the city, a couple of commercial travelers enjoying a welcome weekend respite from their high-powered business affairs.

Soon afterward, Sword ops Charlie Hollinger and Frank Rhodes left the hotel together and strode south toward the casino district. They were talking about things like their luck at the slots and exchanging tips for cashing in big at baccarat and roulette.

A half hour passed before Steve DeMarco and three more members of the Sword advance team—Andy Wade, Joel Ackerman, and Brian Conners—hit the street. The group stood chatting in front of the hotel, casually discussing their separate plans for the rest of the afternoon. DeMarco and Wade said they wanted to see some historic sights. Ackerman mentioned a free Makossa concert in the city park he was anxious to catch, and Conners, who played guitar as a hobby, indicated he'd like to tag along with him. DeMarco suggested that all of them ought to try hooking up with Nimec and Scull at the bazaar a bit later on, maybe going out for dinner afterward. Conners said he wasn't sure, but would probably decide to pass on that, expressing his interest in some local sights he wanted to visit on his own after the concert. And besides, he'd already promised Hollinger and Rhodes he would join them in blowing his week's pay at the tables.

The group stood there talking for another five minutes or so and then moved on.

DeMarco and Wade went right, following the direction Nimec and Scull had taken to the market quarter with only few detours en route.

Ackerman and Conners walked left toward the park together, though Conners would eventually go off on his own.

As had been true since their arrival in the country, all eight men were being watched.

This time, however, they were watching the watchers.

For the second time in as many days Jean Jacques Assele-Ndaki had been shocked and horrified by the photograph of his lifelong friend Macie's gruesome murder. But having the president himself confront him with it *this* time added a new and entirely different element to his reaction.

He'd been prepared to see neither as he arrived at Senateur Moubouyi's colonial mansion and was ushered into the salon by his houseman.

Assele-Ndaki stood in the doorway now, looking into the room with frozen features. President Cangele. *Here.* How was this possible? It was everything he could do not to physically jump when the paneled oak door shut behind him.

"Assemblyman, hello." The president sat at the head of a long table, two of his closest aides to his right, the rest of the chairs filled with more than twelve of Assele-Ndaki's legislative colleagues. "We've been waiting for you with unanimous anticipation. And unanimity among politicians is too rare and short-lived to neglect for any period."

Assele-Ndaki did not move. He felt staggered and weak kneed, as if struck by a hard concussion.

"Mr. President . . ."

"Please, come in," Adrian Cangele nodded toward a single empty chair on his left side. The snapshot of Macie lay in front of him, its lower border pressed flat against the table by the thick fingers of his hand. "Now that you've arrived, there is no reason for you to stand apart. Is there?"

Recognizing the clear edge of sarcasm and double-entendre in the president's remarks, Assele-Ndaki struggled to gain possession of himself. He had expected a huddle of government officials gathered to challenge the power and authority of the very man who was at the table with them and to determine how the UpLink license might be suspended or revoked. Expected representatives of both parliamentary chambers linked by their participation in a conspiracy, and a common warning—which had come to each of them in the form of an anonymously mailed photograph.

Instead . . .

Assele-Ndaki surveyed the room. Only Cangele and his aides were looking at him. All the rest of the men were focused everywhere but in his direction . . . some of them on the two-hundred-year-old rapiers and poniards against one wall, some on the cased set of eighteenth-century French pistols mounted opposite the sword collection, some examining the Chinese porcelain vases and expensive trinkets that filled various cabinet shelves. Others were merely staring at their hands or at vacant points in the air.

Assele-Ndaki turned his attention onto the senator whose invitation he had accepted. Seated at the president's left with his eyes on the table, Moubouyi appeared to sense his gaze. He met it with his own for the briefest of moments, then looked back down.

Cangele's deep-set eyes, meanwhile, continued to scrutinize Assele-Ndaki from his broad ebony face. The smile on his full mouth was quick, and often charming, but also unspontaneous and rarely invested with humor It had a demanding severity even at the most casual and relaxed moments . . . and the mood in the room was worlds from either.

Assele-Ndaki pushed forward across the floor to the table. The president wore an orange and white patterned *kente* batik shirt, collarless with wide bell sleeves. It was unusual attire for him. Cangele typically favored Western dress, custom suits from the renowned European boutiques.

The assemblyman sat.

"I trust," Cangele said to him, "no one present requires an introduction."

Assele-Ndaki gave a silent nod. How could the president have learned about the meeting? About the photograph? Could someone in this room have told him, committed an act of duplicity seeking to curry favor in the belief things would sooner or later come to light? Or perhaps he had found out through his secret eyes and ears throughout the government? But in the end these questions were unanswerable. Nor did his informant's identity and reasons matter. Cangele knew. He knew. One way or another, they would each of them who had planned to obstruct his goals bear the consequences.

"I mean no disrespect, but there are places I would much rather be," Cangele said. His eyes held steady on Assele-Ndaki's face. "Other ways I would have chosen to spend my Sunday afternoon." He triggered his smile again and gestured expansively with his left hand. His right continued to rest on the picture of Macie Nze, its touch flat and heavy. "Instead, I've been pressed into this working visit to Port-Gentil . . . into slipping out of the capital like a thief."

Assele-Ndaki said nothing. His tension was hard to separate from that of his fellow parliamentarians. It was a kind of flux in the room that seemed to radiate from each and accrete into something greater than the sum of its parts. He could feel it prickling his skin like current. When he breathed, it left the taste of steel nails at the back of his tongue.

"Mr. Assemblyman," Cangele said to him, "I know you and Macie Nze had close personal ties, and I wish to express my regrets and condolences over his death. My own direct dealings with him were infrequent, but I remember him as a committed and estimable public servant worthy of respect."

Assele-Ndaki nodded.

"Yes," he said. "There are many who will miss him."

"His savage abduction and murder was a waste. An intolerable act. You may take it as a given that the crime will not go unsolved . . . and that its perpetrators will not elude justice."

"Thank you, Mr. President."

Cangele took a deep breath, then released it through his nose and mouth. He was a large man with a bulging middle and his girth somehow gave the exhalation a tidal quality.

"Although they lack solid proof, my sources have cause to suspect Macie Nze's murder was connected to his falling awry of a mysterious political-influence peddler," he said. "An unidentified foreigner who has sought to hinder my telecommunications initiatives through means varying from financial incentives of questionable legality, to overt criminal bribes. And it pains me to say that some in our government might have been receptive to them."

The president's dark eyes remained clamped on Assele-Ndaki, who looked back at him in silence, not knowing how to answer, afraid to turn away.

"Jean Jacques," Senateur Moubouyi said at last. "Before you joined us, the president was asking our opinions—"

"Off the record, we must underscore," Ali Nagor said from farther down the table. He was an assemblyman from Mounga Province, to the east.

"Of course, I should have mentioned that," Moubouyi said. "President Cangele polled us, informally, about a proposition of amnesty for anyone who may have been lured into accepting the foreigner's inducements. As I understand it, explicit admissions of impropriety would not be required, but rather a simple and confidential pledge among all parliamentarians that none will occur in the future . . . with particular regard to the telecom issue."

Silence again. Then Nagor said, "The president is gratified by the National Assembly's approval of his UpLink licensing policies despite the shadowy lobbies that would have hindered them. And while he welcomes honest and open political debate, he likewise wishes to see the licenses ratified without further sabotage."

Assele-Ndaki did not react. He was trying to plainly understand the meaning of what he'd heard. President Cangele's dark eyes, still fixed on the assemblyman, made it difficult for him to think straight.

"So," Cangele said, then. "What have you to comment?"

Assele-Ndaki hesitated another moment.

"Loyal and good men may make mistakes they regret, Mr. President," he said. "As one who believes in the possibility of atonement, I would prefer such individuals be granted a chance to rectify their mistakes, rather than have their shame compounded by scandal and punishment. And I am convinced most would of them look on it with humble appreciation."

"And yet there is a hesitant note in your voice."

Assele-Ndaki's throat was dry and tight. He drank from the glass of water on the table beside him.

"Only because I would respectfully suggest that some might shy away from the opportunity to make amends out of self preservation," he said, and glanced at the photograph under Cangele's fingertips. "My dear friend Macie Nze was surely innocent of wrongdoing. But it could be that he was under strong persuasion to compromise his integrity, commit an indiscretion that would have weighed on his conscience . . . and was tortured and killed for his refusal. It gives me fear that the same could happen to the guilty who wish to redeem themselves. Or worse yet, to the people they love. These are men with families."

President Cangele was quiet, his smooth features thoughtful. He kept his gaze on Assele-Ndaki a while longer, and then let his eyes slowly move over the faces of the conclaved parliamentarians.

"No one in this room today has seen me. No one in this room has heard me," he said. "None of you . . . are we agreed?"

Heads were nodding around the table. Assele-Ndaki's was no exception.

Cangele smiled his ready, hard smile.

"I know what it is to be a family man. A husband. A father. And to my own bemusement, a recent grandfather," he said. "It is with my growing brood in mind that the commitment I've made toward a democratic future for our nation is constantly renewed. It is for them I wish to see Gabon become a model of social and governmental reform on our continent . . . and in doing so, someday make dinosaurs of autocrats like myself and insatiable bought-out scoundrels such as you gentlemen." He paused, the smile gradually dwindling from the corners inward. The fingers of his right hand tapped the photograph of Macie Nze, his left fist thumping his chest over the wax cloth shirt. "Still, I am African. My blood and heritage is African. I am therefore, by nature, an unromantic dreamer. The reality is that my plans for our republic have come under attack from forces of subversion and terror. And the attack must be repulsed. My pledge here is this: Stand with me now, as one, and you will have my fullest protection. Any past weaknesses you have shown will be excused. But let a single man in this room stand against me, continue his faithlessness, and you will see the offer pulled back from over you, leaving your heads open to whatever may fall on them—again as one. All of you will be reminded that I, too, know how to be terrible and threatening. Remember who I am, good sirs. *Remember my African blood.*"

A hush fell over the parlor. Though he'd continued to address the entire group as he concluded, the president's eyes had momentarily snapped back to Assele-Ndaki. Now he shifted them to the death photograph of Macie Nze, slid it away from himself, calmly leaned back in his chair, and folded his hands over the great mound of his stomach.

The silence stretched out a while longer. His face mild,

Cangele studied the section of tabletop he had cleared of the photograph.

Assele-Ndaki drank from his glass, a long swallow. He knew the question had been left for him to ask.

"How will our unity be announced?" Despite the water moistening his throat, his voice seemed to be issuing from the smallest pinhole.

Cangele smiled, as much to himself as to the others in the room. Quiet and impassive since Assele-Ndaki's arrival, one of the presidential aides turned toward the assemblyman and regarded him with sudden interest, as if having become aware of his presence for the first time.

"We have arranged for an article to appear in the morning paper," he said.

Pete Nimec and Vince Scull waited under the hot yellow sun in the market of Le Grand Village, holding *pain beurre* they had bought on their way into the plaza, the pan fried, heavily buttered breads greasy in their wax-paper wraps. There were throngs of people around them. Hawkers, shoppers, beggars. Many of the latter were children with the filmy stares of *oncho*—a parasitic river blindness—who squatted at the periphery of the square. In a wildlife dealer's stall some yards to the right, a bright green parrot fluttered on its perch in a crude screen cage atop a display table fashioned of two wooden barrels that had been bound together with a thick hemp rope. Fluffs of emerald down clung to the cage's rusty metal bars like dandelion seeds. The newspapers lining the bottom of the cage were covered with a thick dry encrustation of droppings and cracked nut shells. A second parrot lay unmoving in the layer of waste, dead or close to dead. In a bloody canvas sack hanging from a post above the cage, an unseen creature released a shrill animal cry as it thrashed repeatedly against the cloth in a vain struggle to free itself.

Nimec turned from the stall, swallowing a bite of his fry bread without appetite. It was like he'd hurled the food down into a ditch. The happy traveler.

He desperately missed Annie and the kids.

He looked over Scull's shoulder toward the north end of the outdoor market and spotted Steve DeMarco and Andy Wade approaching through a crowded aisle. They were a conspicuous pair. Both men had on pastel short-sleeved shirts, while the Gabonese strongly preferred colorful prints . . . or simple undyed kaftans in the case of the population's devout Muslims. DeMarco's whiteness and Wade's blackness made them even easier standouts. Whites in this country were almost always foreigners—expats or short-term visitors—and lived in a sort of proximate separation with the nationals. Stranger that he was here, Nimec's study of his mission briefs, and his first-hand impressions of the place, pointed toward very little true social mingling between people of different races. They shared the same streets, stayed at the same hotels, and ate at the same restaurants in self-segregated clusters. What interactions they had seemed driven mainly by commerce and politics.

The relaxed companionability of the two Sword ops as they walked together would leave observers with scant doubt they were of another place and culture.

Scull had noticed Nimec looking past him.

"See anybody?" he said.

"Yeah," Nimec said. "DeMarco and Wade."

Scull grunted and bit into his fry bread. He was sweating profusely, his sparse hair pasted to his head, dark rings of moisture staining the underarms of his shirt.

"Ackerman's on his way in, too," he said. "Coming from behind you."

Nimec gave him a nod. That accounted for everybody except Conners, who was decoying.

He and Scull waited in the pressing afternoon heat and humidity. After a few moments the men reached them.

They exchanged nods.

"Hail, hail, the gang's all here," Scull said.

DeMarco looked briefly at him, then turned to Nimec.

"You think we ought to take a walk?" he said.

Nimec jerked his head slightly to indicate the surrounding crush of market buyers.

"I like it where we are," he said. "Best place to be right now."

DeMarco nodded his understanding. A congested area offered its own type of cover—the people in circulation around them would present a constant and changing impediment to an observer's line of sight.

"Okay, let's compare notes," Nimec said to him.

"We were tailed."

"Wheels or heels?"

"Wheels," DeMarco said. "A-B."

Meaning he and Wade had been subjects of a two-car vehicular surveillance.

"The lead driver was a cabbie outside the hotel," Wade said, looking down as he spoke to partially mask his lips from view. "He wasn't interested in fares, ignored a whole bunch of people at the stand. Pulls out behind us, follows slow and tight. Then he turns off, and somebody else in a regular car picks up the tail."

"The hack show himself again?" Nimec said.

"Cruises by about five blocks farther on, disappears," DeMarco said. "I think he might've been worried he got burned."

Nimec stood in thoughtful silence.

"Heels for Scull and me," he said after a moment. "A-B-C."

Meaning the surveillance placed on them had consisted of a three-man foot team. And it hadn't been half bad. There had been a man in an embroidered kufi hat and dashiki talking into a cell phone as he stepped from an apartment building near the hotel. Another two men in casual Western clothes, strolling together on the opposite side of the avenue, moving almost abreast of them. The men across the street had seemed to be conversing with each other, but then Nimec, noticing one of them wore an earbud headset, realized he was also on a cellular. Just as Dashiki had passed Nimec and Scull and turned into a store, Earbud crossed to their side of the avenue, dropping back, taking Dashiki's position at the rear. A few blocks later they pulled another switch. Earbud quickening his pace, then passing. Dashiki reappearing behind them, trailing them again, a quick shopper that one. Meanwhile, lo and behold, Earbud's friend had kept pace across the avenue. The leapfrogging had continued almost the entire way to the market.

Nimec glanced at Ackerman.

"How about you?" he said.

"A pair of gendarmes in a patrol car," Ackerman said. He was shaking his head in the negative, a ploy to confuse hidden eyes. "Right up until I got into the market."

Nimec kept looking at him. "You sure?"

"Positive. Black uniforms. They split off after Conners."

Nimec was quiet again. When DeMarco had told him about being caught on camera at the Rio, the first thing to enter his mind was the possibility of corporate espionage. Several Asian and European telecom carriers had been competing to become the African fiber ring's savior when Planétaire went belly up, and it was conceivable one or more of them could have gotten upset enough to go over the top when UpLink won its contract with the

Gabonese government, figuring they could still gum up the deal. There were also various national lobbying groups that had joined in opposition to yet another dominant foreign company moving in its assets and tried to block UpLink's entry with a passel of legislative maneuvers once they happily bade adieu to Planétaire. A few were still making moves despite the ruling party's obvious support. Any of these interests, or combination of interests, could have decided to do some peeping.

Except Nimec had nothing but questions about what their game might be. Add them to the questions he'd been left with after talking to Pierre Gunville, and there were more than he could count . . . though bundling them all together in his head was almost certainly a bad idea. He had a vague mistrust of Gunville, but at this stage, it was merely that. Nimec didn't know whether it meant Gunville was connected to anything he needed to be concerned about, let alone to whoever was messing with UpLink. The truth was he didn't know what was going on. But the involvement of the gendarmerie was heavy, and he would need to start producing some answers fast.

Nimec took a bite of his fry bread and chewed. Happy, happy business traveler enjoying a treat on his off day . . . and how was he to know talking with a mouth full of food was hell on lip readers?

"The termite that hopped out at you this morning," he said. "You know the real problem?"

DeMarco indicated he did with a grunt as he shook his head no, borrowing Ackerman's little mixed signal trick.

"For every one you spot, there's a hundred more you don't," he said. "If they're infesting us, we'd need a Big Sniffer to find all of them."

Nimec swallowed perfunctorily. The Big Sniffer was Sword's most sophisticated countermeasure sweep unit. But the device was hardly inconspicuous. Used with a boomerang antenna for scanning walls and other surfaces, its microcomputer-controlled instrumentation was carried in what amounted to a medium-size hardshell suitcase.

"If the termites on the surface twitch their feelers, they'll stir up the nest," he said, wiping his lips with his napkin. "We'd get rid of the soldiers and workers, but the breeding colony would just go deeper into the wood."

DeMarco nodded.

"I've been hashing that over," he said. "And I haven't come up with a solution."

Scull shrugged.

"Think garnets," he said.

DeMarco looked at him.

"And ilmenites," Scull said.

DeMarco continued to stare.

"Think *what*?" he said.

"Garnets. Ilmenites. Diamond hunters look for 'em when they analyze soil samples from termite mounds here in Africa," Scull explained, as if the termite reference would surely make the pertinence of his declarations clear. "They aren't worth much by themselves, but come from the same underground layers as diamonds. Termites carry tiny ones up from something like a hundred fifty feet underground, where their breeders live, and deposit them in their little hills. That's how the Orapa mine in Botswana, richest in the world, got discovered."

DeMarco remained clueless. As did the others.

"I have to confess, Vince," he said, "I don't know what the hell you're talking about."

Nimec was thoughtful. The fact was, neither did he.

Scull frowned, put an arm around Nimec's shoulders, turned a hundred eighty degrees to his right, and gestured at random toward a vender's stall. Nimec squared around with him as though to study an item of mutual interest, gazed absently at a woman selling thick cuts of bush meat. They were laid out on a table in the open sunlight, under netting meant to repel clusters of large black flies. The handwritten signs on the table behind them read: *MALLE DE ÉLÉPHANT, SERVEAU DE SINGE.*

"Elephant trunks, monkey brains," Scull said, translating aloud. "In case you're interested in buying, the monkeys around here can carry ebola."

"Thanks."

"Any time." Scull pursed his lips and spouted air up over his face to dry off some sweat, simultaneously fanning himself with one hand. "That problem you mentioned . . . it occurs to me the best idea might be we don't do anything."

Nimec looked at him in silence a moment. Then his eyes narrowed.

"Leave the termites alone?"

Scull squeezed his arm, his expression that of a teacher who had broken through to a slow but earnest student.

"There you go, Petey. We wait. Keep the lights off. Let those droops keep working away figuring they're safe in the dark," he said, using Scullian shorthand for "dirty rotten snoops." "The stuff they leave behind's worthless crap, 'long as we know it's there."

"But it tells us where to find the diamonds."

"You got it. When we're ready, we dig down into the nests where the breeders are crawling around and make sure to bring along our cans of Raid . . . you remember the slogan from those old TV ads?"

Nimec looked at him.

Kills bugs dead, he thought.

DeMarco had joined them in pretending to be interested in the meat seller, comprehension dawning across his features as he listened.

"What do you think?" Nimec asked him.

"If we run with Scull's idea," he said, "I'm guessing our execs and engineers would need to be informed."

Nimec gave him a nod. They would. Informed of everything. So they could know what not to say and do in the false privacy of their hotel rooms or elsewhere.

"It might not appeal much to them," DeMarco said. "I can testify getting naked in the shower this morning wasn't a comfortable experience. And the rest of my personal business was even less fun."

"You don't need to get graphic on us," Scull said. "I just ate."

Nimec looked at them.

"Unless somebody's got a better solution," he said, "they'll have to live with it. The same as we will."

DeMarco took a deep breath, blew the air out with a long sigh.

"I'd hate to be the one who tells that to Tara Cullen," he said.

Aboard the *Chimera*, Harlan DeVane stood looking west over the deck rail as the evening sun swooned into the sea, its sputtering tropical fire reflected in orange dabs on the water's surface.

DeVane's fingers wanted to tighten around his black line cell phone, but he resisted the angry urge, willing the hand to remain steady.

"This word you've gotten from your source at the newspaper," he said into the cellular's mouthpiece. "There is no question about its accuracy?"

"No," Etienne Begela said from his end of their connection. "A declaration of multiparty government ratification of the telecom licenses is to be announced on the front page of tomorrow morning's edition. In accordance with the Cangele agenda, they are to be ratified without further review for a minimum of fifteen years. All key members of the president's parliamentary opposition have adopted a revised stance in his favor, and there is to be a public display of solidarity in the capital." A pause. "I hold in my hand a facsimile of the article's first draft. It is to appear in *L'Union*."

"The government's voice."

"Correct."

DeVane thought in silence, felt the mild heaving of the deck under his feet. The still air smelled of brine and throbbed faintly with the sound of the offshore pumps.

This would look bad for him, and he could not afford it. Not once more could he afford it. While he had always expected his endeavors here would be of finite duration, he would need time to maximize their profitability. And winning it meant taking a calculated gamble.

"When is the UpLink team to tour the headquarters site in Sette Cama?"

"Also tomorrow."

"Their head of security will be among those going?"

"As it stands, yes. I've readied the contingency plan for implementation."

"Its threads must not lead to me. Nor anywhere close."

"That was of highest importance, *naturellement*. My only concern is its amplitude. That the scope of its enactment will lead them to look beyond appearances."

Of course it would, DeVane thought. It was what he wanted—something to stagger and confuse UpLink at its moment of success, and foster insecurities among its financial backers. Let them imagine their enemies coming from all sides, and wonder who they were . . . so long as the answers to their questions remained entwined in mystery.

DeVane stared out at the dying sunlight and nodded. Begela made for the perfect functionary; his mind was like an orderly desk drawer in a drab office. Reach inside, and you would find every needed supply in the right place, but never a single surprise.

"Proceed," he said, and did not wait for a response before terminating the call and going below to send Kuhl his notification.

Big Sur. The balance of the day trembling at midnight's edge. Occasional breezes blowing across the open canyon from the sea, strong and thick with moisture, blurring the long drop down in kettle swirls of mist.

Siegfried Kuhl sat before his notebook computer, reading an e-mail he had received only moments ago, his rigid features bathed in the amber firelight of a kerosene storm lamp on the living-room mantel. Around his desk, the huge black Schutzhund dogs lay quiet. Two of them slept, their sides rising and falling with their slow, regular breaths. The third watched the cabin door at Kuhl's back. It was a pack instinct reinforced through training. By turns, one of the shepherds would remain awake and vigilant at all times.

The coded message displayed in front of Kuhl said:

If the cuckoo calls when the hedge is brown,
Sell thy horse and buy thy corn

In European folklore, the song of the cuckoo heard in September or October—when the hedge is brown—is an ill portent to farmers. An omen that the autumn food harvest is imperiled, warning them to be ready to take counteractive measures, and fill their stores with that which is most precious for survival throughout the long, cold months to come.

Kuhl stared at the computer. *His* time, then, was coming. Coming very soon.

He closed his e-mail program and opened his digital image viewer. Arranged in several rows across the screen now were scrupulously labeled folders of photographic stills. Kuhl opened one of them, selecting an image set of a blond woman he knew to be of early middle age, although his eyes glinted with cold appreciation of her exceptionally youthful appearance. Tall, slender, elegant, and stylishly dressed, Ashley Gordian possessed the refined beauty that came of good genes and exquisite care.

The first series of high-resolution frames showed her lunching with another woman at an outdoor café. In the next, Kuhl saw her through the clear glass walls of Palo Alto's main library branch on Newell Street, the camera following her as she checked out her pile of books at the loan desk and carried them onto the patio. The next group was taken from outside a clothing boutique. Through its storefront window, she had been photographed at the sales counter signing for a credit card purchase, then smiling at the cashier as she was handed her bags, then carrying them to the door. On the street, she had walked directly to her parked Lexus sedan and driven off with her purchases in the backseat.

There were more images of Ashley Gordian that Kuhl could have examined. Dozens more. Ciras and the others had recorded her movements on camera for almost two weeks, storing and sorting them in computer memory, e-mailing the encrypted files to him in Madrid.

But it was not the wife he leaned toward targeting.

Kuhl reached for his glass of mild wine and drank. Then he closed the folder he had been browsing, moved down a row, and selected another.

In this one, he found the daughter. She was lovely in her own right. Slim, dark haired, a firm well-proportioned body. Kuhl saw echoes of the mother in her—the smooth skin, the large green eyes, a certain underlying confidence in the lift of her shoulders, the straightness with which she bore herself.

He carefully studied the numbered screen shots in front of him. They composed a sequential record of Julia Gordian's daily patterns of activity. An album of mundane, forgettable events that would allow Kuhl to plan and execute the unforgettable. There were images of the daughter in the company of friends, male and female. There were images of her shopping for groceries, bringing clothes to the dry cleaner, visiting the post office. There were images of her driving out to the canine rescue shelter where she volunteered her services, turning onto its hidden country drive outside the state park's verdant spread of woodland. There were images of her pulling the vehicle into her garage on her return home. And images taken through her bedroom window. Kuhl studied these for a while, sipped his wine, then moved on. One series of photos followed her as she left the house in jogging clothes, the two race hounds attached to their leash at her side. They seemed to vibrate with tension, their taut whiplike forms emphasizing their predisposition toward flight. Nature had given them swiftness at the expense of courage; their breed was wind without stone. Faced with a threat, they would offer no protection, but attempt to escape from harm. Kuhl could almost see the fear glazing their eyes as they were pounced, their throat-blood spilling over the clamp of toothy jaws.

Kuhl stared at his computer screen and contemplated his mission in silence.

Find what Roger Gordian most loves. Strike at it, and we will have struck at his heart.

But if his heart's utmost love were shared in equal measure by wife and child? Where then to deal the piercing blow?

The wife was a viable prospect, yes. Because she was often in the hardened security of Gordian estate, or with Gordian himself, she would be the lesser target of opportunity as a practical matter. But Kuhl's surveillance also indicated she regularly ventured off alone—and on those instances there would be openings.

Practicality, however, could not be a determinant. Kuhl had studied Gordian for years now. Hard target or soft, he would go after whichever won him the ultimate objective. And for that reason he was leaning toward the daughter for maximum effect.

Gordian's marriage stood on a commitment made by two. On assumptions of mutual responsibility; paired choices, hopes, and dreams. And paired risks. Take the wife, and some part of the foundation they had built together might survive, leave Gordian with the spirit to recover. But the child was meant to carry the future on her wings. The risks they had chosen for themselves were not hers to bear. And *this* child. This daughter. Strong, living freely, forward-moving and sure of herself . . .

With his daughter held hostage, Gordian would be paralyzed, unable to function. And when her wings were crushed, and the hopes and dreams she embodied died in Kuhl's clenched fist, it would irreparably break Gordian, ruin him in every way.

Kuhl sat silently in the lamplight as the marine fog crawled up against his cabin windows and unsettled gusts of wind whipped across its roof. Eyes alert, ears pricked, the watchful black shepherd canted its head up toward the creaking beams and rafters.

After a time Kuhl tapped the keyboard of his laptop and once again accessed Harlan DeVane's secure e-mail server. Then he typed:

A robin red-breast in a cage,
Puts all heaven in a rage.

The message sent, Kuhl turned off his computer and sat still again.

Outwardly, he appeared to be relaxed in his chair.

At his center, he felt Destiny's great spoked wheel rumble heavily through a momentous turn.

SEVEN

From the *Wall Street Journal* Online Edition:

UPLINK AND SEDCO CONNECT IN CENTRAL-SOUTHERN WEST AFRICA
*Lines of Convergence Drawn in Light between
Telco and Power Industry Titans*

SAN JOSE—Less than two weeks after UpLink International finalized its White Knight takeover and development of the African fiberoptic network left abandoned by the sudden pullout of financially strapped European rival Planétaire Systems Corp., UpLink has injected the troubled marine fiberoptics market with yet another surge of stockholder attention, winning an estimated $30 million contract with Texas-based Sedco Petroleum to wire its regional subsea facilities into the carrier system. The new network segment will deliver high-speed phone and Internet/Intranet connections between Sedco's growing string of platforms in the Gulf of Guinea and their coastal offices and is expected to increase the quality and reliability of communications for the oil company's marine-drilling operations.

Financial analysts are in general agreement that the

deal will benefit both parties. Sedco stands to increase production from its facilities and heighten its prestige in a region where competition is intense for the leasing of offshore fields. UpLink likewise will receive a considerable economic and public relations boost from the move, quieting speculative jitters that its African project would sap corporate revenues at a time when most telcos are scaling back the pace of expansion, and investor optimism in broadband remains low due to lingering aftershocks from the dotcom implosion and consumer reticence toward new media technologies, such as video-on-demand and live-event multicasting.

In a symbolic display of commitment for the fast-track prioritization of their plans, Sedco Chairman of the Board Hugh Bennett, and UpLink Founder and CEO Roger Gordian—the latter almost absent from the public eye since his near-fatal illness several years ago—have informed the *Wall Street Journal* that they will attend a formal contract-signing ceremony sometime next month aboard one of Sedco's state-of-the-art drill platforms off Gabon, not coincidentally the hub of UpLink International's African fiber network. Only the size of Colorado, with a population of under two million, the country nonetheless can boast of a relatively stable civil infrastructure and accelerated democratic reforms under President Adrian Cangele, offering foreign companies a lower-risk host environment than its notoriously chaotic regional neighbors—among them Cameroon, Congo, the Democratic Republic of the Congo (formerly Zaire), and Angola.

This is not to suggest that Gabon is anything close to a Western investor's paradise. UpLink's large and formidable private security force has acquired a worldwide reputation. But despite Cangele's reform measures, a complex political landscape and employee safeguard issues have led many other corporations to remain wary of their practical ability to conduct business in the tiny nation. . . .

From *L'Union* Online
(limited content English version):

PRESIDENT CANGELE AND PARLIAMENT SHARE IN JOYOUS RECEPTION FOR UPLINK INTERNATIONAL

LIBREVILLE—In a gathering scheduled for later today, His Excellency El Hadj President Adrian Cangele and senior Parliamentary lawmakers will stand together beneath the graceful marble portico of the Presidential Palace to ratify a fifteen-year grant of the UpLink tele-communications licenses that had been early approved by the National Assembly. This frees the way for Up-Link's installation of a state-of-the-art fiberoptic network throughout the continent, and reaffirms the Republic of Gabon's position as undisputed leader in Africa's technological and economic rise to maturity on the global stage.

By confirming Uplink's long-term franchise, President Cangele has given the company renewed confidence to proceed with its establishment of a headquarters complex in the Sette Cama region without concern that current network building operations could be interrupted by political sea changes. A further provision of the charter enables the Ministry of Transportation to deepen funding for construction of a modern paved highway from Port-Gentil to the Sette Cama, a difficult linkage that currently requires passage by air, river boat, or truck over dirt roads that are prone to flooding in the rainy season and plagued by scattered outbreaks of banditry, acts primarily committed by cross-border infiltrators (see feature article **Cameroonian and Congolese Lawlessness**). While UpLink will be a major beneficiary of upgraded travel to the region, it will also prove a splendid boon to agriculturists and lumbermen in far outlying areas, allowing easier distribution of their products to domestic and international markets. Increased tourism to the Sette Cama's Iguéla and Loango National Wilderness Reserves, long attractive to photographic safari planners and sport fishermen, is viewed as an additional economic dividend for Gabon.

In a demonstration of its openhanded cooperative relationship with the Cangele administration, UpLink International has offered to defray a large portion of the highway's construction cost with corporate funding. While no specific financial amount has been disclosed, its promised subsidy is rumored to be in excess of $10 million U.S., ensuring that no unfair tax burden will be imposed on residents of Port-Gentil and its surrounding districts.

Shortly before this story went to press, President Cangele was asked about media stories of political opposition to his aggressive backing of the UpLink licenses. "The stories were classic sensationalistic exaggerations," he told our reporter, adding, "It is praiseworthy that none such accounts appeared in *L'Union*, our national beacon of journalistic integrity and accuracy."

The president went on to explain that there has been no significant governmental dispute over the idea that UpLink International represents the nation's telecommunications future.

"Any divisions that may have emerged concerned minor timing and procedural issues and were settled by

brotherly, well-ordered debate," he said. "My appearance
with the foremost members of all our coalition parties
will show that, regardless of political or tribal affiliations,
the Gabonese people are joined by common principle,
and a wish to champion West Africa's shift from continuous cycles of violence and revolution to progressive,
harmonious evolution at the dawn of the twenty-first century."

From *L'Union* Online
(limited content English version):

CAMEROONIAN AND CONGOLESE LAWLESSNESS: WHO IS IN CHARGE NEXT DOOR?

FRANCEVILLE—Before sunrise on September 25,
Abasi Aseme, 64, left his home in the village of Garabinzam accompanied by his three adult sons and several
carts packed with furs, ivory, and a modest quantity of
panned gold bought from Minkébé camp diggers, their
little mule train bound for a trader's market thirty miles
to the south at the northern edge of Djoua Valley. They
had made the trip through the lower Minkébé Forest
every week for decades and were welcome callers at supply outposts along their sparsely traveled path. One of
these posts was owned by Abasi's older brother, Youssou.

When the Aseme family did not make their regular
stop around noon, Youssou became concerned: in the
remote bushland, a dangerous stalking ground for animal
and human predators, locals know to travel by daylight
or not at all. By early evening Youssou's concern had

turned to unease, and then to worry. The Asemes still had not appeared. Nor would they after darkness fell. Abasi did not have a telephone, and there was no way of contacting his brother's wife to see whether anything might have occurred to delay his usual market visit.

Early the next morning Youssou and a small party of friends went out in search of his relatives, striking out north toward Garabinzam. Two hours later, the missing traders were found murdered, their wagons and merchandise gone. The killings had been savage. All four victims had their throats cut, their bodies lined in a row on the trail, their legs hacked off below the knees and tossed into the nearby brush, where it must have been evident the body parts would be discovered immediately.

Among Cameroonian bandits, mutilation of the lower extremities is considered a message to those who might be inclined toward pursuit, a well-known signal that they would best keep their own legs from leading them to certain death.

The Asemes are but the latest casualties in repetitive waves of attacks on rural Gabonese by *coupeurs de route*, armed thieves who have fled from antigang crackdowns in Yaoundé and Ambam in Cameroon using graft to buy the cooperation of police and slipping easily through porous border checkpoints along the Minkébé wilderness's mountain ridges. Once believed to pose a threat only at our country's northernmost boundaries, these thugs have in recent months formed alliances of convenience with splinter guerrilla bands made fugitive by Congolese political conflict, and together staged raids on townships such as N'Dendé, deep in our country's interior, with scattered incidents of road ambush reported as far south as the Iguéla, Loango, and Sette Cama Forests near the coast. The stepped up violence has led Gabonese law enforcement officials to ask their colleagues across the border when they intend to take responsibility for apprehending their vicious castoffs. . . .

**From the *Cameroon Tribune* Online
—Editorial
(translated from the French):**

GABON'S NATIONAL CREDO: IF YOU
CANNOT COMPETE, CONDEMN!

by Motmou Benote
Let us begin with the obvious: gang violence and brigandage are unacceptable wherever they may originate. But unless Gabon ceases it efforts to make others accountable for the outlaw problem in its northern districts, casting blame elsewhere rather than engaging in an aggressive pursuit of homegrown malefactors and tribal agitators, its police and military forces will soon be pointing their guns skyward to guard against menaces from distant galaxies. . . .

They toiled in the steamy midmorning heat, a dozen men in jungle fatigues swinging their machetes through the parched brown sedge and waxy clusters of euphorbia beside the dirt road. They kept their sleeves rolled down and wore heavy protective gloves, taking care to cover their skin; the succulents were filled with burning latex juice, and had thorny spurs all along the ribs of their fat, tangled branches.

The men thrashed at the dense vegetation. Their head wraps were drenched with sweat. The camouflage hoods they would put on were still stuffed in their pockets, unneeded as yet. There were no eyes about to see them, and they were not in any hurry to feel the heavyweight Nomex/Kevlar fabric slicken against their streaming wet cheeks and brows.

They worked in the heat, worked ceaselessly, creating clear fields of fire for their ambush. Their shoulder-slung Milkor 5.56-mm semiautomatic rifles were of South African origin, as were the lightweight 60-mm commando mortars and multishot barrel-loaded grenade launchers hidden farther back in their 4×4. Two Shmel RPO-A infantry rocket tubes rounded out their arsenal of heavy weapons, the "Bumblebee" variants designed to fire fuel-air explosive warheads.

A Russian military specialty used to devastating effect during their Chechen campaigns, man-portable thermobaric hardware cannot be purchased cheaply on the black market.

The job's sponsors had been anything but close fisted.

Although some members of the band had equipped their mortar tubes with reticulated, microprocessor-controlled electronic sights, most felt the attachments were burdensome and off-balancing to their aim. Kirdi and Kulani bushmen from northern Cameroon, they had been raised with the bow and arrow as rural Americans might be with the hunting rifle. Where seasonal drought defeats cultivation of food crops, live game is a vital source of protein, and the need to kill or go hungry does more to perfect one's weaponry skills than gun sport. For these men, the ability to acquire a target was basic to their survival, and they were masters at calculating range and determining projectile trajectories.

Five hundred feet ahead of them, the dirt track plunged eastward into a thick, shaded grove of mixed okoumé and bubinga, where a smaller group chopped at the tree trunks with axes, perspiration glistening on their muscled brown arms, their blades snarling in epiphytic vines that coiled up and up around the bark into the leafy green crowns.

The trees crashed down one by one and were rolled across the road. Then branches, brush, and pieces of slashed vines were strewn over the felled trunks to lay a screen of foliage over the ax cuts. Obscured from sight by broken patterns of shadow, the treefall blended into the overgrowth from a distance, and to the drivers of the line of approaching vehicles, would appear to be a natural phenomenon. Long before they might inspect it closely enough to learn otherwise, their convoy would be surrounded on all sides.

Another indispensable survival tool of the hunter is his knowledge of how to exploit the terrain for camouflage and concealment.

The group's construction of their road block took a little under two hours. When they were satisfied the job was done, several of them went over to join their fellows in the copse of tall grass and succulents, while others spread out amid the trees. A single man scaled up a bubinga to saddle himself in a fork of its widespread limbs and find a comfortable position for his Steyr SG550 sniper gun, custom-railed with an AN/PIS thermal, day/night sight.

The men in the copse had also finished their preparations of the area. Their gloves and uniforms tacked with spines and dripping the pasty, whitish secretions of the euphorbia stems, they had cut fire lanes that were as unobtrusive as the log barrier.

Now the band of hired jungle fighters would plant their mortars, and rest, and wait.

It would be a while yet before the UpLink convoy reached them.

A few minutes before the outset of the Sette Cama supply and inspection run, Pete Nimec stood talking with Steve

DeMarco, Joel Ackerman, and Vince Scull at the airport parking area where their UpLink team had gathered. Nimec was leaning back against the driver's side of a modified Sword Land Rover, elbows propped on the hood. The other three faced him in a close ring. Their tight little huddle around Nimec, and the 4×4's bulking frame behind him, would make it tough for anyone watching from out of sight to monitor their speech.

"The company execs ready over there?" Nimec said, and nodded toward a nearby line of Rovers and trucks.

"Tucked into their seats nice and comfy," DeMarco said, "And actually glad to be headed into the jungle after finding out about the termites."

Nimec couldn't say he blamed them. "Freight loaded up?"

DeMarco gave an affirmative nod.

"Okay," Nimec said. "It's a broiler today, but let's be sure we wear our vests. No exceptions. There should be extras stowed in the Rovers for the execs. We all know our jobs. Stay alert."

"Knowing we've got the crawling eye on us," Ackerman said, "it sort of comes easy, chief."

Nimec looked at him. "I'm just being careful," he said. "The bugging surprises me, but it doesn't knock me out of my socks. After Antarctica, our base getting hit hard on a continent where there isn't even supposed to be guns, I half expect anything. You need to remember where we are. This country's surrounded by other countries where nobody's in charge of the farm. Or everybody claims to be. I can imagine how some of the authorities here just might feel threatened by foreigners."

"Even ones bearing gifts," DeMarco said. "You think that could be the reason we're being scoped? Some eager-beaver gendarme trying to impress his bosses?"

Nimec shrugged his shoulders.

"I don't know. Don't get me wrong, I'm not about to downplay the seriousness of it. My gut tells me there's a better than even chance we're onto something else. But until we firm up our information, we should be careful about what we assume." He paused, then shrugged again. "My point right now's really that for the past week or so you've been protecting material assets. Ground freight. Everybody here knows it can put you into a certain mode. Today, with the VIPs going out, things are different. What we need to watch out for is different. There are human beings to protect. And I want to make sure we don't let our guard down for a second. That we do what we always do when there's more than the usual set of considerations about the safety of our personnel."

The men were quiet.

Nimec watched a jet make its takeoff from the runway, gain altitude, and bank in their direction, its airframe reflecting the high sun, a silvery flare of brightness rushing across the open sky. The *shoom* of its turbos grew loud as it flew overhead and then began to fade.

Nimec turned toward Scull.

"What's on your docket while we're gone, Vince?"

"I want to follow up on the business with those French divers," Scull said, and motioned with his chin. "We know the Rover's clean?"

Nimec glanced toward DeMarco for an answer.

"Yeah," he said. "I wouldn't advise you to make any deep personal confessions in standard-issue vehicles like the one I've been driving around town, but these modified babies are checked for bugs at least once a day. Besides, they haven't been anywhere except here at the airport, or over at the HQ site, where we've had men posted around the clock. Nobody besides our own's gone near them."

"What about guides and workmen?" Nimec said.

"They ride in the trucks or the standards. This vehicle's okay, rest assured. If you don't trust me, you can count on its intruder shock or bug detection systems. Take your pick."

"Intruder shock?" Scull said.

"Anybody lays a hand on it who shouldn't gets hit with fifty thousand volts, the same as with a stun gun. The zapper's set every night."

Scull nodded.

"Good enough, I just found myself a phone booth," he said. Then he stepped past Nimec to the driver's door and pulled it open. "You guys chill out a minute, I gotta make an important call."

"Hello, Fred Sherman—"

"Sherm, it's Vince," Scull said into his secure cellular. It was much cooler inside the Rover than out on the blacktop, its mirrored windows blocking the sun's powerful rays. "Since when do you personally answer your phone?"

"Since my receptionist left for the day along with everybody else who works sane hours," said Sherman at the other end of the line. He was one of the top data hounds in Scull's risk-assessment office at UpLink SanJo. "How's it going?"

"Don't fucking ask."

"Nice to hear you sounding happy."

"I try to be consistent," Scull said. "Look, I need some info."

"Sure. Tell me what it is, I'll get on it first thing tomorrow."

"I mean I need it right now."

"Vince, it's almost seven o'clock at night—"

"Not here in Africa, it isn't." Scull glanced at the dashboard clock. "Here in Africa, where I happen to be, it's still before ten in the morning. The day's young and the sun's shining and it feels like a goddamn furnace."

"Vince, come on. Another ten minutes, *five* minutes, I would have been out the door—"

"Good I caught you when I did, then," Scull growled. "Is it a fluke or miracle of God, I wonder?"

"Ah crap, Vince, don't do this to me—"

"You know the submarine cable maintenance outfit we contracted for our Gabon operation? Nautel?"

"Of course, I did most of the research on it—"

"Which is why I don't have to explain how it's the same fleet owner that was doing the job for Planétaire . . . and why I called you and not somebody else," Scull said. "I want to see records from both companies about the African fiber outage back in May . . ."

"Oh. Well, that ought to be easy enough. I already have scads of them in my files . . ."

"And everything they've got on the accident that killed those two Nautel divers. *Everything*, Sherm. Internal review documents, too."

"Different story there." Sherman's tone had lifted and sunk. "Nautel's almost sure to cooperate, especially since we still haven't inked our contracts. But it's hard to get through to anybody who's upper rung at Planétaire right now. With the company going bust, and those irregular accounting practices, quote unquote, being covered in the media, their top execs are all bolting down into hidey-holes. And taking their paper shredders with them."

"More reason to pull the slimebags out by their necks," Scull said.

"Just like that, huh?"

"Right. You figure out where we've got leverage. And use it."

A prolonged sigh of resignation over the phone.

"Okay, I'll try my best," Sherman said. "Where do I fax the docs?"

"You don't. Send them by 'crypted e-mail," Scull said. "You need to talk to me about anything, dial up my cell. And from now on, don't forward any messages to me at the hotel. Not even a hi-how-are-you from my kids. Or that brunette I've been seeing."

"The racked stripper?"

"Amber's a sultry erotic dancer," Scull said. "But, yeah, she's the one."

"Christ, this does sound serious."

"I *said* it was important shit. What the hell, you think I just got an urge to jerk your chain?"

"Christ," Sherman repeated. "I'll get back to you fast as I can."

"Do that," Scull said. "I'm gonna be waiting at my computer."

"Look, rush job or not, this could take a while—"

"I've got a while. In fact, I've got all day. Send me what you can, and make it plenty. Meantime, I need to find an Internet café and plug in."

"You sitting with a crowd of backpacking hipsters at a cyber café? Somehow I can't picture it, Vince."

Scull shrugged in the driver's seat.

"Why not?" he said. "If a guy's main goal is to be an anonymous nobody, there's no better place for it in the whole stinking world."

The UpLink convoy made good time for the first twenty miles of its trip out of Port-Gentil. But it was barely past noon when the populous townships beyond the city thinned out across the low, barren countryside and the string of vehicles left the paved coastal road to drudge over rutted sand and laterite.

At the head of the column, a group of local guides

drove one of the unmodified Rovers. Rumbling along after it was a big, squarish 6×6 cargo truck with a loaded-down flatbed trailer. Pete Nimec occupied the front passenger seat of the tricked-out Land Rover in the third slot, DeMarco behind the right-hand steering wheel, a group of four engineers and company officers in back. Then came another armored Rover for the company honchos driven by Wade and Ackerman, followed by a plain vanilla filled with Sword ops and local hired hands. Next were two more 6×6 haulers. Hollinger, Conners, and an assortment of bigwigs and technicians rode seventh and last in the only remaining armored vehicle.

Soon they were rolling between the southern shore of N'dogo Lagoon and a belt of intermittent jungle and scrubland along the Atlantic Ocean. Sunlight poured down on the trail to throw a blinding white glare off the grainy material spread in uneven heaps beneath their wheels. Nimec could see heat-shimmers over his Rover's wide steel hood as the feeble output from its air-conditioner vents blew lukewarm on his neck and face. Outside his window, slender smooth-barked cypresses rose straight as lamp poles from small island mounds in the lagoon. Storks and egrets stood in the straw-colored reeds at its fringes, some with their long necks bowed to drink. There was no hint of a breeze. Everything seemed still and torpid in the settled dry-season heat. The only motion Nimec observed was from animals along the lagoon bank darting off at the sound of the diesel engines, but it was always out of the corner of his eye, and always too late to catch more than a blurry glimpse of some startled creature—a sleek body, a whip of a tail—as it splashed beneath the surface.

Then lagoon and forest receded behind the convoy, and for a time there was just flat drab savanna spreading out and away from the margins of the narrow vehicle trail.

Sette Cama had been an active British camp in the middle of the nineteenth century. What remained of it now was a loose scattering of wooden huts and bunga-lows that rose from the sedge on either side of the road, and an overgrown graveyard with the names of long-dead colonists etched into its crumbling headstones. Beyond there would be nothing but more deserted stretches of jungle and savanna for dozens of miles.

In his Rover up front, the guide radioed back to call a rest stop before continuing on toward the headquarters site. Then he led the vehicles off the trail over a patch of clumped, flattened grass and treaded dirt toward a large A-framed structure Nimec instantly figured to be the village trading post. There was an old pickup parked in front, a stand with some fruits and vegetables under the roofed porch, and a galvanized water bucket and metal dipper next to a slatted bench by the entrance. Out back was a row of three crude outhouses. Except for a Coca-Cola poster whose red background had faded to a pale pink, the signs taped against the dusty windows were handwritten in French. They seemed to have been put up more in defiance of the tyrannical sunlight than for any other reason. A few well-established palms around the building offered it some weak, spotty shade.

The vehicles stopped, and the locals went to stretch their legs and make small talk with a group of men who came out of the place to meet them, looking glad for a break in their monotony. While they stood and chatted, the members of the UpLink party started to dribble from their vehicles in ones, twos, and threes, a few of them wandering off to investigate the trading post, others just to stand around and smoke, a small number heading with reluctant necessity toward the shabby outhouses. Wearing bush shirts with Sword patches on the shoulders, and baby VVRS guns in sling harnesses against their bodies, some of Nimec's men got out of their vehicles in a loose deployment around the post. They did their best to stay low profile and at the same time ensure they had control of the area, keeping watch over the execs without getting in anybody's way. A single Sword op remained in the cab of each of the three cargo haulers.

Nimec sat beside DeMarco for a minute or two after their backseat companions had wandered off toward the post.

"I'd better work out some kinks of my own," DeMarco said, digging his knuckles into his lower back. "Feel like taking a walk?"

Nimec pulled his head off his back rest, glanced at his watch, and thought about how much he missed Annie. He didn't feel much like doing anything besides getting his job done.

"No thanks," he said.

"You sure?"

Nimec gave him a nod.

"Yeah, Steve, go on," he said. "Think I'd rather wait in here."

The convoy was under way again within half an hour, and soon swung heavily inland through the thickening wilds.

DeMarco glanced over at Nimec as they crawled ahead in their Rover.

"Okay if I ask you something?" he said.

"Why not?"

"Could be it's none of my business."

Nimec shrugged.

"Go ahead, shoot," he said. "I'll let you know."

DeMarco nodded.

"I noticed you've been checking your watch a lot," he said, keeping his voice quiet so it couldn't be heard by the passengers in back. "And I was sort of wondering about it."

Nimec sat looking straight out the windshield.

"Maybe I'm compulsive about the time," he said.

"Maybe."

"Or maybe I just want to keep track of our progress. This WristLink contraption has a global positioning system readout."

"Maybe." DeMarco hesitated, then pointed toward the dash console with his chin. "Except we've got a big, clear, easy-to-see GPS display right in front of us."

Nimec raised his eyebrows but remained quiet a moment.

" 'My Girl,' " he said finally.

"Huh?"

"That old Temptations song," Nimec said. "Remember it?"

"Sure."

"Well, I've got the watch set to play it on the day I'm supposed to get back to the States."

"And see your girl again?"

"Right."

DeMarco smiled a little.

"Nice," he said. "That's nice."

Nimec kept looking straight out the windshield.

"Think so?"

"Yeah."

Nimec cleared his throat.

"Actually it was her son who programmed it," he said. "Annie's got a boy and girl. Chris and Linda."

DeMarco nodded. He briefly took his left hand off the steering wheel and wriggled its third finger. He was wearing a simple gold wedding band.

"I miss my sweetie, too," he said. "Been married going on twelve years, and it's tough when the job keeps us apart. Separations are especially hard for the kids. We have three in our own brood . . . Jake, Alicia, and Kim."

Nimec grunted. "Your wife's with UpLink too, right?"

"A database administrator," DeMarco said. "Her name's Becky. Née Rebecca Lowenstein. My mother was hoping I'd wind up with a nice Italian Catholic girl, keep with the family tradition." A grin filled his face. "Meanwhile, she'll be attending my older daughter's bat mitzvah come next July. *Cosí é la vita* . . . that's life."

Nimec chuckled, and leaned back against the seat. The vehicle rumbled slowly along behind the 6×6's tailgate, forging through clumps of broad-leafed manioc plants that swarmed up on the trail and threatened to close it in.

"You and Annie have solid plans?" DeMarco said after a while.

"For right when I get back to the States, you mean . . . ?"

DeMarco shook his head.

"I mean, are you two *serious*?"

Nimec looked puzzled a moment.

"We're not engaged or anything," he said. "Seems a little too early. But we've been steady for about a year, year and a half."

DeMarco shrugged, holding the wheel.

"How long people have been seeing each other has nothing to do with serious," he said.

Nimec raised his eyebrows.

"I'm not following you."

DeMarco shrugged a second time. "I once dated a woman, exclusive, for almost three years," he said. "Thought she was a great person, got on fine with her, but never considered making things permanent. Just seemed like something was missing between us. Then, bang, Becky comes along, and I know we're a perfect match. Except I'm still involved with that other gal."

"What'd you do?"

"Broke up with her. It's one of those things that's never easy, but had to be done. Then I asked Becky out, popped the question a few weeks later. Cut ahead three months, we're walking down the aisle at that interdenominational UN chapel in New York City, beautiful place. A priest and rabbi co-officiating."

"Never had any doubts you might've been rushing things?"

DeMarco gave Nimec a short glance.

"I'm only human," he said. "You hear these stats about how over fifty percent of marriages hit the mat. And then there are all the timetables society lays on you. You're supposed to date for this long, get engaged for that long, wait so many years to have a baby . . . sure, I had doubts. You don't, it's not normal. But worrying about them seemed like a waste. I knew what I knew. And figured it was enough for me to commit."

Nimec became quiet in his seat as they rocked along over the deeply rutted trail. He turned his eyes to the display console's GPS screen.

"Looks like we're pretty near base," he said, motioning at the readout graphics. "All we have to do now is get there without breaking an axle."

DeMarco nosed their Rover forward, took a hard, jarring bump.

"Or our asses," he said, his hand tight around the wheel.

The sound of engines was close.

They raised their eyes, their heads covered with the heat and flash retardant hoods now. Although the brush around them trembled slightly, it did not part.

Saddled high in the bubinga tree, the man with the Sig SG550 sniper rifle was motionless, camouflage netting wrapped around his face, his cheek against the weapon's nonreflective black stock.

The sound was growing louder, yes. Closer. But its source had not yet entered their fire zone.

The ambushers remained hidden, ready for the moment.

"What the hell," DeMarco said. His foot had slammed down hard on the brake pedal. "You ever ask yourself if the boss finds these green splats on the map just to test us? See what it'll take to drive us crazy?"

Nimec produced a thin smile.

"Sometimes," he said, "I could almost wonder."

DeMarco shifted the tranny into PARK. He had a feeling they might be going nowhere for a while.

They sat looking out their windshield at the cargo hauler's tailgate, their passengers muttering unhappily in the rear. A moment earlier the convoy's lead Rover had come to a sudden halt, setting off a chain reaction down the line. This after their trail had taken them through a thicket of snarled, spiny-limbed euphorbia toward a jungle corridor that had promised some blessed shade from the relentless sun.

The forward driver had exited his vehicle, gone around to the truck behind him, and then paused to talk with some other locals who'd hopped from its cab—the entire team scanning the trail up ahead, shielding their eyes from the midday brightness with their hands. Now he separated from them, approached the Rover, and made a quick winding gesture with his finger.

DeMarco lowered the automatic window, catching a blast of hot air in his face.

"C'est un arbre qui tombe," the driver said to him,

looking dismayed. A man named Loren with angular features and a deep umber complexion, he was an excellent local guide who had already made the trek out to Up-Link's Sette Cama base a bunch of times.

"Ce mal?" DeMarco asked.

One of the execs riding in back leaned forward in his seat, trying to make out the guide's response, unable to understand his French.

"What is it?" he said.

"We've got some downed trees across the trail," DeMarco replied. "Our guide says these things happen sometimes. A tree rots, goes over, hits another, and that one crashes into another."

The exec frowned, but sat back to relay the news to his companions.

"How big a holdup can we expect?" Nimec said to DeMarco.

DeMarco held up a finger, had another brief exchange with the guide in French, then shrugged.

"Depends," he replied after a moment. "There can be two, three, or a dozen trees that need clearing. Loren, a couple guys from his Rover, and the truckers are going have a closer look at the fall, and he wants us to check it out with them so we know the score. He says it doesn't seem too bad from here. If a few of us pitch in to help, we should be able to move soon."

Nimec gazed out in front of him but was unable to see past the 6×6's broad rear end. After a second he turned back to DeMarco.

"Tell Loren I'll be right with him," he said.

DeMarco nodded. "Guess I'd may as well tag along."

"No," Nimec said. "You sit tight."

DeMarco looked at him.

"Any particular reason?"

"Like I told you before, nobody ever gets hurt by being careful." Nimec pushed his molded radio earplug into place and adjusted the lavalier mike on his collar. He thought a moment and then resumed in a hushed tone, "Call back for some of our boys to get out of their Rovers and keep their eyes open to what's around us. But I want them sticking close . . . nobody off the trail. At least one man should stay in every vehicle with the execs."

DeMarco regarded him. The four company honchos aboard their Rovers were talking among themselves in back.

"You sure you don't smell trouble?" he said, his voice also too low for them to overhear now.

Nimec shrugged.

"Not so far," he said.

Then he shouldered open the door to exit the vehicle.

Weapons of war are by obvious definition intended to have ugly effects.

Thermobarics—a military nomenclature for devices producing intense heat-pressure bursts—are uglier than most.

Whether dropped by an F-15E Strike Eagle fighter jet or fired from a shoulder-mounted rocket launcher, a thermobaric warhead will cause vastly more sustained and extensive destruction to its target than a conventional explosive munition. There are numerous designs floating about the open and black international markets, many battle tested, some under development, their payload formulas and delivery systems guarded with varying degrees of secrecy. In its basic configuration a fuel–air warhead has three separate compartments, two with high explosive charges, a third containing an incendiary fluid, gaseous, or particulate mixture. Though Russian arms builders will not confirm it, the RPO-Bumblebee warhead's flammable mix is a volatile combination of petroleum-derived fuels such as ethylene or propylene oxide, and tetranitrome-thane–a liquid relative of PETN, the combustible ingredient used in many plastic explosives.

As the primary HE charge is air detonated, the incendiary compartment bursts open like a metal eggshell to scatter its contents over a wide area. A second explosive charge then ignites the dispersed aerosol cloud to produce a tremendous churning fireball that can reach a temperature of between forty-five and fifty-five hundred degrees Fahrenheit, burning away the oxygen at its center, a vacuum filled in a fraction of a second by a rush of pressurized air approaching 430 pounds per square inch almost *thirty times* that which is normally exerted on an object or human body at sea level. Anyone exposed to its full force will be at once crushed to something less than a pulp, if not entirely vaporized. As the blast wave races outward, many at the nearest periphery of the detonation will die of suffocation, the breath sucked from their collapsing lungs. The casualties may also suffer extensive internal injuries such as venous and arterial embolisms, organ hemorrhages, and actual severing of bodily organs from the flesh and muscle tissues that hold them in place, including having their eyes torn from their sockets.

Pete Nimec had gotten only one leg out of the Rover when the RPO-A warhead erupted at the head of the convoy, and along with his fast reflexes, that was probably what saved his life.

There was a loud eruption from the mass of trees up ahead of him, then a roaring, rushing chute of heat and flame. The concussion struck the Rover's partially open door, slamming it up against him and throwing him back into his seat with his fingers still clutching its handle. He had a chance to glimpse the vehicle Loren had exited just moments before bounce several feet off the ground, then drop back down on its left flank, crumpled and blazing, its windows blown out, completely disintegrated by the blast.

Nimec had seen enough action in his day to realize the six men still inside it would have been killed instantly. Almost without conscious thought about how to save himself, without *time* to think, he dove behind the Land Rover's open passenger door, knelt behind its level VI armor as the blast wave swept over the 6×6, jolting it backward into the Rover's ram bumpers. Debris flew in every direction. Some of it rained down heavily on Nimec. Some drifted in the air around him, burning around him. There were scraps of clothing, foliage, seat covers, lord knew what else. Nimec heard screams in the sucking, broiling wind—from the truckers who'd gotten out of the hauler's cab, from the panicked executives inside the Rover, all their terrible cries intermingled. And DeMarco, shouting at him across the front seat, "Chief, chief, can you hear me, *chief are you okay* . . . ?"

Breathless, dazed, Nimec couldn't answer at first. His left eye stung, something dripping into it, blurring it. The warm wetness streamed down his face. He wiped the back of his hand across his brow and it came away slick and red.

Nimec blinked twice to clear his vision, then found himself almost wishing he could have remained blind to the scene before him. The truckers had been immolated. One of them lay still on the ground, his clothes burned away, his charred body consumed with fire. Near him the scattered remains of another man, or perhaps more than a single man, were also ablaze.

"Chief—"

Up, up, Nimec told himself. Sit up.

He managed it without knowing how, his glance briefly meeting DeMarco's across the seat. And then, somehow, past DeMarco's head, through his side window, he spotted Loren in the grass on the opposite side of the Rover, probably thrown there by the blast wave, rolling in a patch of shoulder-high grass to smother the last of the flames that had eaten away at his clothes, flailing his limbs in pain.

At the same moment, he heard a loud *pop-pop-pop* somewhere at the rear of the stalled convoy. Whooshing, whistling noises in the air. Nimec spun his head around and saw smoke tailing upward from the euphorbia grove, followed by three distinct orange-red bursts behind the last vehicle, the Rover shepherded by Conners and Hollinger. They were getting shelled back there, too. By what sounded to him like light mortars.

Then the unmistakable rattle of semiauto fire from the woods up ahead of him, and the thicket on either side, and the barrels of VVRS III's that had been thrust from gunports on the doors and tailgates of the cherried Rovers amid the confusion, their exterior concealment panels having sprung down as the compact subs were fitted into them from within. The Sword ops who'd already gotten out of their Rovers on Nimec's instruction had dived between bumpers and fenders and tailgates and were also opening up, exchanging volleys with their unseen attackers out in the brush.

Nimec gathered his wits and looked around into the Rover's backseat. Some of its passengers were still screaming. Others had gone still, very still, not making a sound. All their faces wore confused, shocked expressions that probably weren't dissimilar to his own.

DeMarco. Concentrate on giving DeMarco his orders.

"Loren's alive," he said. "I'm going to try and get him."

"You're bleeding—"

"It's just a cut."

"Chief, let me do it."

Nimec shook his head. There were more popping mortar discharges. Then whistles, blasts.

"I'll be okay, listen," he said. "I don't know what the hell kind of setup this is, but they've got us blocked, front and rear. Radio back down the line. Get everybody piled into the armored Rovers. Might not mean anything if they take direct hits, but the rest of the vehicles might as well be tin cans, including the trucks." He thought furiously. "They'll need cover when they move, you decide what's best. Then lock all the Rovers' doors and stay put. Try and keep the passengers cool."

"You run out in the open alone—"

Nimec cut short his protest with a slice of his hand.

"Listen to me," he said. "Contact the base . . . we've got scrambled voice communications, right?"

An acquiescent nod. "Right."

"Tell them to send up the Skyhawk—I just wish we had more than one of those choppers on base. Make sure the crew's warned to expect heavy incoming. Tell them about those mortars. And whatever caught us with that blast of flame . . . some kind of RPGs. I don't know. Also, we've got to have a microwave vidlink with the bird. Can't be of much use to its crew down here till we know the attackers' positions."

"I'll handle it."

"All right." Nimec could still see Loren through the window. "That guide, Steve. I need to get over to him."

DeMarco held up a finger, snapped open a compartment on his door, and fished hurriedly inside.

"You should take this," he said, producing a small medkit. "There's a morphine autoinjector inside. It'll help. And watch out for those cactus plants, or whatever the hell they are. The shit that oozes from them's poison."

Nimec took the medkit and gave DeMarco a purposeful nod.

Then he shut the door with a hard push and dashed back around the rear of the vehicle.

In the expanse of sedge and euphorbia, the bandits had deployed into teams of two, each man laying his mortar about twenty yards apart from his teammate's, and a hundred yards back from the girdled trail.

Crouched beside one member of the gang, their headman watched him feed a high-explosive fragmentation round into his tube, set for drop fire to allow faster discharge than manual triggering with the lever. The round slid down the barrel and hit the firing pin at its base cap. Its primer cartridge detonated at once, igniting propellent charges slotted into the fin blades.

An instant later the projectile launched from the muzzle in a gout of flame and smoke. It rocketed across the sky and thudded into the ground at the convoy's rear, chewing a hole in the trail to hamper its retreat.

No sooner did it strike than the bandit was dropping another round into the tube.

The headman raised his binoculars to his eyes and looked toward the front of the column. Still out of his vehicle, the UpLink security chief had begun shuffling his way back along its side. He held his firearm in one hand, carried something else in the other, a box or case of some sort. . . .

The headman produced a curious grunt. Then he noticed the man writhing in the grass beyond the 4×4. It wasn't possible to get a clear view of him in the patchy thicket, but he believed it might be the guide.

His curiosity became satisfaction, a smile touching his lips. The UpLink security man was rushing toward the guide, exposing himself to try to aid him.

It was almost too good to be true, he thought. His entire reason for stalling the convoy farther up the road had been to bring the security man closer to the trees, into easy range of the sniper who waited with explicit orders to take him out. Indeed, all the orders he'd given his men were clear and explicit, following guidelines of similar specificity from the Congolese warlord Fela Geteye, with whom they were in league. Whom warlord Geteye dealt with on the next level up the chain was none of the men's affair. Such linkages were intricate, preserved in secrecy, and shared only as necessary. What mattered most to the headman's *coupeurs de route* was collecting their portion of the bounty.

It did not mean the headman himself was ignorant of likely connections. His choice of livelihood bore a great many perils, capture or betrayal high on the index, and experience had taught him one should always have a reserve of information worth dealing. He had no qualms accepting jobs on a need-to-know basis. But if those at the top were mindful of their safety, why not he? The trick was to strike a balance—too much knowledge could be dangerous, too little shortsighted and foolish.

The headman knew warlord Geteye had ties to a Cameroonian dealer of stolen arms and technology who had bought favor with many lawmen throughout the region, among them, a police commander in Port-Gentil. The headman knew this commander owed his appointment to an even more highly ranked member of the Police Gabonaise, no lesser than a division chief said to be the puppet of an influential government minister. And although he did not know the minister's name, the headman had heard credible rumors that his strings were, in turn, pulled by a *blanc* of fearsome repute whose name and broad designs were more deeply mysterious than any of the rest . . . and better left that way.

However tempting it was to speculate about the parties' identities, the headman thought it smarter to resist.

He neither knew, nor would have cared to know, that the Gabonese minister was Etienne Begela, that the divisional police boss Begela had called upon to arrange the Sette Cama ambush was an immediate superior of Commander Bertrand Kilana, and that Kilana had been the one to secure warlord Fela Geteye's participation as middleman between the illicit trader and the headman's own band.

Some information was a good thing, yes. But too much knowledge could weigh one down, tip the scale the wrong way. The headman would never wish to become a potential liability to those exceedingly powerful and dangerous individuals who might have concerns about what he could reveal about them under interrogation.

His main interests had been how his gang of killers and thieves played into the scheme, and what was to be gained from their involvement. In that respect, he did not stand above those he led.

Should all continue to go well, their earnings looked to be tremendous. The arrangement with Geteye was one of incentives, each stage of the operation they successfully pulled off boosting their profits. The convoy's interception already guaranteed them a nice sum, with another agreed-upon bonus due if UpLink's head of security was sniped out—a hit the headman believed was about to be accomplished. Were his men able to get away with hijacking the truckloads of multimillion-dollar cargo, they would stand to make a certain fortune, receiving a cut of the loot from warlord Geteye after its turnover by the Cameroonian black marketeer. No restraints had been placed on their taking of casualties . . . as far as that went, the headman had gotten the distinct

sense that a high body count might be preferred. on the
other hand, damage to the precious freight must be
avoided, or at least kept to a minimum. And in that regard, things were about to get tough.

The headman held his glasses steady, watching the be-
sieged line of vehicles through the double circles of their
lenses. The Land Rover in front had been marked for
destruction, and he'd factored in a significant loss to the
cargo aboard the truck at its rear—the RPO-A shoulder
launcher was a ravaging weapon. But he would take no
chances damaging any more of his coveted bounty, and
the nearness of the rest of the conveyances to one another—the last two trucks flanked front and back by what
he now saw to be *armored* vehicles, something he hadn't
been warned to expect—meant a direct hit on any of the
Rovers would have exactly that inescapable, unacceptable result.

The controlled barrage could be sustained only a bit
longer, then. Keeping the convoy paralyzed, and further
softening its defenses by taking out the handful of
UpLink security men that had left their 4×4s.

The headman nodded to himself, thinking.

Soon, he would have to bring his men out onto the
trail for the decisive strike.

Hunkered low between his Rover and the truck behind
it, Nimec swiped more blood off his forehead, and then
propelled himself across the trail.

He drew fire at once. A wild shower out of the trees
that he figured for a subgun volley, then a single heavier-
caliber round whapping the ground inches to his left, too
close, throwing up divots of soil. That one had come
from above. From a *treetop*. A shooter was perched up
there, trying to take him out. The realization brought

DeMarco's question back to mind, what the hell kind of setup *was* this?

He snipped off the thought. No time to worry about it now. The guide was yards ahead of him, down in the sedge, moving, thrashing in agony.

Nimec plunged into the thicket, the folded blanket in his right hand, his unharnessed VVRS gripped in the other, its barrel tilted upward. He squeezed its trigger, sprayed the bubinga grove with fire, covering himself, or doing his best, impossible to take decent aim when you're running full tilt.

Another shot whizzed from above, close again. Closer than it ought to have been. Nimec was a moving target in a tangle of foliage reaching a foot or two higher than his head, and the guy'd gotten off two near hits from several hundred yards. Nobody was that sharp, not unless he had X-ray vision, or was using more than an ordinary telescopic. And Nimec was betting it wasn't Superman up there.

Behind him now, more mortar blasts and subgun volleys. But Loren's screams, those piercing inchoate screams, were the loudest sounds of all, impossible to ignore. They tunneled his awareness, called to it like a maddening beacon. A human being might by dying there before his eyes and was suffering almost beyond comprehension. He had to get over to him, do something to stop those horrible cries of pain.

Nimec scrambled through a cluster of euphorbia, the spiny limbs reaching above his head, twisting up around him, scratching his arms despite his attempt to avoid them. Still, they offered momentary cover from the tree-top sniper. He ran on, hit some more grass, reached his man, and snapped open the medkit DeMarco had given him. Loren was thrashing, rolling, hands slapping his own body. It was as though he were unaware he'd already doused the flames that had eaten at his flesh, and was still trying to beat them out.

"It's okay, easy does it, try to stay still," Nimec said, knowing the guide's convulsive thrashing would only do more damage, thinking he might be in far too much pain to pay attention, possibly didn't even speak enough English to know what he was saying. Sure, why not, there had to be a goddamn *language* problem for him to contend with, on top of everything else.

Nimec squatted down on his haunches, got the morphine autoinjector out of the kit, and pressed the end of the tube to his outer thigh, ejecting the spring-cocked needle that would dispense the painkiller directly through his ruined clothing. He was still urging Loren to hold still in the calmest voice he could manage, It's okay, Loren, we can make it, I promise, we can, only you've got to work with me here, got to *hold still*. He could smell the man's seared hair, his flesh, a sickening, terrible assault on his senses.

And then, suddenly, Loren settled down. He lay groaning—alive, at least—but almost motionless. Nimec couldn't tell why. Maybe he'd understood him after all. Or maybe he was slipping into shock. Nimec simply couldn't tell, guessed it might not be a good sign in the larger scheme of things. But staying here wouldn't prolong his life. He wasn't tossing around, flopping his arms and legs every which way, so it would be easier to bring him back to the Rover, where they'd at least have some protection. The Tom Ricci credo again . . . small steps.

Okay. Next stop, the Rover. He needed to get both of them into it. Throw Loren over his shoulder, drag him, whatev—

There was the crack of a gunshot, the sniper firing another round from the treetop.

Nimec spilled over into the tall grass.

• • •

Steve DeMarco knew how to follow orders without having them spelled out to the letter. Under most circumstances he wouldn't have considered disobeying them.

These weren't most circumstances, though. Which left him to rely on another of the strengths that had gotten him assigned to Nimec's SanJo A-team: the ability to make tough judgments in a hurry.

Get everybody piled into the armored Rovers . . . they'll need cover when they move, you decide what's best.

They had been Pete Nimec's words, not his. *You decide what's best.* Okay, fine, ready and willing to oblige. And moments before DeMarco saw Nimec tumble into the thicket, he'd *decided*, radioing out to the Sword ops inside and outside the Rovers, preparing them for a synched up release of Type IV thermal obscurant from the tail pipes of the armored vehicles. A recent UpLink agent developed for military use, the micropulverized aluminum alloy particles would swirl upward in a buoyant white cloud that provided a thick visual/thermal—or bispectral—fog, shrouding their people from sight as they all transferred to the armoreds. At the same time, the fog would scatter the infrared emissions of whatever it enveloped, everything from the twelve- to fourteen-micron heat signatures of human beings to those radiated by the vehicles, which would be intense even with their engines off after they'd been running for hours in the hot sun. Use ordinary white or red phosphorus, you'd get even wider spectrum wavelength scatter, DeMarco knew. But the stuff burned at five thousand degrees, *hot*, and running through that smoke was liable to blister your flesh and airways on contact. With the Type IV, any thermal gun scopes or heat-seeking rockets the opposition might be using would be totally fouled, while the individuals it was shielding from detection could tolerate short-duration exposure without adverse effects.

DeMarco had decided on his crisp little plan and sent out word over the comlink. One, he would launch a thirty-second countdown. Two, the armoreds would release their bispectral obscurant. And three, the vulnerable UpLink personnel, road guides, and truckers would make their break, go hustling toward the safer vehicles.

DeMarco was at minus twelve seconds, counting aloud into his microphone, ready to push the Type IV fog-release button on the rapid-defense touch pad console beside his left armrest, when he heard the big-bore rifle up in the trees crack for a third time, and saw Nimec drop completely out of sight in the brush.

Stunned, DeMarco called an urgent hold command.

In the Rover behind him, Wade jerked his finger away from *his* control console.

At the tail end of the convoy, Hollinger did the same.

"Chief, you all right out there?" DeMarco said tensely over the shared communications channel.

Silence from Nimec.

DeMarco felt his stomach knot.

"Chief!" He was almost shouting into the mike now. *"Come on, Pete, goddamn it, are you—?"*

"I'm okay," Nimec answered. Flat on his stomach in the grass, his mouth full of dirt, he'd been hauling Loren up beside him as DeMarco's tense radio call went out, too busy to respond at once. "Have to stay low. That son of a bitch in the tree almost took me out with that last shot. I think he's using a thermal sight."

There was momentary silence in his earpiece.

"Hang on, chief," DeMarco said. "I'll get you back in here—"

Nimec cut him short. "Forget me," he said. "I told you to evac those sitting duck vehicles."

CUTTING EDGE **263**

"I was about make the call. Use the Type Four mist for cover—"

"So use it."

"That sharpshooter's got you pinned. You start moving again, trying to lug a wounded man with you, the fucker'll nail you in a second."

Nimec inhaled, wiped blood from his forehead. He'd gotten some juice from a broken euphorbia stem into the cut, and it burned as though on fire.

"If I'm being scoped through a thermal, Type Four's what I need," he said, lying through his teeth.

"That stuff won't disperse fast enough to screen you—"

"I'll keep hugging the ground, find the Rover once the smoke starts to lift."

DeMarco waited several heartbeats before answering him.

"You'll never make it that way," he said at last. "I can use fog oil instead . . ."

Nimec inhaled. He wasn't about to fool anybody here, leaving him to pull rank.

"No," he said. "You've got any sudden ideas in your head, you damn well better shake them."

DeMarco was silent again.

"Steve—"

"Your signal's breaking up, chief. Couldn't hear you."

"What do you *mean* you couldn't hear me?"

"Getting worse, I'm losing you—"

"Don't pull this on me, Steve . . ."

"Lost you," DeMarco said very clearly over their com-link. "Proceeding at my own discretion. Over."

The headman had determined he'd waited long enough. An ambush must have surprise and speed; lose either, allow the situation to become static, and it would fail.

Lowering his glasses so they hung over his chest on their strap, he brought his palm-size tactical radio to his mouth and sent out his command to the men he'd divided up on both sides of the trail. His voice was level and controlled.

In the brush at the convoy's rear, in the forest up ahead, the bandits left their stationary positions and started to converge on the vehicles according to plan.

Moments after breaking contact with Nimec—hanging up the phone on him, figuratively speaking—DeMarco resumed his countdown where he'd left off, twelve seconds minus. He'd moved his finger away from the Type-IV release button on his touch pad to another about an eighth of an inch over to its right.

The lighted button he was now ready to push was marked SGF2, for petroleum smoke-generator fog formulation two, which, in truth, was hardly different from the diesel-and-oil smoke pot formula that had been used on battlefields since World War II. And while it created a quick, dense visual screen and did a good job muddling *near* infrared signals, giving it a considerable degree of efficacy in certain evasive situations to the present day, it didn't work nearly as well as Type IV in degrading the functionality of thermal imagers sensitive to far end IR wavelengths.

That limitation was precisely what DeMarco wanted— no, needed—to put him on more or less equal terms with his opposite number in the treetop.

"Eleven, ten, nine, I want everybody set to go . . ."

An eye on his digital dashboard clock, DeMarco was also getting set, practicing what he preached as he ticked off the seconds over his comlink—only he would be going very much his own way.

". . . eight, seven, send up the smoke!"

DeMarco hit his console button and white SGF2 vapor began pouring from his Rover's tail pipe, Wade and Hollinger releasing it from the exhausts of their respective vehicles at the same instant, the two of them acting on his direct order.

DeMarco looked down at the weapon he'd taken from a hidden underseat compartment, resting all sixteen pounds of it comfortably across his lap even as he'd been having his little clash of opinion with Nimec. UpLink arms designers called it a Big Daddy VVRS, their own version of what master planners with the Pentagon's Future Land Warrior program were dubbing an "objective individual combat weapon," or OICW, which was *itself* a variant of the modular French FAMAS rifles that terrorists had used with grievously damaging results against an UpLink facility in Brazil two years earlier.

Ninety percent of the time, Sword's munitions designers were way ahead of the curve, but every so often they found themselves playing catch up. When that happened, they always compensated by pulling into first place.

The Big Daddy was a single-trigger, dual-barreled, integrated firing system, its lower barrel chambered for 5.56-mm VVRS lethal/nonlethal sabot rounds, and its upper barrel a 20-mm fused multipurpose munitions launcher; a microcomputer-assisted, thermal image/laser dot range-finder targeting scope on top. This was quite the whole package rolled into one.

Hoping it would do the trick for him, DeMarco continued to read the numbers on his dash clock aloud, getting there now, getting there, three, two, one . . .

". . . *Commence evac!*" he yelled.

And gripped the Big Daddy in both hands as he pushed out his door into the churning smoke.

In the 4×4's rear compartment, all four of its terrified passengers sat watching everything beyond their windows dissolve into a blank white void, as if the world were simply being erased before their eyes. Without exchanging a word, they had linked hands on the seat between them, bowed their heads, and begun moving their lips in spontaneous, silent prayer—each according to his or her individual belief, desire to believe, or willing abandonment to the possibility that a higher power might be stirred into turning an ear in their direction.

As one, they petitioned not for their own lives, but for those of DeMarco, Nimec, and the people from the evacuated vehicles somewhere out in the spreading whiteness—

Out there in the hell they could no longer see.

Out, out, and out.

They emptied from the death-trap trucks and 4×4s, a flood of over twenty executives, engineers, and local hands. Their Sword escort closed ranks around them even as they rushed onto the trail, guiding them through billows of turbine-blown oil fog in two groups of different sizes—the larger one running toward the pair of armored Rovers at the head of the convoy, a much smaller number turning the other way, dashing for the single armored vehicle at their rear.

The passengers were not the only ones in need of immediate evac. Three of the Sword ops who'd exited their vehicles for a look-see in the seconds before the raid commenced had taken serious hits—two of them sliced up from shrapnel discharged by exploding mortar rounds, the third bleeding heavily from a gunshot wound to his leg. All had either found or been pulled into temporary cover between the vehicles, all had to be moved out, and in no case was it easy. But while the man who'd taken the slug and one of the shelling casualties were walking wounded, able to stay on their own feet with some assistance, the other was in far worse shape. Semiconscious, the left side of his head deeply gashed, a portion his left cheek torn away in a horrible flap, he had to be brought toward the armoreds in a fireman's carry.

The ops ferried their charges through the mist as hastily as possible. They wore stereoscopic thermal goggles equipped with low-probability intercept, spread-spectrum digital video transmitters, their color-enhanced LPI images appearing on dashboard receiver displays in the trio of armored vehicles. These allowed the security personnel inside the suped Rovers to see everything their exposed teammates saw through the TI goggles, creating a kind of multidimensional collage perspective of their intensely hostile surroundings.

Inside *and* out, the Sword personnel were laying patterns of defensive fire. Careful not to fan the area where Nimec was bellied down in the grass, those on the trail were using the baby VVRS guns with which they'd left their vehicles. At the same time, the men aboard the Rovers were spraying the brush with rounds from their Big Daddies, waiting with their doors partially open for the evacuees, doing what they could to provide fire support as they made their way over from the cleared out vehicles.

For the ops involved in the evac, the SGF2 was proving a tremendous asset.

A matter of seconds after they started hustling the men and women in their care toward the armoreds, they had seen their attackers closing in, advancing on them like Indian warriors around an encircled Old West wagon train. They crept forward through the thicket, rushing with their bodies bent low, dropping, firing, then creeping forward again, their forms radiant in the TI lenses, the hot-spot discharges from their gun barrels appearing as winks of yellow-orange brightness against a gray field.

The rising blanket of fog vastly turned things around. As Pete Nimec had observed only minutes earlier, it was hard to be accurate with a rifle while you were scrambling and doubtful of your enemy's position. But knowing right where your enemy was made it easier. A lot easer when you were fading before his very eyes.

Unable to see the convoy through the smokescreen, the attackers had stopped coming, their arrested movement suddenly turning *them* into blind and confused targets— and the Sword ops were quick to exploit the role reversal. Directing their fire at the IR images outside the blanket of mist, the gunners in the armored Rovers knocked one after another down into the thicket. As the evacuees continued their run toward shelter, their escorts managed to rattle off tight bursts of their own, breaking the ring of ambushers into a scatter of ducking, falling bodies.

Moments later the evacuees were hurrying into the armoreds. They got the wounded in first, the occupants of the vehicles coming out to help them through the open doors, clearing as much room as possible for them in the cargo sections, then assisting the rest, squeezing them inside, slamming and locking the doors behind them.

The transfer accomplished, they were, mercifully and at last, safer.

None of them was at all sure it meant they were saved.

Crouched on one knee outside the Rover, DeMarco was desperately scanning the treetops when he heard the flap of chopper rotors in the distance.

He felt a wash of relief, then took a breath to settle himself. No sense getting too overjoyed. The Skyhawk was coming, okay, but it wasn't here yet. He needed to keep his mind on what he was doing, keep his finger on his trigger.

His gunsight shifted from normal daylight to TI mode

at the flip of a switch, DeMarco could see clearly through the smoke gushing from the 4×4's tailpipe. *Knowing* he'd be able to see in the whiteout was his entire reason for having chosen the oil fog. Type IV's ability to screw up thermal imaging would have hidden the shooter from him, and him from the shooter, but left Nimec visible to the sniper out beyond the edges of the mist, a dead duck without assistance. Nimec had realized this as well as DeMarco, hence their tiff over the comlink. He had not wanted DeMarco to make a target of himself for his sake. And DeMarco supposed he might have felt the same in Nimec's place. Too many heroes here, that was the problem.

DeMarco peered through his eyecup, his cheek to the gunstock, sweeping the rifle from side to side, trying to scope out the shooter.

A special agent with the Chicago FBI for over a decade before hooking up with Sword, he knew how to use a gun. He'd earned high qualifications for sidearm technique, better-than-average rifle certs, and a couple of commendations for situational and judgmental skills. But he was still no expert shot with a submachine gun and, for that matter, had never used deadly force on a human being or anything larger than a cockroach—shit, he even bought humane traps to catch the mice that wriggled into his basement every spring. Only twice in Chi had he been compelled to draw a weapon off the training course, both times getting a hands-in-the-air surrender. There were no dramatic takedowns or feats of marksmanship for him to tell war stories about over beers somewhere; if he was going to help the chief out of his jam, and maybe see another tomorrow himself, he would need to score his first right now.

Perspiration trickling down his face, DeMarco swept the rifle across the trees, a damn lot of them for that bastard to be hiding in, where the hell *was* he up there—?

He abruptly checked the weapon's motion. Through the electronic reticle of its sight, he'd spotted the treetop shooter saddled in the crook of a foliage-swaddled limb, his IR phantom form absolutely still.

It took perhaps a millisecond to realize the sighting was mutual.

His eye to the scope, DeMarco had enough time to see the bore of the sonofabitch's rifle swing toward him in the treetop, *just* enough, the sniper absolutely still and steady up in the treetop except for that one conspicuous movement.

DeMarco could hear his pulse somewhere between his ears as he squeezed back Big Daddy's trigger and felt the recoil against his shoulder, a 20-mm smart round flying from the rifle's titanium upper barrel, the microcomputerized sight processing range and position, automatically calculating the round's best point of detonation for target acquisition, setting it for airburst rather than on-impact explosion. And then an earsplitting blast, the treetop igniting into an orange bouquet of flame, its trunk blowing apart, spewing everywhere, obliterated into countless fiery chunks, shaves, and splinters of wood.

DeMarco felt his heart stroking. Later he would recall his half-surprised glance down at himself as if to confirm it really was still beating inside him, that he really *hadn't* gotten slugged in the chest—here, unbeknownst, was the crowd grabber of War Story Number One for the books.

He returned his eye to the rifle sight, looked through the smoke into the thicket. The gunfire around him had gotten more sporadic. He could hear the whap of copter blades closer overhead. Good signs. Very good signs.

"Chief!" Scanning the vegetation, scanning. His back pressed against the side of the Rover, his comlink channel to Nimec was open again. "Chief, come in, I'm trying to get a visual—"

"I hear you," Nimec said. "Can't see a damned thing, though. Smoke's too thick. Best estimate, I'm ten yards back of the Rover, twenty yards or so deep in the brush."

DeMarco swung his rifle barrel to the left, picked up a pair of low TIs—one man propped on his arms, the other flat on the ground.

"Think I've got a visual on you, chief, hold up a hand . . ."

It rose ghostly and shimmering in his scope's eyecup.

DeMarco breathed.

"Okay, it's you all right," he said. "Hang tight, I'm on my way over."

"Remind me to kick you down for insubordination when you get here."

"Will do," DeMarco said, and tore forward into the vegetation.

Watching the explosion rip through the treetops through his glasses, listening to the sound of a helicopter in the not-too-distant eastern sky, the headman knew it was time to call off his raid, knew irrevocably that it had come to almost total failure. The man marked for assassination was alive, the cargo he'd meant to hijack out of his grasp. Several of his band had been killed or wounded. Any financial compensation he stood to gain from having stopped the vehicles would not offset his losses.

He had become uneasy about his situation the minute he'd noticed there were armored vehicles in the convoy, a feeling that rapidly turned to anxiousness when their chemical fog was released to shroud the trail, and the security teams aboard the enhanced 4×4s had begun fighting off his men. It was not their impressive firepower alone that opened a fissure in his confidence—as a former Cameroonian military officer, he'd learned that no amount of planning could prepare one for every aspect of an engagement, that there were always gaps in what was known about an adversary. What mystified him was that the capabilities they'd demonstrated were in such total conflict with everything he'd been told about them. To have gotten incomplete information was something he could accept. But it made no sense that sources he had always found reliable could so wholly and startlingly *mis*inform him, not unless . . .

The headman's features stiffened, his fierce brown eyes riveted on the enkindled tree where he had placed his sniper. The helicopter would soon appear over its broken, blazing remnants, and when it did, his opposition would be able to scour the ground for him and his men.

There was no time left for further supposition, not now. He would find another opportunity to throw himself open to them.

Trembling with anger, he raised his handset to his lips and called a retreat.

As the copter came flying in overhead, Nimec pressed the TRANSMIT button of his Rover's ground-to-air.

"Pilot, this is CSO, you read me?" he said.

"Roger, sir."

"We've got a mess here. Fatalities. Several wounded, three seriously. They need immediate medevac. There's a burn vic, don't know how long he'll last without treatment."

"Goddamn. The pack of wolves that did this is on the move, I see them heading toward some off-road vehicles—"

"Let 'em go." His eyes on the dash display, Nimec was watching his microwave video feed from the chopper's aerial surveillance pods. "We can't chase them and get these people out at the same time."

"Yes, sir. Hang on, we're coming down. Over."

Nimec cut the radio, exhausted, holding a cotton pad from a first-aid kit to his forehead. It was soaked red.

"Man," DeMarco said beside him. "I feel like I've been clubbed by a giant."

Nimec snorted. He reclined against his backrest in silence.

They sat waiting for the helicopter to land. Stretched out behind them in some cargo space cleared by their Rover's packed-together occupants, Toren released a long, low, wavering moan.

It made the fine hairs on Nimec's neck and arms bristle.

"A few minutes ago"—DeMarco began, then paused to marvel at those very words out of his mouth. He found it hard to believe so little time had elapsed since the windstorm of flame had come raging over the convoy from the mass of trees in front—"When you were out in the thicket, something made me remember Brazil. I couldn't even tell you what right now, my thoughts were racing along so fast. Still are. But the raid there, those terrorists hitting us by surprise, almost wrecking the Matto Grosso compound . . . it feels similar to this in a way."

Nimec looked at him. "How do you mean?"

"Damn thing is, I'm not sure." DeMarco made a groping-at-the-air gesture with his hands. "It's been ages since I read the Shadow Watch case files. But even before we tied it to that maniac Rollie Thibodeau calls the Wildcat, what stuck out at me about the Brazil raid was that it was done by real pros. A HAHO jump insertion, prototype FAMAS assault guns that are just being put into mass production *this year* . . . those guys were seasoned fighters, must've had serious underwriting." He shrugged. "Another thing I could never get was what they were trying to accomplish. Always seemed kind of fuzzy to me, like nothing was what it seemed on its face. And the shit that came down on us now makes me wonder on the same accounts. Motive, tactics, equipment."

Nimec added a fresh first-aid pad.

"I don't know," he said. "The connection's not there for me."

"Maybe it's because there isn't one," DeMarco said. "But who were these guys? Does it seem to *you* we were up against two-bit bushwhackers?"

Nimec considered that.

"I wouldn't lump together every robber gang in the neighborhood as two-bit," he said. "Some are made up of breakaway soldiers. Men who've had combat training from foreign advisers. Russians, Brits, Israelis, our own Green Berets to name a few. The bunch that hit us could fit into that category."

DeMarco shook his head.

"It still doesn't explain their ordnance," he said, and jerked his chin toward the windshield. Up ahead of them, SGF2 mist and dark gray smoke from the burning lead Rover and trees had commingled to blur out the sky and forest, its acrid stench seeping into their ventilation system. "Whatever they used for a showstopper was heavy duty."

Nimec bounced DeMarco's main points against his logic. He really didn't know what could or couldn't be inferred from them. It was hard for him even to think straight. A man was moaning in pain, maybe dying, less than five feet in back of him. Hard to think. At first blush, though, he didn't see that the incidents could be compared. The strike in Brazil had been massive, well organized, perpetrated by an enemy that had carefully assessed and exploited UpLink's vulnerabilities. But their ambushers had gone after a small supply convoy and badly underestimated its defensive strengths. Given the hotel room buggings, and the extent of the surveillance on UpLink personnel in Port-Gentil, Nimec understood there was a very credible possibility that the men who'd struck at them here had backers with a wider agenda and substantial resources—which was a handful of needles and broken glass in itself. To go beyond that at this stage, though . . .

Nimec wasn't ruling anything out, not until he'd had a chance to reflect with a clear head. But he'd been with Roger Gordian's organization long enough to realize it had many disparate enemies, and wasn't about to make any broad jumps drawing conspiracy theories.

He expelled a breath, looked out his window. The Skyhawk was finally wheels down in the grass.

"We'll pick up on this later," he said over the loud whack of its blades. "The guys on that chopper are going to need an assist getting our wounded aboard."

His arms crossed over his chest, Vince Scull sat in front of his idling laptop computer at a cramped corner table in a cyber café called Zèbre Passage, which translated in English as Zebra Crossing, and seemed about as absurd a name to him as Scintillements. More ridiculous, actually. Maybe it was a sign he was getting old, but Scull often looked fondly back on the days when the name of a business would convey most of the information prospective customers needed to know about the services it offered, the products it sold, and whatnot. Macy's Department Store. Woolworth's Five and Dime. Ebinger's Bakery. Howard Johnson Restaurant and Ice Cream Parlor. A customer walked off the street into any of those places, he not only had a very definite idea what he could expect to find, but knew the family name, and in some instances the first and middle initials, or even the *full* name, of its founder. Talk about a lack of consumer awareness, how were you supposed to draw people through your storefront door when the sign above it told nothing about what you were peddling?

Scull made a grumbling sound and shifted in his chair. What the name Zebra Crossing had to do with a joint that served rollups, scones, coffee, and bottled mineral water while providing Internet access to its customers, he didn't know. He also couldn't fathom how the twentyish men and women typing furiously at their keyboards—all of whom were white, and probably the dilettante kids of expat businessmen, and *most* of whom had come in wearing backpacks with padded sleeves designed for their computers—were able to concentrate on their work amid the flurry of other customers placing orders at the counter, carrying food trays past their tables, settling into chairs, or getting books, file folders, and other odds and ends out of their packs. They seemed so damned self-conscious about looking earnest and definite as they clacked away at their machines, some with headphones over their ears. What were they writing? Class papers? Travel articles? Online music reviews? *Books*, God forbid?

Scull didn't understand how they could get anything accomplished. His job assignments took him everywhere on the planet and involved gathering information in every kind of physical environment, but when he actually sat down to prepare a coherent written evaluation, he needed a quiet office, or at the very least a room where he had four walls around him and some uninterrupted solitude . . . none of which was available in good ol' Gabon courtesy of the droops, which was another reason for him to love the country, he guessed. Somebody could stick a gun to his head, tell him to put together a grocery list or else, and Scull doubted he'd be able to do it with all the fucking distractions in here.

But maybe his advanced age of fifty-three *was* why he didn't compute, excuse the pun. Or maybe, just maybe, people thinking they could do honest, roll-up-your-sleeves, get-your-underpants-sweaty work in public places where they could also showcase their lightning-fast notebooks was one major reason so much of everything sucked rotten pigeon eggs nowadays.

Scull produced another low grunt of dissatisfaction and tapped a key on his laptop to wake it from its SLEEP mode, figuring he'd check his e-mail queue to see whether Sherm had come through with any dope on Nautel yet. After five hours of waiting impatiently in this crowded community nowhere, he'd about reached his limit . . .

He abruptly sat up straight. Miracle of miracles. Boldface on his inbox screen was a message from user name F. Sherman with the subject "Hope You Brought along Galoshes and Nose Plugs." Cute, but what was it supposed to mean? Scull hardly cared. He was too busy noticing the little paper clip icon that indicated the message had arrived with a file attachment.

He highlighted the message and clicked it open. There were, in fact, several attached files. Large ones.

The e-mail's body text read:

Per your request, I've got a thigh-high puddle of shit for you to wade through, Vince. And you better believe it stinks.

Scull opened the first file and browsed through it. Within minutes, he was ready to start holding his nose.

EIGHT

From Sledge Online ("The Alternative E-zine of News and Opinion"): Hot Briefs

YANK YOUR GRAND BOUBOU
OUT OF THE CLOSET
UpLink and Sedco Get Down on an Unlikely Stage

by Mannee Almonte

An image of the normally reserved Roger Gordian shaking his derriere at a corporate romp charged with the frenetic dance rhythms of Makossa, Sahelian, and Congo pop musicians is one that would be *muy* quick to grab attention in business and social circles. Add to that picture a dance stage supported by huge pontoons and anchor cables and a background of soaring steel derricks, flying masts, and industrial lifting hooks, and even regular financial observers accustomed to the idiosyncratic styles of a Forbes or Bloomberg couldn't ignore it.

Ever dangle a feather lure over a cat's head? It may be for the very purpose of seizing the media's eye that the event I've described above has been scheduled for next week aboard an offshore drilling platform in the waters of Gabon, an equatorial African republic small

enough to fit on a microscope slide and never heard of
by many American specimens—at least none *we* know.
But there and nowhere else, the head of a telecom giant
renowned for having transformed the role of private enterprise in "advancing global democratization" (Whuz-
zat? Dunno. We're just quoting the *Wall Street Journal*.)
will join the top dog of an ambitious petroleum company
to sign, seal, and celebrate a new partnership that seeks
to compete with the older and slipperier oilfish who have
dominated that aquatic territory for decades. Add their
political hosts in the region, and you've got quite the
must-see must-be jamboree.

"Yank your *grand boubou* out of the closet," enthused
the event's master-of-ceremonies—and Sedco CEO—
Hugh "King Hughie" Bennett in a recently televised Financial News Network appearance, referencing the flam-
boyant embroidered dress costumes worn throughout the
African continent. "Work hard, play hard's my motto;
and we're all getting ready to kick up our heels for this
one."

Having sunk tooth and claw into Bennett's string-and-
feather jiggle toy, your spectacle-susceptible columnist
must confess that his mouth is watering with anticipation
as he prepares to join the crème de la press corps flying
off to the event on Sedco's charter. Which begs the question to those transculturally fashionable, hoity-toity readers who may be past visitors to Gabon—and to our
destination city of Port-Gentil in particular—Can any of
you recommend a Rent-A-Grand Boubou on short notice? The threads are a *must*—just ask King Hughie.

Pointers and discount offers will be welcomed at our
e-mail address, dear friends.

They drove to the airport in an armored Land Rover,
DeMarco at the wheel, Wade beside him, Nimec and

Scull in the backseat. There were several reasons the group was headed out, their wish to shore up security for Roger Gordian's arrival the next day top among them, though all they'd felt free to discuss at the Rio de Gabao was their intention to direct a force buildup at their transit warehouse as a precaution arising from the Sette Cama ambush—provisionally labeled an attempted hijack, though they understood the book on that was a far cry from closed.

Another very pressing reason for their drive was one they would not under any circumstances have discussed in the open.

Scull had something he needed to show Nimec. A crucial document he'd extracted from a series of memorandums and correspondences his man Fred Sherman had been tipped to by an inside source at Nautel, and then had pried out of the company's hands after separately informing three of its highest-ranking executives that UpLink would consider their withholding it from him a flat-out breach of trust and cause for summary abrogation of their as-yet-unsigned outsourcing agreement.

Those statements were no empty threats. The letter had widened Scull's eyes when it came onto his computer screen at the cyber café, and only now in the protective confines of the vehicle—his laptop in a docking station that had swung out from behind its front seat at the touch of a button, the hard copy generated by a color printer integrated into his armrest—was he even moderately comfortable with the idea of pulling it off his hard drive.

"Here you go." Scull took the sheet of paper from the printer's output slot and gave it to Nimec. "A few casts of his line, and Fred got evidence that a mutual pal of ours, identity to be revealed, committed a serious foul."

Nimec put the document on his lap. He felt totally out of sorts—his head cloudy, his stitched eyebrow tugging under its bandages, his ears still ringing from the combustive blast that had almost finished him just twenty-four hours earlier.

"So what do you think?" Scull said.

Nimec shot him an irritable glance. "Give me more than thirty seconds to look this over and I'll tell you."

Vince frowned but didn't say anything.

Nimec went back to reading what he'd been handed, a scanned copy of a letter written on the executive stationary of Etienne Begela, Port-Gentil's minister of economic development and the official who had fêted Nimec's advance team on their arrival. It was addressed to someone named John Greeves II, professional title Principal Claims Investigator, who was with the Risk and Emergency Management Division of a company called The Fowler Group, Ltd.

Nimec looked over at Scull. "Fowler . . . that's a commercial insurer, right?"

Scull nodded.

"One of the ultra-biggies," he said. "Networked with Lloyd's of London."

Nimec grunted and continued down to the text of the letter:

Dear Mr. Greeves,

After giving it every consideration, I must regretfully inform you that I cannot approve your request for permits to conduct an inspection of the offshore site where Messrs. Dupain and Bouchard lost their lives. Please rest assured that my judgment by no means reflects a negative conclusion about your very reputable firm but is rather a matter of having to perform my governmental duties in good conscience.

A complete review of all data surrounding the incident done in consultation with Nautel Submarine Maintenance, and specifically Captain Pierre Gunville, leaves me certain that any manned deepwater procedures would be of great physical hazard to those operating in the area, while yielding no further information that would be helpful to your agency. As you know, Captain Gunville has already completed a postaccident inspection of the site using a remote underwater vehicle, and his report is quite exhaustive.

Though I hesitate to exceed my authority knowing the disappointment this refusal of application shall cause you, it is my personal recommendation that Nautel's findings be taken as definitive insofar as any claims of indemnity that have resulted from the grievous occurrence of 4 May. I am aware that The Fowler Group is the trusted insurance underwriter of many prominent companies doing business in Gabon, especially those involved in petroleum and mineral prospecting. These enterprises fall directly under my ministerial auspices, and I would be saddened if their relationships with you were to suffer from the impression that appropriate compensations for losses incurred during their explorations might be unduly challenged, however erroneous that notion might be.

I am enclosing a copy of Nautel's recommendation to me and will, of course, be happy to provide any other material you may need for your records.

> *Yours Very Truly,*
> *Etienne Begela*

Nimec took a moment to digest everything, then looked up at Scull again.

"Gunville was lying outright at the club," he said. "He told us Nautel didn't conduct an accident inspection, meanwhile the truth is that it did."

"That *he* did," Scull said. "Himself. Personally."

"He also told us nobody else wanted to check out the site, when this Fowler Group was pushing the government for permission."

"And he helped *stop* them." Scull was nodding. "I knew it, Petey. That songbird's chirping was meant to lead us straight into the deep, dark woods. Fucking *blindfolded*."

Nimec was thoughtful. He started rubbing his forehead out of habit, touched the bandage over his eye, felt the wound smart. Later, at the hospital, there would be more tests. He hoped they came with painkillers.

"What about Begela?" he said, jerking away his hand. "You think he was being straight with the insurance man about why he nixed the permit apps?"

Scull shrugged.

"Maybe yes, maybe no," he said. "Could be he's just a careful guy. But the thing that sticks out at me is how strong he went at Fowler. Real heavy-handed. Begela couldn't've made it any clearer he'd be spreading bad word about their coverage if they didn't back off, which to me sounds like political blackmail."

"Agreed," Nimec said. "That's pretty sleazy for somebody who writes about his good conscience. Don't know what kind of fair play laws they have in this country, but in ours, he'd have been pushing toward a serious breach."

Scull nodded.

"Big time, Petey," he said. "Big time."

They rode along in silence a while. The Rover took a sharp turn and swung Nimec to one side, making him a little dizzy as he braced himself in his seat.

DeMarco flicked a glance at him in the rearview.

"Sorry, chief, almost missed our exit," he said. "Guess

I was too busy thinking about what Vince said to you a minute ago."

Scull leaned forward over the backrest. "About what?"

DeMarco shrugged, his eyes on the road again.

"Gunville trying to lead us into the woods," he said. "Because I have to admit, it sounds to me like there are more big bad wolves running around in them than we can count."

"Are you going to come out and say this is the last time, or does it have to be me?"

Roger Gordian paused silently over an open valise on the bed, a starched, pressed, and folded dress shirt in his hands. His wife's question was not altogether a surprise, and he had no wish to avoid it. While Gordian had trouble sharing his innermost thoughts even with those dearest to him, the days when he'd kept them in a lockbox were long past. The sharing wasn't always comfortable, but he did it for those he loved, and because in his heart he acknowledged it was important for him, too. With Ashley, now, especially, he tried. Their marriage had suffered too much when he hadn't.

Sometimes, though, he still needed urging. And if Ashley had intentionally posed her question as an ultimatum to grab his attention, she'd succeeded.

Gordian put the shirt into the valise, then turned to face her. She stood over by the dresser across the room, packing items into a new luggage accessory she'd bought him in one of the designer shops down at the Stanford Shopping Center whose names he could never quite remember. No doubt, the thing was overpriced. Admittedly, it was handy and useful. He wasn't sure what to call it . . . a deluxe travel kit, maybe. Black with two clear-plastic zipper pockets and an opaque nylon pouch below them, it was designed to look like a downscaled

garment bag, hanger hook and all, when unrolled. Roll it
up, buckle the strap, and the bag turned into something
that resembled a cross between a standard shaving kit and
SWAT fanny pack. Clever.

"Don't you think we ought to discuss this before either
us makes any declarations?" he said.

She gave him a look, her large eyes penetrating.

"We can," she said. "But whether or not you care to
admit it, we both know the way it should be."

Gordian was quiet again. Ash's orderliness and thor-
oughness were, as ever, impressive. She had laid the
newfangled travel kit atop their dresser and loaded it with
enough personal hygiene supplies to keep him clean and
scrubbed for months if he wound up cast adrift on a remote tropical island, assuring he would make an impec-
cable presentation of himself when rescuers arrived . . .
or the resident cannibals took him to their leader, whichever came first. Filling the upper pocket were a soap bar
in a lidded plastic dish, nail clippers, cotton swabs, a
deodorant stick, a scissors and tweezer set, a roller-type
lint remover, a comb, a hairbrush, a toothbrush, toothpaste, tooth*picks*, a pack of Kleenex, and a washcloth
folded into a perfect compact square. The pocket underneath held similar contents—sunblock, insect repellent,
disposal razors, a styptic pencil, a small can of shaving
gel, and a Ziploc bag containing smaller bottles of
mouthwash, antiseptic, shampoo, and conditioner. In the
open nylon pouch under the two clear pockets, Gordian
could see an assortment of vitamin, aspirin, and prescrip-
tion drug containers, including a vial of antimalarial tab-
lets he had begun taking a week ago in preparation for
his trip, and the nebulizer he used whenever his breathing
gave him difficulty.

He watched Ashley in silence a moment longer, noticing she was holding yet another little glass bottle in one

hand. On it was a homemade sticker he could tell had come out of her label maker, the word printed across it in red capitals partially covered by her fingers. In her other hand was a round, dime-size piece of aluminum foil she had cut from a sheet beside the rest of the items on the dresser.

"What have you got for me there?" he said.

"Let's not change the subject."

"I wasn't trying," he said honestly. "It's just that I'm curious."

Ashley shrugged.

"The bottle was a sample giveaway of moisturizing lotion," she said. "I finished all the lotion and hung onto it."

Gordian nodded.

"I suppose there's no sense throwing out good bottles," he said.

"None," she said. "That's a complete waste."

"What've you filled it with now?"

Ashley held it up. "See for yourself."

Gordian glanced at the label.

"Astringent," he said, reading it aloud.

Ashley nodded.

"There you are," she said. "You'll be glad to have it with you in the hot weather."

Gordian paused. *Impeccably scrubbed and unblemished.*

"And the foil?" he said.

"A safety seal to replace the original one." Ashley said. She carefully fitted it over the neck of the bottle, pressing the edges tight. "If the cap comes loose and there's a leak, it might ruin something in your suitcase."

Gordian gave her a look that was perhaps nine parts appreciation and one part amusement.

"That's very thoughtful of you," he said.

She nodded, unsmiling. Then she twisted on the bottle cap, took the Ziploc from the second transparent pocket, added the astringent to the rest of its contents, and returned it to the travel kit.

"I have to go, Ash," Gordian said after a while, nothing amused about his tone now. Her dead-serious expression had made him feel a little guilty. "I couldn't avoid the trip to Gabon even when it was all about closing with Sedco. But now it's become about a lot more."

"You feel you have to make a point."

Gordian nodded.

"A show of commitment," he said. "The surveillance on our advance team . . . that hit-and-run on the supply convoy . . . whether or not they're tied together, they make it vital that we move forward as planned. We can't seem to be intimidated by anyone."

She looked at him. "Sedco knows what's been happening to your people in Africa?"

"Dan Parker was briefed, and he's informed Hugh Bennett and the rest of its company officers."

"And they're with you on going ahead with things."

"All the way. Especially Bennett. On Sedco's board, he's got the last word."

Ashley considered that a second.

"I understand your reasons," she said. "But what are his? From what you've told me, he doesn't share your particular interest in supporting nation builders."

Gordian thought a moment.

"King Hughie's used to doing business in difficult environments. He would realize you can't be effective in the region, build upon any accomplishments you've made, by backing down from threats," he said. "And our joint venture aside, my guess is that he believes UpLink to be the prime target of hostile interests in Gabon, figures we'll be the ones to bear the brunt of any escalation." Gordian shrugged. "I also suppose it's possible he simply won't be deterred from staging a corporate tent show with himself as ringmaster. Probably it's a little of this, and a little of that. I'm sure it doesn't hurt that we're providing extra security for everyone and footing the entire tab. In the end, though, it doesn't make a difference. I can be concerned only with my own motivations."

Ashley continued looking at him across the room.

"I know," she said. "And *you* know better than to think I'd suggest that you cancel. But I'm not talking about now. This conversation is about our future."

"I've never asked my people to do what I won't."

"Things have changed, Roger. Sometimes I think everyone knows and recognizes it except you," Ashley said. "You can admit to your physical limitations, handle them, or choose to pretend they don't exist."

Gordian stood by the bed, his gray eyes holding on her green ones.

"I feel fine," he said. "The doctors gave me their full consent."

She shook her head.

"I probably know the results of your checkup better than you do. And all things considered, I'm happy with them. But they don't mean we can erase the damage that's been done to your body." She sighed and leveled her voice. "Two years ago I came closer to losing you than I like to remember. But I'm not able to wish away those memories. We can't afford the luxury. It isn't for nothing that I packed away a nebulizer of albuterol. There's scar tissue in your lungs. Fibrosis. You have shortness of breath sometimes—"

"Be fair. It's generally okay unless I overexert myself. And I've tried hard to be careful—"

"Let me finish," she said. "I'm not accusing you of being cavalier with your health. But you are determined.

Protective. When the stakes are high for the things you care about, you tend to push yourself further than you should. Over the last few weeks, you've taken how many vaccines? Yellow fever, typhoid, diphtheria, hepatitis A. And I'm sure there are some that slip my mind right this instant. Any one of them can have side effects on people whose immune systems never took anything close to the blows yours did."

"Ash, you said it yourself. It's been two years since I got sick."

"You didn't just *get* sick," she said. "You were almost murdered with a biological weapon, deliberately infected with a virus nobody had ever seen before. A strain grown in a laboratory by a process so sophisticated government scientists are still incredulous." She paused and waved a hand toward the window. "Whoever created that germ, whoever tried to kill you, is still out there somewhere. We don't talk about it much these days, I think because you know how it worries me. Maybe we should, though. It's not a trifling detail we can ignore because it's convenient."

Gordian stood there feeling her gaze on him.

"Our marriage is my proudest achievement, what I care about more than anything," he said. "But I've never made you a promise I couldn't keep, and I won't now."

Ashley folded her arms across her chest and gave him a little shrug.

"Then how about trying to make one you can," she said.

Gordian watched her a while without saying anything. Then he strode across the room, came close in front of her, and put his hands on her shoulders.

"I'll think about what you're asking," he said. "Give me until I come back from Africa, and you'll have my answer. I don't know if that does anything to make you worry less. But I want you to feel easier."

She looked at him, then nodded, her eyes overbright. "It's a start, Roger," she said. "It's a start."

There was soft music coming from the jukebox at Nate's, a saloon on San Diego's east side that was an exhausted but tenacious holdout against the pressures of neighborhood gentrification, something that also could have been said of the battered rowhouses shouldered around it on the street like allies in a neglected, fading cause.

Tom Ricci and Derek Glenn sat in a mustard-colored booth toward the back, Ricci sipping a Coke loaded with ice, Glenn drinking imported stout from the bottle and taking long hits on a Marlboro in violation of a clean air law the gray-haired barkeep had resolutely disavowed as unconstitutional, or if not that, then at least undeserving of constitutionality. The four or five other people spaced out along the bar were representative of his dwindling client base, which was almost exclusively male, black, working class, and on the far downhill side of retirement age.

"Business isn't what it was last time I came down to see you," Ricci said.

"Wasn't much, even then," Glenn said. "Notch another win for the civil boosters."

"You sound mad," Ricci said.

Glenn tipped the neck of his beer bottle toward Ricci.

"Sounds like, huh?" he said with a faint smile. "Now I see how you earned your reputation for being an astute son of a bitch."

Ricci watched him take a long pull of the stout. A tall, large-framed black man in his thirties, Glenn headed the bantam security crew at UpLink's regional offices, established in a single renovated warehouse on the Embarcadero waterfront mainly to handle administrative overflow from its Sacramento data-storage facility.

"No reason you have to stay where you are," Ricci said. "I could hook you up at SanJo. A command gig, worth a big pay hike. The rapid deployment team program needs somebody to pull it back together."

A surprised look formed on Glenn's face.

"I thought that was your baby," he said.

"Had to put it down when I went into the field."

"So I heard. But now you're back, and I kind of figured you'd be picking it up again."

Ricci shook his head.

"Decided I work better alone," he said.

"Uh-huh." Glenn looked at him. "It's probably none of my business, but what've you been doing instead?"

Ricci shrugged.

"Catching up," he said.

"Uh-huh."

"Security rundowns."

"Uh-huh."

Ricci hesitated. He reached for his glass, rattled the ice cubes inside, but didn't drink from it.

"And waiting," he said. "Mostly waiting."

"You mind me asking what for?"

"No," Ricci said. "Just not sure I can answer."

Glenn started to say something, appeared to reconsider, and sat listening to the music on the jukebox, a midtempo jazz instrumental carried along by a husky tenor sax.

"I've been hearing all kinds of news about Africa," he said at length. "The hit on that supply convoy, other things besides. What the hell's going down?"

Ricci rattled his ice cubes some more.

"Maybe it ought to be you telling me," he said. "Since you hear so much."

Glenn smiled thinly again. He waited.

"Truth is, I don't know," Ricci said. "I haven't got all the facts yet. A lot of odd stuff's happening over there. All kinds of questions floating around. But it's only been a couple days, and so far nobody's connected anything to anything else. They're not even clear about what the attack was supposed to accomplish."

Glenn exhaled, cigarette smoke streaming from his nose and mouth.

"I guess this makes the extravaganza aboard the oil platform a scratch," he said.

Ricci shook his head.

"Gordian needs to get the Sedco deal done," he said.

"How can they work out a security plan, decide what protective measures to take, when they don't have any idea what to expect? Seems crazy to go ahead with it until they do."

"It shouldn't," Ricci said. "The timing of what happened puts us on the spot. You know the game. The territory we cover, you'll find plenty of uglies who'd love to see us skip out from a threat. That would be giving them what they want."

"Notice we can be intimidated."

Ricci nodded.

"This is bigger than Gabon," he said. "If I were in Gordian's position, I'd do the same as him. He's got to hang tough."

"With some extra manpower to protect him, I hope."

"A fresh Sword detail's flying out," Ricci said. "He'll be fixed okay."

"You mean to join them?"

Ricci shook his head again.

"Pete Nimec can handle whatever comes up," he said. "Better I stay out of his hair, mind the family farm. That way we've got all fronts covered."

Glenn lipped his cigarette, reached both hands into his pants pockets, and fished out a couple of quarters.

"Makes enough sense," he said. "There's nowhere you can feel safe these days. Sometimes I think we're all stuck in the land of Nod."

Ricci's face showed incomprehension.

"You know," Glenn said. "It's from the Bible. Book of Genesis: 'And Cain went out from the presence of the Lord, and dwelt in the land of Nod, on the east of Eden.' "

Ricci shrugged a little. "Religion's never been one of my vices."

Glenn gave him a look.

"I don't suppose," he said.

There was a brief silence between them.

"My offer," Ricci said. "You interested?"

Glenn shook his head no.

Ricci looked straight into his eyes.

"Seems like a fast decision," he said.

"Fast, yeah," Glenn said. "That doesn't have to mean arbitrary."

Ricci kept watching him across the table several moments, then nodded slightly.

"No," he said. "Guess it doesn't."

Glenn finished off his stout, went to get himself a second. Before returning to their booth he stopped at the juke, dropped in his quarters, and punched in some selections.

"Can't find many bargains around these days," he said, sliding back opposite Ricci. "Fifty cents for three good spins on the box is one of the few left."

Ricci's lack of response opened out another spell of silence between them.

Glenn drank his beer, swayed a little to the music in the background. A female vocalist sang to the accompaniment of a piano, its fills running smoothly around her nuanced phrasings.

"The song's 'When October Goes,' " Glenn said after a while. "Singer's Mary Wells. Lyrics by Bobby Mercer, music by Barry Manilow. Nice." He paused and took a deep swallow of beer. "I've dug Manilow since I was in high school."

Ricci looked at him.

"You going to explain your turndown?"

Glenn shook another cigarette from the pack near his elbow, lighted it with a Bic disposable, and sat there smoking. The Marlboro's tip flared on his deep inhale.

"I'll let you in on a little something," he said. "I grew up right in this neighborhood. A rowhouse on Fourteenth Street, two blocks south. All my older brothers wore Crip blue. It's kind of a long story, but I wound up wearing a beret at the opposite end of the color spectrum."

Ricci nodded.

"The flash was black with a wide diagonal gray stripe, yellow borders," he said. "Delta Force, attached to Joint SpecOps. I wouldn't've considered you for my replacement without reading your personnel file."

"I don't suppose."

Ricci regarded him through a haze of cigarette smoke.

"Any special reason you joined the service besides wanting a change of scenery?"

"Like I said, long story," Glenn said. "Maybe we'll get to it sometime. Meanwhile, you can have one crack at guessing where I choose to live nowadays."

"Fourteenth Street. Two blocks south."

"My, you *are* an astute son of a bitch," Glenn said.

He drank, smoked, and listened to his music.

"Family ties why you're back here?" Ricci said.

"Family's gone, one way or another."

"Then what's holding you?"

Glenn's broad shoulders went up and down.

"Maybe it's my volunteer work," he said. "I do a lot with teenage kids."

"Why the 'maybe'?"

Glenn finished his second beer, pushed the bottle aside.

"I think part of it's that I'm just stubborn," he said. "Civil boosters and quick-kill real estate brokers hate the sight of rowhouses. They'd be glad to sweep everybody out of them like litter and doze them flat to make room for more hotel towers, art galleries for rich people who can't draw a straight line to hang their junk, and ritzy apartment lofts where the Swells can live. Try moving into one of those pads—you need to show your broker that you earn fifty, even a hundred times the monthly rent in income."

Ricci looked at him.

"Sounds to me you're on a crusade," he said.

"Could be," Glenn said. "But, you know, the Mexican gangs that smuggle drugs across the border into this city, players like the Quiros bunch we brought down a couple years ago, have a Spanish expression, *plata o plomo*. The silver or the lead. You're either a friend and taking their bribes or an enemy taking their bullets." He shrugged again. "I read a paper by some professors comparing what they do to unfair pressure tactics in business and politics. Fat cat landlords, brokers, and public improvement committees, they just use legal harassment instead of guns. Sometimes to influence each other. Mostly to put the squeeze on tenants. Same principle, different methods."

Ricci sat without offering any comment. The barkeep had dropped onto a chair behind the counter and was watching a ball game on the television above his head, following its action with the volume down—Seattle Mariners, Oakland A's, forty-three thousand screaming fans. Although it was not yet nine P.M., his smattering of customers had evaporated and left him to tend only the two

Sword ops in their rear booth and a skinny old drunk at the bar. The drunk was slouched over a shot glass, mumbling to himself as he threw left jabs and hooks into the empty air. Ricci watched him a moment or two, noticing the punches had snap. Probably the guy had done some real boxing once. *Coulda been a contender.*

Ricci shifted his attention back to Glenn.

"Your answer to my proposition final?" he said.

Glenn nodded.

"Don't get me wrong, I appreciate it. And if you ever need help with something up north, count on me to be there," he said. "But this town stays my home base."

Ricci grunted. He was still rotating his glass between his fingertips.

Glenn leaned forward across the table, pointed to the soda.

"Now you need to tell me if you ever intend to start on that, so I know whether to order another beer or call it a night," he said.

Ricci regarded him quietly, seeming to consider.

"Can't say why, but you quoting the Bible off the top of your head, reading papers by university eggheads, somehow it's no stunner to me," he said. "Explain how you grew up listening to Barry Manilow without the homies kicking your ass every day, maybe I'll stick around."

Glenn grinned, waved his hand in the air to catch the barkeep's attention.

"Settle back and get comfortable," he said.

Ricci gave him the slightest of nods, then carefully raised his glass off the tabletop and drank.

A high-intensity electric lantern in his hand, Siegfried Kuhl strode slowly around the white station wagon and utility van parked near his cabin in the late-night darkness. What he saw satisfied him. The PG&E logo on their flanks, the racked ladder on one side of the van's roof, their yellow safety beacons, every exterior feature was convincing. Indistinguishable from the real thing under his scrupulous inspection.

Kuhl opened their doors one at a time and repeatedly leaned inside with the lantern to examine their interiors from front to rear. Again he was quite pleased. He had studied photographs of the power company's repair fleet and even the upholstery and carpeting matched.

He turned to Ciras and Anton, who stood a few paces from him awaiting his assessment. They had driven the vehicles from a shop outside Monterey where their subterranean customizers had performed the remodeling work.

"Good enough," he said. Then he went to stand behind the vehicles and motioned toward their rear license plates. "You've checked these, too?"

Ciras gave him a quick little nod.

"I was impressed," Anton said. "It must've been quite some trick getting them down right."

Kuhl regarded the spike-haired Croatian with a kind of fascination. Anton's speech bore no trace of the thick Slavic accent, with its hard glottal stops and drawn-out vowel sounds, that had characterized it when he'd been inserted into the United States on a student visa two years earlier. And his capacity to absorb dialect was only part of what suited him for the role of forward scout and intelligence gatherer—the ideal sleeper agent. It was as though Anton could plug into any cultural reservoir and saturate his persona with its mannerisms. While his bluff at the animal shelter had been intended to massage useful information from Gordian's daughter, the performance had gained results that went beyond Kuhl's expectations and had been pivotal to his fixing an operational time-table.

Returning his attention to the license plate, Kuhl shone his light directly onto its face. The tag's reflectorized plastic sheeting material glowed bright under its beam so the alphabetical prefix and serial numbers were illuminated. He stepped back from the rear of the van, moved to one side of the bumper, and again turned his lantern onto the plate.

A vertical row of hidden verification symbols became clearly visible, running down the middle of the tag, dark against its surface. Used by law-enforcement personnel to differentiate authentic license plates from counterfeits, they were composed of tiny glass beads in the sheeting which had been coated with a special polymer that made them nonreflective when viewed at a thirty degree slant. Due to the complex polymerization and embedding processes involved in their production, the coded symbols were the most difficult feature of the plate to replicate. But Harlan DeVane's resources had proven equal to the task.

Kuhl nodded his approval and looked over at the two men. "Move the vehicles into the trees where they can't be seen," he said. "Then join me and the others inside."

He strode back toward the cabin. It was a pleasant night. The air was cool and fresh and the chirping of insects surrounded him. Somewhere in the distance a night bird whooped. He could see Lido watching his approach through a front window, the brute's head silhouetted against the light of the room beyond. A good night, yes. Something of its atmosphere hinted at the best moments of his long *caesura* in Europe—those when he had found a kind of peace at the core of his typhonic restlessness. Perhaps, Kuhl thought, this was because it followed a day on which he had accomplished everything necessary in the way of final preparations, and still managed to exercise his curiosity about something of unrelated personal interest.

Before dawn that morning, Kuhl had gotten into his Explorer and driven west across the Ventana wilderness to the San Antonio de Padua Mission. He carried his fraudulent identification documents in his wallet. Beside him on the passenger seat were his camera and a packet of maps and tourist brochures. The cargo section held a bladdered hydration backpack, a length of rope, hiking boots, his electric lantern, and some basic tools that Kuhl had left in plain sight to ensure they drew no suspicion from military guards—a small wood ax, a collapsible shovel, and a Japanese pull saw.

Kuhl wore an open-collared chambray shirt with a Saint Christopher's medallion on a silver necklace, and had wrapped a rosary around the stem of his rearview mirror. On the vehicle's rear section were a pair of bumper stickers Anton had obtained for him in the city of Carmel. One of them pictured a small map of the original Camino Reál twining in and out of US 101, the sites of the Spanish missions along the road circled and marked by crucifixes. Splayed across the map in large see-through text were the words FRANCISCAN MISSION TOURS, and, below it in a smaller typeface, the name and telephone number of a local travel agency. The other bumper sticker read: I'M ON A MISSION TO SEE THE MISSIONS. An adhesive plaque with the Greek acrostic IXΘYE engraved within the Christian fish symbol was mounted on the SUV's tailgate.

Out past the cattle and horse ranches, Kuhl had wound through miles of rolling scrub country on a steady climb into the Santa Lucia Mountains, where he had seen the sunlight wash up over the wooded lower mountain slopes to eventually flush their bare sandstone peaks with or-

ange. By full daybreak he had reached the edge of the
valley that overlooked the confluence of the San Miguel
and San Antonio Rivers, and made his slow descent into
the basin following road signs to the army reservation
and mission. At length, he stopped at the guard station
mentioned to him by Anagkazo, the dog breeder.

The MP inside the checkpoint booth had politely asked
Kuhl for his driver's license and vehicle registration. As
Kuhl handed them to him through his lowered window,
a second guard had walked around the Explorer, casting
discreet glances first over its body, and then through its
rear windscreen.

They had seen nothing amiss and waved the visitor on
after returning his papers.

On his way toward the mission quadrangle, Kuhl had
passed some branching roads that ran toward a gated can-
tonment and noticed additional barricaded checkpoints
posted with signs reading FPCON LEVEL ALPHA. These
indicated an elevated alert for terrorist activity that had
been implemented as a rule at all military installations in
the United States after the strike on New York City a
few years before—a step up from FPCON Normal, but
significantly below the Bravo, Charlie, and Delta force
protection levels exercised whenever specific threat warnings were issued by federal authorities. Kuhl would not
have chanced his trip if any of the higher stages of alert
had been in current effect, but his men had determined
otherwise, and the mission grounds had been a considerable lure to him—the prospect of an easy penetration
spicing the venture with a provocative element of scorn.

It was also a preparatory drill of sorts. The moment
approached when Kuhl would have to plunge deeper into
hiding than at any previous time in his mercenary existence. Knowing he faced a manhunt of long duration and
unprecedented intensity, he had wanted to test his re-

flexes for survival and subterfuge—smooth any hitches that may have developed over his latent period—in a climate of heightened but nonurgent scrutiny.

More than two hundred years after its founding, a small order of Franciscans still occupied the mission. While some of them chose to live in meditative solitude, others worked in its gift shop and offered guided tours of its grounds on a regular schedule. Kuhl was mostly able to avoid the organized tour groups and prowl the compound alone, stopping to see its olive gardens, its chapel, its cloistered tile-roofed archways, its centuries-old aqueducts and gristmill. Near the end of his wanderings he had found himself in a chamber with simple forms of musical notation painted on the walls. There he studied the instruments on display: a native American hand drum, a violin and cello, a baroque lute and lyre. One wall of the room was covered with a diagram of a huge upraised hand, the front of each finger marked with numbers and Spanish calligraphy. This had caught Kuhl's attention like a barbed hook, and he had stood taking photographs of the diagram, thinking it would be a fine reference for the construction of a possible scale replica, should he ever choose to resume that pursuit.

As Kuhl stood with his eye to the lens, one of the tonsured monks had noticed him from the outer hall and paused in the entryway.

"The chart you see shows the hand signals our fraternal predecessors used to use to teach their Indian converts Western scales," he said. "As new believers, they were taught not only to petition the Lord with their prayers, but exalt him with music."

Kuhl had turned toward the entrance and stared coldly at him over his lowered camera.

"It is good they were given their diversions," he said. "All God's prisoners are in need of them."

Kuhl paid no heed to the monk's reaction. With a slight bow, he had touched a hand to the Saint Christopher's charm around his neck and brushed past him into the hall.

Minutes afterward, he had driven west from the compound. It was not yet one P.M., giving him plenty of time to do his work.

In an oak- and pine-forested stretch of rolling highland some thirty miles back toward Big Sur, Kuhl shifted the Explorer into four-wheel drive, eased it off the roadside into the cover of some scrub growth, and cut the engine. Then he went around to the rear section and got out his hiking boots, backpack, and tools. He changed from his loafers into the boots, loaded the tools into the pack, strapped it over his shoulders, closed the Explorer's tailgate, and started into the brush.

Kuhl had thoroughly scouted the terrain en route to the San Antonio de Padua Mission, concentrating on its prominent rock formations, and was convinced the jutting outcrops would afford the precise geological features he required.

He had searched about for a while before the hollow presented itself to him. At the base of a sandstone rise effaced by weather and the roots of the scrub oak studding its surface, a portion of the hillside had worn away beneath an overhanging ledge to create a moderately deep cave that seemed well suited to his purposes. Here, he believed, was an excellent fallback shelter.

Kuhl had stooped low as he entered the ragged hole of its mouth to investigate, beamed his electric torch into the dark space beyond, and within seconds known his initial impression was correct. The entrance would require covering, but there was an abundance of raw material around him, and he had all the necessary tools in his backpack.

Kuhl found that the long hours he'd spent carving scale miniatures from featureless pieces of wood had yielded a surplus of patience for his work, even a kind of gratification in it, that he would not have known before. Time slipped from his notice as he cut limbs from the trees and underbrush, cleaning the leaves and twigs from the oak branches to form base poles of the proper height, leaving the pine boughs more or less intact, shagged with needles for a rainproof thatch screen. When Kuhl had finished, he sorted the poles and thatching into separate bundles, tied them together with lengths of rope, and brought them into the cave, where they would remain hidden until such occasion as they might be of use.

Returning to his Explorer, Kuhl had checked his watch for the first time since he'd pulled into the thicket. It was just after six o'clock in the evening. The hours had truly gone winging by.

He had been back on the road, headed for his rented cabin, before the last of the sunlight was drained from the sky.

Now midnight had come and gone, and Kuhl could hear the engines of the false power company vehicles awakening as Ciras and Anton started them up and swung away into the darkness. At the door of the cabin, Lido greeted him, licking and sniffing his hand. Kuhl paused to scratch the dog under its muzzle, then strode forward through the foyer. He padded close behind him, treading softly for a creature of its immense size.

Kuhl's bond with the Schutzhunds had been immediate and was strongest with the alpha.

He entered the living room, Lido at his heels. Four men sat waiting there in silence. On the carpeted floor, the two other shepherds peered up at him with their gleaming, attentive black eyes.

Kuhl looked around at his men.

"Let's have one of you put up some coffee," he said. "I want to review tomorrow's action in detail before we rest."

Startled awake by the sound of his own prolonged adenoidal snore, Rob Howell lifted his chin off his pillow and realized the baseball game he'd been watching on TV had been replaced by an infomercial.

Rob glanced at his alarm clock in the flickering glow of the set. It was almost two o'clock in the morning. Wonderful, he thought. The Seattle Mariners and Oakland A's in a match that might very well decide which team won the hotly contested AL West playoff slot, and he'd slipped into dreamland with the score tied at the bottom of the seventh. If that wasn't evidence of a man suffering from acute overwork, Rob didn't know what was.

He groped blearily around on his nightstand for the remote, couldn't locate it, felt for it on the bed, and found it wedged between himself and the vague shape under the quilt that was Cynthia snuggled into a sleeping ball.

"Later for you, Mr. Crap-o-matic Veggie Master," he muttered to the tube, ready to thumb off the power. Then he reconsidered. There was always ESPN to give him the game highlights.

Rob raised the clicker to change channels, landed on the station just as it cut away from a repeat of some NASCAR tournament to a plug for *Sports Illustrated* magazine. Sure, why not, what gave him the right to catch a break? He snorted, thinking he could still look forward to the news crawl at the bottom of the screen when the race footage came back on.

Meanwhile, though, his bladder was sending him an urgent newsflash of its own.

He slipped from under the blanket, tiptoed around the

humongous doggie cushion where Rachel and Monica slept back-to-back—Ross and Joey preferred his wife's side of the bed, while Phoebe had taken a shining to a spot near the head of the baby's crib—and went out into the hall.

It was a chill night—well, *morning*—and after concluding his urgent visit to the bathroom, Rob peeked into the nursery to make sure that Laurie was covered. She was, indeed, nicely tucked in and curled into a ball like a diminutive version of her mother.

Rob blew her a kiss through the half-open door, saw Phoebe's head pop up at him from her favorite nestling place on the rug, blew her one for good measure, and was starting back toward his bedroom when he decided to check on one more thing. He would be leaving for his fill-in shift at the Fairwinds before daybreak and wanted to be certain that he'd put his briefcase of ledgers and files on the little chair Cynthia had stood beside the front door for that single, solitary purpose, hoping to avoid another absentminded misadventure wherein he drove off to work without it.

Sure enough, it was there. Waiting conspicuously for him to snatch it up on his way out to the car.

Rob yawned and turned into his bedroom, having forgotten about a ledger he'd been looking at earlier and set down on the kitchen phone stand before hurrying to watch the ball game's first pitch. Then he climbed back under the blankets with his wife, eager to catch the score—and a few more hours of sleep—beside the familiar warmth of her body.

They would be the last hours Rob and Cynthia Howell spent together in life.

NINE

CALIFORNIA

TIRED, TIRED. AND WHY NOT? IT *WAS* FIVE A.M.

Hitting the SNOOZE control on her alarm clock, Julia Gordian stirred for work on Sunday thinking she could use about four more hours' sleep, which would just about equal the number she'd actually gotten. Not that she felt she had any right to complain. There could be some good, not-so-good, and downright bad reasons for a person to stay awake into the early morning, and though it had been all too long since she'd enjoyed what was undeniably the best of them—plenty of opportunities for *that* had come Julia's way since her divorce, some of them sorely tempting, but she hadn't quite mustered the will to jump back aboard the dating merry-go-round—a baseball game like the beauty she'd watched on television last night made her bleariness seem a fair price to pay.

Julia scooched up under the blankets, fluffed her pillows, settled against them, and drowsed a bit, giving herself a chance to ease into the day. Her mind drifted, touched on this and that like a helium balloon in a light, variable breeze. She wondered if Dad's flight had landed in Gabon yet. Ought to be there by now. Or almost there; he'd left San Jose at three or four the day before. Africa, God. A long, long way for him to go to make a business announcement. He hadn't sounded thrilled about it over the phone Friday night. A necessary spectacle, he'd called it. Then the subject changed. The two of them going on to lament that they'd never made up their postponed lunch date. Things had gotten in the way. Dad's hasty preparations for his trip. Her commitment to the rescue center. Nobody to blame, just the problem with tight schedules . . . so why had they both sounded so guilty? They'd promised to see each other after he returned, and then Dad had transferred the receiver to Mom's hand.

Julia had talked to her for a half hour or so, and then gone out to the grocery to buy some microwave popcorn and other snacks for the game.

She felt her eyelids grow heavy now and lowered them, visualizing its wild final inning. Funny, she thought. Until Craig came along she'd cared nothing for pro sports. Baseball in particular. A bunch of guys packing their cheeks with sunflower seeds, tobacco, and bubble gum as they stood around tugging at their jockstraps. Then she'd watched some games with him during the '98 season and gotten interested. The following year hooked her. Funny, really funny, how her appreciation for what went on around the diamond had outlasted her marriage. But it was *something* positive to carry away from it. And she believed a plus was a plus, worth taking wherever you could.

Last night's game had been one of those simple, fun charges to Julia's battery that helped make it a little easier to be philosophical . . . especially since her favorite team had snatched the win by a hair. Scoreless going into the ninth, Seattle's pitcher throwing a no-hitter. Then a lazy single at the top of the inning, followed by a crushing line drive that led to a one-run ribbie. That had seemed to be the whole ball game right there, but a two-out solo homer by the M's at the bottom of ninth tied it. Then three more shutout extra innings by both teams. Finally, the bottom of the thirteenth, bases loaded, the winning run bunted in on a one-out, two-strike count.

Julia smiled dozily to herself. Poor Rob. He would be driving to the Fairwinds right now with the bill of his yellow-and-green baseball cap pulled down low over his face to hide his dejection . . .

She felt a cold, wet nose prod her hand and slitted open her eyes. Jack and Jill stood at the bedside, fixated on her. Jack was blowing air out his nostrils, a plaintive *murring* snuffle, as though he wanted to dispel any chance of her settling into a deeper doze until the clock bleeped again.

"Uh-uh," she said in a groggy voice. "Get out of town."

Jack paused in his noisemaking, but they continued to stare.

"Can't you guys bring *me* something to eat for a change?"

Jack's ears whirligigged, his head cocked in seeming perplexity. Meanwhile Jill did an antsy little tap dance with her forepaws and rested her snout on the edge of the bed. Then both began to whine in an annoying, sour duet.

"Miserable, rotten creatures." Julia sighed, gave each of them an affectionate bop on the nose with a fingertip. "Better feed you two before the neighbors hear that God-awful routine and accuse me of animal abuse."

She shuffled out of bed toward the kitchen, put up her coffee as the dogs inhaled their food, and then went into her little exercise room. This was her off day from running, and it could not have fallen on a better one. To judge by the chill of her house and leaden sky outside her window, it was going to be another drab gray morning; classic northern California rainy season weather.

Julia did fifteen minutes of stretches at the freestanding ballet bar she'd owned since high school, another fifteen of light weight lifts. Then she showered, downed a breakfast of coffee and banana yogurt, and walked the beasts. By seven o'clock she was in her Honda 4×4 and headed out toward Pescadero.

Julia's drive to the rescue center took under an hour, good time. But traffic was thin at that time of morning, especially headed westbound into the country. Approaching the electric company station across the blacktop, she noticed some road cones arranged around its painted land divider, and then spotted a couple of PG&E vehicles outside the green metal shed—a hatchback in front with its flashers blinking, and a large van pulled halfway behind the shed on its concrete apron. Several workmen stood nearby in hard hats, coveralls, and orange safety vests. One was balanced high on a roadside utility pole, and another two were out in the blacktop by the cones.

This was, Julia realized, the first time she'd actually seen *anyone* at the station, which she'd assumed was either a storehouse or routing center of some kind.

She tapped her brakes and was waved forward by a worker with a SLOW sign in his hand. He glanced into her window as she rolled past, offered her a smile, and she returned it, suddenly remembering the guy who'd stopped by the center last weekend. Barry Hume . . . or maybe the name was *Hughes*. Yeah, that was it. Barry Hughes. He'd mentioned he was a utility man with PG&E and had noticed the center whenever he was in the area. Julia crunched her forehead. Had he ever called Rob for an appointment? She hadn't checked, although he'd really seemed to take a shine to Viv.

A little curious whether he might be among the crew at the station, Julia looked back into her rearview, but didn't see him outside. Of course he could be in the shed or the van, she thought . . . not that it was of particular importance either way.

As Julia reached the wooden sign for the rescue center, it occurred to her that it might be important to find out about any trouble with the local power lines. The clouds had become more threatening after she'd left home, and she had even run into some patchy sprinkles farther east. A heavy fall downpour looked like a sure thing this morning, and since whatever work was being done on the lines probably would have to be suspended once it started, it wouldn't have hurt her to ask the workers what was going on.

Julia considered pulling over, then scratched the notion. She had already hit her right turn signal and started up the drive, and saw no point bothering them right now.

Besides, if the lights at the shop didn't come on when she flicked the switch, she supposed it would be all the answer she needed.

In the false PG&E van's front passenger seat, Siegfried Kuhl waited for the Passport to swing in between the low tree limbs partially overgrowing the bottom of the drive. Then he glanced at his wristwatch.

It was four minutes to eight.

He counted down to himself, heard a few droplets of rain patter against the windshield in the silence.

At precisely eight o'clock he turned to Ciras. Seated behind the steering wheel, he made no more sound than the three Shutzhunds in the rear of the van.

"Confirm that the work on the line has been done," Kuhl said, and tilted his chin toward the utility pole on the opposite roadside, its cables running straight over the treetops to their target.

Ciras reached for his dashboard handset and radioed up. After a moment he gave Kuhl a nod.

Kuhl looked satisfied.

"We proceed," he said.

Rob Howell glanced at his dash clock and groaned in total disgust. A quarter after eight, *damn!*

He'd done it again, only worse.

His Camaro's speedometer needle quivering over the eighty mph mark, Rob shot home from San Gregario Beach along California 84, bearing south-southwest through fog and drizzle, trying to gobble some highway miles without getting nailed by the staties. Under the best driving conditions he would have to lighten up on the gas pedal around La Honda, where the road really started to loop-de-loop, then slow his pace to a virtual crawl as he turned onto the even twistier local routes . . . and he had a hunch the weather would soon become a problem. Slated over with rain clouds, the sky looked about ready to spill its waterlogged guts and compound the hazardously poor visibility with a slick, wet blacktop.

Rob frowned, his face sullen under the bill of his Oakland A's baseball cap. There was no question he'd started out the day on tenuous ground, not from the moment he'd read yesterday's indecent game score on ESPN and abandoned any chance of falling back asleep. But he didn't have any idea how he could have forgotten the weekly payroll ledger. How he could've been so *careless*. And what was more bothersome was that he wasn't sure where it might be.

When he'd finished preparing the ledger on his home computer late the previous afternoon, Rob had copied his entries to a recordable CD, made a paper backup, then slipped both into an accordion folder, which had in turn gone into his briefcase on its chair by the door. That had been about four o'clock, four-thirty. Then, a short while before game time, say six o'clock, he'd pulled the folder just to give the printout a quick eyeball, and compare it with his updated employee list to be certain there hadn't been any omissions . . . and that was where his recollection developed a few critical gaps.

Rob had been trying to mentally retrace his steps ever since he reached the Fairview at seven-thirty this morning, sat down at his desk to transfer the entries onto the hotel's computer, and been dismayed to realize it was missing from his briefcase. He could remember browsing through it on the living room couch, where he had intended to settle in for the A's-Mariner's playoff seed duel. But then Cynthia turned in early—she had been fighting off a head cold for the past week—and he'd decided to keep her company and watch the game on their bedroom TV set. At some point in between, Rob needed to give the baby a feeding and had gone to warm up her formula under the hot-water tap. He distinctly recalled that he'd meant to bring the folder with him, redeposit it inside his briefcase on his way to the kitchen sink . . . but might he have inadvertently carried the folder *into* the kitchen with him?

Could be, he guessed. Either that, or he'd set it down on the coffee table before getting up. What he did remember—or believed he remembered—was that it hadn't been in his hand when he'd entered the nursery with Laurie's bottle, eliminating at least one room as a strong possibility.

Rob produced a long sigh. The drizzle had gotten heavier, and in fact was now closer to a light but steady rain, smudging the road ahead between occasional sweeps of his windshield wipers. He switched them from INTERMITTENT to SLOW and eased off the accelerator before pulling his cellular phone from its visor clip to try his wife again. These days he could barely walk and chew gum at the same time; was he kidding himself trying to simultaneously drive and play detective? But he needed either the CD/R or printout to input his payroll data into the hotel's computer, and it had to be done by tonight. The staff's paychecks were cut by an outside payroll service, and unless Rob electronically transmitted the information so its processors had it waiting in their system first thing Monday morning, nobody at the hotel would get squared away on time next week . . . and he would be the person to blame.

Ah, what I'd give for a home Internet connection, he thought. It hardly seemed an excesive wish. With cash being as tight as it had been since the baby came along, however, anything besides bare bones necessities was out of the question at the Howell abode, and probably would be for a while yet.

Rob was positive he'd feel a whole lot better knowing the folder's whereabouts, but he'd left the hotel in such an agitated rush that he hadn't even thought to call Cynth first. And although he'd been trying to reach her on his cell since eight o'clock or so, she hadn't picked up yet.

He put the phone to his ear and redialed the call, his steering wheel in a one-handed grip. Still no answer. He wondered where Cynth was. She wouldn't take the baby out of the house in this crummy weather, especially since she wasn't feeling well, except maybe to go up to the kennels and check on the greys. But she always brought her cordless with her when she did that.

Rob frowned again, hoping his forgetfulness hadn't gotten contagious.

After a minute's consideration he decided to phone the gift shop. Julia would be at work by now and could track down his wife for him. She had a full plate practically running the shelter single-handedly and Rob didn't like imposing his personal business on her, but he could not imagine a better case for an exception.

He called, listened. The phone at the other end rang. And rang some more. Thinking he might have punched in a wrong number, Rob disconnected, and reentered it. More unanswered ringing. How could there be nobody at either place? He wasn't the type who was quick to worry, but this *did* invite a bit of concern. All Rob could figure was that both Julia and his wife were out back with the dogs. For what reason, he didn't know. He just hoped some sort of emergency hadn't cropped up that required their combined attention.

Rob pressed END, flipped the phone shut, and laid it on the passenger seat beside him. His hands at six and nine again, he gave his engine more gas despite the intensifying rain. The misplaced ledger had suddenly dropped down the ladder in priority, and indeed had almost entirely slipped out of his mind.

He was too busy wondering what the hell was going on at home.

Cynthia Howell was preparing the baby's cereal when she happened to see the accordion folder on the kitchen phone stand.

A box of Gerber's Wheat with Apples and Bananas in one hand, a small pot of warmed up formula in the other, she stood staring at the folder with sudden distress. Hadn't Rob been working on the payroll ledger before the ball game? She believed so. And if that folder contained what she thought it did . . .

"Glumph owwp mooie!" Laurie blurted from her highchair, slapping the food tray with a tiny palm.

Cynthia turned to her, sniffling. Her head felt fat with congestion, and she only hoped the cold germs she'd been carrying around the past few days wouldn't jump to Laurie.

"When Daddy finds out what he left behind," she said, "I've got an inkling he's going to have pretty much the same comment."

"Blehhk!"

"You bet." Cynthia said. "That, too."

She checked the time on the wall clock and frowned. It was a few minutes past eight. Rob had told her he liked to do the payroll the first thing after he got to the hotel on Sundays, get it out of the way to make sure the checks weren't late, and she was surprised he hadn't given her a frantic call by now. But it could be something else had come up that took precedence. Or maybe she was being too quick with her conclusions. This might be a different folder than the one she'd seen him poring over last night. Or he could have removed the disk and print-out from it before he started out this morning, transferring it to a different one for some reason.

Cynthia poured the cereal into the bowl, added a little formula, and stirred them together.

"Pleoww!" Laurie said.

"I know, peapod. Breakfast's coming. Just be patient with me another second." Cynthia set the spoon down on a folded towel. The cereal was a tad too hot and really needed to sit anyway. "I'd better see what kind of upset to expect from Dad."

She went over to the phone stand, picked up the folder, hastily examined its contents, and felt her optimism of last resort evaporate all at once. The CD and printout were inside. Rob had, in fact, forgotten the payroll ledger here at home.

Cynthia reached into a pocket for a tissue and blew her nose. She decided she'd better not postpone inform-ing Rob of her unhappy discovery. The sooner he knew, the sooner he could start back for the folder, or figure out if there was some less inconvenient alternative. As far as she knew, though, he wouldn't be able to get his work done without it.

She read the Fairview's phone number off the bulletin board above the stand, lifted the receiver . . . and to her mild surprise got no dial tone. She frowned, pushed down the disconnect button, released it, and again heard only dead silence in the earpiece.

Perfect, Cynthia thought. Just perfect.

She tapped the button a few more times without any better result, then noticed the keypad lights were out and inspected the phone wire to make sure Laurie hadn't crawled under the stand and messed with it, pulling or loosening the plugs from their jacks. Everything looked to be in place.

"Spo flig?" Laurie cooed behind her in a tone that genuinely sounded as if she understood the problem and wondered what they were going to do to solve it . . . although Cynthia had to admit her maternal pride tended to exaggerate the kid's natural gifts from time to time.

"Wish I knew," she said stuffily, and considered a moment. A few minutes ago she'd heard Julia driving uphill to the center. After feeding Laurie she could take a walk over there, see whether the problem with the telephone was confined to the house. If it was affecting the entire property, and the business phone was down, too, then they would be able to report the trouble using Julia's cell phone.

Cynthia reached into her house robe for another tissue and blew her nose again. That sounded to her like a plan.

She moved to the window. It was a dark and gloomy morning, and it occurred to her that she might have to get Laurie's slicker out of the closet before they left the house. Also let the dogs in from the outdoor pen. Better find out if the rain had started yet.

Even before Cynthia pushed aside the curtain she could hear patters of moisture against the glass. But now something else caught her interest downhill. Two PG&E vehicles were entering the drive. A utility van first and then a station wagon. She watched them approach slowly, the van heading up toward the rescue center, the wagon turning in toward her house.

Cynthia glanced briefly over at the electric range on which she'd prepared Laurie's formula. The indicator light for a hot burner pad was still on, telling her there had been no interruption in electrical power. Nevertheless, she had a hunch her questions about the phone outage were about to be answered.

She stayed at the window long enough to watch the station wagon come to a halt and a uniformed worker get out. Then she started toward her front door, hefting Laurie off her seat along the way.

The baby nestled against her shoulder, Cynthia opened the door just as the worker reached it, and was met by yet another of the young—albeit already eventful—day's surprises.

"Top a' the mornin', laddies and lassies," Julia said, amusing herself with an atrocious cartoon leprechaun's accent. "Shall ye all do your morning toilet, mayhap have yourselves a wee bit of a workout afterward?"

Thirty pairs of keen, curious dog eyes looked at her from gated stalls to the left and right. Before she'd let herself get too settled in at the shop, Julia had decided to step out the back door to the kennels and let the rescues into their exercise yard, knowing they wouldn't budge once it started to rain. Greys were as obsessive about keeping their living areas clean as they were balky about getting wet, and she didn't want them bursting at the seams if the bad weather were to arrive and persist throughout the day.

Julia looked down at Viv, who was already out of her stall beside her.

"You gonna help me open these gates for your buds?" she asked with enthusiasm, dropping the cruddy Irish.

Viv wagged her tail, lowered her forequarters into the play position, and then turned over on her back, rolling about with her long front legs upstretched and her lips pulled into a distinctive greyhound smile.

Julia watched her for a bemused moment, then bent and rubbed her stomach.

"Why do I get the feeling nobody in this joint's got the slightest clue what I'm talking about?" she said.

Over his car radio, the word Rob Howell had heard the WKGO 810 traffic reporter use was *ponding*. As in, "Drivers should expect some localized 'ponding' in sections of the Santa Cruz Mountains, especially along eighty-four near the Highway Thirty-Five turnoff, where we've seen periods of heavy rain over the last hour."

In fact *flooding* would have been a truer description. By the time Rob reached the exit leading onto 35—his usual southbound shortcut—the rain was coming down in buckets and had so completely inundated the ramp beyond that he half expected to see a guy with a grizzled white beard, leather sandals, and a diverse menagerie of critters around him hammering together a wooden ark at the roadside.

Rob checked his rearview, saw there was nobody behind him, then pressed firmly on his ABS brake pedal and swung toward the gravel shoulder. The Camaro's wheels splashed through water several inches deep, their mud guards creating a choppy little wake as he came to an abrupt halt a couple of seconds before he would have made his turn into the exit.

His face tightening into a frown, Rob sat behind the wheel and listened to the steady tattoo of the rain against his car's exterior. From the look of things, the ramp had been washed out by a serious drainage overflow. He supposed it might be worth chancing the turn anyway, but knew he'd be stuck if the backup of water extended out onto the highway. It would be far safer to remain on 84 and take it straight to the Pescadero Creek Road junction—a slower, dippier route, but one the guy in the WKOO weather chopper had mentioned was clear of delays.

The latter it would be, then.

Rob released a long exhale and reached for the cell phone on the passenger seat, wanting to try Cynth again before he got back on the roadway. It had been a while since his last attempt at calling her, and he figured she ought to be within earshot of a phone by now.

But the unanswered rings from both his house and the rescue center did nothing to relax Rob's expression. It just seemed strange . . . Cynth and Julia *had* to be around somewhere. Could the weather have caused an interruption in telephone service? He didn't think it was that severe, at least in terms of the wind being strong enough to blow down lines, or snap any tree limbs that might get caught in them. But you never knew. You really couldn't predict where squalls would kick up when unstable weather systems passed over the mountain peaks and ridges. Lousy as conditions were around him, they could be much worse farther on.

Rob chucked his cellular onto the seat again, returned to the blacktop, and within minutes had persuaded himself he'd gone overboard with his concern. There were a bunch of likely explanations for Cynth not answering, including the one that had just occurred to him. If service had been knocked out, she might be altogether unaware of the problem.

He could just see her wrangling Laurie into eating breakfast about three feet from their kitchen phone, nothing further from her busy mind than the idea that her memory-deficient husband and provider was on his way home right now, and having conniptions trying to get through to her.

"Hi . . . aren't you—?"

"Barry Hughes." Anton produced an effortless smile for the Howell woman, tapping the forged power company name tag on his chest. "I stopped by here last week on my day off—"

"To inquire about adopting a grey, sure," Cynthia said. "You asked if the shop was open, and went to get some information from Julia. I remember you'd mentioned that you were a lineman."

Anton nodded. He stood facing her from the doorstep, his heavy work gloves stuffed into a back pocket of his coveralls. It had started to shower, the rain sizzling on the ground around him, sliding down over the smooth yellow surface of his hard hat.

"Wish I could say I've had a chance to make an appointment to look at the dogs, but life's been all work lately," he said, and paused. "The reason I'm here is to tell you we're doing some maintenance on the cables—"

"Bfow!" Laurie interrupted with a big, gummy grin, reaching a tiny hand out toward him.

Anton chuckled, took it lightly in his own.

"That's exactly right, doll," he said, and then looked back up at the baby's mother. "Anyway, I wanted to let you know your current might be down for a little while.

Five, ten minutes at most. There've been some brownouts in the area . . . nothing major, just some spotty fluctuations . . . and we're trying to trace the source of the problem."

"Oh." Cynthia gave him a questioning look. "I noticed the van heading up toward our kennels."

He nodded. "Your lines look okay, but the couplings are pretty old. That'd be on the poles *and* outside your house and kennels. We're replacing them as a precaution as we go along . . . before things really go *bfow*."

Cynthia gave him a crooked smile.

"I think you might be too late," she said. "Don't know whether it's related to any trouble with the electricity, but my telephone seems to be out of commission."

Anton looked appropriately unprepared.

"Oh." He frowned a little. "Are you sure?"

Cynthia nodded.

"I've been trying to make a call," she said. "No dial tone."

Anton stood there by the door another moment, looking thoughtful. The raindrops continued to dribble off his hard hat.

"Suppose we could have loosened a contact by accident," he said. "Hopefully it'll be something our crew can straighten out right away . . . you've already checked your inside connections, right?"

Cynthia nodded again.

"Just before you buzzed me," she said.

Anton put on another smile.

"With a baby in the house, I sort of figured it'd be your first reaction. Kids always getting into things and all," he said. "If you don't mind, though, I'd like to give it a quick check for myself. Otherwise it becomes an issue with the phone company techs in case we nicked a cable and have to contact them."

Cynthia adjusted Laurie against her shoulder. "Do what you have to," she said, and moved aside to let him in. "It'll get you out of the rain for a few minutes, anyway."

Anton stepped through the doorway, wiped his boots on the mat, let her guide him to the kitchen, and held the receiver to his ear as she stepped back to give him some room.

"Nothing," he said, and made a small show of examining the jacks. "It's out for sure."

She shrugged.

"I was just about to feed the baby, walk up to the center, and ask my husband's assistant—"

"Julia . . ."

"Right, I almost forgot, you met her the other day," Cynthia said. "Anyway, she has a cell phone, and I'm going to need to make an important call."

Anton abruptly hung up the phone and turned to her.

"I'm afraid I can't let you do that," he said.

His tone flatly declarative.

No expression on his face now.

Cynthia stood there in baffled silence, looking as if she was certain she had misheard him.

"Excuse m—?"

"I said you can't do that," Anton broke in, and then flicked his right hand into the utility pouch on his belt and produced the weapon he had chosen for the job. A Sig P232 .380 ACP. White stainless-steel frame, blued barrel. Powerful, accurate, and easily concealed.

Her eyes wide, her lips a wide circle of confusion and fear, Cynthia stared as he raised the pistol, stared uncomprehendingly at the terrible black hole in the center of the gun barrel. She instinctively pulled Laurie close, arms wrapped around her, backing away until she came up short against something hard. The table, a chair, a counter, Cynthia wasn't sure what in her fear and incomprehension.

That gun. That great black hole pointing at her. Aimed at her from across the kitchen.

"No," she said. Clasping the baby tightly against her chest. Laurie crying now, sensing her terror. "Whoever you are . . . *no*."

Anton cocked the hammer of his pistol, a sound that sent a physical jolt through Cynthia.

She held her daughter close.

"No," she repeated in a breathless moan, waves of desperate panic sucking the air from her lungs. "Please . . . take anything you want from me . . . please, *please* . . . just don't hurt the baby . . . *I'm begging you don't hurt my baby*—"

Anton leveled his gun at the spot where the screeching infant was clenched in her mother's protective embrace, the small body against her chest, their hearts pressed together, beating together.

"It won't hurt," he said, and pulled the trigger.

Kuhl heard the dogs start to bark moments before Anton radioed him from the house.

"Phone lines are down," Anton confirmed. "Everything's cleaned out in here." A pause. "The robin has a cellular."

Pulled to a halt in front of the rescue center, Kuhl listened to him over the van's radio and then had Ciras contact the two men posing as utility workers back on the road. They had strung a chain across the foot of the drive to bar access. The signs hung from its temporary posts—one facing the eastbound lane, one facing west—advised visitors approaching the center that it was closed for the day due to emergency electrical repairs. Anyone who attempted to disregard the warnings and somehow tried to enter the drive would be verbally redirected by the men or, if required, stopped by more extreme means.

Kuhl stared out at the rescue center for perhaps thirty seconds, rain beading his windshield, drumming on the roof of the van with increasing rapidity. The silver Honda Passport belonging to Julia Gordian was the only other vehicle in the dirt parking lot. Inside the center's front door were two signs, one of particular interest to him.

Customized in the shape of a greyhound, the sign on the upper portion of its glass pane read:

Welcome to the In the Money Store

A smaller changeable message board below it read:

Back in 15 Minutes

It was the latter that held Kuhl's eye.

He regarded it silently as the penned dogs downhill continued their raucous barking. He had expected his target to be inside the shop. The operation, then, would have been a fast and uncomplicated piece of work—his team entering as utility men, catching her off guard. Instead, they had found her sign on the door. And yet she must be on the premises even now. If not in some backroom of the shop, then certainly on the grounds. Her vehicle was here. She had not been seen leaving the drive on foot. And he doubted some unknown exit from the property existed . . . where could it lead? There was little but woodland for miles in every direction.

Kuhl listened to the husky, agitated barking of the greyhounds. He must assume the Gordian daughter had also heard it and could not wait for her to become alarmed.

Very well, Kuhl thought. Very well.

He shifted in his seat so he could see Ciras as well as the pair of men behind him.

"Prepare yourselves," he said. "We take her now."

Julia had been giving the rescues some exercise out back when the first droplets of rain sent the squeamish dogs into a mass retreat from the yard . . . all except Viv, who'd continued to play the role of devoted sidekick, sticking to her like glue even as the rest of the greys piled up against the cinder-block structure that held their kennels.

Conceding defeat to the weather, Julia let the dogs inside and returned each to its individual stall.

She had no sooner left the kennels, Viv close at her heels, when she heard the barking down at the house. A loud, excited commotion that abruptly gave her pause.

If you're looking for a watchdog, the greyhound isn't for you. I'd tell you a grey's bark is worse than its bite, but you're not too likely to notice one of them doing either.

It was a line Julia had used on the Wurmans the previous weekend, and, her efforts to discourage their interest in adoption aside, it was also the absolute truth. The outburst from their backyard pen wasn't just unusual; she'd never heard anything quite like it. Not out of her own dogs, Rob and Cynthia's, or any of those awaiting placement at the center. Greys just weren't barkers. Julia knew a deep, throaty woof was about the biggest fuss you could expect to hear, and would be a rare occurrence from even *one* dog at a time. She also knew from experience that a single barking grey normally wouldn't set off its companions in a group . . . but from where she stood outside the kennel door it was clear that several, if not all, of the Howells' five dogs had joined in the up-

roar. Which made things seem that much more conspicuously odd to her.

Julia didn't get it. And Viv's distressed behavior was
a fair indication she felt the same. The dog had sidled up
against her leg for reassurance, her whole body shivering
with tension.

Julia stood there in the rain midway between the kennels and the shop's rear entrance, laying a hand on Viv
to comfort her.

"It's okay. Be cool." She stroked Viv's neck as the
barking persisted, then remembered the dogs *had* let out
a few sounds of complaint last week when a doe and her
two fawns came straying from the nearby woods to graze
in Cynthia's herb garden. Although they'd stopped once
the deer were scared back into the trees, Julia supposed
the visitors could have returned with braver attitudes than
before. There was no reason for her to conclude the
racket meant anything was seriously wrong.

Still, Julia wasn't inclined to ignore it. Viv was still
trembling against her thigh. The dogs behind the house
hadn't settled down in the least. And she couldn't help
but wonder why Cynthia hadn't stepped out and quieted
them by now.

"Come on, kiddo, how about we go see what's doing?"
Julia said. A moment later she moved on, starting to hook
around the shop instead of heading for the back door,
wanting a straight, unobstructed view of the drive farther
downhill.

Hesitant, ears pinned against her head, Viv lagged behind a second, and then went slinging after her.

Their course change proved a short one. Julia had
taken only about a dozen steps before she halted again
with a sudden, extremely potent blend of surprise and
caution.

She reached down toward Viv, this time pressing a

firm hand against her chest to stop her in her tracks. About twenty yards ahead at the side of the shop, a couple of men in power company uniforms stood by a window in the falling rain. One of them was leaning forward to peer through it with his face almost pressed to the glass and his hands cupped around his eyes. The other stood with his back to him, gazing out across the property toward the wood line, his head moving from side to side.

The discovery gave Julia the creeps. It was a strong reaction, sure, and she was ready to admit the uncharacteristic barking of the Howells' dogs might have quite a bit to do with its provocation. She had, after all, passed the linemen working down near the roadside transfer station, or storage depot, or whatever it was. Julia guessed it might be possible they had attempted to reach her at the shop for some reason, found its door locked, and decided to see whether she might be located in a back room.

Possible, yes. Except she didn't believe that in her heart. There was a lurking quality to their presence she would not allow herself to dismiss as anything else. Since when did utility workers go snooping through windows if you didn't answer the door? She'd adjusted her message board to say she'd return in fifteen minutes—not a long wait by any account. Not even if they had urgent business. And as far as the guy facing away from the shop, his head turning ever-so-slightly left and right as his partner leaned up against the windowpane . . . Julia couldn't help it, but he struck her as being on the *lookout*.

She debated what to do next. If she hadn't left her cellular in her purse, and her purse in the shop, a logical first step would have been to check in with Cynthia down at the house. Minus that option, she could reverse direction, skirt around the back of the store to the other side, and take a look at what was happening downhill from there . . . or maybe from the woods edging the property. It seemed paranoid, sure. Could be she was letting herself get very carried away with things. And say she *were*. Besides possibly winding up soaked to the bone, what did she stand to lose by being careful? At worst she'd feel foolish later on, have a laugh at her own overactive imagination as she was drying off with a towel. And at best—who knew? Really, who knew what these guys were doing out here?

Or what they might have done at the house to get the dogs so upset, Julia thought, aware of their undiminished barking.

She backpedaled, her hand still on Viv's breast, gently prodding the greyhound to join her, wanting to move behind the shop where the men couldn't see them.

Viv didn't budge. Her fur was slick from the rain but she seemed indifferent to it, almost oblivious, and was staring at the two men in coveralls with her ears raised stiffly erect and turned forward. Although her body remained tense, she was no longer trembling.

These were not encouraging signs. Julia had found that Viv took to baths with less complaint than many greys, but she was still water shy, and like all members of the breed highly sensitive to changes in temperature. Under ordinary circumstances a chill downpour would send her into a squirmy run for cover. Instead, she had not moved from her alert set and was studying the men with her head pointed toward them like an arrow.

Julia gave her another little push.

"Let's go, Viv," she said in a low, insistent voice. "Now."

The grey offered a final bit of resistance and then complied.

Moments later Julia was hurrying past the shop's steel back door. Viv stopped once to look behind them, but

Julia got her attention with a light tap to the head and urged her on.

Julia had gone just beyond the door when she saw a second pair of men in power company uniforms rounding the opposite side of the building.

They spotted her at the same time, locking their eyes on her, staring straight at her through the driving rain.

Then they started walking rapidly toward her.

Julia froze with alarm. She did not know who these people were, or what they wanted. Didn't understand what was happening. But there was no longer any question that they meant trouble.

A heartbeat later, she realized how serious it was.

As she watched the men approach, Julia saw both of them reach into their coveralls and suddenly bring out weapons, guns of a sort she knew weren't pistols, but thought might be Uzis or something very similar.

She glanced over her shoulder, her heart lurching. The men she'd seen at the west window had turned the corner of the shop and were advancing on her from behind, those same compact assault rifles also having appeared in their hands.

They were closing in.

Four armed men.

Closing in on her from both sides.

Julia stood rooted in place another second, trying to think despite the terror whirling through her mind. She couldn't go forward, couldn't retreat, and recognized it would be hopeless to consider making a run for the woods. *What*, then? What was she supposed to do?

Her eyes darted to the back door of the shop. If she could make it inside, get to a phone fast enough, she'd at least have a chance to call for help. The police, her father's security people . . .

It was her only option.

"Viv!" she shouted. *"Come on!"*

Julia hurled herself at the door, tore it open, and ran into the shop, Viv sprinting after her, following her inside a half second before she slammed and locked it behind her. She passed through the storage and orientation rooms to the rear of the counter, lunged for the phone by the cash register, snatched it up . . . then suddenly felt every ounce of blood in her veins drain toward the floor.

There was no dial tone. No sound in the receiver. Nothing but the flat, crushing silence of a dead line.

All at once Julia remembered seeing the workers, the men who'd been *posing* as workers, high up on the utility poles as she'd driven in from the road a little while ago.

The telephone wires, she thought.

Whoever they were, they had cut the wires.

She stood for the briefest of moments, her breath coming in broken gasps, Viv pressing against her leg in the cramped area behind the storefront counter. Then she heard a loud thump outside the storage room, another, and knew her pursuers were trying to break their way in through the door. One chance left, and not much time. She tossed down the receiver and grabbed her purse off the counter, snapping open its clasp, reaching inside.

At the rear of the shop, a crackle of automatic gunfire, then the sound of the back door bursting open. Steel or not, the bullets would have destroyed the simple cylinder lock in its knob.

She groped in the purse for her cellular phone, pulled it out, flipped open its earpiece. There were footsteps behind her now, hurrying through the storeroom. Only seconds left. Julia's heart racing, she fingered the cellular's ON button, listened to the inane electronic theme that sounded when it was powering up, waited with maddening helplessness for the little smiley face welcome image to pop up on the LCD screen—

She had enough time to see the figure of a tall, broad man appear outside the storefront entrance, *just* enough to note his utility worker's uniform through its glass pane before the door exploded inward with a loud crash, the little clutch of bells above it jangling wildly, its wood frame fracturing, splintering apart as something stormed into the shop ahead of the man, an animal, a huge black-pelted dog, hurtling forward at his shouted instruction, coming straight at her, all fur and teeth.

That was when Viv leaped out from behind the counter.

Kuhl had kept his stubby MP5 subsonic extended as he kicked in the rescue center's door, ordering Lido forward with the German commands demonstrated by Anagkazo.

The sight of a greyhound dashing out around the end of the counter caused him some small surprise and perhaps even a cold flash of appreciation for its pluck. But his cardinal rule was to be ready for the unexpected . . . why else had he acquired the Schutzhund dogs?

The grey leaped at his alpha in a blur of speed and collided with it midair, knocking it down onto the floor with its own momentum, snapping at it with a kind of rumbling growl. Its teeth sank into the alpha's shaggy black hide and slicked its breast and neck with blood.

Kuhl swung his carbine at the greyhound from where he stood in the door, squeezed off a rapid three-round burst. Crimson spurting from its flank, the grey emitted a shrill yelping scream that sounded almost human, rolled from his alpha in a flail of limbs, and then lay heaped on the floor.

The situation remedied, Kuhl shifted his attention to his target. She stood behind the counter, staring at the greyhound's still, blood-splashed form with mute horror. There was a cell phone gripped in her right hand.

Kuhl did not pause. He held his MP5 straight out and crossed the room toward her, simultaneously calling Sorge and Arek from the parking area. Back on all fours near the sprawled grey, his lead dog seemed essentially unharmed despite the deep bites it had sustained.

Kuhl ordered the alpha forward again.

"Voran, hopp!"

Go on, over.

Lido reared toward the four-foot counter, bounded over it, and fell upon the Gordian daughter—a leaping drive that knocked her back against the wall and then down onto the floor under his mammoth weight. Fixing its eyes on her right hand, interpreting the phone it gripped as a possible weapon, the alpha took quick action to disarm her and buried its fangs in her wrist.

She produced a sharp cry of pain, her blood mixing with the alpha's saliva, smearing its teeth and gums with red-laced foam.

Kuhl saw the open cell phone drop from her hand and go clattering to the floor as the great canine held her arm in its bite. He came around the counter, slid the phone out of her reach with his booted toe, and reached down for it.

It was an UpLink, he noted aridly.

Kuhl examined its backlit main display screen and determined there was no active connection. Then he pressed the mouse key and went through its menu selections until he found the call history feature. The Gordian daughter's recently dialed phone numbers appeared in the order the calls had been placed. Satisfied that the last she had made was not a 911, he highlighted the number and pressed SEND to determine who the recipient might have been.

An answering machine picked up after two rings, its greeting in the Gordian child's voice—her home phone.

Kuhl disconnected. Most likely the purpose of her call had been to remotely check incoming messages, but he wanted to assure himself she had not left a message intended to alert anyone who might discover it as to precisely what had occurred here.

When they learned, it would be at his will.

Poised over his captive behind the shop counter, Kuhl turned his MP5 down at her, peripherally aware his men had gathered in the small back room to his right. Sorge and Arek sat at wait behind him.

"Give me your remote play-back code," he told her.

Silent in her pain, her eyes bright with defiance, she glared at him over the barrel of the submachine gun. Blood dripped from her arm over the alpha's clamped, bristling jaws.

There was, Kuhl realized, much of the father in her.

He pushed his weapon closer to her face, decided to make a threat of what already had been done.

"The code," he said. "Give it to me, or I will order the woman and infant in the house downhill killed."

She kept looking up at Kuhl, her eyes boring into his own.

"I do not bluff," he said.

A flicker of hesitation on her features. A blink. Then her silence broke.

"Six-four-eight-two," she said.

Kuhl recalled the home phone number, interrupted her recorded greeting with the code. There were no incoming messages stored in the machine.

Good, he thought. His assumption had been correct. She hadn't had time for hasty warnings.

Kuhl hit the END button again, moved the scroll bar down to the next listed number, and then dialed it as an added precaution. He listened to a prerecorded announcement for the business hours of a sporting goods shop. Yet another prosaic call.

Good and better.

"The people down at the house," the Gordian daughter said in a croaking voice. Her arm still locked in the alpha's mouth. "I don't know what you want from me . . . but promise you won't hurt them."

Kuhl said nothing. He motioned to his men.

They closed in around her, rifles leveled.

"Wait, please." A single tear spilled from the corner of her eye and tracked down her cheek. "My dog . . . at least let me take a look at the dog . . . I can't just leave her—"

Kuhl interrupted her with a shake of his head.

"No, my caged robin," he said. His face set. "No promises, no negotiation."

TEN

It was nine o'clock when Rob Howell finally saw the wood-burned sign marking his hidden drive in front of him. As he sloshed his Camaro toward the foot of the drive, Rob glanced up at the utility pole near the PG&E routing station across the road and didn't see any downed or sagging phone wires, but knew he couldn't draw any conclusions from that alone. A service outage could have occurred elsewhere in the grid, or resulted from a loose contact that would be discernible only on close inspection.

What couldn't have been more evident was that the area had been under heavy showers for a while. The concrete circle around the station where utility workers would sometimes park had been set off the road at a slight incline, and Rob didn't remember ever noticing a significant rain buildup on its surface. But a deep sheet of water had covered and overflowed the empty apron, gurgling down its lip to swell the drainage culvert at the margin of the blacktop.

Rob's quick glance at the station evoked a twinge of residual annoyance at the two power-company vehicles that had sped past him in the opposite direction about five miles back, soon after he'd turned onto Pescadero Creek road at the Highway 84 junction. A van and a wagon, he recalled that he'd seen them hurrying toward him on the deluged road, slowed his car, and expected their drivers to do the same out of common sense—if not simple courtesy. Instead they'd continued along at a full tear and splashed his windshield with a blinding curtain of water that threw him into a brief swerve. Rob had been astounded by their recklessness, and was certain he'd have landed in a ditch if his experienced driver's reflexes had been a whit slower.

But there were other things to occupy his mind right now. Pulling into the driveway, Rob glimpsed Julia's Honda Passport straight ahead outside the rescue center, then saw his doddering old Ford pickup over to the left next to his house. These seemed sure signs that both Julia and his wife were around. The big question, then, was where?

Rob drove the thirty feet or so toward the house, coasted left onto the dirt-and-gravel track branching toward it, and suddenly heard the dogs barking like crazy out back in their pen.

A sense of foreboding crept over him. There was no way Cynth would leave them in the pen under any circumstance, not in this torrent. What they were doing outside? And what in the world could *possibly* be causing them to make so much noise?

As he ducked out of the Camaro to the front door, keys in hand, Rob had time to note almost unconsciously that nobody had come to the window upon hearing him pull up.

Oblivious to the accordion folder on its stand beside him, Rob paused in the doorway to wipe the soles of his shoes on the entry mat, an act of habitual normalcy in a life from which every trace of the normal was about to depart. He would never recall anything else from the time he swung off the road until after the police arrived. He would not even remember mustering the presence of mind to call them on his cell phone . . . this hole punched in his memory by shock and horror the only mercy availed him that day, and perhaps all that kept him sane in the countless tormented days and nights to come.

For Rob Howell, the chasm between before and after would open with that automatic, momentary pause.

So absurd and yet so natural.

Wiping his shoe bottoms on the mat.

"Cynth?" he called from inside the door.

No answer.

"Cynth? You home?"

Still no answer.

Rob moved farther through the house, saw the kitchen light was on, and found his gaze suddenly drawn to a puddle of wetness on the small section of floor visible through its entry from his angle in the middle of the hallway. Something was spilled there on the floor. Something red. Splashed across the floor tiles, tendriled out into the thin puttied spaces between them. A gleaming puddle of red on Cynth's precious new kitchen tiles, which Rob had painstakingly laid himself not three months earlier as a fifth anniversary present to her.

His heart thumped.

"Cynth?"

Not a sound except for the greys barking outside.

Dread perched on his shoulders like some cruel taloned bird, Rob rushed into the kitchen, looked down near the feet of the table, and began screaming wildly into the silence of the house, his legs melting away underneath him, the world blurring out in a gush of tears, screaming, screaming, his wails of horror and grief rising from the bottom of his lungs until they shredded off into hoarse, hysterical sobs.

What he had seen was an abomination.

• • •

"Hey, Roger, you made it!" Hugh Bennett said in a bassoon voice, coming over from the parlor entry. "Been looking forward to this a while . . . heard you were finally on the way from the airport! Guess it's been quite a haul for all of us staying here—except Tom o' course!"

In Gabon only a few hours, Roger Gordian was not too surprised to find King Hughie waiting for him at the large colonial home of Thomas Sheffield, an expat Sedco official whose guest he would be for the next couple of days.

What *did* catch him unprepared was the retinue of perhaps eight or ten suited, seated Sedco executives in the parlor behind Hughie.

"Good to see you." Gordian looked into his large, broad-cheeked face. Bushy white eyebrows ran together under the forehead like, a solid raft of clouds. "Everyone's here for dinner?"

Bennett slapped him on the back as they shook hands.

"And an informal meeting, Gabon-style!" King Hughie said. "They say people like doing business at night in these parts! And *I* say, great! No time beats the present for ironing out the details of tomorrow's ceremonious occasion!"

Gordian looked at him. Did he really believe everything that left his mouth had exclamatory value?

"I hope you'll understand that I need time to freshen up," he said. "It *has* been a long trip."

Hughie looked over at Sheffield, who had been standing beside Gordian in apparent mortification.

"Not a problem!" he said. "Tom's got himself a damn well-stocked wine cellar . . . and his cook went and prepared some *beee-eau-ti-ful* hors d'oeuvres to tide me over while I do my sampling!"

• • •

The two police detectives arrived first thing the next morning with an attitude of impatient irresistibility.

Megan's response was to be patiently immovable.

She had sized them up the moment they entered her office and known they were poised to intimidate. Perhaps because they were men addressing a woman, or law officers accustomed to throwing around the weight of their authority, or for some combination of those or other reasons. She didn't really care. They had stated what they wanted. She was determined to learn more about why they had come before offering her compliance. But although they wore their game faces as well as she did, and a sense of pressing urgency could be felt on both sides of her desk, Megan thought her clearer view of their relative positions might give her a bargaining edge.

The leveler was how much their presence worried her. She couldn't afford to let them see it.

"Ms. Breen, we need to speak to Roger Gordian about his daughter," said the senior investigator for the third time. His name was Erickson. Probably in his late forties. Big squarish face, cornflower blue eyes, a crop of wavy, canary blond hair wet from the rain outside. He sat with his right leg across his opposite knee, wearing brown off the-rack mufti under his open raincoat. "You say he's traveling someplace?"

"He's abroad on business," she said. "In Africa. It's no secret."

Erickson studied Megan across her desk. "Even so, you must be able to reach him. Or his spouse." He paused, added, "We've tried their residence but no one seems to be present."

Megan converted the tension in her facial muscles to an expression of firm resolve. Erickson seemed dogged but not confrontational. He might be the one to deal with.

"I believe Mrs. Gordian is visiting with relatives," she

said. "But you have my full attention. As the senior executive at UpLink in his absence, I'm responsible for managing its affairs. They include observing Mr. Gordian's privacy and keeping him from being unnecessarily distracted. If you'll tell me—"

"How about you make those job responsibilities include giving us some cooperation?" interrupted the other man.

He'd introduced himself as Detective Brewer, strong emphasis on the job title. Thin, narrow-eyed, and about ten years younger than his partner. A small-town cop from Sonora who was suffering from an overkill of TV crime dramas and thought tactless and pushy equaled urban tough. He wore no topcoat over his navy suit and had left his umbrella in the stand out in her reception room.

Megan directed her response at Erickson.

"If I'm to contact Mr. Gordian, I need to know generally what brings you here," she said.

The older cop sat very still. His eyes showing a flicker of compromise before the flat resistance dropped back over them.

"We need some information about his daughter," he said.

Megan concealed her disappointment. It was only when she braced for the question she needed to ask that her control almost faltered.

"Has anything happened to Julia?"

Erickson took a breath, released it. Megan saw his foot move up and down over his knee.

"We have to get in touch with Roger Gordian," he repeated again, clinging to his laconic manner.

Megan waited before she answered. Her office was silent. The double-pane glass of its windows completely deadened the lash of wind and rain against them, some-

how increasing her awareness of the dark splotches of
moisture on Erickson's coat.

"So far we've been talking through a wall," she said.
"It's difficult to come together that way. How about we
step around it and see if it works any better?"

Brewer shook his head angrily, almost rising off his
chair. "We don't have to do anything or step anywhere.
We are conducting a police investigation, and you should
be aware you're on the brink of obstructing—"

Erickson got his partner's attention with a tap on the
knee, held up a preemptive hand. He looked embarrassed.

"Consider us as having stepped," he said.

Megan kept her eyes off Brewer's flushed face as he
settled back in his chair. Compounding his belittlement
would serve no useful purpose.

"I realize that whatever has brought you here must be
very serious," she told Erickson. "And you can rest assured I'm ready to help you reach Mr. Gordian and anyone else who has to be contacted. If there's bad news to
be broken, however, I intend to be the person who does
it. As a second in this company and a close family friend.
But I obviously can't until you tell me what this is
about."

Erickson sat there looking at Megan another moment,
shrugged, and uncrossed his legs.

Then he leaned forward and told her.

"Still ain't heard nothing from Africa?" Thibodeau said.

"Not yet," Megan said. "Pete's on his way to tell Gord
right now."

"Seems like it's taking a while," Ricci said.

"When I spoke to him, he was outside the city. It's
night in Gabon, and I don't think there are any passable
roads through the jungle. He's flying back to Port-Gentil
in one of our helicopters."

"What was the problem reaching Gordian yourself?"

Megan looked at Ricci across the small conference table. "He's staying as a guest at a local Sedco executive's home to avoid the bugs in the hotel walls, and they're behind closed doors having a late consultation about that affair on the oil platform. Hughie Bennett and his entire court are in attendance, and I don't want the boss to hear this news over the phone under those circumstances." She paused. "Better Pete tells him in person. He should be there any time."

Ricci did not answer. His glassy calm eyes gave no clue to what he might be thinking or feeling. Megan saw her reflection in them and could not keep her own nerves from becoming exposed. That was unlike her, and she resented him for it—how much more of herself might be revealed on the mirror's surface?

She sipped from the glass of water beside her to relieve her parched throat.

"I don't know, Rollie," she said. "My mind is everywhere at once. I know I'll pull it together, but for now I just can't center."

Thibodeau nodded grimly.

"Soup to soup," he said. "Be a Creole saying I heard a lot growing up. Ain't no food for the pot tonight, we find something to put in it tomorrow."

She gave him a thin smile. "I'll try to remember that one."

"*Oui.*"

Megan was quiet a moment. With the detectives in her office, she had called Nimec to break the news about Julia, then phoned Ashley Gordian's sister's house in Los Angeles, gotten the answering machine and left an urgent message for Ashley to get in touch. After that she had summoned Ricci and Thibodeau down here into one of

UpLink SanJo's underground safe rooms—a spare rectangular enclosure that was little more than the conference table and four windowless, two-foot-thick concrete walls webbed with an array of interstitial countersurveillance systems.

It hadn't taken her long to share what she knew, and none of it was encouraging. Julia Gordian was gone from the animal shelter where she did volunteer work a number of days a week. The woman whose husband operated the shelter had been shot dead along with her infant daughter, their home a crime scene Erickson had described as beyond horrible.

"This Rob Howell," Ricci said now. His eyes went to Megan as he spoke. "Those cops figure he's clean?"

"He's under no suspicion of having been involved," she said. "His co-workers saw him arrive at the hotel Sunday morning, then rush back home—he'd forgotten a bookkeeping file of some sort. His cell phone LUDs show the calls that were placed from his car to his house and the greyhound rescue center. He uses FastTrack for his bridge tolls, and account deductions were recorded both ways at the plaza lanes off Highway One into San Gregario. He also bought gas with a credit card on his return trip. In both cases the systems show when those expenses were paid and back up his story."

"Don't tell us nothing about what he did before he left his place," Thibodeau said. "Or after he got back."

Ricci looked at him, then shook his head.

"You consider travel distances, average road speeds, and the time Howell's call to the police was logged, it narrows things far as opportunity," he said. "My guess is the operation was planned for when he wouldn't be around. Pro all the way. The phone lines disconnected at their feeder pole, more than a single type of weapon used.

There were fresh tire tracks showing several vehicles at the center and at the utility station near the pole." His eyes returned to Megan. "Is Howell available? In case we need some information from him."

"I don't know." She took another drink of water. Her tongue and throat continued to feel as if they were lined with sandpaper. "I suppose I should have thought to ask—"

"You done your'n fine," said Thibodeau. "Those detectives gave you enough to think about. Ain't likely they would've been generous with that information anyway."

Ricci kept looking neutrally at Megan.

"You told me the cops found blood at the animal shelter."

"Yes, I did."

"That it might be Julia's."

"Yes."

"What makes them think she's not a third murder victim?"

Megan stabbed a look at him, her shoulders rising a little.

"Let's not try to be too delicate."

"I was asking a question."

"About the boss's daughter. And my good friend."

"I have to know what there is to know," Ricci said. "You don't like my way of phrasing things, I'm sorry."

But he did not sound apologetic. Megan's posture remained very straight, her eyes green fire in a face pale with strain.

"There was blood at the shelter," she said. "And, yes . . . it's believed to be Julia's. But Erickson suggested that whatever took place in there seems of a different nature from the violence that occurred at the house."

"Any concrete reasons?"

"He wasn't about to submit an itemized evidence list

to me, and I didn't press my luck. We could profit from a good relationship with him if he doesn't shy away."

Ricci studied her a moment.

"You find out what line those cops are working, or decide that was out of bounds, too?" he said.

In her anger, Megan could have balled her hands into fists until the knuckles were white, dug her fingernails into her palms. She held her composure and folded them on the table instead.

"Nobody broke into Julia's SUV. There was nothing stolen from the shelter, or the house where the mother and baby were killed. Nothing to indicate robbery was a motive," she told him. "I heard a lot of words from Erickson about processing the crime scene, looking at the evidence, reconstructing what happened without assumptions. But you were a police detective. Do you actually believe they would come right out and tell me they think Julia Gordian was abducted? Right now Julia's status is a question. She's a phantom. A 'whereabouts unknown.' I don't even know that we've reached the time period when she can be officially declared a missing person."

"Doesn't effect what we do, except maybe giving us the chance to get a jump on the feebs," Ricci said. "Once this gets ticketed a kidnapping they'll be all over it."

"I can't see how that's bad," Megan said. "It's not us against them. They have resources. Expertise in the field—"

"And we know how their main office loves sharing intelligence," Ricci said.

He was quiet and still. The silence was like a knot bunched in tightly around his thoughts.

"Won't get us anywhere to sit here talking," he said at length. "I'm heading out to the scene while it's warm. Before it gets too worked over."

Megan wanted to catch Thibodeau's eye but knew

Ricci would not miss the slightest glance. She chose to wait, and Rollie didn't disappoint her.

"No sense you going alone," he told Ricci. "Better you and me get a look at things together."

"I can handle it myself."

"That ain't the matter. We got to figure the local police won't be thrilled by our visit. Be tougher for 'em to shake off two of us than one."

Megan was quick to move in.

"Rollie's right," she said. "He should go, too. I'll make some calls and pull whatever strings I can from here."

Ricci regarded her closely. "That a suggestion or an order?"

"It's how I want it," she said.

Ricci kept his eyes on her a moment longer and then shifted them to Thibodeau.

"She can give you directions to the shelter," he said, and stood. "I'll wait down the hall."

Thibodeau caught up to him as he was holding his palm to the biometric scanner to bring an elevator for the garage level. He looked to be sure Megan was still back in the safe room before putting a hand on Ricci's arm.

"Keep talkin' to me like I'm some junior rover, it'll get settled between us in good course," he said in a low voice. "But what you said about the boss's girl being killed . . . you don't want to give touch to that around Megan. Don't want to go near it."

"You think it's something we should rule out?"

"I think we all got experience enough to know the could-be's, and Meg sees things clearer than anybody you ever gonna meet. But ain't no cause for you adding to her pain."

Ricci shrugged.

"Fine," he said. "Next time we meet on the subject I'll

be sure to raise the possibility the boss's daughter took off on a cruise to nowhere."

Thibodeau brushed his gaze over Ricci's face.

"Take a look in the mirror some day," he said. "You going to see one cruel son of a bitch."

Ricci stood there a second or two without a word. Then the elevator dinged its arrival.

"Sure enough," he said, and turned to enter the car, leaving Thibodeau to follow him through its open doors.

There were two Sonoma police cruisers parked across the foot of the drive as Ricci's VW Jetta approached in the falling rain. Pulled abreast of each other, the black-and-whites faced in opposite directions and had sawhorses erected on either side of them.

About thirty feet west of the blockade, Thibodeau nodded toward the right shoulder of the road.

"We might want to stop here, stroll on over to them," he said, ending a silence that had lasted for their entire ride to the rescue center. "Be less apt to get their backs up."

Ricci said nothing in response, but whipped the car onto the puddled shoulder.

They got out and continued toward the drive on foot, raindrops rattling hard against their umbrellas.

The cops exited their cruisers in dark waterproof ponchos, walking around from either side as officers will do when strangers come toward them, cautiously, neither trying to hide nor be too conspicuous about the readiness of their draw hands, but keeping them just near enough to their holsters to exert a subtle, nonprovocational psychic weight.

Ricci took note of their guarded stances with an evaluative eye. He had met unknown persons the same way on hundreds of occasions in his decade with the Boston force.

The first cop came forward carefully.

"Gentlemen." A little nod. Calm, polite tone. "What can we do for you?"

Ricci told him their names, flashing his Sword insignia card in its display case.

"We're UpLink private security," he said. "You might've heard of us."

The uniform checked the identification. He nodded.

"Sure," he said. "Good things. I once checked out job opportunities on your Web site. There are some tough prereqs just to snag an interview."

Ricci did not comment.

"Our boss's daughter," he said. "She's your missing person."

The cop gave another nod. He had dropped his showroom face.

"Julia Gordian," he said. "This is a damn bad one."

"We need to take a look around the C.S."

The cop paused a moment. He wore his cap under the hood of the poncho and its bill shed droplets of water as he shook his head.

"Not possible," he said. "The area's been secured."

Ricci stared at him.

"We drove all the way from SanJo," he said. "Make an exception."

Thibodeau tried to moderate Ricci's harshness.

"We understand you got physical evidence needs to be protected and want to feel comfortable," Thibodeau said. "And we won't give it no nevermind if somebody from your department sticks with us, make sure we don't disturb nothing."

The cop gave him a curious glance. "Louisiana?" he said.

"And proud of it," Thibodeau said. "Didn't think any-body could hear no accent."

A grin.

"Went down for Mardi Gras once. Beats the hell out of me how you people can take eating that spicy food."

"Secret's to line the gut with moonshine."

The cop's grin enlarged a bit.

"Look, I really wish I could do something to help, but we have rules about restricting access to unauthorized parties."

Thibodeau made his pitch. "No special considerations for fellas you hear such great things about?"

"None I have any pull to give. You'd need to arrange for special clearance."

Ricci briefly let his glance range over the cop's shoulder. A crime scene van and other police vehicles stood farther uphill. Small clusters of technical services and investigative personnel were everywhere. He noticed a plainclothesman in a raincoat moving between them on the drive. He was hatless, carried no umbrella, and had both hands in the pockets of his coat.

He turned his attention back to the uniform.

"Who's the scene coordinator?"

"That would be Detective Erickson—"

Ricci cut him short. "Then stop wasting our time and call him over."

The cop managed not to look flustered. But his partners were drifting slowly over from outside their patrol cars.

"Unless there's some urgent reason, my orders are to see the investigation isn't interrupted," he said after about ten seconds. Rain bounced off the front of his cap. "I think the best way for you to proceed is leave your contact information so I can pass it up the line."

Ricci stared at him with cold intensity, ignoring the other three uniforms.

"The detective in charge," he said. "Call him over."

His expression no longer friendly, the cop looked about to react to the outright challenge.

Then a new voice: "You two Ricci and Thibodeau?"

Ricci turned and saw the man in the raincoat hurrying around from behind the crosswise-parked cars. His blond hair was wet.

"Erickson," Ricci said.

The detective moved his head up and down, then flicked a glance at the uniforms. They backed off and returned to their black-and-whites.

"Megan Breen just called on my cell," he said. "She told me you were coming, explained you'd like to view the scene."

Ricci nodded.

"She's been very cooperative," Erickson said. "There are certain restrictions on where you can and can't go. You guys agree to abide by them, I'll try to return the favor."

Thibodeau didn't hesitate for an instant.

"Be appreciated," he said.

Erickson nodded.

"Follow me," he said, and then turned to walk back up the drive.

They followed.

An eight-month stint in Antarctica had raised Megan Breen's command of her patience to a sublime level, and she had done everything she could to keep herself occupied while awaiting word from Africa and Ashley's callback. Whatever else was happening, she had a company to manage, as she'd had an ice station to run amid a wide spectrum of crises brought on by both man and nature throughout the polar winter. Her waking nightmare had begun today with two small-city detectives arriving out of the blue to deliver the most unexpected and shocking of messages. The tense, rapidly called huddle with Ricci and Thibodeau had followed without segue in Megan's numbed mind. But the constant reminders that it was still a day at the office were among the nightmare's most surreal components. There were matters she needed to track in every area of operation. Routine decisions to make, clusters of problems to address, requests to grant, deny, or put on hold. Many of them were duties she would have normally considered headaches but counted as blessings right now in her attempts to stay busy. She did not expect to give better than partial attention to anything in front of her, nor stop her fears about Julia from obtruding on her thoughts. Still, Megan could only believe that being partially diverted, maintaining even the flimsiest semblance of normalcy, was preferable to giving in to the sense of helpless, useless, agonizing despair that would be the sure and terrible alternative.

When the e-mail arrived, she was at her office computer making an immense effort to focus on a contractor's bid for the expansion of an UpLink optics and photonics R&D facility outside Seattle. On any other morning, she almost certainly would not have noticed the new inbox item for quite a while. Though she had never bothered to disable the sound notification option on her messaging program—default settings tended to remain in place on her machine out of casual apathy—Megan considered its bell tone an annoying nuisance given the large volume of electronic correspondence she received, and for the most part left her desktop's speakers switched off. Typically, she would check for messages at semiregular intervals throughout the course of her workday—while having her morning coffee, before and after her lunch break, then again perhaps an hour or so before heading home.

Today, however, was not normal. Not typical, no. Not regular or routine by any stretch of the imagination. Today Megan had turned on the speaker volume control thinking she wanted to leave every line of communication open, and it was for this reason that she heard the chime that signaled a message had jumped into her queue. It was the tenth she'd opened in under an hour. Eight of the previous messages were work related. The last had been a nasty bit of junk mail that managed to squeeze through her software filters and, because she was distracted, trick her into opening it with a moderately devious subject line that would have been otherwise identified for what it was by her mental antispammers to prompt a quick delete. All nine were long-term or short-term ignorable.

Until this one.

This turned out to be the message Megan had sought and dreaded, and nothing could stop the cold slide of ice that began to work through her intestines the instant she read its subject, causing her to break into visible shudders as she opened it with a hurried click of the mouse.

Much as she'd tried prepare herself, nothing.

"Don't think I have to reconstruct what happened back here," Erickson was saying. "You can see for yourselves."

Ricci and Thibodeau stood with him outside the rescue center's back door, studying its demolished lock plate and frame.

"Somebody fired a lot of rounds," Ricci said. "Wanted past the door in a rush, didn't care about surprising anyone with the noise."

"Right," Erickson said. "We can thank this rain for

making the ground damp enough to give us some decent
shoe impressions to photo and cast. There were four attackers from the looks of things, came around from either
side of the main building in pairs. Your boss's daughter
must have left those kennels out behind us, seen them
closing in, and hurried through this entrance to try and
get away from them."

Ricci had closed his umbrella and crouched to examine
the door frame.

"You must've pulled a lot of slugs out of this," he said,
running a latex-gloved finger over the pocked, splintered
wood. "What caliber?"

"Nine mil Parabellum," Erickson said. "The ammunition was fragged, but the spent cartridge casings we recovered told us right off."

Ricci glanced over his shoulder at Erickson.

"Big, deep punch for nines, even fired up close," he
said. "There a brand name on those casings?"

Erickson gave a nod. "Federal Hydrashok."

"Premium make."

"That's right."

"Expensive."

"Right."

"You able to tell anything about the guns from the
ejection pattern?"

"Not definitively."

Ricci responded to the cop's knee-jerk hedge with a
look of overt impatience.

Erickson hesitated a moment, exhaled.

"Off the record," he said, "I believe the weapons used
outside this door were subs."

Ricci considered that.

"Outside," he repeated.

Erickson nodded.

"Were shots fired inside?" Ricci asked.

"The shop seems a different story." A pause. "Put on those booties from my kit and I'll show you."

Erickson led the Sword ops through the entrance and back rooms to the area behind the sales counter.

"Be careful where you step." He motioned to several dark brown splatters on the linoleum that had been bordered with tape. "The stains were partially dry when I arrived yesterday morning. Maybe a couple of hours old. It was clear on sight they were blood, but I swabbed and did a Hemodent test to confirm."

Thibodeau studied them a moment, then raised his eyes to Erickson.

"You know whose blood?" he said.

The detective appraised his grave features, the cheeks pale above the dark beard.

"Julia Gordian's purse was left on the countertop," he said. "She carried one of those Red Cross donor cards, and her type matches."

Perspiration glistened on Thibodeau's forehead in the chill dampness of the room.

"Une zireté," he muttered under his breath.

It is something atrocious.

Erickson was still looking at him. If the literal meaning of the words eluded him, their underlying emotions were easy to translate.

"I'm not saying anything for sure, but it doesn't appear she was shot." The cop knelt, pointed to the rust-colored stains. "The bleeding wasn't that heavy—"

"No spray patterns like you'd expect from a bullet wound, either," Ricci said.

Erickson glanced up at him.

"Right," he said. "From the way the drops struck the floor and their cast off angles . . . you see these streaky lines trailing toward the wall . . . I'd guess she fell back against it in a struggle and got cut or something."

As he spoke Ricci shifted his eyes to a much larger stain crusting the floor of the shop.

"Must've been a more serious wound left that one over there," he said, gesturing across the counter top. "You have a theory to explain it, too?"

Erickson straightened and turned to him.

"The main thing you need to know is that our tests fixed the blood group as different from Julia Gordian's," he said.

Ricci regarded him curiously.

"Any bullets or casings picked up in the storefront?"

"No."

"Ideas how the blood got there?"

"We're still narrowing down the possibilities."

Ricci tipped his chin toward the front entrance without taking his eyes off Erickson's face.

"I can see from here that door got kicked in," he said.

Erickson nodded.

"Wouldn't have been hard for a strong man," Ricci said. "It seems pretty lightweight."

Erickson nodded again.

"Means there was probably a fifth perp," Ricci said. "At least a fifth."

"Right."

"So maybe the blood stain was left by whoever came crashing through the door."

"I told you we're looking at the possibles."

"You going to have more for us on them soon?"

Erickson took a moment to answer.

"We'll see what develops," he said. "Meanwhile, it would help if you could come up with the names of anybody who might have grudges against your employer, knowledge of his family . . . whatever you think is relevant."

Ricci's gaze remained fixed on the detective.

"Share and share alike," he said. "I want to take an-other quick swing around the grounds before we leave. Got any problem with that?"

Again Erickson was quiet.

"I doubt you'll find much that can add to what you know evidence-wise, but can't see why not . . . with some stipulations," he said. "The residence downhill is still be-ing processed, and we're considering whether to extend the crime scene to the woods. That puts them off limits."

"Howell off-limits, too?" Ricci probed.

"Couldn't stop you from talking to him if he were here, but he's staying with family."

Ricci grunted.

"Okay, what else?"

"I stay with you," Erickson said. "Acceptable?"

Ricci nodded.

"Come on," Erickson said. "We'll start out back, work our way down to your car. So I can do you two fellas the final favor of seeing you off."

The Sword ops showed no hint of amusement in their expressions.

A moment later they all went out into the rain.

"That e-mail, Pete. Did you get it yet?" Megan asked over his radio headset.

In the bird chopping west from the hospital at Lam-baréné, Nimec could hear a distinct tremor in her voice.

"Hold on," he said. "These goddamn gadgets . . . the co-pilot had to reset the display mode for me. Okay, it's coming through now . . . I need a second to check it out."

Nimec stared at the helicopter console's multifunc-tional readout panel. The message on its GMSS comlink display left no question about what had left Megan so badly shaken and stretched his own control to the limit. He felt a sick, lancing anger.

Delivered to Megan's computer from an anonymous proxy server, the e-mail now bouncing across uncounted miles of world to Nimec via satellite bore the subject line:

Aria D'entrata—For the Life of Julia Gordian

Nimec had opened it immediately and read the text:

She wears freedom on her shoulder. A combination of ideographs discreetly tattooed on the upper left side. When she goes for a jog with her dogs, alternate mornings, the body art can be seen on her sleeveless arm, as green as her eyes and lovely against her white skin.

自 = *Ji* = Oneself.

由 = *Yuu* = A reason, or meaning.

自 由 = *Jiyuu* = Freedom.

The father's dream on her shoulder.

What we have taken we can return. The father is to make an announcement tomorrow on the Sedco oil platform. Its nature will be revealed to him in advance of the designated time. The words are to be honored or the daughter will be killed.

Shi is the Japanese word for death.

Its ideograph is 死

The tattoo needle will apply it to her dead face twice, a black kanji symbol below each dead green eye. The arm that carries the dream will be cut off and discarded before her dead body is tossed into the waste.

Defy us and the father will see all this and worse.

Nimec finished reading it and took a deep breath.

"Those first couple of words in the subject, Meg. You know what they mean?"

"*Aria d'entrata*. Italian. I think it's an operatic term for a vocal passage sung when a performer makes an entrance."

Nimec felt that white-hot spike in his gut again. They were being taunted.

"The tattoo . . ."

"Julia told me she was going to have it done," Megan said. "It must have been the last time she stopped by the office. A month ago. Maybe more. I'm not even sure Gord knows about it yet. She made me promise to stay mum, wanted to spring it on him in person. You know how she likes to get a rise out of him, Pete—"

"Meg—"

"Yes?"

"Listen to me," he said. "The description's to confirm this e-mail isn't a hoax from somebody who might've found out what's happened through a leak. Something of that nature."

"There's a lot of information," Megan said. "The reference to the color of Julia's eyes. Also that part about the jogging. Her greyhounds. Even her schedule."

"She's been watched."

"Yes." Megan took an audible breath. "Pete, what do you think whoever's behind this is after? If she's being held for a ransom, what sort of *announcement* can they want?"

"Wish I could give you an answer. All I know is somebody likes playing games. You can feel the spite here."

"Yes."

Nimec thought aloud. "The boss might have some ideas. He has to see the e-mail. I've got to show it to him right away."

"I don't know how he'll manage to handle everything. It's so much at once."

Nimec was quiet. He felt the vast spread of distance between them.

"Ricci up to snuff?" he asked after a moment.

"He's at the rescue center now. With Rollie. I haven't contacted him about the message."

"Better do it in a hurry," Nimec said. He thought some more. "We need to rely on him, Meg."

"I'm not sure I can."

"You've got no choice. If there are any solid leads, Ricci's the one to find them. He's the *one*, Meg."

Silence.

"I know," she said. "But knowing it doesn't give me much comfort."

Nimec stared out the chopper's canopy into the rushing blackness of night.

"Sometimes," he said, "we can only go with what we have."

As far as his statement to Ricci went, Erickson had been candid: There wasn't much of anything helpful to be found outside in the way of evidence.

Not on the grounds per se.

Accompanied by the detective, Ricci and Thibodeau had again walked back to the greyhound exercise pen and kennel, both empty now with the dogs taken into temporary care by the ASPCA. They had reinspected the sides and rear of the shop, then strode along the periphery of the bordering woods. Finally they went out front to the parking area to take a look at Julia Gordian's Honda Passport, and the muddy vestiges of tire prints the cops had already lifted the previous day.

They were standing over by the Honda in the rain when Ricci noticed a car parked among a group of police cruisers a yard or two farther down the lot—a Ford Cutlass, standard-issue plainclothes unmarked in precinct requisition lots. Its window was open slightly more than a crack, a man in a navy blue suit working on a laptop computer in the front passenger seat.

Ricci looked more closely and saw something on the armrest beside the man. It raised a thought.

He broke away from Erickson and Thibodeau and hastened over to the car.

"Got a minute?" Ricci said, crouched under his umbrella. He motioned his head back toward the Passport. "I'm with Erickson."

Surprised by the sudden interruption, Navy Blue glanced out at him, pushing the computer screen down out of his angle of sight.

"You one of those guys from UpLink?" he said.

Ricci nodded, came up close to the window, and shot a look inside at what he'd recognized as a pad of graph paper on the armrest. But he had no chance to catch more than the briefest glimpse of the sketch on its top page before Navy Blue reached over and turned it facedown where it lay.

"This is a crime scene," he said. "I've got important things to do."

"Like I said," Ricci said. "Not more than a minute."

Navy Blue continued to regard him from inside the Cutlass, his expression at once standoffish and warily curious.

A grunt. "Something I can call you besides Man From UpLink?"

"Name's Tom Ricci."

Navy Blue sat a moment, pushed the button to lower the window about halfway.

Ricci figured that was all he would need.

"I'm Detective Brewer," the cop said. He still sounded suspicious. "Go ahead and make it quick."

Ricci did, but not in the way Brewer expected. Before the other man could react, he thrust his free hand through the window, turned Brewer's laptop toward him, and raised the lid so he could see it.

Brewer flinched in his seat.

"Hey, what the hell are you doing?" He pulled the computer back around, snapped it shut.

Ricci's face was calm.

"Didn't mean to surprise you," he said. "Might be none of my business, but I thought I saw you using that crime scene diagramming software. Figured I'd check for sure. Maybe offer some advice."

Brewer glared at him. "You want advice, keep your fucking hands to yourself—"

"No harm intended." Ricci held a low, level tone. "I was on the job once upon a time. Boston. Found out the hard way these computer sketches aren't worth jack on the witness stand. You want to impress a jury, don't lose your original hand sketch on that pad. Accurate's good. Sometimes giving them a feel for what you saw can be better."

Brewer stared at him in angry confusion. Ricci knew he wouldn't believe his excuse for the grab. It didn't matter. Nor did it matter that he'd incidentally happened to be telling the truth about the testifying part. He'd gotten his look at the screen image. Not a long one. But long enough.

"There a problem here?"

The voice was Erickson's. Ricci half-turned and saw the detective standing behind him. He and Thibodeau had come over from the Honda.

Ricci left the explanation to Brewer. He doubted the cop would mention anything about the laptop, embarrass himself by admitting he'd been caught off guard.

As expected, pride won the day.

"No," Brewer said. He was trying not to seem abashed. "The two of us were having some shop talk."

Erickson gave his partner a long look, hands in the pockets of his raincoat, water dripping from his hair.

"Shop talk," he repeated.

Brewer nodded inside the car.

"Ricci used to be a cop," he said. "We were comparing notes about procedures. How they've changed and so forth."

Erickson's gaze dissected him another moment and then swung onto Ricci.

"Didn't do much comparing with me before," he said.

Ricci shrugged under his umbrella.

"We had other things to talk about," he said.

Erickson was silent. Thibodeau was silent. Both of them were looking at Ricci and had separate reasons for being skeptical and displeased.

"Okay," Erickson said at last. He gestured the Sword ops toward the road. "I think maybe it's time I walk you two back to your car."

Thibodeau hadn't taken his eyes off Ricci.

"Guess it would be," he said, and started traipsing down the gravel and mud drive in the rain.

"I get to find out what was going on between you and that other detective?" Thibodeau said.

"Sure," Ricci said. "I aim to please."

Thibodeau waited. They were back inside Ricci's Jetta on the shoulder of the road, rain dashing against the roof and windshield.

"Erickson was holding out on us," Ricci said. "I knew he wouldn't give up whatever it was and played his partner on a hunch."

Thibodeau looked across the seat at him.

"That hunch pay off?"

"Yeah." Ricci told him how he'd seen Brewer in the car with his graph paper and laptop, gone over to check it out, and gotten a look at the crime scene diagram on Brewer's computer. "It was all right there for me on his screen. The stain on the floor. Its location and measurements. And an outline of a dog. The word greyhound lettered right over it."

Thibodeau was shaking his head, his brow creased.

"A dog," he said. "Don't get it. Erickson said—"

"I heard what Erickson said. Kept it nice and vague for us. Except vague only works when it's consistent, and he wasn't making sense. The blood left behind isn't Julia's and he's thinking about other possibles. Maybe one of her attackers, maybe not. But if not, who? If he isn't looking at anybody besides Julia being in that store when things went down, it would've had to belong to whoever came after her."

Thibodeau tugged at his heavy beard as it all sank in.

"Be damned," he said. "Be damned if it didn't slip right by me."

Ricci stared out into the rain.

"At first I figured he was lying straight out. That the cops had somebody in custody and wanted to keep it secret," he said. "Wouldn't have guessed those possibles he mentioned didn't include human beings."

Thibodeau was quiet a moment, still plucking his beard.

"We got to be concerned with Erickson. He hear tell about what you did . . . how you did it . . . he gonna shut us out altogether."

Ricci shrugged.

"Let him," he said. "Gives me one less person to second guess."

Thibodeau shook his head some more. "I ain't trying to start a gripe, just saying you might've warned me. Never know when we gonna need him. We'd put our minds together, consulted, we might've figured a way to get the information out of him so we don't lose his trust—"

Ricci pitched a glance across the seat at him.

"I don't want anybody's trust," he said. "Just want to know why the cops are keeping that dog's body under wraps. And where it is."

Thibodeau started to say something, quickly cut himself off.

"Any thoughts about how you gonna do that?" he said with a kind of yielding resignation.

Ricci thrust his key into the ignition and brought the Volkswagen to life.

"Yeah," he said. "I do."

ELEVEN

VARIOUS LOCALES

"**THIS THE STREET?**"

"Sheffield's place is just ahead of us." DeMarco motioned to a dormered Old Quarter house on the right as he turned a corner in their Land Rover. "When I drove him over from the airport, the boss was in a pretty decent mood. Bushed, you know, but kidding with Wade and Ackerman in the backseat about it being a fancier Motel 6 than the one where he usually grabs a bed." He shook his head. "I never would have thought I'd be here again tonight, bringing the kind of news we've got."

Nimec glanced at him across the front seat.

"There's no good time for bad news," he said. "When things hit us over the head, we cope. Timing isn't part of the bargain."

DeMarco checked his mirrors and pulled to the curb. It was almost ten o'clock at night, twenty minutes having passed since he'd met Nimec's chopper at the same field where Gordian had arrived some hours earlier.

The two men sat quietly in the vehicle's dark interior.

"You think about how you're going to break it to him?" DeMarco said.

Nimec's smile was catacomb bleak.

"If I do that," he said, "you can forget about me coping."

He exited the Rover, strode into the building's fore-court, and went up the steps to its entrance. The penguin who answered his ring reminded him of the waiters at the Rio de Gabao dinner reception. When did the black suits and ruffled white shirts come off?

A hurried introduction. Nimec said he needed to see Roger Gordian alone, was told Monsieur Gordian was in a meeting with his host and fellow house guests, explained he'd come about something very urgent, was then led into a side parlor, and invited to have a seat while he waited.

He stood instead with his back to the plush sofa.

Gordian was smiling as appeared through the parlor's sliding walnut doors minutes later.

"Pete, hi," he said. "I heard the doctors were checking you out and didn't expect to see you until sometime to-mor—"

He caught Nimec's sober, uneasy expression and stopped in the middle of the room. The smile had faded.

"What's wrong?" he said.

Nimec quickly went past Gordian to the doors, drew them shut, and then turned to face him.

"Boss," he said. His hand went to Gordian's arm. "It's Julia."

"That's Rob over there on the tennis courts with the dogs," Meredith Wagner said from the Jetta's backseat. She motioned to the small community park on their left with her head. "He wanted to take them running while the rain gives us a letup."

Pulled up by the park entrance, Ricci and Thibodeau looked out at the solitary figure of Rob Howell on the other side of a high chain-link fence surrounding the courts. His back to the plastic-coated mesh, hands deep in the pockets of his barn coat, Howell stood watching the dogs chase each other in repeated energetic circles around the wet artificial turf.

Thibodeau shifted around to face the woman.

"We won't trouble him any more 'n we need," he said. "I promise you."

She nodded without turning from her window. Dressed in jeans and a light brown corduroy jacket that closely matched the color of her hair, Meredith Wagner was about thirty-five, plain, thin, soft spoken, and visibly worn. They had found her at the ranch-style house she shared with her husband, Nick; three-year-old daughter, Katie, and, since yesterday, her brother Rob and his five greyhounds in a quiet suburban development outside Sonoma.

"He's so used to caring for those animals . . . I don't think he could make it if not for them," she said. "I don't think he'd have anything left to keep him in one piece."

Thibodeau did not comment. He wasn't sure whether she had been addressing him or thinking aloud to herself. In either case, he could say nothing except what she would already know—that he wished things were otherwise, wished events hadn't brought them to where they were right now.

He thought in silence a few moments. When you went fishing for information, you could never predict which facts would take a long cast of the reel to pull in, which ones would jump into your hands, and which would lead you toward a rich bounty of others. After Ricci had reminded him how he'd gotten Erickson to let out that Rob Howell was staying with relatives, Thibodeau had thought it might be a while before they could identify the particular family members and track them down. But that had proven to be as easy as stopping at a gas station to buy the Monday-morning edition of a regional newspaper called the *Mountain Journal*. Though they had originally picked it up to see what the police and emergency freq chasers might have found out about the crime from early dispatcher–respondent radio exchanges that would flurry over the air before law-enforcement put a stopper on open communications, it had been of far greater help than they'd bargained for. The paper's freelance police stringer had picked up on the double homicide near the state park in time to get a jump on local television stations, learn where Howell had gone through his homespun contacts, and include the sister's name and town of residence in his story. Once they read it, Ricci had only needed to call directory information for her phone number and street address.

And so they had found themselves here not two hours after leaving the rescue center. Thibodeau was convinced it was partly just luck that had delivered them to the Wagner family's front door before a crush of media vans—if it wasn't profane to use a word such as *luck* under these circumstances. The violence at the center had taken place on a Sunday morning, when the TV and radio crews were skimpiest, especially in the state's more remote, unpopulated areas. What had given the *Mountain Journal* a chance to trump the competition also gave the police some time to go into clamp-down mode and keep the name of Roger Gordian's daughter from surfacing as part of their investigation . . . for the time being. With the weekend over, things would start to percolate. The *Journal* people would want to spread its story around to make certain they got credit for breaking it first. Morgue beat reporters would get on the trail. Big-market newshounds with deeper and wider sources than some country redbone with a police band radio in his Chevy would smell blood—literally smell blood, Thibodeau thought—and reports would be flying everywhere by the evening news cycle.

He and Ricci were ahead of the pack but Thibodeau believed it wouldn't be long before the rest caught up. And while Ricci's gut might fill with acid when he thought about the FBI joining the case, his own concern was having the press toss themselves into the mix. For reasons that didn't exactly align, both men were very eager to talk to Rob Howell before others got wind of his whereabouts.

As a result, Thibodeau could sense the impatience with which Ricci glanced at their passenger's pale, exhausted face in the rearview mirror.

"Okay," Ricci said in his peculiar uninflected tone. "You want to go tell your brother why we're here?"

Meredith Wagner nodded and reached for her door handle.

"I'll let you know when he's ready," she said.

She went and talked with Howell for a couple of minutes. They saw him abruptly turn toward their parked car, saw him look back at his sister and talk to her some more. Then she waved them over, waited for them to approach, and sort of drifted off along the tennis court's painted white foul line. Giving them room for privacy, Thibodeau supposed, but remaining close enough to cut short their conversation if Howell became too upset.

"Mister Howell—" Thibodeau began.

"Rob's fine." He shook their hands. "Meredith says you work for Julia's dad. Private security, is it?"

Peripherally aware of the dogs in their circular sprint around the court, Thibodeau nodded, gave him their names, told him how sorry they were for his loss, and explained that what they wanted to ask wouldn't take long.

"We know you been through everything with the police, ain't about to put you on that go 'round again," he said.

Howell cast his sunken eyes down at the ground a moment. Then he raised them to Thibodeau's face and shrugged. "It's all right. If it can help you find Julia, I don't mind."

Ricci looked at him. "Julia," he said, "and the people who took what they did from you."

Howell turned his way.

"My daughter was only six months old," he said.

Ricci remained tunneled on his eyes, noticing their glazed appearance. *Tranquilizers. A CNS depressant. Probably lorazepam.*

"I'm sorry," he said.

"I got a call from him this morning, you know. The detective in charge. He didn't want me to talk to anybody about what happened, mentioned you two in particular. In case you showed up at Merry's."

"He say why?"

"I guess just what you'd expect," Howell said. "Something about how they don't want their investigation compromised by outside parties."

"You're allowed to talk to whomever you want. Nothing legal they can do to stop you."

"I figured that," Howell said. "And if he's right and we're wrong, I can always claim not to remember his words."

Ricci nodded a little.

"The medication," he said.

"Yeah."

"Besides," Ricci said. "We aren't at Merry's."

A faint, desolate smile touched Howell's lips, revealing little white flecks of dried saliva at their corners. He checked on the dogs with a glance over his shoulder, thrust his hands back into his pockets, and quietly bowed his head toward the synthetic grass again, his thoughts slipping into their own nebulous, faraway space.

"We were at the center before," Ricci said. "The cops gave us a look around. Probably decided to phone you because I got on their nerves asking questions they didn't want to answer."

Howell brought up his head, slowly, working against the heavy resistance of the tranqs.

"What sort of questions?"

"There was blood on the floor of the shop," Ricci said. "Near the door. The detective was ready to tell me it wasn't Julia's, but he wasn't so ready to tell me the blood came from a dog that'd been shot."

Howell nodded.

"Vivian," he said.

"That be one of the rescues?" Thibodeau said.

Another nod.

"Julia favors her. The first day she came to work for me, I remember lecturing her about how our policy's not to become too attached." Howell gestured toward the whirling dogs behind him with a slight roll of his shoulder. "Being firm's how I wound up with five of my own."

Ricci looked at him. "With all the things the police shared with us, we have to wonder how come they kept quiet about the dog. Vivian."

Howell's mouth worked.

"Evidence," he said after several moments. "She's just evidence to them. It's why they won't let me anywhere near her. They call it a safeguard."

Ricci let his eyes rest on him. "It's important for us to know what's happened to her body."

Howell's expression was odd.

"I'm not sure what you mean," he said.

Ricci paused a beat.

"When a pet's remains have to be examined during an investigation, the police bring them to a lab for tests," he said. "Depends on the case, but they'll usually give them back to the owner after they're through—"

Howell was shaking his head.

"You don't understand," he said.

Ricci looked at him.

"Don't understand what?"

"Viv's alive," Howell said.

Aware Gordian would want to see it with his own eyes, Pete Nimec had hardcopied the e-mail aboard the chopper, printing it out on a single sheet of paper he'd folded into his wallet. Behind the closed sliding doors of Sheffield's visitor parlor now, he sat on the couch with him and heard that paper rattle in his trembling hand.

"There's nothing else?" Gordian said. His face was chalky. "This message is *it*?"

"So far," Nimec said. "Yeah."

Gordian shook his head. "Ashley . . ."

"She doesn't know yet. Meg's been leaving messages for her to get in touch."

"I'll contact her myself."

Nimec looked at him and nodded. He heard the paper rattle.

"You're sure it's the truth . . . about the tattoo?" Gordian said. "Because if Julia had gotten something like that put on her body, she'd tell me just to see my face turn red. You know her, Pete. How she is. She acts like it's *amusing* when my dander's up. She'd tell me—"

"She told Megan. Some kind of secret thing between them. I think she was going to make a presentation of it the next time you saw her."

"My God," Gordian said through a harsh exhalation. "If not for that poor woman . . . her baby . . . killed, shot *dead* . . . I'd think it was all some kind of hoax. That maybe someone who knows Julia found out she'd gone out of town, sent this poison over the Internet for a sick thrill . . ."

He let the sentence trail, recognizing the uselessness of trying to bind it in logic and reality. Nimec heard his agitated snatches of breath, the paper rattling again between his fingers in the silence of the room.

"Who's on it?" Gordian said.

"Ricci and Thibodeau. If there are any leads, any paths they need to follow, every man, every resource, everything we've got is available in a heartbeat. You know that."

Gordian nodded.

"I need to tie things up, get back home right away—"

"Boss," Nimec interrupted. "You can't leave Africa."

Gordian looked at him. "No," he said.

"Gord—"

"I know what you're thinking. It doesn't matter. Somebody has to be with Ashley."

"Meg plans to stay with her, look after her for as long as she has to—"

"No, Pete. Forget it. I won't let you decide this for me. That demand in the message . . . the announcement I'm supposed to make . . . we can't jump to the conclusion it has anything remotely to do with the actual motive or motives for what's happened. It could be a red herring. Meant to throw us off."

"Or not," Nimec said. "You really feel we're in a position to take chances right now?"

Silence clapped down over them again. But now Gordian became very still, staring at the wall opposite him, the printout no longer rattling in his hand. The thick doors and walls of the room blocked out any sounds from elsewhere in the old French mansion.

After a long length of time, he turned to Nimec.

"The path you need to follow starts here," he said, and put a hand to his chest. "Whatever the reason for what's happened to Julia . . . those other innocents . . . they've fallen into the middle."

Nimec said nothing for a while, and then nodded pensively.

"Find who's at the other end," Gordian said.

UpLink SanJo. Mid-afternoon. Their secure conference room's sound-baffled, audio-secure walls once again enclosing them in an electronically fortified cocoon of silence. On one of those walls, a flat plasma screen jacked into a digital viewer showed an enlarged image of the e-mail Megan had received hours earlier. It struck the eye like the Mark of the Beast, a reminder that nothing in this technological age can make us impervious to its stain.

"We need to find out what evidence they're pulling from that greyhound," Ricci said. "We can't wait."

Megan looked at him. "You're positive it's that important."

"I'm positive the cops think it is," he said. "We cruised past that veterinary clinic a bunch of times. Saw a team of uniforms cooping outside in a patrol car. And I guarantee they weren't going anywhere."

"What makes it a sure thing is that they ain't letting Howell in to see the dog," Thibodeau said. "He tells us the vet be a good friend of his. Know him for years, care for every one of his hounds. Most're more dead than alive when he bring them from the track. Some of 'em need surgery. Howell say you have to treat runners different from other breeds. They ain't able to tolerate certain kinds of medicine or anaesthesia, need lower doses, you know."

"One reason the cops brought the dog there is that

Howell insisted on it when he found her alive," Ricci said. "The clinic is only a few miles from his rescue center out in the boonies. Good break for him, trying to save that dog. Not too convenient for the badges."

Megan was looking at him. "Why not?"

Ricci's expression seemed to say the answer should have been obvious. "If they're under orders to keep watch over it, they'd prefer bringing it someplace near an all-night diner, where they can tank up on free coffee and muffins the whole time. If it bleeds out on the way, so much the better. The dog becomes meat. They don't have to worry about its carcass disappearing from a locked refrigerator drawer in a police lab, but a live animal in a country vet's infirmary makes them insecure." He paused a second. "Howell had some strong persuasion, though. The vet's no bumpkin. Used to be with the San Francisco Zoo. Has a diploma in veterinary forensic pathology. The cops would have to call on somebody like him for the necropsy anyway . . . probably couldn't find a better qualified man for the job."

Megan was thoughtful. "And yet Howell doesn't know why the police are so interested in the dog, am I right?"

"Right."

"No idea despite his long-standing relationship with the veterinarian."

"Right."

She shook her head. "I don't understand that."

There was a crackle of impatience in Ricci's stillness.

"Once the vet becomes a fact finder in a criminal investigation it obliges him to clam up," he said after a moment. "He leaks anything and it's a violation of professional ethics."

"I still think he'd be entitled to a general explanation," Megan said. "Terrible as it sounds, we're so focused on

Julia, we risk losing sight of what Rob Howell's suffered. He's lost his entire family."

Ricci turned toward her.

"You know how tight the cops can be with eyewitnesses in protective custody," he said. "Maybe the dog had a clear look at the perps and they want her status kept secret till she's well enough to make them in a lineup."

Megan was silent. The sarcasm had caught her off guard.

"Wasn't any call for that remark," Thibodeau said from his opposite side. His large body shifted in his chair. "This ain't no joke—"

"Stay out of this." Ricci cut a hand in his direction, held his gaze on Megan. "You're the one who might as well be joking. You don't have the right to speak for me. You don't know where I'm focused. You don't know, or act like you don't know, that the cops are putting an extra-heavy lid on things to keep us out. You sit here throwing words around a table when that e-mail on the wall says everything. We need to get busy."

Megan remained quiet, staring back into his eyes. "What's your recommendation?"

"We have to get Erickson to share that evidence from the dog. Whether he likes it or not."

"I'm convinced," she said. "But I also prefer we don't alienate him. He has legal authority over the investigation and—as you've implied—can withhold anything he wants from us. We, on the other hand, have no license to meddle. If we plan to get somewhere we need his voluntary permission. Or maybe cooperation's a better word. And I think the best way to obtain it would be to exert pressure on Erickson through behind-the-scenes channels."

"Those channels have names attached to them?"

Megan nodded. She drew in a breath.

"Until now I've kept any knowledge about the e-mail within our organization to give us elbow room, but that changes tomorrow," she said. "Since it's safe to assume Erickson's department would have put the FBI on alert for possible involvement, I can't see a reason not to contact our old friend Bob Lang at Quantico in the meantime and ask him off the record to make a request of the local field office. That would be the San Francisco division. It won't be long before the case winds up under its bailiwick anyway. And at that point they can share evidence with whomever they wish."

Thibodeau was nodding as he mulled her words over.

"Sounds reasonable enough to me," he said. "Beats going to war with Erickson."

Ricci ignored him, continuing to look at Megan as if it were just the two of them in the room.

"Lang's your old friend, not mine," he said. "You want to visit wonderland with him, it's your choice."

A taut silence between them again. Megan's eyes became narrow.

"What are you suggesting?" she said.

Ricci sat a moment, then slowly shrugged and rose from his chair.

"Nothing," he said. "You're the boss, you make the calls. I just want to get back to work."

When the phone rang in Derek Glenn's office, he was at his window admiring the new 120-foot-tall naval shipyard cranes that soared prominently in his view of the waterfront. They had appeared there about a month earlier, and he hoped it was a permanent spot. Keeping a vigilant and appreciative eye on the cranes had come to occupy a large part of his day, and Glenn supposed that if he ever looked out to discover them farther up or down the harbor—or, worse, altogether gone—it might be a sign he'd have to find something else about the commercial harbor that might be of interest, which had been tough before their arrival. Or something other than standing by the window to keep him occupied. Either way, it would be a development worthy of consideration at UpLink's San Diego overflow warehouse.

His lookout interrupted, Glenn went over and lifted the receiver.

"Yup, I'm here."

"Glenn. It's Tom Ricci."

Glenn was surprised. Not a word from the guy for over a year. Then a phone call, a visit, and a second call in the space of a week.

"Lo and behold," he said. "Knew I should have explained my picking up the tab the other night was a one-time deal—"

"I need help."

Glenn's face suddenly became serious.

"What is it?"

"Something you maybe don't want to take on," Ricci said. "Might not even want to know about, because just knowing puts you in it to where you have advance knowledge."

"As in the sort of knowledge that might not be any good for my job status?"

"Could be," Ricci said. "Could be that won't be the worst of it. You say good-bye right now, it's fine. You decide to take a pass, I'm okay with that, too."

"How long do I have to think about this?"

"Till I hang up the phone," Ricci said. "If you're in with me, you have to be up here tonight. Early as possible."

Glenn thought it over a few seconds, the receiver cradled against his shoulder, his eyes wandering toward the high, reliable cranes framed by his window.

"Go ahead," he said. "Let me hear it."

A country route near Portola State Park, half past eleven at night, a ground mist spreading over the roots of the oaks and madrones. Under a low roof of clouds the sky was moonless and starless.

The shingle outside the square, flat, single-story brick building read PARKVILLE VETERINARY CLINIC, KENNETH W. MOORE, D.V.M., PH.D., but there was scarcely enough light seeping from the windows on the clinic's north side—and from the dashboard of the police cruiser parked out front—for someone even a yard or two away to see the sign with his unaided eye. Discerning the doctor's name and credentials would be almost impossible.

In the thick woods that belted the clinic's parking lot, Ricci would have known what the lettering said without having to use his portable night-vision binoculars—the vet's name being one among many details he'd marked while driving past the clinic with Rollie Thibodeau almost twelve hours earlier, doing a canvass for reasons he'd kept to himself. Still, he found the definition with which it appeared in the high-mag, IR-boosted illuminator tubes exceptional. A clear, close, fully stereoscopic image. It was not so many years ago that night vision optics gave you green ghosts moving among ghost-objects and a poor sense of their spacial relationships. The ability to read a sign in pitch darkness at fifty yards and judge its distance was an asset he would have coveted as a SEAL, and later as a Beantown homicide cop. He did not take it for granted.

But now Ricci's gaze held on the sign for only a moment before shifting elsewhere. A single prowl car did not automatically mean that two cops inside made up the entire watch. There could be others on foot patrol, though he'd have bet against it.

Beside him, Glenn's thoughts were running to the contrary as he scanned the wide pool of shadows around the clinic through his own NV binocs. A hidden frown creased his brow under a black nylon balaclava.

"This just doesn't wash," he said in a hushed voice. He lowered the glasses and normal darkness poured into his eyes. "The police have a murder on their hands. The daughter of a famous businessman kidnapped. A war hero. And you tell me there might be important evidence in that animal hospital. But they've got one cruiser guarding it. No backup I can see."

Ricci looked over at him.

"As of this minute, it isn't an official kidnapping," he whispered. "Tomorrow there'll be feds all over the place."

"Still . . ."

"Don't think UpLink. Or U.S. Army," Ricci said. "Think small-town police force. They haven't got many resources. Don't have a clue anybody besides Howell knows the dog's alive, being kept here in the middle of nowhere."

A grunt. Glenn raised his lenses again. Both cops were slouched against their headrests, relaxed, chatter from their police radio faintly reaching the trees. They had their windows open—the driver's window lowered about a third of the way, his partner's almost completely down on the other side.

Glenn wished it had been the latter facing him. He would need to make a perfect shot. If he missed by a couple of inches up or down, his .50-caliber plastic sabot—fired from an original VVRS, sound-suppressed barrel, his version of choice—would either strike the driver's window or the rack lights atop the cruiser, jolt the patrolmen into alertness, and all hell would break loose. If his aim strayed a little to the right of his desired line of fire, he might hit one of the cops. Their heads were vulnerable. Their upper bodies, too. And even discharged at its lowest barrel speed a variable velocity round could inflict serious physical damage. It was why the military shied from the term *nonlethal* in preference of the *less-than-lethal* or *reduced lethality* designations. A weapon was a weapon was a weapon. Glenn knew cap guns could kill under freak circumstances, and the VVRS was no toy.

He turned his attention from the car windows to those on the near side of the clinic. All except the first of three or four running toward the back had their blinds raised. Glenn saw an overnight attendant in lab whites filling out paper forms at a desk behind the last window. Insofar as he could tell through his lenses, they were charts comparable to the sort nurses and doctors would hang from beds in hospitals that treated patients of the human variety. There was, he noticed, bluish light flickering from somewhere in the room . . . probably a television set. It wouldn't hurt if the attendant had its sound up.

"Okay," Ricci said. "You ready?"

Glenn nodded.

"Give me exactly two minutes." Ricci tapped the face of his WristLink. "Remember . . . anything goes wrong, head straight for the car and take off."

Glenn hesitated. This had been another point of disagreement between them, but Ricci had been relentless in his insistence on drawing the heat if there was a foul-up.

Ricci stared at him in the dark, waiting for his second nod. He gave it with slow reluctance.

"I thought it'd be 'In for a penny, in for a pound.' "

"Bullshit," Ricci said. Then he slipped away toward

the left, bent low under the ponderous boughs of the hardwoods.

Hoping the cops would continue to lean back in their seats a bit longer, an eye on the tritium dial of his own watch—not quite as jazzed as Ricci's, but accurate— Glenn knelt into position with the rifle.

Ninety seconds later he sighted through its night scope, counted down the final half minute to himself, and then pulled the trigger with a silent prayer.

The muted crack of the subsonic round leaving his weapon was no louder than the hammer click of a dry-fired revolver. It traveled straight through the cruiser's open window, skimmed between the cops and the windshield, and struck the interior of the passenger door's frame.

The startled cops jerked in their seats as the sabot burst open on impact to release its superconcentrated fill of dimethyl sulfoxide and zolpidem—a soporific aerosol formulated to be instantly absorbed into the bloodstream on contact with skin or mucous membranes. Glenn knew a microscopic amount of the agent would be enough to knock out someone the size of a pro-basketball center within moments, and neither of the cops was built like Shaquille O'Neal.

They dropped off into unconsciousness, spilling over each other in the front seat of the car. The two probably hadn't had time to wonder what was happening to them. Their exposure to the chemical incapacitant would leave them with pounding heads, queasy stomachs, and a whole lot of confusion when they recovered. But they would be alive and well.

Glenn produced a long exhalation of relief, slung the rifle over his shoulder, and looked out past the treeline with his binocs.

Ricci had emerged from the woods and was hurriedly moving across the parking lot toward the patrol car.

Extending a gloved hand through its partially open window, Ricci unlocked the passenger door of the cruiser, pulled the senseless cop in the shotgun seat upright, and propped his weight against the backrest to ensure he'd remain in that position. Then he reached down between the seats for the prone driver's dislodged cap, careful not to lean too far inside. Any residual trace of the DMSO/zolpidem agent that hadn't been biologically absorbed should have become inactive within seconds of its release into the air, but he did not want to take unnecessary chances.

He started toward the front of the clinic. At the entrance Ricci donned the uniform cap, knocked, and waited with his head bowed almost against the peephole. Moments later, he heard footsteps on the other side of the door.

"Back already?" The night attendant. Standing there behind the door. "Fella, the way that coffee passes through you, you're gonna have to start drinking a weaker blend."

"Or less of it," Ricci said from the shadows, speaking quietly, his face still turned down so all the attendant would see through the peephole was the peak of the officer's cap.

He heard the snap of the turning lock, braced himself. The door began to swing inward, light from the clinic's vestibule filling the open space.

Then the night attendant spoke again as the space widened: "C'mon in before y—"

Ricci quickly shoved through the door and locked his arms around the attendant, a full body tackle that landed him on his back, the wind leaving his mouth with a grunt of mixed pain and surprise as he struck the floor. Down on top of him, Ricci grabbed hold of his arm, wrenched it hard, got him onto his side, twisted the arm some more to make him flip onto his stomach, then pressed a knee into his spine below the shoulder blades. Another pained grunt escaped the attendant. He tried to lift himself up, pushing his free hand against the floor. Ricci dug his knee in deeper to keep him still, got a spray canister of DMSO/zolpidem out of his belt holster, held it to his face, and thumbed the nozzle.

The guy went limp. Pain gone; one, two, three.

Ricci rose to his feet, hustled across the vestibule and waiting area, and then passed through a swing door into the rear section of the building. There was a short hallway. Two examining rooms to his left, an operating room, a cubbyhole office beyond them, then a fourth room near the end of the hall to the right. All were doorless.

He hooked into the last room and immediately saw the cluttered desk where the attendant had been working on his charts. On a table beside it, the television that had cast a flickering glow through the window was tuned to a late-night talk show, its host mugging at his viewers. Otherwise the area was very sparse. There was a steel gurney in the middle of the floor. Some file cabinets stood against one wall. Another wall was lined with a dozen or so boarding kennels, the four largest on the floor, the rest above them on wide metal shelves.

Ricci scanned the kennels from just inside the entryway. Most were vacant. Each of the few containing animals was tagged with a case number and what was presumably the pet-owner's surname. He saw a house cat watching him curiously from an eye-level shelf. Several kennels apart from it on the same shelf, a small furry dog was curled up into a sleeping ball.

In a big kennel on the floor, a greyhound lay on its side facing him, its bandaged flank rising and falling with its slow, heavy breaths, an IV tube running into it from a drip bag mounted above the kennel's wire-mesh door. The dog's eyes were open, staring, and blank. Ricci couldn't be certain whether it was aware of his presence.

The tag below the door read: 03-756A-HOWELL CENTER.

Ricci's gaze held on the dog a long moment, went to the file cabinets. *No*, he thought. *Not there. Case is too fresh, too outstanding.*

He turned toward the desk and noticed a rack holding several plastic clipboards, their neatly labeled tops facing outward. The board with the number and name matching those on the greyhound's kennel jumped out at his eyes almost at once.

Ricci pulled it from the rack, hastily inspecting the notations on the attached sheets of paper.

His eyes widening, he heard his own sharp intake of breath.

Ricci needed under a minute to take digital snapshots of every handwritten page with his WristLink. After he was finished, he replaced the clipboard, went through the desk drawers, located the tray that held the sealed glass vials and transparent evidence bags referenced in the vet's notes, and photoed them as well before returning them to the drawer in which they'd been found.

He had taken a half step toward the entryway when he paused, turned to look back at the wall of kennels, and went over to crouch in front of the wounded greyhound.

His fingers reached through the mesh and gently, gently touched its snout.

"Good girl," he whispered. "You're a good girl."

Then Ricci was up on his feet again, racing from the clinic into the night.

TWELVE

VARIOUS LOCALES

THE *CHIMERA*'S MASTER BEDROOM. WEARING A SILK robe dyed the shaded grays of twilight by the handloom weavers of Andhra Pradesh, Harlan DeVane sat at his computer in the depths of the African night and appraised the second e-mail to his enemy. He wanted to carefully reread the words he had written and view the animation his technicians had embedded with graphic image files, assuring himself that each component enriched the other, that the entire product met his every criterion.

In his intense, unmoving concentration, DeVane's tightened lips were the same noncolor as the rest of his features. He almost could have been a waxwork figure, showing no outward sign of his satisfaction with the message's wording and form.

Yet, satisfied he was.

Here was an example of manipulative power wielded with brilliance. Here was real *wallop*. How often was a hoodwink conceived to smack the eyes with its falsity . . . make one aware he was being toyed with?

It brought a symmetry to things that DeVane did not believe he could have manufactured, but could only have wrested from existing circumstance.

Pain did indeed cut many different ways; the child that

was loved could bring about the father's fall as surely as the child shunned and hated.

Locked onto this thought, fascinated by its many ironies, DeVane fired his ultimatum into electronic space.

Palo Alto. Morning. A downcast brow of clouds over the hills threatened another day of chill rain and mist.

In the Gordian home, Megan Breen had been running on coffee and nervous energy for hours and found her caffeine level in increasingly frequent need of a recharge. She had spent the greater part of the night doing what she could to comfort and support Ashley, and the rest of it conferring with the Sword ops who'd turned the living room into an ad-hoc base of operations. Inside, their surveillance techware occupied every available surface. Outside, their vehicles had crowded the entire drive. The thirty-acre estate had been secured by armed patrols to ensure Ashley Gordian was as safe from physical harm as anybody on earth . . . but Megan knew her heart could not be protected in similar fashion, and that very deeply worried her.

The e-mail arrived at the precise tick of eight o'clock. Ash had fallen off into a doze that not even total exhaustion would sustain for too long. Megan was in the kitchen dumping a soggy coffee filter into the waste bin with one hand and scooping fresh grinds into the maker's basket with another.

One of the ops—Lehane—thrust his head into the entry.

"Ms. Breen," he said. "Something's jumped into your queue. We think it could be—"

Megan didn't hear the rest as she ran past him into the living room.

The subject line of the e-mail read:

Aria di Bravura: A Song of Love and Sacrifice

Megan dropped into a chair, started to reach for the computer mouse, and then realized she'd carried the heaping plastic coffee spoon from the kitchen.

"Will somebody take this damned thing from me?" She passed it off to one of the men without turning her eyes from the display. "Thanks."

The op stood with his hand out and glanced downward with mild surprise.

She had let go of the coffee spoon before he'd managed to reach for it, spilling a small heap of dark roast on top of his shoe.

Roger Gordian watched the e-mail open on the screen of the notebook computer he'd set up in his guest suite at Thomas Sheffield's place.

The image that filled most of the display was of a large upraised hand of fire, its glowing orange fingers spread wide. Gradually materializing across its open palm in black text was this message:

> The conditions of Julia's release are simple. We demand no ransom, no portion of the father's wealth. Only a promise made to all the ears of the world— and has not reaching them been his lifelong goal?
>
> At nine o'clock tonight aboard the Sedco oil platform, Roger Gordian is to renounce his dream of freedom through information, declare UpLink International and its subsidiaries utterly and permanently dissolved, and require that its stockholders forsake their shares by legal agreement without any form of compensation, including financial reimbursement from insurers.
>
> All UpLink's corporate operations will then cease.

All personnel must be evacuated from its facilities worldwide. All its projects must be abandoned, its communications networks dismantled.

Full implementation of these terms is to occur within a time frame not exceeding 48 hours after the announcement or Julia Gordian will be executed.

The black text remained in place for thirty seconds and then coalesced into a rotating sphere that rapidly underwent another smooth transformation against the fiery palm, changing colors, reshaping itself into the UpLink logo: an Earth globe surrounded by intersecting satellite bandwidth lines.

Another half minute passed. The hand clenched into a fist, morphed into an red-orange fireball, and brightened. Then it suddenly plunged to the bottom of the screen like a falling comet, leaving behind an empty white void.

Gordian turned from the screen and looked over at Pete Nimec in the chair beside him.

"What's this about?" Gordian said. His face was ashen. "Say I complied with the declaration to pull up stakes, how could anyone think I'd be able to go about convincing our investors to do the same thing? It's inconceivable. You're talking about fortunes. There are thousands of our employees *alone* who have their life savings attached to our stock. Tens of thousands. They'd be wiped out. I'm not even sure what they'd be expected to *do* with their shares." He paused a moment, running a hand through his thin hair. "But I don't know why I think I can apply sane reasoning to these demands. Not one of them is grounded in reality. There's no way they can be met . . . not if I had months available."

Nimec took a breath.

"Nobody expects you to meet them," he said. "The

whole thing's outrageous. It's meant to put you through your paces."

Gordian was shaking his head. "But if that's the case—"

Gordian fell silent. Nimec waited. They exchanged glances.

"If that's the case, Pete . . . and this is all about *taunting* me . . . causing me heartache . . . then what's going to happen to my daughter?" Gordian stared at Nimec. "What are the people who took Julia planning to do to her?"

Nimec hesitated, dismissing every hollow word of encouragement that came to mind. Gord deserved better from him.

"I don't know," he said. "I really don't know."

His name was Fred Gilbert, and he was vocally irate about someone ringing his telephone off the hook at seven o'clock in the morning. According to what he'd already told Glenn three or four times during his lengthy rebuke, the fact that it was a business call only worsened his unhappiness.

"This is an outrageous imposition," he said. "Or don't we agree a man has a right to choose his own schedule?"

"Of course, sir," Glenn said at his end of the line. "And I apologize for having disrupted your routine—"

"My *sleep*."

"Yes, sir. Your sleep—"

"Of which I require eight full hours," Gilbert said. "You took my contact information off the club's home page, is that correct?"

"Yes," Glenn said. That much of his story, at least, had been true. "Mr. Gilbert, I've tried to explain—"

"If the times I'm available weren't posted on the site, you might have some excuse. But they're quite clear for anyone to read."

"Understood, Mr. Gilbert. Again, though, I did mention—"

"I know. I have listened. You are here in California on overnight business, flying out to Baltimore at ten o'clock, and need to leave for the airport in an hour," Gilbert said. "It is still no justification for discourtesy. Rules cannot be ignored simply because they may be inconvenient. Whether you are in town for a day, a month, or a decade, respect and discipline must be observed." A pause. "Canines no less than humans learn by example, and I suggest you foster these qualities in *yourself* if you mean to own a Schutzhund trained dog."

Glenn sat across the kitchen table from Ricci looking wearily frustrated. Having gone the entire night without shutting his eyes except to blink the crust from them, it was hard for him to commiserate with Gilbert. In the long hours since their arrival at Ricci's apartment, the two men had worked steadily to upload the digital photos of forensic evidence and notes from the Parkville clinic to a desktop computer, sort through what they'd learned, and decide how to move forward with it. Both had centered on the items that first caught Ricci's attention at the clinic—a numbered and labeled vial containing strands of black fur, and a cross-indexed handwritten entry on Moore's notepad that read:

9/03
7:00 p.m.
Canine fur & dermal matter extracted from grey-hound's subgingival maxilla and mandible. Primarily lodged bet. right and left upper canines and lateral incisors, lesser quantity collected from inner cheek and anterior premolar surface (see accomp. dental chart). <u>*Prelim: grey inflicted bite wound upon another dog*</u>*. Unusual, follow w/DNA workup*

*of blood at scene. Visual & microanalysis of fur
samples (detailed breakdown t.c.) match shepherd
characteristics. <u>Prelim: black longhair possible.
Rare. (Attack dog?)</u> Follow w/comparison test. Reference specimen needed (FBI Hair & Fiber File?)*

Showing Glenn the notes, Ricci had pointed to the
phrase "attack dog," gotten an oddly distant expression
on his face, and shaken his head.

"That's close, but not right," he had said. "It'd be a
Schutzhund. An animal he could totally control."

"He?"

Ricci had glanced at Glenn, looking almost surprised
by the question.

"Whoever took Julia," he'd said and left it at that. As
if no further explanation were needed. "We've got to find
out who'd sell those dogs in this area."

And by six A.M. a relatively swift Internet search had
furnished an abundance of material about the classification in general, and some very specific information on
the North Bay Schutzhund Club, of which Gilbert was
founder, president, and breed warden.

Now Glenn held the receiver away from his mouth,
ballooned his cheeks, and exhaled to release some of his
tension.

"Sir, you can trust I'll take your advice," he said after
a moment. "I definitely recognize my mistake . . ."

"I would *hope* so."

"But since the harm's been done, and you're already
out of bed, I'm hoping we can turn that mistake . . . in-
excusable as it is . . . into something productive—"

"Anagkazo," Gilbert said abruptly.

"Excuse me?"

"You told me you'd seen an individual walking a black
German shepherd from the window of a car."

Glenn remembered the hastily improvised line he'd fed him. "Yes, that's right, a taxicab . . ."

"Told me it was a longhair."

"Right."

"Told me you wish to look into acquiring such a dog to guard home and family while you travel on business. Which is commendable."

"Right . . . ah, and thanks . . ."

"I try to recognize positive traits in all species," Gilbert said with no hint of sarcasm whatsoever. "At any rate, if you'd taken the extra time on your computer, you would have found the Schutzhund USA registry's online genetic database. It lists DNA-based evaluations of each and every certified dog's pedigree, physical conformation, and susceptibility to hip dysplasia and other health problems going back five or more generations. It also would have shown you that pure black longhairs are quite scarce. Just a handful of breeders sell them in this country. Virtually all have been imported from Europe or sired by imported breeding stock—"

Glenn wanted to get back to what Gilbert had said at the outset of his lecture.

"I don't meant to interrupt, sir, but that word you used a minute ago . . ."

"Word?"

"Started with an 'A,' I think . . . ana-*something-or-other* . . ."

"Anagkazo."

"Right, right . . ."

"That's a name," Gilbert said testily. "John Anagkazo. Good respectful fellow up in the hills. Our homepage has a link to his Web site. If the shepherd is indeed Schutzhund qualified and was purchased in the state of California, you can be guaranteed his farm is where it came from."

•   •   •

About eighty miles west of San Jose, the Anagkazo ranch sat on multiple acres of rolling grassy field laid with training tracks, hurdles, agility and obstacle course equipment of various configurations, and a large open pen area for the dogs out back of the main house, a restored woodframe that might have been a century old.

Ricci and Glenn found the breeder waiting at his door when they drove up at nine o'clock. As they exited their car, Ricci turned on his cellular and saw a half dozen new voice messages for him. The log showed four with Thibodeau's office number. The two most recent ones had come from a phone with Caller ID blocking—Breen at Gordian's house, he would have bet. Ricci wasn't prepared to return any of them. The Parkville Vet Clinic didn't open till ten, but he figured the cops outside would have awakened by now. Or if they hadn't, they'd have been found by their fellow police checking up to see why they hadn't responded to routine radio checks. Erickson would know the clinic had been broken into, recognize it was a slick job, smell right away it was tied to the kidnapping. But Ricci had left nothing out of place, and that would throw some question marks into his head. Anything Erickson thought couldn't be more than be a guess. And whoever made Julia disappear would probably top his suspect list. Would UpLink be on it? Not as an organization. Ricci thought he might rate on his own, though. Maybe high enough for Erickson to conduct some inquiries before eliminating him . . . even if that other detective, Brewer, was too afraid of getting jammed to admit he'd given him a peek at that crime scene diagram. Erickson nosing around UpLink could be trouble, and Ricci couldn't afford to worry about it until later.

He turned off the phone, snapped it back into his belt clip, and a moment later joined Glenn at the door.

"Hi, I'm John Anagkazo." The breeder smiled through a thick beard, putting out his hand for them to shake. "I saw your car from way down the road . . . I'm guessing you must be Misters Ricci and Glenn. With Uplink International, is it?"

Glenn nodded and showed his Sword ID.

"Corporate security, Mr. Anagkazo," he said.

"Sure, sure. You told me over the phone. I hear super things about you folks." Anagkazo looked curious. "C'mon in . . . and call me John, please. No need to wrestle with the second name."

Ricci was looking past him through the door at the head of an enormous, large-boned German shepherd.

"Long as your friend won't mind," he said, nodding at the dog.

Anagkazo smiled.

"Bach's fine," he said. "Won't bother anybody who doesn't bother me."

They followed him into a living room with a strong Southwestern feel—earth-toned geometric patterns on the rugs and upholstery, hand-crafted solid-wood furniture. The shepherd trailed behind them, waited for Anagkazo to lower himself into his chair, and stretched out beside him, nuzzling a leather chew toy on the floor.

"It must've been quite a ride for you out of San Jose," Anagkazo said. "I can put up some fresh coffee . . ."

"Thanks, we're okay," Ricci said. "I'd kind of like to get right to why we came."

Anagkazo shrugged. He waited.

"We've been trying to get some information about black longhaired shepherds," Ricci said. "From what we hear, you're the only local person who breeds them. And gives them Schutzhund training."

Anagkazo nodded.

"At every level," he said, "including specialized training. I've been at it a while, and about sixty percent of my business nowadays is with police and fire departments all around the country . . . I'm very proud of that."

And the pride looked real. As did his friendly, helpful demeanor. Ricci had studied his face and body language for any changes and seen none indicating he might be on the defensive.

"So, what sort of questions have you got?" Anagkazo said. "I need to tell you right off there's a wait on long-coated sables."

"They're that popular?" Glenn said.

Anagkazo shrugged.

"It isn't really about popularity for me." He reached down over the armrest of his chair and scratched his dog's neck. "Black-and-reds like Bach here are very well established lines in this country, and we've got a wide pool of sires and dams. But I just introduced the sables a few years ago—four generations into it now—and I don't want to risk overbreeding my stock. That's how you pass along congenital diseases, temperament problems, a whole bunch of weaknesses you'd rather see go away." A pause. "A dog has to be at least a year and a half old to qualify for basic Schutzhund classification. There's a litter of blacks due in January, plus two sixteen-month-olds that are almost ready for placement and have full deposits on them. Which is too bad—"

Ricci broke in. "You sell any lately?"

"That's just what I was about mention," Anagkazo said. He was still scratching his shepherd. "If you're interested in blacks I'd have to say this is crummy timing. The deposit on the pair of dogs came a few days ago from a big-time movie director who's got a South Hampton estate in New York. And I sold my only other three

beauties a couple weeks back to a photographer who's
staying right over on the Peninsula . . . well, actually,
drove out and *delivered* them to his cabin, way off the
beaten path in Big Sur country. Three dogs. Some guys
who work for him had prepaid last month. I guess while
he was getting settled into the place."

Ricci looked at him.

"He have a name?"

"Estes," Anagkazo said. "Nothing confidential. He's
new in the country, I think . . . from Europe."

Ricci kept looking at him.

"Where in Europe?"

"Didn't say. Or I don't remember him saying, anyway.
But I got the sense he's one of those people who's lived
everywhere. Money to spend, you know. Has an accent
you can't place . . . sort of a worldly mix, reminded me
of how Yul Brynner, the actor, used to sound. It's why
he could play the part of a pharaoh, the king of Siam, or
a Mexican bandit, and it always seemed believable."

Ricci felt something unnameable rear inside him. Felt
its *teeth*.

"The photographer," he said. His eyes were on the
breeder's face. "Describe him to me."

Anagkazo straightened a little in his chair. The curiosity he'd first shown at the door had become laced with
a certain unease.

"Square chinned. Tall. Strong-looking . . . a real hard-
body type." He moved his hand up from his shepherd's
neck to his armrest. "Has this fella done anything
wrong?"

Ricci's jaw muscles worked. It was as though, suddenly, his brain had locked around whatever words he
might have given in answer, perhaps even his ability to
articulate any response at all.

Glenn glanced his way, saw his fixed expression, and turned toward Anagkazo.

"John," he said. "You'd better tell us exactly where we can find him."

Thibodeau had spent the morning at his desk answering phone calls, but as each hour passed he had grown increasingly convinced the one call he'd been hoping for wouldn't come.

When his latest jump at the receiver proved him wrong, he immediately found himself wondering whether to be glad or sorry.

"Ricci. Where're you now—?"

"Never mind," Ricci said. "All you need to worry about's what I tell you."

"I been leaving messages on your voice mail, waiting to hear from you for hours," Thibodeau chafed. "Same goes for Megan—"

"Save it and listen."

Thibodeau reddened. "We got Erickson poking around, trouble piled on top 'a trouble. And you act like keepin' in touch be something gonna stunter you—"

"You want to find Julia Gordian and the murdering scum you like to call the Wildcat, you better shut up and listen."

Thibodeau fell silent, breathing hard. After Erickson had phoned him that morning to ask questions about a break-in at the animal clinic, he'd immediately known Ricci was in it up to his neck . . . known and only wanted some sort of accounting before he could hang that miserable neck from a rope. But he'd taken care not to alert the detective. Even in his anger, he'd wondered if Ricci might have found something to go on.

Julia, he thought. The Wildcat . . . *le Chaut Sauvage*.

Thibodeau would not in his wildest stretch of imagination have believed he would hear them mentioned in the same sentence.

"Go on," he said. He was almost panting now. "Can't waste time."

"I'm headed to Big Sur. It'll take me maybe an hour to get up there, and I'll need support. Ed Seybold from my old team. Newell and Perry if you can get hold of them. Maybe a half a dozen other men, but no more . . . have Seybold pick the rest."

Thibodeau swallowed. "Big Sur cover a lot of ground, you gonna narrow it down—?"

"Just make sure those men are pulled together, I'll be in touch with you," Ricci interrupted.

And then the line went dead in Thibodeau's hand.

Siegfried Kuhl was pensive.

Looking out through his terrace doors into the rain, watching it spill down the precipitous wall of the cliff in windblown whirls and ripples, his mind had returned to his abduction of the robin who was now bound to a chair across the room from him, his mind bringing him back to the moment Lido had been attacked by the greyhound.

The bite had done little to injure the Schutzhund, its thick coat preventing the other dog's teeth from sinking too deeply into its flesh. And Kuhl had been quick to finish things with his weapon. Yet he had wondered ever since if the true harm might have been to his plans, occurring the moment the animals made contact.

The dead flesh and bones of the dog he had shot— might it not hold clues that could eventually lay a path to him? He had been unable to dismiss the thought that there might be blood, fur, or other traceable physical evidence that could identify the shepherd. It was an uncommon creature, after all. And if the evidence were direct enough, and the breeder Anagkazo spoke to those in search of Gordian's daughter . . .

If he spoke to them before Kuhl's men were able to take care of him, the time left until he needed to head out to the fallback might very well be limited to hours, if not minutes. And though the storm would make travel there difficult, he had ordered Anton and Ciras out to fill the Explorer with basic supplies—water, protein bars, first aid—so that he might vacate the cabin as soon as possible.

After all Kuhl's preparation, it staggered him to think the success of his task might be threatened by a simple miscalculation of how the greyhound would react to his forced entry of the rescue center.

Kuhl turned from the terrace to his captured robin. He looked into her eyes over the cloth gag knotted around her mouth. That particular restraint had been unnecessary except as a precaution, he mused. Realizing she was in a place where cries for help would be of no use, she had held a silence Kuhl found admirable. She had showed no frailty, done no pleading save for the lives of the woman and infant at the rescue center, and the dog that attempted to protect her.

Even now, Kuhl thought, her steady gaze did not present him with any sign of weakness.

He moved away from her, went to the desk where he had sat long nights at his computer, and looked inside its top drawer. Waiting there was the tool steel combat knife he would use when the moment to dispose of her finally came.

Her head pulled back from behind without warning, a deep cut across the throat . . .

In his admiration, Kuhl would give Julia Gordian as sudden and painless a death as his expert hand could render.

It was, he thought, the very least she deserved.

• • •

The clouds had reasserted themselves throughout the morning to form a massive gray band that stretched along the coastline from Half Moon Bay southward to Point Conception and was widest from the Santa Lucia Mountains on east across the Ventana wilderness and Los Padres National Forest. By midday, rain was falling heavily again, the charcoal gray sky cat-clawed with lightning, thunder rumbling like great millstones in its turbulent lower and middle altitudes.

Ricci and Glenn watched two men exit the cabin and stride toward a white Ford Explorer parked only a few straight yards from where they were crouched side by side under cover of the trees. One of the men carried a portage pack, his companion a couple of nylon zip duffels.

Ricci's eyes briefly went to Glenn.

"I'm betting that's survival gear," he whispered.

Glenn nodded.

"Looks to be," he said.

Water spilling from the porous roof of leaves above them, they observed the pair in silence. In what had seemed almost a reenactment of their previous night's work at the animal hospital, they had left their car about a half mile back and then climbed the rest of the way up the hillside on foot. The thick frock of woodland on the slope offered vital concealment and also made for some tough going—steep grades, impassable thickets, streams swollen by the unrelenting rains, and patches of soggy ground with unsafe footing had forced several detours. But they'd pushed forward and were mostly able to stay within eyeshot of the paved road, sticking close whenever possible. After about an hour's hike, they had finally seen one of the huge limestone gateposts described by Anagkazo off to their left, picked up the dirt route that led to the crest of the bluff, and then stolen alongside it to their present spot.

Now they continued to watch as the two figures from the cabin strode around back of the SUV, keyed open its hatch, raised it, loaded the bags inside, and then pulled the cargo shade over them.

Ricci unholstered his sound-suppressed Five-Seven from his belt.

"You set?" he said.

Glenn took a breath and gave him another nod. He had a leather slapper flat against his palm, preferring its directness to the DMSO spray.

They shuffled over several feet to put themselves behind the Explorer, then waited a moment. Ricci pointed to the man on the left, pointed to himself, and got a final affirmative nod from Glenn. He held up three fingers and started to sign the count.

His third finger ticked down and they sprang.

Though large and muscular, Glenn was clear of the dripping brush and on top of Mr. Right in a flicker. He struck the back of his head with the sap, his blow pounding onto the base of the skull, and the man buckled in a heap.

Ricci had simultaneously rushed out behind Mr. Left, locked an arm around his throat, and put the bore of his gun against his temple. The guy snapped back his head, trying to butt him hard under the chin despite the chokehold and pressure of the nine mil—guts, good reflexes. Ricci slipped the move, spun him around by his shoulder, and brought a knee up into his middle below the diaphragm.

Mr. Left sagged back against the Explorer, the wind knocked out of him.

This time Ricci got the nine right into his face, pressed its barrel to the side of his nose, right about at the nub of the tear gland. Quickly patting the guy down, he found a Sig .380 in a concealed shoulder holster and a card wallet in the back pocket of his slacks.

Ricci tucked the Sig under his belt and flipped open the wallet's ID window.

"Barry Hughes," he said, glancing at the driver's license. "That who you are?"

As Mr. Right started to nod against the upward pressure of his gun, Ricci tossed the wallet into a puddle and drove a fist into his cheek. Something gave at the hinge of the jaw.

"Give me your real name," Ricci said.

The guy was silent, blood overspilling his lower lip.

"Your name." Ricci stared into his face, pushing his Five-Seven deeper into the corner of his eye. He could see the skin below the socket crinkle under the end of its barrel. "Let me hear it or I'll kill you."

The guy looked at him without answering for perhaps three more seconds.

"Anton, you fucker," he said at last, front teeth smeared red, his speech already distorted from the fractured jaw. It came out sounding like *Antunnn yfuker*.

Ricci nodded. At the periphery of his vision, he saw Glenn unlock the Explorer's passenger door with the key he'd pulled from its hatch, reach in to give the ignition a quarter turn, then lower the window and cuff the other guy's wrists around the vertical bar of its frame.

Grabbing his man by the shirt collar now, Ricci pulled him off the flank of the vehicle with a sudden wrench.

"Anton, I know your mouth hurts, but you'll need to talk to us about a few things before giving it a rest," he said.

There was a door at the side of the cabin that offered admittance to the kitchen and, directly beyond it, the living room.

Ricci had Anton lead the way to the door at gunpoint, one hand clamped over his shoulder, the other holding the Five-Seven to his ear behind the loose, misshapen swell of his jawbone. Behind them, Glenn had the stock of his VVRS cradled against his upper arm as he held it forward at the ready.

"Open the door," Ricci said. He nudged Anton with the gun. "No surprises."

Anton turned the knob, pulled. The rain was a constant susurrus that muffled the sound of its opening. Listening carefully, however, Ricci could hear a faint rustling in the brush to his right.

Okay, he thought.

Standing at an angle to the door, hidden from within behind the outer wall of the house, Ricci flung a glance around Anton through the small unoccupied kitchen. Past the living-room archway, three men were at a table playing cards. A fourth seated on a sofa to the extreme right seemed to be dozing there, arms folded behind his head, his legs outstretched and crossed at the ankles. The sables were lying at rest on the carpet between them. One of the dogs raised itself a little at the sound of the opening door, recognized Anton's familiar presence across the length of the two rooms, then lowered its shaggy head back onto the floor.

Ricci turned slightly, motioned with his chin, and side-stepped.

A burly hand came around Anton's bloodied mouth from behind, clapped over it, and pulled him back into the rain. Ricci heard the hiss of released aerosol to his left, then a shifting of foliage as Anton was ditched out of sight.

Thibodeau emerged from the wet vegetation, relieved of the unconscious man, slipping a DMSO canister into his belt holder. The rest of the entry team was in position on either side of the door.

Ricci looked at Thibodeau's bearded face for the barest instant, then turned toward the open door again. Anton had spilled plenty outside the Explorer, and had seemed scared enough to have been telling the truth when he said the Killer was upstairs—which would mean the dogs would be no threat down here. They would do nothing belligerent without his personal command.

"I'm going in," he whispered and ran into the cabin without a backward look.

Ricci's estimate of Anton's honesty under the gun proved right on. The flunky had told him the short spiral staircase would be in the living room, past the archway to his immediate left, and there it was, exactly where it was supposed to be.

His Five-Seven out in his hand, he crossed the kitchen in a dash. Ahead of him, the Killer's men were springing to their feet, but then Ricci swung toward the stairs, and bounded up onto them, and suddenly the commotion and movement was behind and below him. He took the steps several at time, vaulting up them, knowing he had seconds at best to get to the bedroom. There were shouts, exchanges of gunfire, more shouts, all distant echoes outside the narrow, winding, ascending shaft of his awareness. Behind, below, outside, somewhere in another world. Ricci cared only about getting up to the second floor, and the taste in his mouth, the taste of his *want*.

And now he was at the upstairs landing and off it into a short hall. He paused a beat. How long since he'd entered the cabin? Five seconds? Ten? Maybe he'd have five more. Tops, five. Four, three . . .

There were a couple of wide doors along the hallway to his right, adjacent to each other. Another narrower one

to his left—a closet. That second door on the right, Anton
had told him it was the master bedroom, was where the
Killer had her, where the Killer would be. . . .

Ricci made his choice, lunged forward, stopped for
half a heartbeat, kicked his foot out against the *first* door
at the point where the latch met the hasp. It flung open,
crashed back against the wall, and he burst into the room,
his Five-Seven in a two-handed police grip—

His back to the open doors of a terrace overlooking
the seaward plunge of the bluff, the Killer stood across
the room by a plain wooden chair.

She was in it. Gagged. Trussed. Hands bound behind
her with rope, bound to the chair.

Above the gag, on her face, an expression of terror
without surrender.

Ricci reached into himself for her name, pulled it
through the atavistic howl of rage filling his mind.

Julia.

She. Was. Julia.

The Killer was holding a combat knife to her throat.

"Let her go," Ricci said. His eyes on the Killer's eyes.
The Five-Seven thrust out in front of him. "Let her go
now."

The Killer did not move.

The blade in his grip, its honed edge against her throat,
he did not move.

Ricci unwrapped the fingers of one hand from the gun,
reached back, felt for the door, pushed it shut. Somewhere behind it, on the other side, the shouts and gunfire
were fading. There were footsteps coming rapidly up the
stairs.

The Killer kept staring at Ricci in silence. He did not
move the knife from Julia's throat.

The footsteps had reached the door now. Behind it, an urgent shout:

"Ricci!" Glenn's voice. "Ricci you in there?"

Ricci didn't answer.

"Ricci—"

"Stay out," Ricci said. "Tell everybody to back off."

Through the door, Glenn said, "What's happening? Is Julia—?"

"She's okay," Ricci said. "Thibodeau and the others will be right behind you on those stairs. Just keep everyone down the hall. Don't ask questions."

Ricci looked at the Killer.

"Let her go," he repeated a third time. "It's finished."

The Killer did not move his knife.

"She's piecework to you. Nothing. Just another job," Ricci said. His gun remained level with the Killer's heart. "You do her, I do you, what's the point? But there's still something in this room you want. Something you've wanted since Khazakhstan. Since Ontario. And I'm giving you a chance to have it. I'm promising you the chance."

The Killer watched Ricci's face.

Studied it for another long, long moment.

Then he dropped his knife hand from the soft white flesh of Julia's throat, went behind the chair, cut the ropes around her wrists with one quick slice, crouched, severed her ankle bindings, and straightened. Only the gag remained uncut.

Ricci nodded slowly.

"There's been no circulation in her legs," he said. "Step away from the chair—two steps to your right—so I can help her up."

The Killer stepped back.

Still covering him with the gun, Ricci moved toward the chair, slipped an arm around Julia, and eased her to a standing position, not letting her stumble, holding her erect with his own strength, gradually feeling her legs take over. Above the gag, her face remained composed.

"You can make it on your own now," Ricci said to her. Then he tilted his head back toward the door, raised his voice. "Glenn . . . you hear me?"

From outside the door: "Yeah. Hearing you fine. Sounds like they've got things under control downstairs."

"Good," Ricci said. "I'm sending Julia out. Stay away, don't come near the door. Don't let anybody else get close to it, either. No matter what, got me?"

"Ricci—"

"*Got me?*"

A pause.

"Yeah," Glenn said, then. "Yeah, man. I do."

Ricci backed toward the door, his gun on the Killer, his free hand on Julia, steadying her, guiding her along with him. He reached behind him again, opened the door just wide enough for her to pass through and nodded for her to leave.

She hesitated, looking at him.

"Go," he said. "It'll be all right."

Julia held her gaze on him for another moment. Then she nodded and went through the opening.

Ricci slammed the door shut behind her.

"We're almost ready," he said. His weapon pointed at the Killer. "Better slide that chair across to me."

It was pushed forward. Ricci swept it around his body and leaned it against the door, wedging its back under the doorknob. Then he set his gun down on a small table he'd seen out the corner of his left eye.

Outside the door, he could hear Thibodeau's voice shouting up from downstairs, then Glenn answering him, telling him Ricci had gotten Julia out, that she was free of any threat. There were some more words exchanged between them, followed by the tread of heavy ascending footsteps.

Ricci saw something like a smile on the Killer's face as he dropped his knife to the floor, and then pushed it aside with his foot.

"Now," the Killer said, "we take our chances."

Ricci nodded.

"Now," he said.

Kuhl and Ricci advanced on each other, sidling for position as they moved into the center of the room.

His fists clenched, his sinewy arms raised to protect his head, Ricci bounced a little on his knees to loosen them up. His opponent had a good three inches on him, a longer reach. Probably twenty or thirty more pounds of muscle slabbed over his broad frame. He would have to get in close and tight, rely on speed to overcome those advantages.

Kuhl shifted now, feinted toward him. Ricci didn't buy it. His hands still blocking, he wove around him, found an opening under the massive arms, came in low with a right uppercut meant for the chin.

Faster than he looked, Kuhl parried the blow sidearm, tried grasping hold of Ricci's outthrust wrist to pull him off his feet. But Ricci slipped the grab, got back away from his reach, and then rounded again, setting himself to throw another punch across Kuhl's body.

This time Kuhl was even more prepared, his left foot snapping out at the moment before contact, getting between Ricci's legs to kick the inside of his opposite shin and throw him off balance. Before Ricci could recover, a right hook came smashing hard against his cheek.

Ricci went staggering, the side of his face exploding with pain, blood filling his mouth, his vision momentarily dimming. And then Kuhl was coming in on him again, hitting him with a series of powerful jabs, his fists repeatedly, brutally pounding Ricci's face and neck.

Ricci felt gravity pulling him down, dragging at his legs and head, and managed to resist it barely in time to duck an overhand right that seemed to shoot straight for his eyes out of a grainy nowhere. He sucked in a breath to fill his chest with air, inhaled again, again, and then shuffled a little to get his heart pumping and dispel the motes of swirling nothingness from his vision.

Kuhl was not about to give him that opportunity. He launched forward, his fingers pointed outward, going for Ricci's eyes, trying to blind him, gouge his eyes from their sockets with the tips of those stabbing fingers. Ricci shifted back, bobbed down under the hand, swallowed more air, got more of the blackness out of his face, and then came up under the Killer's throat, came up *fast*, jamming his cocked right elbow into it with all the strength he could muster, connecting with it right below the knob of his Adam's apple.

Kuhl grunted, swayed a little. A small, moist sound escaped his throat. Ricci pressed him, knowing this might be his only break, needing to make the most of it. Chin low, feet planted wide, he bored into Kuhl, pistoning his fists into Kuhl's stomach and sides, pounding him with lefts, rights, jabs, pressing, pressing, his knuckles hammering him with one blow after the next.

Then Ricci felt the Killer loosen up, or maybe slip, he wasn't sure, didn't care, just knew he had him where he wanted him, and rammed his kneecap up between his legs, digging it into his groin.

Kuhl went down to the floor, kneeling, sagging forward, attempting to brace himself from going flat on his face with his outspread palms. But Ricci stayed on top of him, kicking his face, arms, legs, and body, making him bleed, opening wounds all over him, watching the redness spurt from his torn, lacerated flesh.

Wanting to bring him down as low as he possibly could.

And then, suddenly, coming up in the Killer's fist, a bright flash of steel.

The combat knife.

He'd gotten the knife off the floor.

It flicked up, and then out, as Kuhl successfully thrust the blade in Ricci's direction, jabbing its point into the back of his right leg.

Ricci felt its hot/cold penetration deep in his thigh muscle, swung a final kick at the Killer's hand with his opposite foot, managing to land it between his wrist and elbow.

Kuhl's fingers opened, dropping away from the knife handle. Lurching forward, his head bowed, blood and saliva pouring from his mouth, the Killer propped himself on his knee, tried to thrust himself to his feet, failed, and started to topple forward.

Ricci caught him by the front of the shirt on the way down.

"Here, murderer," he said, the knife still sticking out of his thigh. "Here's a little help for you."

He hauled Kuhl up onto his rubbery legs, simultaneously turning him toward the terrace, forcing him backward, standing him up against the glass doors, using his own weight to prop Kuhl's limp, weakened body against the doors as he reached out over his shoulder, slid one of them partially open by its handle, and again pushed him backward—through the opening now, into the wind and rain, back and back and back across the terrace to the guardrail.

The rain swirling around them, lashing them, washing their blood down onto the terrace floor so it mingled together in flowing, guttering cascades that went spilling over the lip of the terrace into the drop, Ricci held the Killer up and looked into his face, shaking him hard, his fists around the bunched wet fabric of his shirt, holding him, holding him there against the iron guardrail above the vertiginous, storm-swept plunge of the canyon and staring into his eyes for one last, long moment of time.

"You son of a bitch," he said. "You son of a bitch, we did this to each other."

And pushed him over into the abyss.

Thibodeau had heard the crashing in the room on the cabin's second floor and wondered what in the name of everything holy was going on.

Upstairs now, working his way down the hall past Derek Glenn, Julia being hustled out of the cabin behind him, it was the room's sudden dead silence that had gotten his mind racing everywhere at once.

Thibodeau tried to push in the door, found it blocked, and ordered the men behind him to put the ram to it.

Moving through the splintered doorframe into the room, he noticed two things that made his eyes grow wide.

The first was Ricci sitting on the floor, rain blowing over him through an open terrace door. He had propped himself back against the wall, a wide pool of blood under his right leg, a slick reddened knife on the floor beside him.

The second thing Thibodeau noticed was that he was alone.

Thibodeau put away his questions for the moment, rushed across the room, and crouched over him.

"You're bleeding like a stuck pig, gonna need something to stop the flow," he said. Then he saw that Ricci had gotten open the tac pouch on his belt and was struggling to fish something from inside it. "What're you looking for in there? I can help you get it out . . ."

Ricci looked at him, hesitated a beat.

"Wound-closure gel," he said, nodding for him to reach inside.

THIRTEEN

SAN JOSE
GABON, AFRICA

ENTERING HER DINING ROOM, ASHLEY GORDIAN glanced up at the wall clock above the Sword op's head and was amazed to see that morning had turned into afternoon. What sleep she'd gotten since Julia's disappearance had come only when she let her guard down against it, and in each instance she hadn't kept her eyes shut for long. Ten minutes here, fifteen there, she wouldn't let herself yield to more than that. Ashley's reluctant submissions to fatigue had felt more like automatic powerdowns than true periods of rest—the physical equivalent of going offline for system maintenance, she supposed—and between them she had lost all sense of time's orderly progression. Yet afternoon it was. The hands of the clock had moved on since she'd last been in the room . . . even if the Sword op hadn't since she'd last entered it.

Seated below it at a mahogany lowboy he'd been using as a workstation, his shirt sleeves rolled up, he was hunched over the laptop computer in front of him, staring at the screen. Ashley wasn't sure of his name; his ID tag was on his jacket, and his jacket was slung over the back of his chair. There were so many of her husband's security people around the house and its grounds giving everything of themselves, working well past their scheduled shifts, defying exhaustion in ways she couldn't fathom. Some were men and women Ashley recognized, others were people she'd never seen until a day or so ago, but all wore the same look of implacable resolve on their faces. Her admiration and gratitude went beyond words, and she'd provided whatever assistance she could, making them as comfortable as possible, bringing them food and drinks to keep them going, little things that made her feel useful in a way she paradoxically thought almost selfish. She needed to do something, needed to participate, even though her participation hardly seemed to measure up to their efforts. The alternative was to succumb to the crushing sense of futility and helplessness that always seemed to be lurking just past the next moment,

Now she stepped over to the op, noticed the remains of a pizza crust on a paper plate at his elbow, and placed a hand on his shoulder to catch his attention.

"I brought you this slice hours ago," she said, taking the plate. "You look like you haven't budged since."

He glanced blearily up at her from the screen.

"Hasn't been that long," he said. And paused. "Has it?"

The puzzled expression on his face made Ashley smile in spite of herself.

"Why don't you take five," she said. "I can set you up on—"

She broke off, a stir in the adjoining living room turning both their heads toward its entrance. Everyone in the makeshift command post was suddenly moving, exchanging hurried questions and answers, bringing cell phones out of their pockets.

Ashley felt sweat slick her palms, felt her legs tremble beneath her. Whatever news had broken and spread through the command center like a wave was critical, good or ill, and the op beside her could not hide his recognition of it.

"Mrs. Gordian." He was suddenly on his feet beside her, motioning toward his vacated chair. "Ma'am, why don't you wait here while I—"

"No." She shook her head. "I'm okay, really. Let's just get in there."

She rushed toward the living room, almost running into Megan Breen as they converged on the entry from opposite sides.

Megan was gripping a cellular in her hand, tears streaming from her eyes. It was the first time Ashley had ever seen her cry, and the realization seemed to bring her heart to a standstill.

Then she noticed the smile beneath her tears, wet with her flowing tears, and took what she would always remember as the deepest breath of her entire life.

"Ashley—"

"Meg—"

"Julia's on the phone," Megan said, and held it out to her. "She's on the phone, they've found her . . . and she wants to say hello to her mother."

The Sedco oil platform. Offshore Gabon. Roger Gordian stood behind a podium in the glare of high-mounted kliegs, grim eyes staring from faces where smiles were to have held, silence around him where festive music was meant to have been played.

In each of his pants pockets was a folded sheet of paper. On each sheet, a different speech: the one near his left hand a scripted concession to madness, the other written in stubborn, unrelenting hope of its defeat.

Gordian glanced at his watch, then back at the solemn faces lined in rows before him.

Moments to go, and bitterness sat at the back of his tongue.

He would mouth the words that needed to be spoken. For his daughter's life, for the slimmest *chance* at saving her life, he would do that, do anything necessary. Whoever had taken Julia from him, whatever monstrous intent was behind the act, her kidnapper had known an essential truth:

In Gordian's heart, the Dream had been born. But while the past and present were things of hard reality, only the future lived in a man's dreams . . . and Julia was truly, beyond all doubt, the child who carried it on her shoulders.

He stepped forward, took the podium, began to slowly reach for the words in his left pocket.

And suddenly caught sight of movement beyond the faces, the eyes. Someone racing toward him the blinding lights.

An excited shout: "Boss . . . *Gord* . . ."

Roger Gordian stood stock-still as Nimec came closer, pushing between the rows of men and women seated before him. His heart knocking in his chest, Gordian found himself no longer thinking about words that had to be spoken, but only caring about those he wanted more than anything to hear.

"We've got her!" Nimec shouted. "She's safe, she's okay, *we've got her!*"

Gordian took a breath.

Perhaps the longest, deepest breath he'd ever taken in his life.

And then he reached into his right pocket and carried on.

The Gulf of Guinea. One thousand feet below the ocean's surface. The crewed submersible launched from the *Chi-*

mera's hold eeling toward an escape platform off the Cameroonian shore.

In the small aft passenger cabin, Harlan DeVane stared past Casimir and his co-pilot into the watery gloom outside the forward dome. Behind him in abandoned waters, toasts to good fortune were being made on the Sedco platform, its beacon lights radiating far into the night. Broadcast to the world, Roger Gordian's words of success had been statement enough of DeVane's failure. Transmitted in secret, his own unanswered communiques to Kuhl had been mere redundant verification.

The robin was free. Father and daughter would be reunited.

Father and daughter.

DeVane stared into liquid emptiness, his bloodless face without expression, despising the thoughts that filled his mind like some baneful toxin. Was there relief from them knowing what was in store for Etienne Begela . . . that before the night was over his brains would pour from a bullet hole in his skull not quite as neatly made as the rondelle he had been given? Or would he find greater comfort in the past?

DeVane pictured his long-ago return to the high tower of his father, its doors unlocked for that second visit by the secret video he had taken of his couplings with the widow Melissa Phillips, and his genetic proof of paternity of the child she had birthed out of wedlock . . . the misbegotten product of their ardent clasps in the night.

His small teeth bared themselves in what might have been a smile of recovered satisfaction. DeVane had studied his father's life thoroughly after their first meeting at the long table of glass. There were two legitimate sons, and a daughter . . .

Her surname at birth had been VanderMoere. After her marriage to the multimillionaire president of an inherited commodities empire, Arthur Phillips, she had adopted her husband's surname, retaining it after his untimely death.

DeVane learned everything he could about the widow Melissa Phillips . . . everything he could well before the day he stepped up to his half-sister's brownstone in New York City and allowed her to think she had begun her seduction of him.

In fact, it had been other way around.

Oh, what flimflam that turned out to be—the father who had taken pains to hide any knowledge of his whoreson's existence from his family rewarded with a twice-misbegotten grandchild. The payoff DeVane extorted from both father and daughter to keep their vile secret providing ample startup capital for the first of his own business endeavors. And the son DeVane had fathered . . .

He closed his eyes now, resting his head back in his contoured seat as the submersible sped him away through the depths.

That little bastard had been left to fend for himself in some adoption home.

EPILOGUE

MORNING SUNSHINE POURING OVER MOUNT HAMIL-
ton in the crystal-clear distance, Roger Gordian was
about to pop his daily capsule of flaxseed oil—rich in
omega 3, good for the pump, Ashley insisted—when his
direct line rang.

He put down his glass of water, plunked the capsule
back into the weekly pillbox Ash filled for him every
Sunday night, and picked up.

"Gord," said Dan Parker at the other end of the line.
"I've finally got it!"

Gord furrowed his brow.

"Got what?" he said.

"The word."

"What word."

"C'mon, don't play dumb. That day at the steakhouse . . .
when you said how you were content with everything
you've accomplished, but didn't want things to stay exactly the way they were. How you wanted to stop and
not stop. You told me were looking for a perfect word
to describe how you felt, remember? For what it was you
wanted."

Actually, Gordian hadn't recalled telling him until that
moment, what with everything that had happened over

the past month. The thought, however, had been very much on his mind.

"So," he said. "Give it to me."

Parker paused over the phone.

"Retirement," he said. "How's *that* one, my friend?"

Dressed for her regular jog, Julia Gordian opened her back door and went to lasso up the hounds. It was a gorgeous morning—the hard rains of September long past—and the dogs had been lounging in the sun since she'd let them out an hour earlier. But now it was time for them to get some exercise . . . even the slowpoke.

"Jack, Jill, let's go!" she called. Then looked over at the third dog stretched in a bar of sunlight behind them. "You, too, Viv! Old wounds only count so much for excuses in this house!"